VISION OF DARKNESS

Coulter was about to leave when the hair on the back of his neck rose. A sensation came out of the northwest. He turned, and saw a golden light threaded with black. It flowed like a river through the sky, but the light had a beginning and an end. The light had a feeling. It drew and repelled him at the same time.

He got a sense of Arianna, as if he were with her, as if he were almost a part of her. She was in great pain, extreme pain, pain so severe it was ripping her from the inside out.

He fell to his knees with the power of it. He wasn't in pain—he knew it was her pain—but it felled him just the same. "Ari," he whispered—

And then the feeling was gone as if it had never been. He raised his head toward the sky. The light had passed. The presences were gone.

"Are you all right?" Leen asked.

Coulter put a hand on hers. He had no words for what he had just felt. "I'm fine," he said, "but something has changed."

"What?" she asked.

"I don't know," he said. "But I don't think things are going to be quiet anymore."

THE BLACK THRONE SERIES

THE
BLACK
QUEEN

Kristine Kathryn Rusch

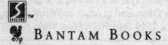

BANTAM BOOKS

New York Toronto London Sydney Auckland

THE BLACK QUEEN

A Bantam Spectra Book / August 1999

ISBN 0-553-58115-5

Published simultaneously in the United States and Canada

Bantam Books are published by Bantam Books, a division of
Random House, Inc. Its trademark, consisting of the words "Bantam
Books" and the portrayal of a rooster, is Registered in U.S. Patent
and Trademark Office and in other countries. Marca Registrada.
Bantam Books, 1540 Broadway, New York, New York 10036.

PRINTED IN THE UNITED STATES OF AMERICA

WCD   10   9   8   7   6   5   4   3   2   1

For Loren and Heather Coleman, with love.

ACKNOWLEDGMENTS

Thanks on this one go to Anne Groell for the brainstorming and for taking chances; to Merrilee Heifetz for staying the course; to Dean Wesley Smith who helped me find some important solutions; and to everyone who asked me what was going to happen next.

THE SIGNAL

THE SIGNAL

CHAPTER ONE

THE ECCRASIAN MOUNTAINS were the tallest mountains Gift had ever seen. Even though he had lived near them for the last five years, he still marveled at their height and their power. Their faintly red rock made him feel as if he were at home, but their rounded peaks spoke of an age, a timelessness, that he hadn't seen anywhere else in the world.

He stood outside the Student's Hut in the Protectors Village and waited for Madot. Dawn had just touched the tips of the mountains, the sunlight a pale yellow as it rose over the ancient peaks. It would take another hour before the light reached him.

The village was quiet. Many of the Shaman were already busy with their daily tasks. Others, the night guardians, slept. It had taken him almost a year to get used to the rhythms of the Protectors. They gathered much of their food, and the rest was brought to them by the nearby Fey Infantry garrison, a custom that was hundreds, perhaps thousands of years old. No commerce took place here. Protectors Village served two functions:

it housed the Shaman dedicated to guarding the Place of Power, and it gave the young apprentices a school of sorts, a place to train where they would be undisturbed by the outside world.

Fifty stone huts huddled on the plateau. They were round and made out of mountain rock. They had no windows and only one door. Some of the huts were built for several inhabitants, like the Student's Hut. Some were built for one person: a full-fledged Shaman who had to, by rights, live alone.

Gift wasn't a Shaman yet, and he wouldn't be for a long time. He had decades of training ahead of him. Madot, his main teacher, believed that he could cut his training short because of the power of his magic, the unprecedented strength of his Vision, but she was only guessing. There had never been an apprentice like Gift in the entire history of the Fey. His magic was unique—his heritage was unique—and because of those things, his future was uncertain.

He rubbed his hands together in the early morning chill. Madot had instructed him to wear only his apprentice's robes. She was going to take him to the Place of Power, several years before most apprentices were ever taken. It was said that a goat herder found this cave, and took his family inside. When they came out, they were Fey.

Simply entering the cave did not create a Fey. There was magic in a Place of Power that when tapped, altered everything. That much he knew without being taught. He had discovered a second Place of Power fifteen years before, and had lived in it for several weeks. There he had seen things he still did not comprehend, things that had changed his life forever.

He would not be standing here if he hadn't lived in that place.

He shifted from one bare foot to the other. His toes were growing cold. The bottoms of his feet had become hard from use. He rarely wore shoes—they were frowned upon by the Shaman—but usually he was moving. He almost never stood still.

Madot saw that as a flaw. She saw many things about him as flaws. He had been raised by adoptive parents who had no idea how to control his Visionary magic, and he had used his talents in ways that the Shaman here frowned upon. That his spells had been successful didn't matter, nor did the fact that with them he had saved hundreds of lives. That he had misused the magic was the important thing, the thing they wanted to corral in him.

Wild magic, or so Madot called it. She said his wild magic and his impatience were his greatest faults. Until he had come here, he thought his wild magic was his greatest asset. He hadn't even known he was impatient until he had come to a place where time seemed to have stopped.

There were no regular schedules as there had been when he lived in a Fey military camp, no rhythms as there had been when he lived in the rural areas of his homeland, Blue Isle. Here the Shaman went about their business as if they were being governed from within. He always felt at loose ends. He wanted to stay busy, although sometimes there was nothing to do.

Madot said he had to get used to quiet. He thought that the most difficult thing of all.

He glanced up the mountainside. The Place of Power was a morning's climb from the Protector's Village. From here, he could see the silvery shimmer that marked the cave's entrance. His stomach jumped slightly. He had no idea how different this Place of Power would be from the one he discovered on Blue Isle. On Blue Isle, the Place of Power contained items from the Isle's main religion, Rocaanism. But Rocaanism wasn't practiced anywhere on this continent, known as Vion. Here, at the foundation of the Fey Empire, the word "religion" wasn't used at all.

Finally, he saw the door to Madot's hut open. She stepped outside and sniffed the air, as she always did, as if the faint fragrances on the breeze gave her information that Gift could never get. To him, all the smells were familiar: the dusty sharpness of the mountains themselves; the pungent odor of the ceta plants that grew perennially behind the Student's Hut; the stench of the manure that he and the other students had spread on the communal garden just the night before. Nothing stood out, and nothing was unexpected. Once he had asked her what she smelled, and she had smiled.

The future, boy, she had said. *Just the future.*

It also took him a while to get used to being called "boy." He was thirty-three years old, a full adult in most places. To many Shaman, though, a thirty-three-year-old was still in his childhood. Most full Shaman didn't begin their solitary practices until they were ninety or older.

The Shaman were the longest lived of the Fey, and it was a good thing, because so few had the ability to become Shaman. Of those who did, even fewer chose the work. It was arduous and its rewards were few. He still thought of the Shaman who helped raise him—a woman he thought of as his father's Shaman, even though his father hadn't been Fey—and of the sacrifices she had made so that her Vision, her dream for the future, could come true. She had died for that dream. Apprentices did not become Shaman until they were ready to make that supreme sacrifice. It was the one area that Gift was confident he would pass. He had sacrificed so much over the years that sacrificing his life seemed a very small thing indeed.

Madot was watching him. Her eyes were dark against her wizened skin. Her white hair surrounded her face like a nimbus. The hair was the unifying feature of all the Shaman, the hair and the desiccated look of the body, the skin. It was as if in training their Vision to See and Foresee, they had lost something vital, something that nourished them from within.

Gift had none of that look. He favored his Fey mother in most things, but it was obvious that Gift was not fully Fey. His father had been the King of Blue Isle, and the people there were short, blond-haired and blue-eyed, with skin so fair that it turned red in the sun. Gift's Fey heritage showed in his height, his hair, and his faintly pointed ears, but his Islander heritage diluted his skin to a golden brown, made his cheeks round instead of angular, and gave his eyes a vivid blueness that usually startled any Fey meeting him for the first time.

Madot found Gift's appearance cause for concern. He had been having Visions since he was a child, and he had first used his Visionary powers when he was three. Thirty years of such extreme magic should have taken a toll on his skin, his hair, his face, but it had not. And that worried her. Once she had mumbled that perhaps he hadn't tapped his full power yet, and once she had said that perhaps his magic was something Other, something so different that the rules no longer applied.

"You are being impatient," she said as she approached him, her dark robes flowing around her. Her voice was high and warm. He would have called it youthful if he had heard it without seeing her. Yet she was among the oldest of the Shaman in the village, and one of the most powerful.

He smiled at her accusation. She was correct. He was impatient. "I was trying to wait," he said.

"Trying forces you to be impatient. You must not try. You must simply be."

He shook his head slightly. "You've been telling me that for five years."

"And for five years you have not understood me."

"Then perhaps the problem is with the messenger, not the recipient."

She smiled at him, and her eyes twinkled. The expression filled her tiny face with wrinkles and made her look like a wizened infant. "That's the argument of the impatient."

He shrugged. "Well, we've already established that."

She laughed, then put a hand on his arm. "Are you ready for a climb?"

"I have been for years."

"No," she said, the smile suddenly gone. "You have not. You have wanted to go for years. But you have not been ready."

"And you think I am now?"

"I didn't say that either."

He waited. Word games were part of a Shaman's business. It was canon here that information given too easily was wasted on its hearer.

"You want to ask me," she said, looking up at him.

"I do. But I'm trying to be patient."

"That 'try' word again." She sighed. "Ask anyway."

"Why are you taking me up there today?"

She looked away from him. " 'The hand that holds the scepter shall hold it no more, and the man behind the throne shall reveal himself in all his glory.' Have you heard that before?"

"No," he said, startled. He thought he had heard all the prophecies about the Black Throne.

"Four had visits from the Powers last night. Those were the words given." Four meant four of the Shaman, probably those guarding the Place of Power. The Powers were the spirits of the Fey dead who, from the planes beyond, guided the living. At least that was how they were once explained to him. The Shaman believed that the Powers were more than that, and that their abilities were indescribable to mere mortals.

Madot was watching him closely.

He shook his head slightly. "I don't see the connection."

"Shamanistic Visions are always about the Black Throne."

"I know that," he said. "But I thought the Visions could foretell any future point from now to a thousand years from now."

"This wasn't a strict Vision. No one Saw events. All they heard were words. They believe it to be a Warning."

A shiver ran down Gift's back. But he kept his mind focused on the conversation. He didn't want to speculate, not yet. If he had learned anything from his teachers, it had been that speculation could dilute a message.

"I still don't understand why that made you decide I'm ready for my first visit to the Place of Power."

"It is not your readiness we are dealing with," she said, and he knew that the "we" in that sentence did not refer to him, but to the full Shaman in the village.

"Then what is it?" he asked.

"Your presence."

"You may ask me to leave?"

"I didn't say that." Her grip tightened on his arm, and she led him around the Student's Hut to one of the many paths that led to the steps carved into the mountainside.

His entire body was tense. What he had thought a reward for progress in his studies was turning out to be something else altogether. A test of some sort. A decision, perhaps already made, to treat him differently than the other students or to make him leave.

He didn't want to leave. He was born a Visionary, the most powerful Visionary in the history of the Fey, and a Visionary had two choices: he could lead or he could become a Shaman. Gift had had a taste of leadership. He had seen the compromises it caused, the responsibility it held for other people's lives. He had seen how Visionary Leadership could be corrupted, and how such a Leader could often rely on no one but himself.

Visonary Leadership also required a harshness, a warrior's nature, a willingness to sacrifice one life for the good of all others. Gift had watched his grandfather, his great-grandfather, his father, and now his sister make such decisions. He wanted no part of it.

The life of the Shaman appealed to him. Never did a Shaman take a life. If he did, he would lose his powers. The Shaman's nature was at its heart peaceful. Madot had once said that put Shaman at odds with all the rest of the Fey.

At the time, Gift hadn't cared. His sister Arianna, in her role as Black Queen of the Fey, had been attempting to alter the nature of the Fey. She wasn't full Fey any more than he was, and she had been raised an Islander. For fifteen years she had held the Fey Empire together using diplomacy and tact. Before that the Fey Empire had been a conquering empire, and its hereditary ruler was often the best warrior among the Fey. Arianna had a warrior's spirit, but she lacked the conqueror's drive. She believed the Empire would become stronger by consolidating its holdings, and using its resources to grow richer, not to expand. So far, it had been working. In fact, it had been working so well that Gift felt he could leave her side and immerse himself in his apprenticeship.

Was that what the Warning was about? If Arianna died now, childless, Gift would inherit her Throne. The Black Throne only went to those of Black Blood. The Black Blood passed through his mother, Jewel. Gift was the eldest. Arianna only held the throne because he had given it to her willingly. It had been something he felt she was more suited to than he.

He knew better than to ask Madot any more about the Warning. She would answer him in her own time. She led him to the stairs.

They were ancient and well tended, carved out of the mountainside. Their surface was smooth and shiny, but not slick. Every morning and every evening, one of the Protectors swept the stairs. Once a week, another Protector washed them. If the stone cracked or wore too thin, the Shaman told one of the Infantry when the food deliveries came, and within the week, Domestics who specialized in stone masonry arrived to fix the problem. The Domestics also spelled the stairs so that no one could slip on them or fall down them. The spells were as ancient as the stone, and in all the centuries that the Protectors had guarded the Place of Power, no one had been injured climbing to or from the cave.

As he climbed beside Madot, Gift wondered if the Domestics also spelled the stairs to make the trip easier. His legs felt lighter, as if the muscles in his thighs had to do no work at all. He almost felt as if he could sprint up the mountainside, but he restrained himself. The climb was a long one, and he knew that running would only exhaust himself later.

So he savored the trip. The ancient staircase was carved deep into the rocks, and as he moved, he could see the veins of red running beneath the surface, like blood beneath the skin. Partway up, he traced a finger along one of the veins: it was warmer than he expected. Madot watched his movement, and smiled.

She said little and that was not like her. Usually she used every moment to teach him. There were seven apprentices in Protectors Village right now, and most were taught by all the Shaman. But Gift had Madot as his main teacher because the Shaman had been divided about his presence from the beginning. Some had been frightened of him. He was the first Shamanic candidate of Black Blood ever, and many did not believe that he was here to become a Shaman, but rather to learn how to dismantle them.

He understood the belief. It showed that the Shaman understood the kind of cunning that had ruled his grandfather's and great-grandfather's lives. If Gift had been like them—and he wasn't in any way that he knew of—he would have found some way to infiltrate the Shaman, especially now.

A ruthless ruler would want to destroy the Shaman, and the Place they guarded. Ever since the second Place of Power had been discovered, the Shaman had been worried. Fey legend said this: *There are three Places of Power. Link through them, and the Triangle of Might will re-form the world.*

For centuries, the Fey had debated what the prophecy meant. Did "re-form the world" mean that everything would be destroyed? Or did it mean that the world would become strictly a Fey place, a place where all diversity was destroyed? Most agreed, though, that discovering the Triangle would benefit the Fey, as discovering the cave had benefited the goat herder and his family by giving them powers undreamed of before. Controlling the Triangle, most believed, would make the Fey gods.

Shaman believed that once the second Place of Power had been discovered, the third would be easy to find. A Shaman would stand within the first Place of Power, another Shaman would stand in the second, and together they would triangulate the power, and learn where the third was located.

But discovery of the Triangle frightened everyone. Gift had set up, at his sister's request, guards for the second Place of Power. Those guards did not allow a Shaman into it. The Black Family, at least Gift and Arianna's branch of it, did not want anyone to have access to the Triangle. Gift and Arianna could have attempted to triangulate the power and learn where the third Place of Power was. So far, they had chosen not to. Arianna believed, and Gift agreed, that there was no need to unleash more magic upon the world.

The Shaman, on the other hand, had requested an opportunity to triangulate the Places of Power, and Arianna had refused them. Then the Shaman had made it clear that they guarded the first Place of Power and they did not want a member of the Black Family to enter it. The Shaman feared such power in the hands of the Black Family, and would have done whatever they could, short of fighting the family themselves, to prevent the Black Family from controlling the Triangle.

The Shaman believed that warrior magic, as represented by the Black Family, would use the Triangle for harm. They believed that only Domestic magic should control such power, and they guarded this Place of Power to prove their point.

Yet they were taking him there now—and the fact that he was one of the few who had ever seen the second Place of Power made this event even stranger.

He wondered what the Protectors had said. They were the main guardians of this Place of Power, and they had fought his entry into the village. They hadn't relaxed their vigilance in five years.

Halfway up, he and Madot stopped. A platform with benches carved from stone indicated that this was the designated resting point. Madot sat in the left bench and indicated that Gift sit in the right.

He didn't want to. He wanted to keep climbing. But that was the impatience she was trying to train out of him. He sat.

The bench was cold beneath him, but then it had no veins of red running through it. It faced westward, providing a spectacular view.

The Eccrasian Mountains extended as far as the eye could see. In Vion, distances were vast, and the countries were sparsely populated. These mountains bisected Vion; another shorter range provided its western border. The Fey originated in the mountains, and were like no other race in Vion. Gift could see why. It took a hardy and combative people to survive in this place.

It was early spring, and there was still snow all the way to the tree line on most of the mountain peaks. This one, known as Protectors Mount, never had snow, no matter what time of year. Some said it was because of the Place of Power. Others believed it was because this mountain was alive. Whatever the cause, it made life in Protectors Village just a little easier than it would have been otherwise.

The wind was bracing here. It whipped at Gift's cheeks. He threaded his fingers together. His bare feet were warm on the stone platform. He knew if he looked down, he would see more veins of red below. But he continued to stare over the mountains.

He hadn't been this high before. The rugged peaks were white or gray, and then tapered into a lush greenness provided by a crop of sturdy mountain pines. The valleys down below were lost in morning mist. It was as if he were floating above the clouds.

He could feel Madot's gaze. When he turned, he expected to see her usual indulgent smile. Instead, he saw a deep and unusual sadness on her face.

A small shiver ran through him.

"Let's go," she said, and stood. This time she did not take his arm. She walked ahead of him on the stairs, establishing a pace that was more strenuous than the one before.

He was able to keep up easily, however. The lightness in his legs he had felt earlier was still there. The only difference now was that the stairs were steeper, and he had no chance to observe the sights around him. He had to concentrate on keeping up with Madot.

He had never seen her move so fast. It was almost as if revealing her sadness had embarrassed her.

Or perhaps she had revealed too much.

They reached a second, smaller plateau, and from there he could feel it, the power of the cave ahead. It drew him like a woman's touch. He was familiar with this feeling. It was how he had discovered the Place of Power on Blue Isle. He also had to live with a muted version of it in Protectors Village. Live with it, and deny it at the same time.

Here there was no denial. He allowed the feeling to guide him. He gazed up, and saw the entrance glowing silver. His heart leaped. That sense of homecoming had returned.

Madot was watching him again. "The feeling is strong in you," she said, and the words were a statement, not a question. It almost sounded as if she were disappointed by what she saw.

"Shouldn't it be?" he asked, unable to take his gaze off that entrance.

She didn't answer him. Instead, she led him up the last flight of stairs. These were so steep they were almost a ladder. He had no trouble negotiating them, but he wondered if others did, if the design was purposeful, to prevent unwanteds from coming to this Place of Power.

The stairs ended in another ledge, this one carved flat and maintained to a polished perfection. Pelô, one of the Shaman Protectors, stood at the top of the stairs.

He was skinny and tall, his white hair as chaotic as Madot's. He wore a dark Shaman's robe to blend in with the mountain. He carried no weapon, only a large staff carved from esada wood. He stepped back as Gift climbed onto the ledge. His dark eyes held disapproval, and something else, something even more unsettling.

"One shouldn't test a Warning," Pelô said to Madot.

The look she gave him was dismissive. She didn't bother to reply.

"He has friends at the other Place of Power," Pelô said. "You know we cannot let him inside."

"There are no Shaman currently on Blue Isle," Madot said.

"But there are powerful Visionaries."

Gift stood perfectly still during the exchange. The wind was stronger here, and colder. It buffeted him and he had to constantly shift his weight to keep his balance.

"I am doing what my Vision told me to do five years ago," Madot said.

"Why did you not do it then?" Pelô asked.

"Because there was no need."

"I do not believe there is a need now."

"The Powers issued a Warning."

"Did they?" Pelô asked. "There was no Vision attached."

Gift shifted. Had Madot acted on her own? He didn't like that. "I have never wanted special treatment," he said. "I want to be an apprentice like the others. Bring me up here when the time is right, for them and for me. Please. If this is wrong—"

"No one has said it's wrong," Madot snapped.

Pelô raised a single eyebrow. The effect made him look like a quizzical dog. "I haven't said it, but I should have. It is wrong. The boy does not belong here. He belongs with his family."

"Near the other Place of Power?" Madot asked.

Gift had never seen her agitated before. She wasn't certain of what she was doing either. "I don't want to leave," he said gently. "I do want to learn how to use my powers for healing magic, not warrior magic. I am not a Domestic. I'm a Visionary. The only choice left to me is to become a Shaman."

"You have the Black Throne," Pelô said. "By rights—by Fey law—you should be sitting on it. You and your sister, with your wild magics, believe you are above Fey law and Fey custom. You believed you could give her your Throne. But the Throne chooses whom it will, and for centuries it has chosen your family. Your sister has denied her Feyness all her life—"

"She is more Fey than I ever was," Gift said.

"She was raised by outsiders," Pelô said. "She does not know our customs. She is fierce, but she is no warrior. We have taken no land in fifteen years."

"More than that," Gift said. "My great-grandfather Rugad took no land for twenty before that. He was waiting to hold Blue Isle."

"And now we have Blue Isle. Tradition says we move to Leut and conquer it."

Gift's mouth was dry. He was suddenly thirsty. He and Madot had brought no water or food with them. He wondered if that were customary or an oversight.

"I have never heard a Shaman argue for war before," he said.

"We uphold Fey tradition," Pelô said.

"There is much to Fey tradition," Gift said, "besides war."

"We do not believe in indiscriminate fighting," Pelô said. "But now two Places of Power are known. It is time to follow the prophecy—"

"Enough," Madot said.

"No," Gift said, turning his head toward Pelô. Gift had always thought of that movement as the royal movement, a command without giving a verbal order. "I'm curious."

"And you are an apprentice," Madot snapped. "You do as I say."

"I'm only an apprentice when it suits you," Gift said. "If I were truly one, I would be below, learning how to control my Vision with the others."

"You could control your Vision since you were ten," Madot said. "You have no need for such tricks. Which is why you can never be an ordinary apprentice."

"Then why did you allow me to come here?" he asked.

"We almost didn't," Madot said.

"Who denies the true Black King of the Fey?" Pelô asked.

"I am not the Black King." Gift spit out the words. "I am not and I will not be."

Pelô acted as if the words meant nothing to him. He turned to Madot, moving so that Gift was cut out of the conversation. "Do not take the boy any farther."

"I will not take him to the heart."

"Then why have you brought him?"

"Come with us and see."

"I cannot leave my post."

"Then you will find out after the boy does." She held out a small wizened hand to Gift. "Let's go."

He didn't take her hand. He stood for a moment, looking at Pelô's thin back, at the staff which guided his protective powers, and at the shimmer beyond. The entrance to this Place of Power was plain. The Fey had left it unadorned, so that it looked like a common cave to the untrained—or nonmagical—eye.

"Gift," she said.

He looked at her. If he went with her, he was doing something many of the Shaman did not approve of. If he stood up to her, he was acting like a member of the Black Family. And if he left Protectors Village, he gave up all his dreams. He could not be a true apprentice; he knew that now. He had always thought the Shaman's hesitation reflected their attitude toward him. He hadn't realized it was also because of his own talents, his wild magic.

"Gift," she said, and he recognized the tone. This was the last time she would ask him.

He put his hand in hers. Pelô grunted and turned away.

The shimmer was bright. Gift had seen the entrance to the other Place of Power as a living blackness, not as a silvery light. That seemed odd to him. Still it pulled him forward.

But Madot did not walk toward the entrance. Instead, she went to the side of the platform. Hidden there, between two boulders, were more stairs. They twisted among the rocks, descending out of sight. These stairs were not as clean as the others. No one had maintained them in a long time.

"What is this?" he asked.

She placed one hand on the nearest boulder. "Is it customary among your people—" and whenever she used that phrase in such a sneering way she was referring to the Islanders—"to ask unnecessary questions?"

"I was raised among Fey," he said again, knowing she knew that. Knowing she knew everything about him.

"You were raised among Failures."

The harshness of the word took his breath away. No one spoke of that. No one ever mentioned how all the Fey who had come to Blue Isle in the first invasion force were later killed by the Black King for failing in their mission. He had lost his adoptive parents in that slaughter and to this day he had not forgiven himself for being too far away to save them.

"They were Fey," he said softly.

"There are holes in you, Gift," she said. Her body blocked the stairs. "And a darkness that worries me."

"You've been telling me all day why I am not suited to this place. You used to be my greatest supporter. Why did the Warning change that?"

Instead of answering, she started down the stairs.

"Dodging my questions isn't the best procedure," he said.

"I am still in charge of your program here," she said as she turned the sharp corner. "I may do what I want."

He could no longer see her. If he wanted to know why she brought him here, he had no choice but to follow.

These stairs were slick with dirt. They had once been as polished as the others, but time and wear had destroyed that. There were no handholds, and the corner steps were tricky. He braced his palms on nearby boulders, hoping to keep his balance.

Madot was so far ahead of him that he could only see the edge of her robe. She was like a dream image, ever elusive, impossible to catch.

The farther down he went, the darker it got. No sunlight reached here, and in the little patches of dirt beside the large rocks, nothing grew. But the air was warmer than he expected, and smelled faintly of flowers. He didn't know where the scent came from.

After a final twist, the stairs ended. Another platform surrounded by high rock walls greeted him. Above him he could see patches of blue sky, but it felt as if he were indoors.

No Shaman Protectors greeted him here. Only Madot waited, her hands clasped before her. She looked ancient and small, standing beside the black-scarred stone.

There was something about this place, a feeling of great history and great age, a feeling that much had happened here—more than Gift could take in at one moment.

"Did you have a Vision last night?" Madot asked.

He shook his head. "I haven't had a Vision since I came to Protectors Village." If he had, he would have told her. She knew that. Apprentices were required to report their Visions.

"You felt nothing last night?"

"Nothing," he said.

His answer didn't seem to satisfy her. He didn't know why. It wasn't unusual for Visionaries to go years without a Vision. Some Visionaries only had three or four in their entire lives. A Shaman was trained to invite Visions, but Gift hadn't reached that stage of his training yet.

"Have you ever Seen this place?" she asked.

He understood the question. She was wondering if he had had a Vision about it. He looked around. The stone here wasn't black. It was red, a deep, deep red, the color of drying blood.

"No," he said.

She frowned, but said nothing. With a quick movement, she spun and headed into the darkness. He followed. They went under an overhang that hid a doorway. This may have been a cave at one time, but it had been so long ago that he couldn't tell. It didn't look like a cave. It looked like a building carved out of the rock. The doorway's dimensions were uniform, its edges smooth. The floor was the same polished stone, the walls sanded smooth. Beside the door were Fey lamps. Gift recognized their construction. The Fey lamps he had been raised with carried the captured souls of enemies, and when someone touched the lamp in the proper place, those souls flared with a brilliant light.

These lamps, though, were not warrior lamps. They were filled not with the souls of enemies, but the souls of volunteers—Fey who had died of illness or old age, or who chose to serve their people in this final way.

Madot picked up a lamp and handed it to him, then took one herself. Gift touched the base of the lamp before grasping the metal handle. The lamp flared, revealing several souls inside. They still had their Fey form, and they looked at him through the glass as if he were the curiosity.

Over the years, he had learned not to pay the souls inside a Fey lamp too much attention. The worry was that they would flare to light whenever they wanted, and burn themselves out early. He gave them a small smile, then looked around the room.

It was empty. There was no furniture or built-in benches. The far wall had been scorched as if a fire had burned against it, and another wall bore the imprints of hangings long gone. Madot walked across the room and disappeared through an interior doorway.

Gift followed.

The door led to a long hallway, again perfectly formed. Other doorways lined the walls, and some of these had the remains of wooden doors still hanging in them. But there were no decorations or furnishings, or anything to indicate who—or what—had lived here.

The air was surprisingly fresh and very warm. Even though the floor was covered with a thin layer of dirt, there was no dust. Madot walked as if she had seen all of this before. Gift wanted to stop and look, but knew he could not.

The hallway gradually widened until both of them

could walk side by side. Several branches broke off the hallway here, and a flight of stairs went both up and down, indicating other floors.

At the end of the wide hallway was a set of double doors, made of stone and decorated with highly polished brass. Madot stopped outside of it and passed her hands over the knobs as if performing a ritual to open them.

Gift raised his Fey lamp to help her, and in doing so, something caught his eye. Above the double doors was a crest. It had been carved into the stone, and then covered with a paint that had somehow lasted through the years.

For a moment, he thought he had seen the crest before: in his father's palace on Blue Isle. His family's crest had stood above the throne there: two swords crossed over a heart. But this image was different. Here he saw two hearts pierced by a single sword. He didn't know what it meant, but he knew it wasn't a coincidence.

Madot glanced at him, saw where he was looking, and then smiled. She pushed the double doors open, and stood aside.

The room beyond the doors glowed red. The entire floor was alive with the veins he had seen in the mountainside. The walls were decorated with jewels: large emeralds, sapphires, and diamonds were mixed with shiny black stones and shiny gray stones. They pebbled the wall in a repeating pattern that reflected and at the same time held the red light.

Madot nodded at Gift. He stepped inside. He was shaking, and he wasn't sure why. The place had a vibration to it, a feeling that made him conscious of how small and frail he was. He could almost feel that place inside his head where the Visions lived. It seemed to lift up, to float, as if joining with the red light.

"Is it safe in here?" he asked.

Madot did not answer him. She remained in the doorway.

He took another step inside. She would stop him if it wasn't safe, wouldn't she? He could see his own image reflected in the shiny red floor. As he walked, streaks of gold and silver flowed through the red, like hairline cracks in glass.

He turned. Madot stood in the open doorway, hands clasped behind her back. Watching. She looked like no one he had ever known. A stranger, judging him.

He swallowed and went forward. The gold was taking over the red, brightening the room. The diamonds refracted it into a hundred colors. Across the far wall, a large image slowly appeared. The two hearts again, pierced by the single sword. They rose above a blackness that seemed complete, corporeal.

That blackness was a live thing. He could feel it, drawing and repelling him at the same time.

He glanced over his shoulder. Madot had come into the room. She was walking behind him. No streaks of color appeared on the floor beneath her feet. The light remained dim where she was. He realized, suddenly, that some of the light came from above him.

A single ray of light beamed down from the ceiling, encircling him. He took a large step forward, testing it, and the light moved.

"What is this place?" he asked.

"Go farther," she said.

His palms were damp. He had to remember to take a breath. The blackness drew him deeper. He took another step forward, and then another. The blackness coalesced into a form, into something he could recognize.

A throne.

The Black Throne.

It really existed.

"By the Powers," he whispered. He had never seen anything so magnificent.

The Throne was large enough to seat three full-grown Fey. Its back rose up the wall so high that if Gift stood on the seat, he would have to reach up to touch the top. Its seat, though, was in the normal place, and looked comfortable. Very comfortable.

It looked as if it were made for him.

He made himself stand still. He couldn't move backward, but he wouldn't let himself move forward either. His sister sat on the Black Throne, at least metaphorically. She was the one who ruled the Fey, not he. He had no right to be here.

"What is the point of this?" he asked.

"The Black Heir is supposed to sit in the Black Throne."

He was shaking. "You felt you needed to tempt me? Why?"

"Go closer."

"I'm close enough, thank you."

"It is your Throne," Madot said.

"It is my sister's Throne."

"She has not sat in it."

"She didn't even know it existed. Neither did I."

Madot stood by his side. "Which is why every Black ruler has a Shaman. The Shaman takes the ruler to the Black Throne. Once the Fey ruled from here, but since we have expanded our Empire, this room is largely symbolic."

"My great-grandfather was here?"

"Rugad sat in that chair," Madot said. "I watched him. It frightened him, as it frightens you."

Gift remembered his great-grandfather. Nothing seemed to frighten that man. "I am not frightened," Gift said, not sure if he was lying. "I just don't understand why you need to tempt me now."

"The Warning," she said.

"Repeat it to me." He heard command in his voice. He had tried to purge command from his entire system, but it kept reappearing.

He had to leave.

She said, " 'The hand that holds the scepter shall hold it no more, and the man behind the Throne shall reveal himself in all his glory.' "

"And you believe that I am the man behind the Throne?" he asked.

"Your sister will leave the Black Throne. So the Warning says."

"It says nothing about the Black Throne. It could refer to Blue Isle."

"Blue Isle is a small place compared to the Fey Empire."

"Blue Isle has a Place of Power. It may be small in land, but it is large in the history of the world."

"Still," Madot said. "Your sister sits on Blue Isle's throne, too, does she not?"

"I have never been behind her. I am not even an advisor any longer."

"You are the heir. If she dies or leaves, she has no children to follow her. It will be your hand that holds the scepter."

"So you say," Gift said. "But I see nothing of that in this Warning. And why, if I take the Throne, is this a Warning? I am of Black Blood. I am, as you say, the legitimate heir. This should not be a problem."

She tilted her head slightly. "Blood against blood," she whispered.

He felt another shiver run through him despite the warmth of the room. Members of his family from the Fey side could not fight against each other. The Fey phrase "Blood against blood" referred to that. Gift had been taught the meaning like this:

Black Blood could not fight against Black Blood. It led to chaos and death. The last time Black Blood warred on itself, centuries ago, three thousand people died. It was said to be a raging madness that made fathers turn upon sons, sons upon mothers, mothers upon daughters. And it happened throughout the Fey Empire. Only one in ten survived. The Fey Empire was small in those days. Now it covered over half the world.

"I would never kill my sister," he said. "Even if I didn't care for her, I know what happens when people of Black Blood kill each other. I understand my responsibility to the Fey."

"I have Seen it," she whispered. "There is a madness loose."

"Loose? Or will it be turned loose by something we don't know?"

She took his hands. Her fingers were like ice. "Touch the Black Throne," she said. "For me."

"Why? So that you can become Shaman to a Black King?" His words were harsh, his voice as cruel as he could make it. He hadn't expected this here. He had experienced it in the palace on Blue Isle, and it had been the reason he had not seen his Uncle Bridge in Nye. But he hadn't expected it among the Shaman. He hadn't believed, until this moment, that Shaman could have ambitions.

"I do not want to be Shaman to a Black King." Her entire body was rigid. She almost cringed before him. There was something else then, something he didn't entirely understand.

"It's a test," he said. "You want to see if I am lying to you, if I really want the Black Throne."

Her nod was almost imperceptible. If he hadn't known her so well, he wouldn't have seen it.

"Why isn't my word good enough?" he asked.

"The fate of the world rests on your shoulders," she whispered.

"The fate of half the world," he said. "My decision only influences the Fey Empire."

"Whoever sits on the Black Throne determines how big that Empire will be," she said.

He hadn't been this angry in years. She had no right to test him like this, no right to doubt his word.

And then he heard his own thoughts, how entitled they sounded, how much like his great-grandfather. She had a right. She needed to know if she was bringing him into the fold as a Shaman or as a future Black King. The Shaman did not want the next Black King here.

He took a deep breath, then let it out slowly. "If I do as you ask, then you must promise me one thing."

She raised her head. Her eyes reflected the red in the room. The light gave her face an eerie cast. "What?"

"If I prove that I do not want the Black Throne, promise you'll train me as a Shaman. You'll give me the full training, including the parts you've been denying me because you're afraid of what I might do with the learning."

She looked away from him. That movement was

confirmation that she had been denying him, that even she was afraid of him.

He stood at his full height, hands clasped behind him, feet slightly apart in military style. The stance of a ruler. He knew it. He did it deliberately. He wasn't making this agreement with her as an apprentice. He was making it as an heir to the Black Throne.

"All right," she said without looking at him. Her voice was soft. "I agree to your terms."

"Good." He started toward the Throne and then stopped. He had to know one more thing before he touched it, before he did as she asked. "If I touch this Throne," he said, "does that obligate me to rule the Fey?"

"No," she said. "If anyone could touch the Black Throne and become ruler of the Fey Empire, this place would be heavily guarded. Only true heirs will be drawn to it, and only the one who will sit on the Throne will be comfortable in it."

He glanced at the Throne, at the swirling blackness of its base. It looked comfortable to him. Too comfortable.

"Why hasn't anyone brought Arianna here?" he asked.

"She has no Shaman."

"If this is important, then a Shaman should have gone to her."

"One did," Madot said. "Arianna will not leave Blue Isle."

That wasn't entirely true. Arianna saw no need to leave Blue Isle. She believed she could rule as well from there as she could from any other place in the Fey Empire. Apparently, no one had explained the Black Throne to her. The Shaman had probably demanded that she come here, and Arianna, stubborn as always, hadn't bowed to a demand.

Madot was watching him. For the first time since he had come to the mountains, his impatience had left him. He didn't want to approach the Throne but he was drawn to it at the same time, the same way he had been drawn to the Place of Power. All those years here he had controlled that feeling.

What would giving in now do?

His dead mother's face flickered across his Vision. It was a brief flash, and then nothing. She had never done that before. Usually she spoke to him. He could only see her in a Place of Power, and then only when she wanted to visit him. She hadn't visited him in over a decade.

He tried to conjure her again, but could not. Whatever had passed across his Vision was gone now. The near Sighting had left him cold and a little shaken. Had she been trying to warn him? Or had he simply seen something he'd wished he could see? Someone who could give him advice at this moment?

He did not look at Madot again. He took a deep breath. Did he want the Black Throne? No. He had never wanted to rule. From his childhood, when his grandfather had died and Gift had been left in charge of the Fey on Blue Isle, he had not wanted to rule. But he had ruled, and he had hated it. He couldn't imagine a life like that. It was not a life he wanted to live.

The Throne pulsed. Its blackness seemed to move outward. The crest on the wall behind it seemed even more vibrant, more alive than it had earlier. The sword glistened in the reddish light. For a moment, he thought he could see blood dripping out of the impaled hearts.

He took one step closer. With his right hand he reached out, and touched the Throne's arm. It was cold. The chill shocked him. Then it warmed and he felt how very comfortable it would be. It would hold him, embrace him. It would be so easy to slip into the Throne, to become part of it.

But something within him resisted the simplicity of it. The Throne was calling to his Black Blood, not to him. He did not want to sit there. Now or ever.

He started to pull his hand away, but the blackness reached out and enveloped him. It felt like the warm and reassuring grip of a friend, questioning him, warning him that he was making a mistake. He stared down, saw that his hand was covered in blackness.

"No," he said and yanked.

As the Throne released him, golden light shot from his hand and the place he had touched. It was so bright he had to close his eyes. He tumbled backward and the fall seemed to take forever.

He could see the light through his eyelids. He brought an arm over his eyes, but it was too late. The light flowed inside his mind, illuminated all the dark corners, and threaded through his Vision. He tried to push the light out, but he could not. Instead it reached inside that part of him where his magic lived, and tapped.

The familiar feeling of the world spinning, the only acknowledgment that a Vision was coming, entrapped him. He tried to prevent it. He wasn't sure if this was a Vision sent by the Powers or something triggered by the Throne. And he wasn't sure if those two things were all that different.

He felt his body land on the stone and then the spinning began in earnest. He could not open his eyes. But he Saw—

—His long-dead great-grandfather alive as if he had never died, sitting on the throne in Blue Isle, smiling at him—

—And his sister was standing before the Black Throne, looking at it with such longing that it frightened him. He wanted to warn her, to tell her to stand back, but he almost didn't recognize her or the look on her face. He took a step toward her—

When everything shifted again.

—He was in water, thrashing, an undertow pulling him down. Water filled his mouth, tasting of brine and salt. The old Fey in the boat—his great-grandfather again? Or someone who looked like him?—reached for Gift, but if Gift took his hand, the old man would die. And Gift didn't want that. He didn't want to cause someone else's death—

—His sister, her face gone as if someone had drawn it and then wiped it away, calling his name—

—His long-ago best friend, the man to whom he'd always be Bound, Coulter, kissing a Fey woman, kissing her, and then Gift grabbed him, pulled his head back, and put a knife to his throat. He had to—

—His sister, screaming—

—In the Places of Power, two Shaman stood at the door, preparing to find the Triangle of Might. He couldn't stop them. He was trying, trying, but he didn't have the strength—

And then the spinning stopped. He was lying on his side on the strange stone floor. Gold and silver spread out around him, but the rest of the floor was red. Madot hovered over him. She hadn't touched him. She knew better. Visions were sacred things.

"How long was I out?" he whispered. His throat was dry, his voice nearly gone. Sometimes Visions took half a day from a Visionary's life, and sometimes only an instant.

"I don't know," she said. "I thought maybe you were dead. You hit the floor so hard."

Her voice was shaking. What would it have meant if he died here? Would she have been punished? Would the Shaman as a unit? Would Arianna have finally come to the Eccrasian Mountains? Would it have taken his death to bring her to the Black Throne?

He sat up slowly. His whole body ached. It felt as if the light had poked and prodded him, had used instruments on him to see if he hid something that wasn't there. He closed his eyes. Nothing had been taken from him, and so far as he could tell, nothing had been added. He just felt like a room that had been thoroughly searched.

Madot put a careful hand on his back. Her touch was gentle, but he wanted to shake it off. Had she known what would happen when she brought him here?

"Did you have a Vision too?" he asked.

"No."

And that was odd in itself. Usually a series of Visions was powerful enough to trigger any nearby Visionary. By rights, all of the Shaman in Protectors Village should

have Seen something. And Madot's Vision should have
been as powerful as Gift's.

He opened his eyes. Her face wasn't far from his, her
small mouth pursed, her lower lip trembling.

"Did you know this would happen?" he asked.

"No."

He waited.

She swallowed, hard, his mentor no longer. Something in their relationship had changed. Something
fundamental.

"I wanted to see," she said slowly, "if the Throne
would hold you. I thought it would. You're the oldest
child of the direct line. It should have held you whether
you wanted it to or not."

"And if it had, you would have stopped my training."

"A warrior has no place among the Shaman," she
said. "A Black King cannot serve as his own advisor."

Gift pushed himself off the floor. He was shaking. A
gold outline of his body remained in the spot where he
had lain. Slowly it returned to red, in all places except the
points where his feet still touched.

"It did hold me," he said. "It grabbed me and it was
going to pull me in and I pulled away."

"That's not possible," she said.

"I did."

"You cannot separate yourself from the Black Throne."

"I did." His body still ached from the strain of that too.

"It wanted you?" she whispered.

"And I said no."

Her eyes widened. "That's not how it's supposed to
work."

"Oh?" He was regaining control of his voice. He made
it sound cool. "Was I supposed to disappear into the
Throne, and then try to yank command from my sister?"

"She would have Seen. She would have given command to you. It would have worked."

"This was your Vision?"

"Once," she said. She raised her head and looked him

straight in the eye. "I Saw your sister hand her Throne to a tall Fey with coal black hair. I did not see his face, only hers. But when you came here, I knew you were the younger version of the man I Saw in my Vision."

He didn't know how she could know that. He had learned, in his thirty-three years, that Visions were not so easily deciphered. "Have you told anyone else about this Vision?"

"Of course." It was standard procedure for a Shaman—for any kind of Visionary—to share a Vision with another. Sometimes the other Visionary had a similar Vision, and together they would assemble the truth as if it were a puzzle. "I told the entire village. Others had Seen changes in the Black Throne, but none had Seen you. We decided to wait, to give you training, and to see what it did to you."

He touched his hair. His still-black hair. "You expected me to turn white."

"And to age," she said. "When you did not, we knew you were the one in the Vision. No one else looks like you."

"From the back, I'm not so sure."

Her gaze was soft. "We have thought of these things."

"You've thought of Sebastian?" He was referring to the stone being whom he called brother. "He's my Golem. He was created in my image."

"He does not look like you. I have Seen him. His face is cracked."

"His face. But from the back, he could be mistaken for me."

"No," she said. "He moves differently than you."

Sebastian did too. He moved slowly, as if each action took extra thought. Just from his movements, it was possible to tell that Sebastian was not made of flesh and blood.

"And then there's my sister," Gift said. "She's a Shape-Shifter. Have you thought that the person you saw was a Shape-Shifter as well?"

"She was handing the Throne to this person. He had to be of Black Blood. She is the only Shape-Shifter of Black Blood in recorded history."

Gift sighed. Madot had a point, but it still made him uneasy. His own Visions, the recent ones, haunted him. Why was he seeing his great-grandfather? Rugad had been dead for fifteen years, slaughtered with his troops near the Place of Power on Blue Isle by Gift's Islander father and the former leader of the Islander religion. They had believed that Rugad, the greatest warrior of all the Fey—the Black King who conquered the most territory in his reign—was an evil, ruthless man who had to be eliminated. Was his appearance in Gift's Vision a symbol of someone else, someone equally as ruthless, who would wrest the Throne from Arianna? And who would that be? He could think of no one of Black Blood who could do such a thing.

"You do not believe me," Madot said.

"I do not believe that I was the man in your Vision." He ran a hand through his hair. He ached everywhere, and he hadn't been this exhausted in years. What had happened to him here? And did he dare tell the Shaman of it? Or would they see that as yet another sign that he was not worthy of their profession, not capable of their magic?

"You did not See what I Saw."

He frowned. "I have never Seen myself on the Black Throne."

"Just because you have not Seen it," she said, "doesn't mean it won't happen." One of the main tenets of Vision. A Visionary never Saw the entire truth.

"I know," he said.

"But you Saw something else, something that disturbs you." She spoke softly, referring to his recent Vision.

He didn't want to answer her, not yet. He needed to talk to the others, but he would do so before all the Shaman. He had had some of these Visions before, when his great-grandfather had first arrived on Blue Isle. Gift did not think the return of the Visions a coincidence.

"What was that light?" he asked Madot.

She glanced at the Throne and shook her head. "I have never heard of anything like it. But then, no one has rejected the Black Throne before."

He had put that much together himself. "But what do you think it could be?"

Her face went flat, as if her emotions were so strong that she had to struggle to hide them. "The Throne absorbs magic. Magic often comes in the form of light."

"You think the Throne was releasing magic?"

"Yes," she said. Her voice shook. "And I hope I'm wrong."

CHAPTER TWO

*T*HE ARGUMENTS WERE old ones. Arianna gripped the arms of the old wooden throne in a vain attempt to maintain her patience. No one had ever explained to her that the main duty of a ruler was to listen to people blather about things she thought she had already made herself clear on.

The audience room was full. Her Fey guards stood against the wall, arms at their sides. Several other guards were in the hidden listening booths, just in case someone got out of hand. Because she hated this duty so much, she often put it off, and then petitioners piled up. She knew that she would be here for most of the afternoon. There was a line of supplicants outside, most of them in chairs her Domestics had provided—spelled to keep anyone waiting calm.

It was amazing to her how small this chamber felt when it was filled with people. It was actually one of the longest rooms in the palace, and had the same width as some of the larger suites. But the ancient spears lining the walls seemed to make it smaller, as did all those guards—not to mention the fact that there were no windows to open. She had spent too many years Shifting from one animal or bird form to another. The outdoors was, in some ways, more comfortable to her than an interior room with no fresh air, and filled with torches that couldn't quite make it light enough.

The chamber was too hot and smelled of nervous sweat—the petitioners', not her own. She wasn't nervous about anything. She was just hoping she could make it through the afternoon without losing her temper, providing more stories for the gossip mill. The Islanders loved her, the very first Queen of Blue Isle, or so she heard. They called her colorful, and gave her a lot of leeway because she was a war hero, and because she had Fey blood. Her mercurial moods had become something the placid Islanders were willing to forgive because she had tainted blood.

The bastards. The Fey didn't see her as mercurial. Which probably proved the Islanders' point.

That mercurial label was probably the reason she hated these sessions most of all. In her other role as Black Queen of the Fey Empire, she did not need to hold such formal audiences. Sometimes she thought of combining the roles, but she had tried that once, about twelve years ago, and all it managed to do was upset the Islanders and confuse the Fey.

So she was stuck with days like this. A day full of spring sunshine, and she had to spend it inside, listening to people who had placed all their hopes on this single meeting.

The pair in front of her were prosperous men from the city's seafaring merchants society. They were Islander, but they wore Fey cloaks over their linen shirts and tight pants. Their boots had been made in Nye. She wondered if they dressed that way to prove how cosmopolitan they were, or to show her how important trade with other continents was.

The oldest one, a man with so many lines on his face that she knew she would have to count them if he went on much longer, was arguing that Blue Isle needed to resume its trade with Fillé, the country on the Leut continent with the most accessible ports. Every quarter since Arianna had become Queen of Blue Isle, some of the older Islanders came before her, asking her to resume trade with Fillé. And every quarter, she turned them down.

Leut was not part of the Fey Empire. It was supposed to have been the next stop on her great-grandfather's long series of conquests. But the Fey Empire stretched over half the world already. It had enough wealth to sustain itself forever, and to keep its people happy and well fed. Arianna, who had been raised Islander, not Fey, did not see the point of continuing the conquest when there was nothing to be gained but more land. Her main focus as Black Queen had been to retrain the Fey, to get them to think about building instead of destroying.

It was an uphill battle, and she didn't need distractions like trade with a non-Fey country to remind the Fey that they used to conquer people instead of set up diplomatic relations.

Of course, she couldn't explain that to the merchant who was droning on and on and on. She had never explained that. This was one instance where she relied on her mercurial reputation. When he was through with his presentation, and when his elderly friend was through with his, she would wave a hand and say in a particularly dismissive tone, "Petition denied."

They would be disappointed, of course, and because she never gave a reason for denying this particular petition, they would try again—or other merchants would—next quarter. In keeping her reasons to herself, she doomed herself to a long afternoon four times a year.

As the first merchant finished, something caught her eye. She looked up. A broad flat light, gold laced with black, flowed into the room. It was wide, like a river.

She blinked, and felt the light pass through her. No one else seemed to notice. She blinked again, and the light was gone. She almost turned to see if it flowed through the wall behind her, but she didn't. She wasn't even sure she had seen it, not really. Maybe she had imagined it. Surely someone else would have noticed.

The second merchant stepped forward. He opened his mouth and she wished she could close her eyes. Her head was beginning to ache. Lights, headaches. She really hated this part of her work.

"Highness," he said. "If we open trade with Fillé, we not only have the Fey Empire, but an entire new . . ."

She wasn't listening anymore. She felt not quite dizzy, but not quite solid either. Light-headed. Black dots swam before her eyes. Inside her mind, something moved.

". . . products we have no use for throughout the Empire. Our productivity is up. We have space to grow new crops, items that will . . ."

Moved, raised up, awoke. She wanted to put a hand to her head, but did not.

". . . revenue for Blue Isle. Even though we are an unconquered part of the Fey Empire . . ."

Which was so important to the Islanders, she thought. And perhaps in some ways it was. She willed herself to focus on his words.

". . . could use trade of our own. We are not asking for the Empire's blessing. Just yours, as Queen of Blue Isle."

Pain exploded behind her eyes. She gasped and bent over. For a moment, she saw only blackness. It was as if she had crawled inside her own mind.

The pain ran through her head, down the back of her neck, and into her spine. She couldn't move if she wanted to. It felt as if something were being forcibly separated from the inside of her skull.

"Highness?"

The voice was soft. She made herself focus on it, willed herself to think despite the pain. With great effort, she sat upright. The two Islanders stood before her, their pale skin and blond hair in sharp contrast to the Fey darkness filling the room.

The wooden throne felt sturdy beneath her, the only sturdy thing about her at the moment.

"Highness?" one of the Islanders said again.

She should know who he was. She should know who all of them were. But she didn't. It was as if they were at the same time familiar and unfamiliar. She had never felt like this before.

"Highness?" The other Islander took a step toward her.

Highness. Using titles was an Islander tradition. It felt wrong. She was Fey. Fey did not use titles. She almost opened her mouth to say that, but she couldn't think as to why she would. She was Queen of Blue Isle and Black Queen of the Fey. The Islanders could call her "Highness" if they wanted to. It was correct.

She put a hand to her forehead. "I must postpone this meeting," she said. She didn't even know what the meeting was about, not at the moment. And she should. She should.

But she did know better than to admit weakness.

"My advisors will tell you when I am ready to resume." She stood, not too slowly to tip off anyone as to how very ill she felt, and not too quickly in case she fainted. The pain stabbed into her brain as if it were digging to pull something loose.

She walked off the platform, through a side door, and into the cool hallway. The hallway was lined with tapestries depicting Islander events she didn't remember or understand. One of her Islander guards came out of the listening chamber. He too looked familiar. And concerned.

"Arianna," he said and that sounded strange too. An Islander using Fey traditions? He was short, like they all were, blond, and his face had lines. But it was familiar. And dear. She knew it, knew it well, had trusted it . . .

She was frowning. The hand she had placed on her forehead in the throne room was still there. No matter how hard she tried not to look ill, she failed. "Get me a Healer," she said, and put her other hand against the wall.

She would not faint. Not here. Not anywhere. Fainting was weakness and no one of Black Blood showed weakness.

And then the feeling of determination passed as if it

had never been. She looked up to see if her friend the guard had left. He had. She would sit beside the door, in this corridor, until she felt better. She would sit—

HER EYELIDS FLUTTERED and then she opened her eyes. She was in bed, with a sheet and a blanket covering her. The windows were open to the garden. A robin flew past the window, pausing to look inside. She smiled at it, wondering if she had met it when she Shape-Shifted into her bird form. The light breeze blowing inside was cool and fresh, and felt good on her hot face.

She pushed the pillows back and eased herself up. The headache was gone. Only the memory of it remained, as a kind of absence—a feeling that if she probed too hard, the pain would return. She made herself relax and take in the safety of the room.

This had been her room from infancy. Once it had been the nursery. Her Fey mother had played with her stone brother Sebastian here, and her blood brother Gift had slept in this room for less than a week before he was kidnapped by the Fey. After Arianna's birth, she spent all her time here. She and Sebastian bonded here, and she had always come to this place when she needed comfort.

She needed comfort now, although she wasn't exactly sure why. She had had headaches before, and the normal illnesses that plagued everyone: colds and an occasional flu. But she had never felt as if she couldn't hold herself upright. She had never felt such pain in her whole life. For thirty years, she had been healthy and strong. Was that suddenly going to change?

"Health is what we believe it to be." The voice came from the corner of the room.

Arianna turned slowly. Seger sat in the chair beside the cold stone fireplace. Her nut brown fingers were threaded together, her delicately aging face placid. She had been the Black King's Healer once, a woman of such talent that she had been allowed to touch Arianna's Fey great-grandfather. After his death, Seger had shown her loyalties to the Black Family, and Arianna kept her as her own personal Domestic, the Healer who spent more time looking after the staff in the palace than Arianna herself.

"What?" Arianna asked. Her voice cracked. How long had she been unconscious?

"Health is what we believe it to be." Seger stood and threaded her hands into the sleeves of her white robe. "You were sitting there, worrying that your health had gone."

Seger did not read minds. No Fey did. But she had known. "Was it that obvious?" Arianna asked.

"Your face is a book to me, child."

"I'm no child," Arianna said.

"In my world you are."

"I've been ruling your world for fifteen years."

"We shall hope that you rule it for a hundred more." Seger crossed toward the bed and sat on its side. "Tell me what happened."

Arianna frowned. She wasn't sure what happened. She had seen something before the headache, but the memory was tantalizingly out of reach, as if something held it hidden behind a wall. Instead of telling Seger about that (was there something to tell?), Arianna explained the headache, the suddenness of it, the confusion it brought her, and how the pain finally felled her. She couldn't describe that feeling of alienness, of having thoughts not quite her own, so she didn't.

"Have you eaten anything unusual?" Seger asked, putting her warm hand on Arianna's forehead.

"No."

"Slept normally?"

"Yes."

Seger tilted her head. "What do you remember before the headache struck?"

"I—" Arianna stopped herself. She closed her eyes, trying to remember. She had—seen?—something.

"Ari?"

She shook her head, sighed, and opened her eyes. "We were talking about opening trade with Leut. The leaders of Jahn's seafaring merchants came to speak to me about the possibilities."

"Don't they have enough business trading through the Fey Empire?" Seger asked. She was clearly trying to distract Arianna. She knew that Arianna had forgotten something and she was trying to give Arianna's mind a chance to recover the memory.

Arianna smiled at her. "I didn't know you were interested in policy."

"And I didn't think we were going to expand our borders beyond Blue Isle."

"Trading with countries on a brand-new continent frightens you?"

"Worries me," Seger said. "Open the door a crack, and someone will push it wide."

Arianna nodded, surprised to find that the movement didn't hurt. "It worries me as well. But the Islander merchants remember a time when trade with Leut was common."

"Before you."

"Long before me. Long before the Fey found Blue Isle."

Seger took Arianna's right hand and stretched it before her, poking at the center of the palm. Then she twisted it slightly, exposing the underside of the wrist, and traced the entire length of the arm to the neck.

"None of this hurts?"

"No," Arianna said. "I feel fine now."

"Hmm." Seger frowned. "Nothing happened to you in that discussion? No one touched you? No one cursed you?"

Arianna leaned as far back as she could so that she could see Seger's face. "You think this was a magical attack?"

"I am trained to look at all options." Seger took Arianna's other hand and began the same procedure.

"I was speaking to Islanders," Arianna said.

"Your father is an Islander."

"My father *was* an Islander."

Seger tilted her head slightly. They disagreed about her father. Arianna believed he was dead; Seger believed he was not. Arianna's father, King Nicholas, had gone down one of the tunnels in the Place of Power fourteen years ago, and hadn't been seen since. At first, Arianna had been unwilling to accept the loss. Now she knew it was what made her rule on the Isle possible. If her father had still been alive and visible, none of the Islanders would have accepted her.

Still, any thought of her father saddened her. "All I meant," she said carefully, "was that the average Islander does not have magical abilities."

Seger smiled. "Sometimes it is clear that you are a Shape-Shifter. You have a Shifter's arrogance."

Arianna rolled her eyes. "All right," she said. "The average Islander has no idea whether or not he has magic. And certainly couldn't use it on me."

"There were no Fey in the room?"

"My guards."

Arianna took her left hand back. Seger's silence was profound.

"What have you been trying to remember?" Seger asked.

Arianna bit her lower lip. Seger was right; she saw everything about Arianna clearly. Too clearly. "I saw something before the headache. A—light?"

"What kind of light?"

Arianna shrugged. "At the time, I thought I imagined it. No one else seemed to notice."

"Perhaps you saw it with your Vision."

"Or perhaps it was part of the headache."

Seger stared at her. Obviously, Seger did not believe the light to be part of the headache.

"What makes you think this was a magical attack?" Arianna asked.

"The fact that I can find no residual pain in your body. The suddenness of it."

"I have known people to die suddenly of extreme headache," Arianna said, thinking of one of her father's guards, a loyal man who had put a hand to his head, complained of pain, and then passed out. When he awoke, he could no longer speak or move, and two days later he died.

"Yours is not the same pattern," Seger said. "You should summon other Shifters on the Isle, see if they had the same experience you did."

"What of other Visionaries?"

"Is that where the pain was? In your Vision?"

Arianna shook her head. "It was all over my brain, as if something were digging into my mind, and peeling away layers of thought."

Seger placed a hand on Arianna's forehead, and then put her other hand on the back of Arianna's skull, as if she wanted to hold Arianna's brain together. The movement pulled Arianna forward slightly.

"Do you feel as if you've lost anything?" Seger asked quietly.

"No," Arianna asked.

"As if anything's been added?"

"No."

Seger let go of her head. Arianna could still feel the imprint of her hands.

"Do you know what this could be?" Arianna asked. "Does it sound like a magic you're familiar with?"

"No," Seger said. "But Fey and Islander families have started intermingling. Magic is no longer as controlled as it was. You and Gift are evidence of that."

"And Sebastian."

Seger smiled. "Your stone brother is old magic. I worry, sometimes, about his longevity."

"Perhaps he felt something," Arianna said.

"We can ask."

Arianna nodded. "Find him. Tell him I want a private conference. You can listen."

"I plan to," Seger said. "I will accompany you from now on."

Arianna crossed her arms and leaned back against the pillows. "Now you give orders to the Black Queen?"

Seger looked at her oddly. "It is my function," she said, rather stiffly.

Arianna wondered what she had said that was wrong. Seger had never given her that look before.

"If you can't find anything wrong with me," Arianna said, "I'm going to go back to work."

"As long as I accompany you." Seger was holding fast to that. Arianna stared at her.

"You will not divulge anything you learn in private meetings."

"I never have," Seger said. "I don't plan to start now."

Arianna threw the covers back. She felt fine. In fact, she felt better than fine. She had more energy than she had had in weeks. She grabbed the gold ceremonial gown she had been wearing before and slipped it over her head. She didn't know who had undressed her, and she didn't care. Her people did their duty as they saw fit, and their first order of business was to take care of her.

She cinched the gown at the waist with an ornate gold belt made on Nye. She had decided about five years ago to start mixing the cultures that the Fey Empire had conquered. If she wore something, the rest of the Empire did too. She could think of no better way of supporting unity than mingling products, ideas, and commerce in as many ways as possible.

Her long black hair was flowing free. She wrapped it into a bun and held it in place with gold and black painted L'Nacin sticks. Then she slipped her feet into sandals made here on Blue Isle, hating the feel of shoes against her skin. She had always hated shoes, but she wore them now. The birthmark on the base of her chin marked her as a Shape-Shifter, and the golden color of her skin marked her as part-Islander. She didn't need other things, like her preference for bare feet, to set her apart from the people she ruled. They had enough trouble with her unusual attitudes without being reminded that she had a slightly different heritage than all of them.

Arianna opened the door to her room. A young Islander page stood outside, his simple brown clothing marking his lowly status. He bowed when he saw her.

"Get the Islander merchants back in my audience chamber," she said, "and apologize for the abrupt end to our meeting. Tell them I will join them shortly."

The page nodded and started down the hall.

"I haven't dismissed you yet," Arianna said.

The boy froze, his back rigid. He couldn't have been more than twelve, and he was probably terrified to work in the palace. Still, he had to learn protocol.

"Is my brother in his rooms?"

The page swallowed visibly. He bowed again. "No, ma'am. He left his rooms a few moments ago. I believe he was going to the gardens."

Of course. Sebastian's favorite place on the entire Isle. Arianna placed her hand on the page's shoulder.

"Thank you," she said to him. "Now you may go."

He started to run, then remembered himself and slowed down. He headed for the stairs, toward the royal portraits of all the past Islander rulers, and looked up as he did so. He seemed startled by all those round blonds facing him. Arianna was nothing like them.

She suppressed a smile. As a child, she used to stand before those portraits and wonder how she fit in. She had hated how different she looked. Now she looked at her own portrait and saw how she did fit. Her long narrow face and angular features were a heritage from her mother, but the roundness to her cheeks and her expression came from her father. She also saw, in that portrait, what people had remarked on since Gift came into her life years ago: that she and her natural-born brother were male and female sides to the same face. Outside of identical twins, she had never seen two people who looked more alike. Not even Gift and the man who literally had been modeled after him, Sebastian.

Arianna went to the end of the corridor and peered out the bubbled glass window. The garden was barren except for the plants that remained green year-round.

She saw them as splotches of color against the brown. Sebastian had to be down there somewhere.

She turned, and almost collided with Seger.

"For a woman who was concerned about her health," Seger said, "you seem most energetic."

Arianna shrugged. "I'm happy to be feeling well."

Seger grunted as if she didn't quite believe her. Arianna wasn't sure she believed herself. She used to have this kind of energy as a young woman. Since she ruled the Fey, she couldn't remember feeling this kind of buoyant joy.

She grabbed her skirt in one hand, and hurried toward the stairs. Seger followed. Arianna took the shallow steps two at a time, something her personal guards had complained about. But the stairs were built for little short Islander legs, and she was one of the tallest of the Fey. She felt more comfortable going down the stairs in this way.

She reached the ground floor, took a side corridor, and pushed open the double doors that led into the garden. The air was even cooler here than she expected, and smelled of freshly turned dirt. She would get the hem of her skirt filthy, but she didn't care. She stood on the flagstone patio that one of her advisors had begged her to add so that she and Sebastian could hold an occasional meeting outside without ruining their clothes, and then she stepped off into the dirt.

Sebastian was leaning against the palace wall, his gray cracked skin blending in with the stone. He wore his usual black, which set off his black hair, and made his gray eyes seem even lighter than they were. He could never be handsome—his skin prevented that—but he had an arresting charm that she was certain had come from Gift.

Sebastian was a Golem, created by Domestic Fey long dead to replace the infant Gift when he was kidnapped. According to most rules of magic, Sebastian should have died weeks after he was created, but he did not. He was

thirty-three years old, ancient for a Golem, and had survived two shatterings that Arianna knew of. He was
made of stone, but inside him was a person. The materials of his personality had been supplied by Gift over the
years. The two were Linked from infancy. In some ways,
Sebastian was a part of Gift that had lived separately
from him since they were babies.

Arianna went to Sebastian and took his cold smooth
hands in hers. They had been close since she was born,
and more than once Sebastian had saved her life.

"Sebastian," she said. "What are you doing out
here?"

He turned his head slowly and looked at her. Because
of his extremely slow movements, and the cautious way
he spoke, some thought him feeble. But he wasn't. His
stone body had great limitations, most of which Sebastian had tried—and failed—to overcome.

"I . . . scared . . . my-self," he said in that broken way
of his. His voice was raspy and had no melody at all.

She held his hands tighter. "How?"

"That . . . voice . . ." he said. "The . . . one . . . I . . .
found. The . . . one . . . you . . . and . . . Fat-her . . . said . . .
I . . . could . . . not . . . use."

Her entire body went rigid. The voice he was referring
to was Rugad's voice. The voice of the Black King, Arianna's great-grandfather. With his bizarre magical abilities, Sebastian found the voice and thought it a good
substitute for his own. When he had used it after Rugad's
death, however, he had so frightened his family that they
asked him never to use it again.

"What about that voice?" she asked.

"I . . . spoke . . . with . . . it."

"On purpose?"

He shook his head in his own distinct way. One
careful movement to the right and back again. "It . . .
came . . . out . . . of . . . my . . . mouth. I . . . could . . .
not . . . stop . . . it."

"What did it say?"

His fingers had wrapped around hers. His grip was so strong she felt her bones rub together, but she said nothing. He was terrified. She hadn't seen him terrified in years.

"It . . . said . . ." He closed his eyes. " 'Where is that girl?' "

The voice that came out of his mouth was not his. Arianna took a step backward, wiping her hands on her skirt as if she had touched the body of her dead great-grandfather. Hearing his voice again made it seem almost as if he were alive.

She turned, saw Seger behind her, hands clasped over her heart. "Don't let him do that again," Seger said.

"Sebastian," Arianna said. "Sebastian, open your eyes."

He did. They were filled with tears. "It . . . hap-pen-ed . . . again, did-n't . . . it?"

She nodded.

"What . . . does . . . it . . . mean, Ari?"

She didn't know. Seger stepped forward, almost as if she were coming between the two of them on purpose. "When did this first happen?" she asked.

"Not . . . long . . . ago. I . . . saw . . . a . . . light. It . . . went . . . through . . . me. Then . . . the . . . voice . . ." He shuddered. "After . . . that, I . . . came . . . here."

"Did you say anything else?"

Sebastian shook his head.

"Did anyone hear you?"

Sebastian shook his head again. One of the tears left his eye and ran down the cracks in his cheek. "Did . . . I . . . do . . . something . . . wrong?"

"No," Seger said. "You did something right by coming here alone. When the voice comes, can you anticipate it?"

Sebastian looked at Arianna. She wiped away another tear that hovered on his lower lid. "I . . . do . . . not . . . know."

"You closed your eyes before you used the voice. Was—"

"I . . . did . . . not . . . use . . . it!" Sebastian's lower lip was trembling. "It . . . used . . . me."

Seger let out a small sigh, as if she had expected that and feared it at the same time. Arianna looked at her. "What is it?"

"That light was important. I wish I had seen it. I don't think it's a coincidence that after it went through you, you had a headache and Rugad's voice developed a mind of its own," Seger said.

"You . . . are . . . ill?" Sebastian asked Ari.

"Not now," she said. "Seger helped."

"What . . . is . . . hap-pen-ing?"

"I don't know," Seger said. "But I think we've been very careless. We shouldn't have let you keep Rugad's voice, Sebastian."

"He's had it for years. Nothing has happened." Arianna slipped an arm around her brother. He was shaking. Sometimes he seemed much younger than he was.

"I know," Seger said. "But I think it's time we removed it."

"Can you do that without hurting Sebastian?" If the answer was no, Arianna would forbid any attempt. Sebastian was one of the most important people in her life, perhaps the most important since her father had disappeared.

"I don't know," Seger said. "I've never removed a voice from a Golem before."

"I . . . want . . . it . . . gone," Sebastian said. He took Arianna's hand again. "I'm . . . sor-ry . . . I . . . found . . . it."

Arianna smiled at him, giving him reassurance she didn't feel. Everything seemed like it had changed suddenly, and she didn't know why. Or how.

"I'm going to need help," Seger said. "I suspect what we're facing is something greater than Domestic magic can deal with."

Arianna froze. "What do you mean?"

"Let me do some investigating first, and then I'll tell you."

"So you're not going to follow me anymore," Arianna said.

"I'll be with you as much as I can. But this is strange, and the fact it has attacked both of you is worrisome. If Gift weren't with the Shaman in the Eccrasian Mountains, I'd be concerned for him as well. But if anything has happened to him, they'll know what to do."

Gift. Arianna hadn't thought of him. "Why do you think something would have happened to Gift?"

"You and Sebastian are powerful targets. Perhaps someone is going after the entire branch of your family."

Sebastian leaned forward slightly. "You . . . do . . . not . . . know . . . if . . . others . . . were . . . hurt. Be-fore . . . you . . . think . . . con-spir-a-cy, check . . . on . . . that."

Seger smiled at him, a smile as fond as the ones Arianna sometimes bestowed on him. "I'll do that, Sebastian," she said. "I will check everything. Let me know if the voice returns. And you—"she looked at Arianna—"make sure someone is beside you to help you if the headaches come again. I'd suggest Luke. He did well finding me the first time."

Arianna felt a slight jolt. The guard who had helped her, the one she hadn't recognized, had been the captain of her Islander guards. Luke. He had been family for years. Not recognizing Luke was like not recognizing Sebastian.

"Ari?" Seger frowned at her.

Arianna swallowed. "I will," she said. And then, because this may have been worse than she initially thought, she added, "Do this quickly. Speed may be as important here as knowledge."

"I know," Seger said, and left the garden.

Sebastian pulled Arianna into a hug. She let him. His solid body was familiar against hers. "I . . . do . . . not . . . want . . . his . . . voice."

"Seger will help."

"What . . . if . . . she . . . can't?"

"We have the entire Fey Empire now," Arianna said. "There'll be someone in it who can help you."

She hoped. Because she wasn't thinking so much of the removal as the warning Seger had given about that voice when it first reappeared. *If you use someone else's voice too much, you take on part of his soul.*

Arianna had been the one to recommend that Sebastian keep the voice. She had thought they would need it to convince the Fey that she should be Black Queen. But the Fey had accepted her easily, just as she had been told they would, and no one thought of Rugad's voice again.

Until now.

They had been careless. They had put Sebastian at risk. *She* had put Sebastian at risk. She hugged him close. He was so gentle and precious. She couldn't lose him now.

"Do . . . not . . . wor-ry, Ari," he said. "We . . . will . . . be . . . all . . . right."

But she wasn't sure. She wasn't sure of anything anymore.

Chapter Three

COULTER SAT BEFORE the five swords guarding Blue Isle's Place of Power. The swords were huge, twice as tall as he was, carved with an ancient magic. They stood, points down, in a triangular pattern in front of the door, a single sword in front, two behind it, and then two more. Their jeweled hilts glinted in the spring sun, and their blades, brightly polished, reflected him as a square blur of pale flesh and blond hair.

He could see the entire valley from here: the Cardidas River flowing red as it always did through the Cliffs of Blood; the village of Constant, now more of a town, huddled against the base of the mountain; and the ridgeline where, long ago, the Fey had initiated an attack that should have won them Blue Isle.

Instead, Blue Isle remained intact. Ruled by the daughter of Blue Isle's King, in an unbroken line that had existed for over a thousand years. That the Queen of Blue Isle also had Fey blood showed the cunning of her parents; they had foreseen their unity as the only way to keep Blue Isle's unique culture intact, and to keep the Fey from constantly attacking. The Black King of the Fey, Arianna's great-grandfather, had wanted Arianna to become fully Fey, to lose her Blue Isle sympathies and become a ruthless military leader, but he had lost that battle early. Then here, on this mountainside, he had lost his life.

Coulter should have liked this place for that very reason. But it was here, in this cave, that he learned his own limitations. He had lost the only parent he had ever had, and had been so stunned by grief that he had endangered the lives of the only people he loved. Arianna and Gift had forgiven him, but he had never forgiven himself.

That was part of the reason he was here: he was serving penance. He kept a chair up here that he had made in Constant, and sometimes he spent entire days sitting on it, contemplating the valley below. Gift had asked him, five years before, to be the guardian of the Place of Power, and Coulter couldn't refuse him. This place was too dangerous to be left unguarded or to trust in the hands of unknowns. If people had any inkling at all of the place's magic, they would be able to come in here, use the items stored inside to overthrow Arianna, and take power. Or do something even worse.

Coulter wasn't the only guard, of course. Gift had put others up here, others that he trusted. But Coulter was in charge, and he took that responsibility seriously. No one who didn't belong here would ever gain access to the Place of Power.

The air was cool this afternoon, but it had a fragrance to it that he hadn't smelled in months. Things were starting to grow. The winter on the mountain had been a harsh one. He had climbed the broken steps many times wearing heavy boots with a Traction spell he had learned from some Fey Domestics on its soles. He had performed that spell for the other guards as well; the last thing he wanted anyone to do was slip on the ice and fall.

Since the Place of Power had been rediscovered, no snow fell on the mountainside. It fell on the other mountains all the way down to tree line. He found that strange, but he found many things here strange. He tried to accept them anyway.

He leaned the chair back on two legs, and the top of his head brushed the broad, flat sword blade. There was no magic in these giant swords—if there had been, he would have felt it—but the jewels in the hilt focused and aimed any magic that came through them. He liked to lean against them, though, to draw strength from them. They made him feel the ancient power that he was able to share. The power he was only beginning to be able to control.

Coulter, whose parents were Islander, was born an Enchanter. That was the Fey term. The Islander term varied depending on which region of Blue Isle heard of him. Here, in the Cliffs of Blood, where his birth family was from, he would have been known as "demon spawn." But his parents had been smart enough to leave, and he had been born on the other side of the Isle. His parents were slaughtered in the first Fey invasion, and a Fey Shape-Shifter recognized his magical abilities and took him to be raised by the Fey.

Only they didn't raise him. They neglected him. But he got to observe their magic, and by the time he was five, he knew how to use it—not well, not correctly, but enough to save Gift's life one horrible night. In doing so, Coulter had Bound the two of them together, mingled their life forces so that if one of them died, the other would too.

That Binding had been a mistake—there was a less risky way to perform the spell, one that didn't tie their lives together—and it had been the first of many. Coulter hadn't received real training until Arianna became Black Queen. She sent for the only remaining Fey Enchanter from the Galinas continent, as well as a group of Spell Warders, to train Coulter.

Even then, he wouldn't go to her. She had wanted him to, and he wouldn't because he was afraid their emotions would run away with them. He loved her. He had from the moment he met her, and he was afraid if he were at her side, he would hurt her somehow.

So he had forced the Enchanter and Warders to come to him. He let them train him, and now he was using that training in other ways. When he was not up here, guarding the cave, he worked in Constant, teaching Islander children with wild magic how to control and use their powers. Without planning to, he had started a school, and in the last year, parents had sent him students from other parts of Blue Isle, places where Fey and Islanders had intermarried and were creating children with new, stronger powers, powers that sometimes frightened Coulter with their intensity.

So now when he came to the mountain, he came here to rest. When he was in his school, he had to be on his guard constantly. The problem with half-Fey, half-Islander children was that they were born with their magic powers fully formed. The Fey didn't come into their magic until puberty. So the Fey child had already learned about life, about control, before his magic overtook him.

But the interracial children and some of the Islander children had no such buffer. Parents who had no magical ability or whose magical ability had been effectively suppressed by the Islander religion didn't know how to deal with two-year-olds who could create fire simply by snapping their fingers.

Coulter did. He could remember being such a child, and the way the Fey would grab his hands, deflect his spells. He had help now with these little ones—Domestics who were used to raising children, the Warders who had come to train him, and the Enchanter brought in by Arianna. That Enchanter was not nearly as skilled as Coulter was, but helpful nonetheless.

Coulter had a hunch the need for his school would grow, and if he allowed himself to dream, as he sometimes did, sitting in his chair with his head leaning against the sword, he imagined schools like it all over the Isle.

"Anything?"

The voice wasn't unexpected. Coulter had sensed

someone coming up the stairs for some time now, but it hadn't been anything he concentrated on.

He brought his chair down on all four legs, and stood. The Fey woman at the edge of the carved stone plateau was taller than he was—but then they all were—and she held herself with a soldier's grace. Her face was narrow, her eyes slanted upward in an angle that matched her sharp cheekbones. She wore her long black hair in a single braid, revealing her pointed ears.

"Leen," he said in greeting. "It's quiet as ever up here."

And then she smiled. It was her smile that had once intrigued him. He had thought it like Arianna's. He and Leen had tried to be lovers once, several years before, but it ended quickly when they both realized that the only woman he'd ever wanted was a woman he could never have.

"Rue the day when it's no longer quiet," she said, putting a hand on his shoulder as she passed him. She bent down and picked up the chair, moving it away from the swords and the boulders that blocked her sight.

She had very little magic—she was a minor Visionary, good enough to lead an Infantry troop, but not good enough for anything else—and she had come into that magic late. She had been twenty when she had her first Vision. By then, she had already lived through the loss of her family, slaughtered by the Black King as Failures, and the battle against the Black King himself. All her life, she had been a valued member of Gift's extended family. That was why she was here; because she too could be trusted to guard the cave.

"You think a day like that will come?" he asked.

She carried the chair to the edge of the platform, perilously close to the stairs and the ledge. If she wasn't careful, she would fall. He picked up the chair, as he always did, and moved it back a few feet.

Ritual. They both enjoyed it. It was like a silent banter between them.

"I'm Fey," she said. "I'm suspicious of quiet."

"I rather like it," he said.

She nodded. "They want you in the school. It seems you had a visitor again today."

"Matt."

"Yes."

Coulter cursed under his breath. Fourteen-year-old Matt was a powerful Enchanter, as powerful—maybe more powerful—than Coulter. But his parents had forbidden him to come to Coulter's school because the Fey ran it. They taught him using the Book found in the Vault beneath the Place of Power. He was learning the ancient magic without learning the controls that the Fey had modified for their own magic over thousands of years.

Matt wanted that control, and he knew he could get it from Coulter. But Coulter was afraid that if the boy was discovered at the school, the boy's father would retaliate. That confrontation would be horrible.

"Did you tell him I was here?"

"Yes," she said. "He said he wanted to come back tonight. And bring his brother."

Coulter swore again. "That's just what I need."

"You can't deny them. They may be more important than all your other students combined."

"I know," he said. "But they're dangerous too."

She didn't say any more. She knew how dangerous. And she knew why. "Things are never easy."

"I never said I wanted them to be."

"Oh? Didn't I hear that a moment ago?"

"No," he said. "I want things quiet, not easy."

She sat down. "I guess I can accept that."

He double-checked the chair's position. Even if he was no longer her lover, he still cared about her. She was a unique woman, one who deserved better than what he had given her. "Who relieves you?"

"Dash, at twilight."

Dash was one of the few Islander guards. He was young, had great strength, and was one of the best with a sword that Coulter had ever seen. He also had incredible night vision, and could see so well when light was uneven or poor that it was better to have him on the mountainside as things grew dark than a Fey who relied too much on magic and not enough on skill.

"Good," Coulter said. He was about to leave when the hair on the back of his neck rose. A sensation came out of the northwest. He turned, and saw a golden light threaded with black. It flowed like a river through the sky, but the light had a beginning and an end.

"What is it?" Leen asked.

She couldn't see something like that; she didn't have the abilities for it. "I don't know," he said.

He frowned. The light had a feeling. It drew and repelled him at the same time. And beneath that feeling was a vibration that echoed through him, making him realize how very small, how very frail he was. Something ancient flowed in that light, something that had great power and great history.

It flew over him and along a trajectory that would take it over the Cliffs of Blood to the Infrin Sea. As the light passed, he got the sense that he knew it, or part of it. He had met it before, in a different form, a familiar form. A hated form? He wasn't sure. All he knew was that even though he had never seen a light like this, he recognized it as something other than what it was.

"Coulter?" Leen sounded concerned.

He held up a hand. It wasn't over. He felt a very strong magic behind him. He turned toward the cave, the entrance to the Place of Power. He sensed several beings standing in the cave's mouth. This was a familiar sensation: he had felt it years ago when Gift's dead mother Jewel had returned as a Mystery, a ghostlike creature that wasn't alive but hadn't ascended into the Powers either. Gift and his father Nicholas had been able to see her, but Coulter hadn't. He had sensed her as a solid person-shaped mass of magic.

He hadn't sensed her in a long, long time. Not since

King Nicholas disappeared down a tunnel inside this very cave.

Coulter walked toward the mouth of the cave. "Jewel?" he asked, knowing that she wouldn't be able to answer him. But as he got closer, he realized that his first impression had been correct: there were several magical shapes here. If he concentrated, he could separate them one from another. He counted seven at the edge of the cave door, and ten in a row behind it, and more behind them, more than he could count.

All of the Mysteries? It wasn't possible, was it? Had they been summoned by the light or were they drawn to it as he was? Or were they watching it for another reason?

He wished he could talk with them. He didn't entirely understand the Mysteries. They had been people once, all of them murdered, all of them after their death granted by the Powers the ability to affect a minimum of three people: the person they loved the most; the person they hated the most; and a third person of their choice. The Mysteries weren't always benign. They were often as they had been in life: complex and difficult, with a mixture of good and bad.

"Coulter?" Leen was beginning to sound worried.

He took a step closer to the Mysteries, if indeed that was what he faced. He walked around the two outside swords, past the one that guarded the door to the cave. From his position, he could see the white marble stairs and the strange light that always bathed the place. He could hear the faint burble of the fountain far below. If he didn't sense the magic, he would have thought he was completely alone.

"Something happened," he said to them. "Something important. Please help me, if you can. I need to know—"

And then he got a sense of Arianna, as if he were with her, as if he were almost a part of her. She was in great pain, extreme pain, pain so severe it was ripping her from the inside out.

He fell to his knees with the power of it. He wasn't in

pain—he knew it was her pain—but it felled him just the same. "Ari," he whispered—

And then the feeling was gone as if it had never been. He raised his head toward the sky. The light had passed. It was probably over the sea now on its way to Leut.

Leen had come up behind him. She put her hands on his shoulders as if she wasn't sure if she should comfort him or help him up.

The presences were gone. A wind blew past him, into the cave, as if proving that nothing blocked its way.

"Are you all right?" Leen asked.

Coulter put a hand on hers. He had no words for what he had just felt. "I'm fine," he said, "but something has changed."

"What?" she asked.

"I don't know," he said. "But I don't think things are going to be quiet anymore."

CHAPTER FOUR

*B*RIDGE FACED THE window, controlling his temper. The early spring sunlight, usually something that cheered him, now only irritated him. He spread his legs out and clasped his hands behind his back as he often did when contemplating the city below him: Nir, the capital of Nye, where he had spent all but eighteen years of his miserable life.

How often had he looked out this window at the street vendors hawking their wares, the stone buildings and the cobblestone streets, the brightly colored flags waving in the faint breeze? He hated the flags more than anything else. They still had a nationalistic air that he had tried to breed out of this wretched little country. Blue flags for stores that carried only Nyeian merchandise; yellow, green, red, and purple for items made in other countries; and the new addition since Nye had become part of the Fey Empire forty years ago: the black flag, for items that came from some unidentifiable part of the Fey Empire.

When his grandfather Rugad had left to conquer Blue Isle—and to die there, the arrogant old bastard—Bridge had banned those flags. But the Nyeians found a way to impart the information anyway. Blue ribbon binding fabric or a bit of blue cloth in the front of a display window. The issue of the flags caused so much surreptitious behavior that Bridge actually worried it would lead to a rebellion. Eventually he brought back the flags as a gesture of goodwill. But he hated them. He saw them as a symbol of his failure as ruler.

Behind him, a chair squeaked. So his daughter was growing restless. Good. Let her and that fop she had chosen for a husband stew for a moment. Bridge wanted to deal with them calmly, not in full temper as she expected.

He tightened the grip on his own wrist. Between her silly request and the strange feeling he had had all day, controlling that temper would be difficult. He made himself take a deep breath.

Below him, Nyeians, in their thick, frilly clothing, went in and out of stores, stopping at the street vendors, and carrying large purses into the new Bank of Nye. The new Bank of Nye. He smiled, this time truly amused. The new Bank of Nye was forty years old. It was the brick building across the street that looked prosperous and settled against the cobblestone. His palace was the old Bank of Nye, an ancient stone building shaped like a fortress. His grandfather had claimed it as Fey headquarters when the Fey conquered Nye, and the Black Family had lived here ever since.

This branch of the Black Family anyway. The poor relations. The branch with lackluster Vision. What other epithet could he think of? Probably every one his grandfather had hurled at him in the years after Bridge's sister Jewel died. Now the Empire was being ruled by Jewel's daughter, a half-breed who had never been to Galinas, had never been out of her little Isle. And she had decreed that the years of Fey conquest were over, that the Empire was complete.

His grandfather's spirit had to be restless. The girl was changing everything the Fey stood for.

No more conquests meant no more warriors. And the

Fey had always been warriors. With increasing frequency, Bridge had to deal with loose bands of Foot Soldiers attacking random targets, trying to create trouble where there was none. He had heard stories like that throughout the Empire.

This Arianna, so unlike her historical namesake, didn't know the trouble she had brought with this long peace. Sometimes even he forgot what war felt like, and he had spent his first eighteen years in battle.

A discreet cough sounded behind him, reminding him of the folly of his own children.

"Daddy?"

His daughter Lyndred had no patience. That was one of the reasons she sat behind him now. She thought she could control him by putting pressure on him. And, to her credit, she had once been able to do so, until he realized that she was just like his sister had been: brilliant and manipulative and talented.

She wouldn't manipulate him today, even if he hadn't made that decision years ago. She wanted to marry the Nyeian beside her, and have babies with the weaselly twerp. Dilute the Black line so badly that no one would recognize those children as part of the Black Family. He would not have approved the match no matter how much she manipulated him.

He hadn't done well by his daughter. Her resemblance to Jewel, his sister, had always made him cool toward her. And that had been a mistake. Lyndred was the only member of his immediate family with enough Vision to lead the Fey. Black Blood did indeed run thin through him, and he was aware enough to know it.

The sun disappeared behind a cloud that loomed over the large stone buildings. It seemed like a sign. Better to take care of things. His daughter had waited long enough.

Bridge turned, and resisted the urge to go to his desk. Standing behind the solid mahogany, he would have a barrier between himself and this man—this boy—who believed he could marry into the Black Family. But Bridge needed no barrier to hide behind. Not in this instance.

So, he kept his hands clasped behind his back and raised his chin slightly, knowing the power the stance gave him. The older he had gotten, the more he looked like his grandfather: craggy features in leathery skin, black hair with just a touch of silver, a thin mouth that sometimes spoke of meanness. The main difference was in the eyes. Rugad's eyes had a brilliance that Bridge's never would. He had known that even as a boy, when he had seen his father stand beside his grandfather. The look of the Black Family was a uniform one—it was easy to see that the men were father and son—but his father's eyes didn't have that brilliant ruthlessness in them either. And that somehow dulled his features, made him seem like a lesser man, even though that was the only difference.

Bridge tried to will his grandfather's forcefulness into his own expression now. He had to be doing pretty well, because the fop sitting next to his daughter cringed.

Bridge took a step forward. His daughter had chosen a typical Nyeian. The boy had pasty skin and no muscle tone. He wore his brown hair long, the edges just brushing the frilly white collar that accented the pallor of his face. He was dressed in the Nye formal style: a tight embroidered jacket over a white shirt that had ruffles on the neck and sleeves. His pants were velvet and were tucked into a pair of thigh-high boots with fringe at the top.

Lyndred sat beside him on a matching wooden chair, clutching one of his long hands in her own. She wore standard Fey warrior clothes: a simple leather jerkin over breeches, with her hair braided down her back, not because she wanted to, but because Bridge wouldn't let her in the palace if she dressed like a Nyeian.

"Daddy," she said again. "I thought you agreed to meet with us."

"I agreed to meet with you," he said.

She tilted her head slightly, like a cat examining him. She had the sharpness in her eyes, like his grandfather's, like Jewel's. Only unlike them, she didn't use it. She seemed determined to live a normal Nye life: parties all evening, shopping all day, children trussed in three layers of clothing even on hot afternoons.

"Then you also agreed to meet with Rupert," she said.

Rupert. What kind of name was that? It was a Nyeian name, one that wouldn't work in battle, just like all the other Nyeian names he had heard. Percival, Rupert, Chauncey. He couldn't imagine shouting those names in the heat of the moment.

Names were important things. The Fey had always known that, and had chosen their children's names accordingly. Many Fey adopted the naming tradition of the conquered countries: Bridge and Jewel had been named according to the L'Nacin tradition of using descriptive words for names. But Bridge was aware that his name was symbolic as well and that part of the reason he had remained in Nye was to provide a bridge between the Fey on Galinas and on Blue Isle.

And eventually, his grandfather had hoped, on Leut.

Only now Arianna was not planning to go to Leut. Perhaps there never would be a bridge between the great continents of the world. Perhaps Blue Isle was where it would all end.

"I did not agree to meet with Rupert," Bridge said. He inclined his head mockingly at the boy. The boy blinked at him, then looked away.

No spine, just as Bridge thought.

"I want to marry him, Daddy," Lyndred said.

"Of course you do," Bridge said. "But you will not."

"Daddy, he's from one of the best families in Nye."

"The best families in Nye are not worthy of polishing our boots," Bridge said, keeping his gaze on the boy. Color filled those pasty cheeks. *Stand up to me, boy, and maybe I'll let the girl wallow in her own folly, make her understand that she is making her own mistake, always questioning my opinion.* He wondered if the boy had even considered standing up to the Fey ruler of Nye.

Probably not.

So much for the good family.

"You don't understand," Lyndred said.

"I understand too well."

"You hate Nyeians."

He turned his gaze to her. "There's not enough about them to hate. At best I feel a mild contempt." And then, because he could not help himself, he said, "Think you can overcome mild contempt, boy?"

Rupert raised his head. His eyes seemed bigger than they had a moment ago.

Of course not. The boy couldn't even speak to his prospective father-in-law. This simply would not work, even if Bridge liked the boy, which he decidedly did not.

"Why do you want to marry this—Rupert?" Bridge asked.

Lyndred put her other hand over the one she had clasped in Rupert's. "He's good-looking and smart. We have great conversations, and we love to spend time together. We would be blending our houses, one of the best families on Nye and the Black Family, just like my aunt did on Blue Isle."

"And you expect your children to be as special as your cousins."

"It's always good to mix Fey blood with new blood," she said, repeating one of the tenets of Fey belief, one which had been born out in repeated conquerings. Mixing Fey blood with that of other races kept the magic strong.

"There's a wild magic on Blue Isle," Bridge said. "There's nothing wild about Nye."

"Everyone thought Blue Isle was a group of religious fanatics who would be easy to conquer. Maybe you're as wrong about Nye."

"You forget," Bridge said softly. "We conquered Nye forty years ago. Easily." He looked at Rupert. The boy kept his gaze downcast. What did she see in him anyway? "Your people rolled over quite quickly, Rupert."

The boy jumped at the sound of his name.

"What makes you think you're worthy of my daughter?" Bridge asked.

The boy raised his head again. He was beginning to remind Bridge of a badly whipped dog. Head up. Head down. Head up. Head down. He wondered if the boy would heel if he asked him to.

"I asked you a question," Bridge said.

"I love her." The boy's voice broke midway through the sentence, as if he were still going through puberty.

"You love her," Bridge said, his tone flat. "I suppose you have written her sonnets?"

"They're lovely, Daddy."

"Let him answer," Bridge said, keeping that even tone.

"Yes," Rupert said.

"And made her chocolate in the Nyeian tradition?"

"Yes."

"And you have written your own ballad to honor your love?"

"Yes."

It took all of Bridge's restraint to keep from rolling his eyes. "These things, then, make you a worthy candidate to become a member of my family?"

"Sir?" The boy was shaking. Lyndred held his hand tightly as if she were afraid he would bolt.

"You are asking to become part of the greatest family in the world. What do you bring to us besides love?"

"Sir, I—my family is one of the oldest on Nye. We have great wealth. An interest in the Bank of Nye. We—"

"I own the Bank of Nye," Bridge said. "Just like I own the entire country. Fortunately for your family, the Fey believe in allowing people to continue holding property even after the Empire has taken over a city. Your wealth is on my sufferance, and I could take it in a heartbeat if I so chose. Now, what do you bring to my family?"

The boy opened his mouth, closed it, and opened it again, like a fish. He looked at Lyndred, who for the first time could not meet his gaze. Perhaps the boy loved her, and perhaps she was infatuated with him, but she knew the answer to the question her father was asking, and she knew the boy did not measure up.

"I am one of the greatest poets on Nye," the boy said

at last. "My family's talent in the arts is beyond compare. We have always bred great poets."

"And how will great poets help the Fey conquer Leut?" Bridge asked. "Will we have you all stand and recite your verse in the hope of boring the Leutians to death?"

"Daddy!" Lyndred said. "We're not going on to Leut. Everybody knows that. Rupert's family understands there's more to life than war. He'll bring us sophistication, and help us lose our roughness. He'll teach us how to be cultured."

"Cultured," Bridge said. He gazed at Rupert. "Cultured?"

"The Fey have no poetry and little music, and their art—"

"Our art is magic. Our poetry are battle stories, and our music battle cries," Bridge said. "You want to narrow our focus, make us like Nyeians?"

"We know how to be peaceful." The boy had some spunk in him after all.

"The Fey have not warred on anyone for fifteen years. We know how to be peaceful as well, but we do not lose our edge."

"Daddy," Lyndred said.

He held up his hand to silence her. The anger he had been holding back had finally come to the surface. "You do not bring anything of worth to my family," he said to the boy. "You bring your Nyeian ways and think those are the only ways. You, with your silly name and your love poetry and your 'interest' in the Bank of Nye. You have courted the cousin of the Black Queen of the Fey, and say you would bring culture to our family. Our family which has experienced more cultures than you can imagine. Our names reflect it. I am named in the L'Nacin tradition, and Lyndred in the Tashil tradition. I have lived in five countries, and have ruled this one for fifteen years. I know your culture, and I despise it."

He spat out the last sentence, then took a step closer

to the boy. The boy recoiled visibly. If he had been standing, he would have backed away until he hit the wall.

"You are not worthy of my daughter. You are not worthy of an audience with me. You are not worthy of ever coming near a member of this family again. Am I making myself clear?"

The boy swallowed. "Yes, sir."

"You will destroy the love poetry you have written for my daughter, and you will never sing your ballad again."

"Daddy!"

"If I hear of it, I will destroy not only you but your family. Is that clear?"

The boy swallowed again. He was full of more nervous ticks than a prisoner. "Yes, sir."

"Good. Now get out of here."

The boy yanked his hand from Lyndred's and ran for the door, not pausing to look back. Lyndred watched him go, a stricken expression on her face. Then she rose, slowly, to face her father.

In the last year, his youngest child had grown as tall as he was. Eighteen and beautiful. And smart. He couldn't tell her how proud he was of her, not now, when she stood before him, her powerful eyes flashing with an anger that matched his own.

"You had no right to do that," she said. "I will marry him whether you let me or not."

"You could," Bridge said. "If you wanted to marry a coward."

"He's no coward."

"Then why did he run?"

"You told him to leave."

"Would you have left if his father had ordered it at that moment?"

Her jaw worked, but it took her a moment to say anything. Her anger was shifting from him to the boy. Good.

"No," she said. "I would not."

She sank back onto the wooden chair. It creaked beneath her weight. Bridge put his hand on her shoulder and squeezed. She hadn't loved the boy, but she didn't know that. She had only felt infatuation, flattery, pleased that someone had courted her so formally and in such a romantic way. One day she would thank him for this. But not now.

He took the boy's chair, and turned it so that it faced her. "You convinced me of one thing today," he said.

She raised her head. She wasn't crying, and she should have been, if the boy had been her true love. But she didn't know that either. Bridge remembered how he had felt when her mother died. Loss like that tore a man from the inside out. That was love. The belief that you could not live without the other person, and when the other person left and you did live, that you were no longer living as you had before.

"What?" she asked.

He almost smiled at the anger in her voice. Perhaps that had been her problem. He had not gotten her angry often enough.

"You've convinced me that you need to leave Nye. You've taken on too many of this country's ways."

"I know there are other places. You've made me go all over Galinas."

He had too. He had even made her spend a summer in an Infantry training unit run by her oldest brother, Rugan. She had been an able student, Rugan had said, but she had no fire.

Bridge did not know how to give her fire.

"Yes," he said. "You've seen Galinas, and all of its countries. But you have never been to a place completely different from Nye, a place where there are no Nyeians at all."

She crossed her arms. "I do not think you have to send me away because I fell in love."

"I'm not." He folded his arms on the back of the chair, and then he rested his chin on them. "I hadn't realized until today how much of the Nyeian culture you had accepted as the way things should be. No Fey raised as I was would have seen love poetry from a boy like that as anything more than a joke."

"It was no joke," she snapped.

"Not to you." His voice was gentle. "But it should have been. You come from a long line of warriors, Lyndred. You are named for one of the most ruthless generals of all the Fey. If a warrior wrote you love poetry, I would be the first to tell you to treasure it. But that boy was no warrior."

"That's why I liked him."

"You wouldn't have liked it after a year of marriage. He also had no backbone. You would have bent him to your considerable will and when he did not fight you, you would have snapped him in half. I saw your face. You were surprised just now when he ran off instead of defending your love."

"You said it." She raised her chin in an unconscious imitation of Bridge. "He's no warrior."

"And you need one," Bridge said. "If you're ever to marry."

"What do you mean, 'ever'?" she asked.

"It is not a requirement, as long as you have children."

"Arianna has no children."

Ah, the mysterious cousin. The competition that Bridge had felt with his own sister, he sometimes felt he had passed on to his daughter. She seemed focused on Arianna, determined to be better.

"That's right," he said. "Arianna has no children. And neither does her brother. That's a serious mistake. If they were killed tomorrow, the Black Throne comes to us. If they never have children, it will be our branch of the family that will rule the Fey, not theirs."

She was frowning slightly. He had never said this to her before, and he wished he had. It would have saved her from the debacle with the Nyeian Poet of Good Family.

"Now do you see why it's important to learn what your mate will bring to our family?"

Her chin went up one more notch. If it went any higher, he thought with amusement, she would be looking at the ceiling. "I think poetry is a fine thing to bring to this family."

"I agree," he said. "As long as it is not the only thing."

The edges of her mouth twitched. He knew the look. She was trying to fight a smile, trying to hold on to the anger she felt. She had done that since she was a little girl, tried to contain the smiles that he could always create within her. But it rarely worked.

He wasn't going to push it now. She had a right to be mad at him, and he wasn't going to jolly her into forgetting that. He wanted her to set this whole incident aside.

"So," she said, "where are you sending me this time?"

"I'm not sending you anywhere," he said. "I'm accompanying you."

"Where?"

He stood abruptly and walked over to his desk. This time he needed the buffer. "We're going to pay our respects to the Black Queen."

"What?" Lyndred stood too. "Daddy, we haven't been invited."

"I know," he said. "Not once in fifteen years. She hasn't asked to see any of her uncles, and why should she, really? All of us were passed by. None of us were deemed worthy of the Black Throne."

He couldn't quite keep the bitterness from his voice. When he had been a boy, his grandfather had groomed him for the Black Throne, saying that if something happened to Jewel, he would get it. But he had made too many mistakes in the Nye campaign. He had led an Infantry unit and had not seen the trap they were walking into. He had managed to save them—if he was good at anything it was recovering from his own mistakes—but a true Black King, his grandfather said, would never have led them there in the first place.

Bridge knew the truth of that statement, just as he knew he didn't have the tactical genius needed to sit on the Black Throne. But if Arianna had tactical genius, she wasn't showing it. She was doing no more and no less than Bridge would have done in her place.

"So why are we going?" Lyndred said.

"Because you need to get out of Nye." He tapped his fingers against the polished mahogany. He didn't say that he needed to get out as well, but he did. He had almost forgotten what it was like to travel. He had been here too long, and he had grown as accustomed to the place as Lyndred. "And because I would like to talk to my niece about her plans for our people."

"You don't like how she's ruling us."

He sat in the leather chair behind his desk. "I hate it. This is not how the Fey live."

"Will she listen to you?"

"She might. Perhaps she hasn't had real Fey advice. Perhaps I should have gone long ago."

"Why didn't you?"

How could he explain to his daughter the effect of that Scribe, coming into this very office, repeating Arianna's message word for word? Lyndred didn't remember it. She had been three years old. Her mother had been alive, and had been relieved at the message. But Bridge had seen it for what it was. An insult from a girl, a girl who had not even been raised Fey. At the time, Arianna had been younger than Lyndred was now.

We would like you to continue your good work on Nye. We need a ruler of your abilities to maintain the most important port city on Galinas, and to keep the peace within its home country. We shall resume trade, of course, and begin contact with all parts of the Fey Empire. We appreciate your support in all ways.

The veiled threat, the veiled insult. A ruler of his ability. She had already known where he belonged, and she kept him there. She had probably known that, before he learned of his grandfather's death, he was preparing his own battle fleet to come to Blue Isle. If Bridge had timed it better, he would have arrived to support his grandfather, and if his niece had died by accident in the struggle, then Blood against Blood would not have happened. But from the moment his grandfather died, Bridge lost his opportunity to seize the Black Throne by accident. He lost his opportunity to be anything more than the man who maintained the most important port city on Galinas.

"Your mother didn't want me to go," he said. It was true enough. And it seemed to be enough to satisfy his daughter. "Besides, Arianna needed to establish power on her own. If I had arrived within a year of her ascent, she might have thought that I threatened her rule. She might have initiated the Blood against Blood."

"Surely she wouldn't have," Lyndred said. "She knows about that."

"She wasn't raised Fey," he said. "I couldn't be sure of anything."

Except that she was a Shape-Shifter, the first in the Black Family, and a powerful Visionary. He wasn't much of a Visionary at all, and that stopped him too. He respected his own people enough to know that they needed a Visionary Leader if there was one available. A man who ruled by hunch and instinct always failed.

As if reading his thoughts, his daughter asked, "Have you Seen something?"

He shook his head, feeling a sad smile cross his face. "All I have Seen, baby, are small things. Hints of trouble that make no sense to me. Two hands holding a scepter as if they wanted to pull it apart. A Fey man whom I do not know drowning. Two hearts pierced by a single sword."

She was quiet for a moment, her eyes downcast. And suddenly he realized what a fool he'd been. She'd come into her Vision a year ago, and he had never asked her what she'd Seen. He only listened to what she had volunteered.

"What have you Seen?" he asked her.

When she raised her eyes, they were filled with tears. "I don't want to go to Blue Isle, Daddy," she said.

His heart started pounding, hard. "Why not?"

"There's a Golem that will try to kill me," she said. "And a blond man who will give me a child I do not want."

Bridge felt his breath catch. "What else?"

"You'll die, Daddy. It must have been yourself you Saw in the water. Because you'll drown. On the way to Leut. You'll die."

She was protecting him. He ran a hand over his face. No wonder she wasn't upset about this Rupert. She hadn't loved him. She had been using him as an excuse to stay on Nye. If she didn't go, she probably assumed, Bridge wouldn't go either.

"Is that all?" he asked.

"The Black Queen," she said, "has a very cruel face."

All day long he had had the sense that Arianna needed him, that he should go to Blue Isle. Had he been wrong? Had the feeling simply been a wish from his own heart? A wish that he were more important than he was?

"Have you spoken to a Shaman about these Visions?" he asked.

She nodded. "Last week, when I went to see Rugan, I stopped in L'Nacin and saw the Shaman there."

"And what did he say?"

"He said that we never see complete Visions, that we can try to prevent them, but we won't know if we succeed until the moment passes, and sometimes not even then." Her voice shook. "He also said that I cannot prevent your death. You are my father, and it is the way of things that children outlive their parents."

Those words may not have calmed her, but they calmed Bridge. It *was* the way of things. And the Fey were not supposed to be afraid of their futures.

"So you would keep me in this place for the next hundred years?" he asked.

She wiped at her eyes with the back of her hand. The Fey were long-lived and the Black Family particularly so, if they weren't killed in battle. She knew that asking him to live forever in Nye was asking him to spend the rest of his life in a place he hated.

"She didn't ask you to come," Lyndred said. It sounded like a final attempt at getting him to change his mind, an attempt she didn't seem to think would work.

"No, she didn't," he said. "But all day I've had a feeling I should go. That's like a minor Vision, isn't it?"

He was asking his youngest child, a girl barely in adulthood, whether a feeling was a Vision. He was as pathetic as his grandfather had said he was. At his age, Bridge should know the difference between a feeling and a Vision.

"Maybe you should see the Shaman," she said.

"Maybe." Then he might find out if the Shaman had Visions about this trip as well. Of course if he had a Vision that he felt could be prevented, it was his duty to tell Bridge. No one had spoken to him.

"You won't, will you?"

Bridge shook his head. "If I stay in Nye much longer, I'll be little better than your Rupert. And if you stay here, you'll lose touch with all things that are important. I am going to deliver you to the Queen's court, so that you learn how the Black Throne works. That way, if Arianna dies without issue, you or your children can take over."

Lyndred swallowed. "It won't be that easy. If she dies without issue, everyone will fight for the Throne."

His smile was small. He had been through this once. She hadn't. "No one fights over the Black Throne, baby," he said. "We all fear the power of Blood against Blood too much. If a strong leader who has a hereditary claim to the Throne takes it, no one dares argue."

"So that's why you never challenged Arianna."

His daughter was too smart by half. But that was part of what he admired about her. He sighed. "I could have challenged her, I suppose," he said. "But I lack the Vision. That's been clear since I was a boy. And at that time, no one in my family had such Vision either, not since Jewel died. Arianna had a right to that Throne."

"But she stole it from her brother."

"Not according to the Scribe. According to him, the brother didn't want it."

Lyndred's back straightened. "I would have wanted it."

"I know, baby," Bridge said softly. "That's what I'm counting on."

CHAPTER FIVE

I DON'T KNOW," Alex said. "Sneaking out seems wrong."

Matt suppressed a sigh. Sometimes he wondered how he and his twin could look so much alike. They certainly didn't think alike.

Matt sat on the center of his bed, his legs crossed and his feet on the blanket their mother had embroidered specially for him. She would be furious if she saw him sit like that. These blankets, created for the boys before they were born, were supposed to adorn their beds until they died.

Alex's was tucked in all the corners of his bed, looking pristine, like usual. He sat with his feet on the floor, and with a good view of the window his father had made at the boys' request when they were little more than toddlers.

His father had been sort of normal then. At least he had done things that fathers did. He played with the boys, made them things, disciplined them. Now such tasks were up to their mother, and every time their father looked at the boys or spoke their names, she would get a soft, sad, and sometimes frightened expression on her face.

"I've been sneaking out for a long time," Matt said.

"I know." Alex glanced out the window at the birch tree in the backyard. Beneath it, his uncle had been buried before they were born. His mother had erected a small memorial made of stones around the tree, and the boys used to get in trouble if they even approached it. "I always thought you were wrong for doing that."

"I'm learning things. You're not," Matt said, resisting the urge to raise his voice. His mother was cleaning up in the kitchen. He could still smell the beef stew. She was probably keeping some of it warm for his father. He hadn't made it back yet. Matt really didn't want to go to the Vault to find his father again.

"But what are you learning?" Alex asked. "*Their* ways?"

Whenever Alex used "their" in that manner, he meant the Fey. He had picked up his father's hatred of the race that had overrun Blue Isle long before the boys were born.

"Coulter isn't Fey."

"But he was raised by them. He has Fey friends."

"So do I," Matt said softly. "They know more about magic than we do."

"We don't need to know more. Father will teach us—"

"Father can't teach anyone," Matt said, "and you know it."

Alex's hands clenched. "He's fine," Alex said, without looking at Matt. "He's just thinking of otherworldly things."

That was their mother's phrase, although she hardly used it anymore. Now, she just kept herself and her fourteen-year-old sons away from their father. Sometimes, Matt thought, she seemed to hope their father would never return.

"No," Matt said. "He's going crazy. It's in the Words. It happens."

"To people who abuse their magic." Alex's knuckles were turning white. "He never did that."

"He used magic to save the Isle, before we were born. Him and King Nicholas. They killed the Black King and saved Blue Isle."

It had risen to the level of myth in their family. Their father was a hero and a religious leader. A Great Man. Everyone treated him that way, even now.

"Then King Nicholas should be crazy."

"King Nicholas disappeared a long time ago. His daughter rules."

"His half-Fey daughter." Alex spit out the words. Matt cringed hearing them. Alex's attitude wouldn't help at all. Alex needed guidance, and he wasn't getting any.

"Just tonight," Matt said. "Please. Someone will be able to help you with those hallucinations of yours."

Alex closed his eyes. "Maybe I'm going crazy too," he whispered.

Matt understood the fear. He had felt it for years, as he watched his father deteriorate. Matt had vague memories of his father as a strong, sensible man who could draw people to him if he needed to, back in the days when his father had restarted Rocaanism, the Islander religion. His father had trained new Elders and Danites and Auds. He had sent them out to preach that there were other ways to control magic, other considerations besides Fey considerations.

And the Queen had allowed it. She had even given it her blessing, although she refused to allow certain parts of Rocaanism to be revived because they were harmful to Fey. So there were no ceremonies with holy water, for instance, but Matt's father hadn't minded. He had said that ceremony had false trappings, and he was re-creating the religion according to the real Words, and the current experience.

In those days, when Matt had been little, his father had seemed all powerful. Now his father was an embarrassment, seeing things that were not there, speaking with people who had been long dead.

When his father was lucid—which wasn't as often as it used to be—he would warn his sons not to use their magic. *It has a cost,* he would say. *It will take your mind, like it is taking mine.*

"I don't think you're going crazy," Matt said. His brother was watching him, tears in his eyes. They were both lanky boys, with their father's blond curls and their mother's strong features. She was a beautiful woman, and Matt knew, they would be handsome men. Their father wasn't handsome, and probably never had been, but once he had been brilliant, one of the greatest scholars on Blue Isle.

Before the Fey came.

"Then what is it?" Alex asked. His voice was husky with repressed emotion. "I saw another one today."

Matt knew that. He had walked in on his brother in the middle of the hallucination. Alex had been sprawled on the bed, eyes rolled back in his head, body twitching slightly as if he had the chills. Matt had placed his hand on his brother's back, felt the rigid muscles, and waited. When it seemed like Alex would come out of it, Matt slipped through the window and ran to Coulter's school.

But Coulter was on the mountain. The only person Matt saw was Leen, and as friendly as she was, he couldn't talk to her. She was Fey. She wouldn't understand his fear.

But she had understood his need to see Coulter. And she had told him when Coulter would be back.

"That's why you need to come with me," Matt said. "Coulter will know what to do."

Alex licked his lower lip, and then bit it, as if he wanted to stop it from trembling. "Father said once that Coulter was just like him."

Matt remembered that. He remembered how it startled him, because he had thought the two men very different. His father was a lot older, but he also seemed unhappy. Coulter didn't. Coulter seemed to have command over his life.

It was that comment, the one that frightened Alex away from Coulter, that made Matt want to seek him out. "Coulter's had Fey training," Matt said. "Father hasn't. Maybe that's the difference."

Alex wiped at his left eye, a surreptitious movement. Matt pretended not to see it. "Father's older. Maybe he used more magic."

"Maybe." Matt swallowed. "But wouldn't it be better to learn from the man whose mind is still intact?"

The question was harsh, and it made Alex flinch. But for the first time, Matt felt as if he had gotten through to him.

"But what if what's going on with me isn't magic? What if I'm just going crazy?"

Matt had thought about that as well, but he didn't want to admit it. What if he was the only twin who was really sane? How long would that last? Maybe the insanity just came to Alex earlier than Matt.

"Then I expect Coulter will tell you," Matt said.

Alex snorted. "No one could tell someone that."

"Coulter can."

"How come you have so much faith in this guy?"

Matt ran his hands along the thin fabric covering his thighs. To admit this was to tell Alex how much Matt had cut him out of his life. "I've been going to the school for two years," Matt said. "I've watched him."

"Two years!" Alex raised his voice. Matt shushed him. "You can't have gone for two years. I'd have known."

"I went when you were asleep sometimes, or when I could get away. I haven't been able to go regularly like Coulter wants, but it's helped. I haven't made fire in my sleep for a long time, have I?"

Alex looked away. "Father forbade us to go to that school."

"Father can't remember what day it is."

"Mother can."

Matt nodded. "And I think she knows where I've been going. She just hasn't said anything."

Alex's jaw tightened. He wasn't going to go. Matt knew it.

"Come on, Alex," Matt said. "Father's supposed to train us, but he hasn't been able to do that for a long time. You haven't even told him about the hallucinations, and you've been having those since you were twelve."

Alex shook his head slightly, and then he stood. "What do we tell Mom?"

"Nothing," Matt said. "We go through the window."

"Sure," Alex said. "Then she comes to get one of us to go to the Vault and we're missing. She'll appreciate that."

"She won't know."

Alex raised his head. "Do you know how many times I've covered for you?"

Matt didn't, but it didn't surprise him. "She won't let us out this close to dark. I think we risk it."

Alex ran a hand through his curls. "She knows I haven't been feeling well. I'll tell her I'm going to bed."

"And what about me?"

"What you tell her is your business," Alex said and left the room.

Matt cursed softly, and then, by force of habit, looked around to see if anyone had heard him. This was a religious household. Cursing was even more of a sin than it was in other households. His friends got reprimanded if their parents overheard a mild oath. Matt got punished.

Words are important, his father used to say. *More important than you realize.*

Matt ran a hand through his curls just as his brother had done. What would their mother say if she knew that Alex was having hallucinations? What would she say if she knew that Matt was trying to find him help?

She would probably tell their father, and then they'd have to spend another week in the Vault, listening to him rant. Matt shuddered. He couldn't do that. He couldn't risk it.

He pulled the door open and walked across the hall. The kitchen was the best room in the small house. It had the big stone hearth, and a large wooden table his parents' friend Denl had made when the boys were very little. The kitchen always smelled good, and his mother was usually there, making up small potions or cooking.

She was there now, a tall woman with vibrant red hair that was slowly losing its vibrancy. Streaks of silver covered it like a veil, stealing the color, and making her look older than she was. Her greenish blue eyes were sharp, her lips thin. She still wore the apron from dinner, and it was covered with the flour that she had had Matt purchase that morning. Her hands were on her hips, and she was staring at Alex.

Apparently his lie hadn't worked.

She sat Matt standing in the doorway. "What's this I hear?" she asked. Her lilting voice used to soothe him, remind him that there were places other than the town of Constant, that people lived happily away from the Cliffs of Blood. "Yer gettin' yer brother to lie for ye?"

Matt swallowed. "No."

"Then what? He's never come to me with this tale afore. Ye've always been the one to tell tales, Matt."

He felt color rise in his cheeks. He supposed he deserved that. Alex had his head down. He wasn't going to get any help from his brother.

"I want to take Alex to Coulter's school," Matt said, deciding, since his mother had challenged his truthfulness, to actually be truthful.

Alex rested his head on the table as if that sentence had been a physical blow. Matt himself cringed, expecting her to yell.

But she didn't. She glanced at him, and then at his brother, and then back at him. "Why would ye do that?"

"Because," Matt said. "We need some help, and we can't get it in the Vault."

He used that phrase on purpose. The religious items for Rocaanism in all its one-thousand-year history lived in that Vault, along with the Words of the religion, and instructions on how to use the magic that the Roca had once let loose upon the Isle. But his mother would also know that he meant one other thing when he said "the Vault." He meant he wasn't going to get any help from his father, either.

"Yer da is na well."

"And he never will be again."

His mother turned away. Alex kept his head on the table, as if he were ducking the whole fight.

"You know that, Ma. You know it. You just won't accept it."

"Yer da is a special man," she said, without looking at Matt. "He has a kindness—"

"It doesn't matter." Matt had heard that speech a hundred times: *He has a kindness that most cannot see; he has saved us all; he even saved the Isle. He did it at great personal cost . . .* "It doesn't matter what he did, Ma. What matters is who he is now. And he's not the kind of man who can help us."

She put a hand on Alex's head. "Ye've been havin' stray magic?"

Their father had once explained how he had magic and hadn't realized it, how all of his powers had leaked out, causing damage when he actually thought he was in control. Only he hadn't used the word "magic." He never did. Only their mother was not afraid to call things as they truly were.

Alex shook his head without raising it from the table.

"Then why do ye need Coulter's school?"

Matt had started this and he was sorry. But there was no turning back now. "Tell her, Alex."

Alex shook his head again.

His mother looked at Matt. Matt hated that expression. It was strong and demanding and powerful. "If he will na say it, 'tis up to ye."

Alex would never forgive him. "He thinks he's going crazy," Matt said, and his mother winced. Alex shoved away from the table, but his mother grabbed his shoulder and held him in place.

" 'N why is that now?" she asked Alex.

Alex was looking at Matt with murder in his eyes. "It's nothing, Ma," Alex said.

"It must be somethin', if yer willin' ta lie 'bout it."

Alex's face was turning red. Matt hadn't seen him that mad in a long, long time. "I see things sometimes."

"Things?" his mother asked.

"Hallucinations," Matt said.

To his surprise, his mother asked no more. Instead she let go of Alex's shoulder and sank into a chair. "Lord hae mercy," she said, and buried her face in her hands.

Alex's mouth dropped open, and Matt felt himself gasp. His mother didn't act like this. She was always strong and demanding. She should have told them not to leave. She should have told them if they were going to go anywhere it was the Vault. She should have forbidden them from having anything to do with Coulter.

"Am I going crazy then?" Alex asked.

But she didn't seem to hear him. She brought her hands down and stared at the fire burning low in the hearth. "I told yer father," she said. " 'Twas wrong the names he gave you. Matthias, my son, ye shoulda been Jakib after me brother, and Alexander, ye shoulda been Marcus or even Nicholas after the King. I coulda bore having a son named Nicholas. But yer da, he insisted. Matthias and Alexander, like the sons of the first Roca. Maybe he was losing his mind even then. He thought he could do right this time, but it don't seem right is possible na more."

And then she burst into tears. Both Alex and Matt went to her side, putting their hands on her shoulder. Alex looked lost, his blue eyes haunted, and Matt suspected he had the exact same expression on his face.

"Ma," he said, crouching beside her. "What're you talking about?"

She raised her head. Tear streaks marked both cheeks. Matt couldn't remember ever seeing her cry before. " 'Twas two sons the Roca had," she said. "Alexander, the one with subtle magic, sightin's a the future 'n such, 'n a way with him that 'twould make anyone do what he wanted.

'Twas him that was the ancestor of the royal family. The second son was Matthias. He was like yer da, all wild, with the ability ta do most a what he wanted when he wanted. I worried about ye, Matty. I thought ye'd be the one to go—"

She didn't finish that sentence. She shook her head as if trying to shake the words out of it.

"I dinna think 'twould hit Alex too."

"What?" Matt asked.

"It's in the Words," Alex said. "I thought you were supposed to read them."

"I read them so many times they make no sense," Matt said.

" 'A man cannot have the powers of God,' " Alex quoted. " 'It will ultimately destroy him.' The Roca wrote that after he learned what had happened to his son, Matthias. Don't you remember?"

Matt didn't. He had studied what his father had told him to study and nothing else. He hated the Vault, hated the smell, the glass dolls, the drums made of skin, the old vials of blood. Most of all, he hated the way his father's eyes lit up when they went inside, and the golden light flowed off the small altar holding the leather-bound book of Words.

" 'Tis na story but history," their mother said. "The son, Alexander, used the subtler powers only when he needed to. Creatin' a warmth, a way of rulin' that bound people tagether. The other son, Matthias, used every power givin' him through the Roca's blood. By the time the Roca returned, when he got his second life, the life when he wrote the Words, Matthias was insane."

She whispered those last words.

"So?" Matt asked. He had heard the story before and never understood its significance. Perhaps he had never wanted to.

"There are some what believe that yer da is the Roca come again. Him and Nicholas, parts of the same whole, created to stop the scourge the Fey had become. And they did. Then yer da and I have sons. And he names them like the Roca named his. And ye have powers, Matty, from a little boy, like yer namesake."

"Like Father," Matt said. "Father was the same."

"Aye," his mother said, her gaze meeting his. "He was."

Matt felt his stomach clench. He didn't want to think about this, but he had never been able to stop himself from imagining it. He was named after his father as well. Matthias, destined to go insane. That was why he went to Coulter, to help him prevent his own destiny.

"But why," he asked, and as he did his voice changed slightly, that uncontrollable squeaky rise and fall that had been happening for the past two years, "why would Alex's hallucinations change that?"

His mother looked at him, then closed her eyes. "I tole yer da 'twas na good, keepin the Fey terms from ye. But he hoped ye'd be pure for the Islanders. He hoped ye'd be the hope of the New Rocaanism."

"Ma," Alex said, sounding slightly annoyed.

"I am na an expert. But I dinna think Alex's havin' hallucinations." She brought her hands to her shoulders and squeezed her boys' arms. Her fingers were like ice. "Go. Dinna tell yer da, and I wilna either. But dinna lie if he asks."

Matt met Alex's gaze. Alex shrugged.

"Do you want us to get Father on our way back?" Matt asked.

"No," his mother said. "I'll bring him his dinner. 'Tis na a task I should be givin' to ye boys anaway."

She let their hands go and stood, then brushed off her apron, smearing rather than removing the flour. When the boys hadn't moved, she looked up at them, first Alex, then Matt.

"Go," she said. And they did.

Matt was the first out the door. The backyard was dark, although Matt could still see sunlight on the mountainsides. The air smelled fresh and held the beginning of a deep cold. Spring was here, but it was new: the nights still felt like winter.

He wished he had a coat, but he knew better than to go back inside. He didn't want his mother to change her mind.

Alex joined him a moment later. He was carrying both their coats—long warm woolen ones their mother had made two years ago. Then the coats had been too big. Now they were getting too small.

"She didn't want us to be out late and get a chill," he said. The flatness of his tone hid the cadences his mother would have used. Once Alex would have tried to mimic her, but apparently the night was too serious for that.

Matt was looking up. Stars shone faintly against the orange and pink sky. "She's worried, isn't she?"

"Frightened is more like it," Alex said. "I didn't expect her to give permission."

"Is that why you told such an obvious lie?" As he watched, the sky darkened. The oranges were turning red.

"Let's just go," Alex said.

Matt looked at him. His brother's face was shrouded in shadow. "I'm trying to help you."

"Maybe I don't want help."

"Maybe you're a bigger fool than I thought." Matt walked across the lawn. The grass was spongy with dew. When he reached the road, he stayed on the side, so that he wouldn't get too much dirt on his only pair of boots.

After a moment, he heard Alex's footsteps behind him. Matt no longer wanted to talk to him. If his brother wanted to be stupid then it was his problem. Matt had done all he could.

He shoved his hands in his pocket and walked, head high. The neighborhood hadn't changed much in all his years. The stone houses still looked forbidding in the darkness. Most of them had no windows, although a few added windows after Matt's father created one for the boys.

The streets were silent after dark, but Matt could see lights in the main part of the town, where the plaza was. There was probably a bazaar going on. Constant seemed to have them all the time now that the city was open to trade. When his parents moved here, Constant had been ruled by a group of Wise Ones who tried to keep the town isolated from the rest of the Isle.

It was isolated no longer. There was even an enclave of Fey on the Cardidas side of Constant. They lived in wooden buildings their Domestics had assembled and they had the most beautiful gardens Matt had ever seen. His father had forbidden them to go to that side of town, but sometimes Matt snuck there, to see what was so frightening about these people his father hated.

So far, he hadn't been able to tell.

The school, though, was in a building on this side of Constant. It had once been a stone house, like Matt's, only someone had built onto it. So instead of one small dwelling with three rooms besides the kitchen and living area, it looked like several pushed together.

There were only five live-in students right now, but Coulter had once told him there would be more as time went on. A lot of parents moved their magical children to Constant, and lived near the school, so that the kids had families as well as education. Matt envied them. Their parents helped them instead of getting in the way.

He led Alex down the dirt path that led to the school's back entrance. Instead of a garden or a yard, the school had a dirt playground, filled with equipment that Matt didn't understand, and didn't ask to have explained. They called it the magic yard. Once he had seen a group of students hurling fireballs at each other, and he realized that some of the reason for the dirt was to prevent serious injury. But he had also seen a solitary boy out there one afternoon, drawing pictures in the dirt with a knife. The magic yard wasn't used as much as Matt would have thought.

Lights were on all over the building—wasteful, his mother would have called it. Some of the lights were magic sticks—an exercise that Coulter assigned the live-ins—and the rest were torches, burning in their holders. Their light looked odd with the sun still on the mountains, but he knew as soon as the sun set completely, he would welcome the flicker of fires.

As he and Alex crossed the magic yard, Matt saw a short Fey man sitting on a chair in front of the door. He was cleaning his fingernails with the edge of a knife. A plate covered with crumbs and sausage wrappings lay on the ground next to him.

The little man looked up. He was older than most Fey Matt had seen, his face square, the angles lost in age and a few extra pounds. He smelled of soap and leather, with just a whiff of garlic from the sausage. When he saw Matt, he grinned.

"Can't stay away, huh?" he asked, and then he cackled. "Your God always gets his revenge."

Alex grabbed Matt's arm and tugged, but Matt reached over and trapped Alex's hand. "It's all right," he said.

Alex didn't look like it was all right. Alex looked frightened.

"Coulter's expecting us, Scavenger," Matt said with a strength that he didn't feel.

"Coulter doesn't even know you're coming," Scavenger said. He turned his knife over so that the blade glinted in the torchlight. As he did, he watched Alex. Matt could feel his brother tremble. "I bet no one knows you're here."

"My mother," Alex said, and Scavenger laughed.

"That's right," he said. "And the Black King's alive and well and running Blue Isle."

"No," Matt said. "We did tell her."

"What happened?" Scavenger asked. "That evil puss-face of a father of yours die?"

"Hey!" Alex started for him, but Matt's grip tightened, holding his brother in place.

"No," Matt said. "And Coulter does know we're coming. I told Leen."

"You think she tells Coulter everything?" But Scavenger stood up, kicked the chair aside, and pulled open the door. "You two had dinner yet?"

He asked this last in a warm tone, as if he hadn't said

any of the other things. Coulter had once told Matt that Scavenger was unpredictable and perhaps even slightly crazy, but that he knew more about magic than any other Fey alive. Matt had always thought that strange, because one afternoon Scavenger had told him that he had been a Red Cap, the nonmagical Fey who, in the days when the Fey were trying to conquer the world, took care of the bodies of people who died in war.

"Yes," Matt said. "We've had dinner."

"Too bad," Scavenger said. He stopped in front of the wooden worktable and picked up a knife. "We have this wonderful sausage from L'Nacin. You haven't tasted anything like it. I haven't in years. I've been here so long I'd forgotten how good food is in the rest of the world."

The kitchen was hot. The stone walls kept in the heat from the day's cooking, and the hearth fire still had active coals. The room was large with a high ceiling and some open vents that the Fey Domestics had installed years before. Even those didn't cool off the heat, though.

A cistern stood on the wall opposite the fireplace. The wall bisected the cistern, with half of it outside so that it could collect rainwater. Scavenger set the knife down, picked up a bucket from beside the table, and walked to the cistern. He fastened the bucket to the rope pulley and lowered it. After a moment, Matt heard a splash.

"Well, you'll at least want something to drink while you wait," Scavenger said. "It's hot in here."

"I don't plan to wait," Matt said. "Where is Coulter?"

"I'll get him." Scavenger brought the bucket up, then dipped a cup into the water. He handed the dripping cup to Matt, who did not refuse it. He was thirsty after the walk. Alex looked at him as if he were crazy, taking water from a Fey. Matt met his brother's gaze, then took a long drink.

The water from the cistern was cold and tasted so fresh that after the first time Matt had had it, he hadn't wanted other water. It made him ask later if the water was spelled. Coulter had laughed and said no, that they were lucky to have found a building with a cistern that went so deep. The water inside, he had once said, wasn't just rainwater. There was a ground spring beneath it as well.

Matt drank half the cup, then wiped his mouth and handed the cup to Alex. Alex frowned, but didn't refuse. He knew better. He was as polite as their parents had taught him to be. He took the cup, sipped, gingerly, then drank greedily, as if he couldn't get enough. He had been thirsty too, and unwilling to admit it.

Scavenger watched with a slight smile. He dipped one more cup in the water and set it on the table. "You can wait here."

"No," Matt said. He'd been through this game with Scavenger before. Scavenger would claim to get Coulter, leave Matt in the kitchen, and never return. Coulter would say later that he didn't get the message. "I'll go."

"We'll both go," Alex said, water droplets on his lip. He set the cup down, wiped his mouth, and stood beside his brother.

Scavenger's smile was broad. "Don't trust me?"

Matt shrugged. "Trust you enough to drink your water."

Scavenger laughed. "I like you better than your father, boy."

"I would hope so," Matt said. "It seems like you hate him."

"I don't hate him anymore," Scavenger said, picking up the second cup for himself. "I loathe him now."

Matt heard Alex let out a hiss of air, and knew that to be a sign that the two of them needed to get out of there before Alex lost his temper. Matt put a hand on the small of his brother's back and pushed him to the door near the hearth fire. Alex looked over his shoulder at Scavenger, eyes narrowed, and Scavenger laughed again.

"Someday, boy," he said, "maybe you'll get up enough courage to ask me why I think your dad is evil incarnate."

"My dad thinks the Fey are," Alex said. Matt shoved harder. Alex dug his feet in.

"Some things never change," Scavenger said.

"Come *on*," Matt said. He moved ahead of Alex, then opened the door and tugged Alex's arm. Alex came. The dining hall outside the kitchen was cooler, but not by much. Some of the heat from the hearth fire had carried into here.

There were still dishes on the long wooden tables and crumbs on the benches. Two Fey Domestics were talking near another door, and started when Matt and Alex came out of the kitchen. The Domestics were young—not much older than Matt—and apparently not doing the work they were supposed to do.

He didn't care. All he wanted to do was find Coulter. He walked over to the Domestics. They were as tall as he was, both of them girls, their dark skin flushed with something like embarrassment. One was so lean that she looked almost feral. The other had a softness to her dark eyes. Matt met her gaze.

"Hi," he said. "I'm looking for Coulter."

"He's in the library," she said.

"Thanks." Matt glanced at Alex, who hung near the kitchen door, watching him. His brother had run a gamut of emotions today, and beneath them all, Matt realized, was terror. Matt remembered feeling afraid the first time he had talked to the Fey, but that had been a long time ago, and gradually, he realized they were as different from each other as they were from him, just like Islanders. You couldn't judge one on the basis of the others.

But Alex didn't know that. He had listened to their father more than Matt had. In some ways, Alex had believed.

"Come on," Matt said to his brother, this time softer.

The Domestics smiled at Alex as if sensing his discomfort, but not knowing the reason for it. Alex walked around the benches, and to the door, and stopped beside Matt.

Matt thanked the Domestics and then went into the corridor. Once this building had been a house similar to the one he had grown up in, the one in which he still lived, but now it was very different. Some of the walls

had been removed or had holes knocked through them.
The rooms had been expanded or someone had added on
to them. The feeling was not so much that of a unified
building, but of a labyrinth.

Alex noticed it too. He stayed close to Matt, so close
that Matt could feel the warmth of his brother's skin,
hear his uneven breathing. Matt had gotten lost in this
labyrinth before, had felt like Alex felt now, only with no
one to guide him. Sometimes Matt thought it one of
Coulter's tests: anyone who could find him in the maze
would be worthy of his help.

The library was around several corners, past a number of wood doors, and up half a flight of stairs. The
stone here was newer, and clearly part of one of the addi-
tions, but which one Matt couldn't tell from the outside.

He liked the library. Its fireplace was small, but it had
lights everywhere, most of them near chairs designed for
comfort. Books lined the walls. Some were Islander books,
taken from the larger kirks, a few saved from the cata-
combs beneath the burned Tabernacle in the city of Jahn.
Many were from faraway lands, hand-printed in languages that Matt could not read: Nyeian, L'Nacin, Ghitlan. Very few books were in Fey, and those that were
seemed ancient. The Fey placed little value on scholar-
ship. They were a people who believed in action, in the
future, not in the past.

This room was cooler than the hallway. Just about
perfect, Matt thought, feeling the sweat run down his
back. The library smelled faintly musty, of books that
had sat too long on shelves, but over that was the smoky
incense of the fire. Coulter liked to place a stick of a foreign wood that Matt could never remember the name of
on top of the fire itself, to give the room a slightly spicy
odor. It somehow made things feel more homey.

Coulter was standing in the corner, near one of the
ladders that had wheels on its base so that it could be
moved around the room. The ceilings were high here as
well, and books went all the way up. Matt had never
seen what was on top.

Alex sneezed, then put a hand to his nose. "What's that smell?"

"The fire," Matt said.

Coulter turned, saw them, and smiled. He was a short man, with hair blonder than most in Constant, and sharp blue eyes. He was square as well, with muscles that made the sleeves of his linen shirt bulge. He closed the book he was looking at, replaced it on the shelf, and crossed the room.

Alex remained close to Matt.

"So," Coulter said. "Leen told me you'd bring your brother." He gave an odd, formal little bow. "It's a pleasure, Alexander."

"Alex." Alex sounded young, hesitant, the fear coming out in the shakiness of his voice.

"Alex," Coulter said. He glanced at Matt. "Things were risky when you came alone, but your family will know that both of you are coming here. It's not something you'll be able to hide."

"We told my mother," Matt said.

Coulter raised his pale eyebrows. The expression was almost comical. "What did she say?"

"She cried," Alex said.

"I told her we needed some help, and we couldn't get it from the Vault." Matt had almost said his father, but he didn't. He was more loyal than that. "So she let us come."

"It wasn't that simple," Coulter said.

"No," Matt said. "It wasn't."

"I'd be interested to know what swayed her."

Matt swallowed. His brother wasn't looking at him again. Why did Matt have to do everything? "Alex swayed her."

"I did not!" Alex said. "I don't want to be here. There are Fey here."

Coulter's look at Alex was measuring. "You are your father's son, aren't you?"

"Yes," Alex said fiercely. "I believe what he does."

"Then I can't help you," Coulter said. "And anyone who feels that way about the Fey isn't welcome here."

"No," Matt said. "Please. You don't know it all."

Coulter turned to Matt. Those startling blue eyes had a flatness to them that Matt had never seen. "I know that your father killed hundreds of Fey with his hatred, and then he killed the one hope the world had for peace. We've managed to struggle through since, but not because of your father."

"He saved us," Alex said. "He saved everyone."

"From the Black King?" Coulter actually sounded bitter. "Maybe. But the actions your father and King Nicholas took wouldn't have been necessary if your father hadn't murdered Nicholas's wife, Jewel."

Matt's heart twisted. He hadn't known that.

"My father does not kill people," Alex said.

"No," Coulter said. "Your father kills Fey. Knowing that, and knowing how you feel about the Fey, many of whom are my friends, I do not want you here."

"Please," Matt said, taking Coulter's arm. "You're the only one who can help us."

Coulter did not shake free of Matt's grasp, but he stared at Alex. Alex's eyes filled with tears. Matt saw them glinting in the light.

"Please," Matt said again. "My brother won't kill anyone. We were raised to respect life. My mother is a Healer. Coulter, you know that."

The muscles in Coulter's arm shifted. For a moment, Matt thought Coulter would break his grip, but he did not.

"I know your mother," he said. "It's amazing to me that such a good woman would love a man like your father. But then, the heart is sometimes a mystery to me."

Alex bit his lower lip. Matt waited, thinking maybe he heard conciliation in Coulter's voice.

"She cried when you spoke to her about coming here?" Coulter asked. "I'm curious as to why."

"Because Alex is having hallucinations," Matt said. "And she doesn't think Father can help."

A tear ran down Alex's cheek. Alex started to wipe it away, then stopped when he seemed to realize that would draw attention to it.

"She's upset about this because she thinks you're losing your mind like your father has?" Coulter was looking at Alex as he spoke.

Alex's lower lip trembled. "No," he said. "It's more complicated than that."

"Hmm," Coulter said.

"It's got to do with history," Matt said. "Something about the Roca."

"You'll have to explain it to me," Coulter said. "I'm not a Rocaanist. I never have been. I was raised among the Fey."

Interesting choice of words—"among" rather than "by." Matt had been around Coulter long enough to know that Coulter usually spoke quite deliberately.

"No," Alex said. He pulled Matt's hand off Coulter's arm. "Let's go. I don't need anyone's help."

"If you're having Visions, you need someone's help," Coulter said. "Visions are meant to be shared. And there are other powers that some Visionaries have, powers that can be either fruitful or harmful depending on how you use them."

"Visions?" Matt asked. "You mean what's happening to Alex is normal?"

"For some people," Coulter said. "You boys have the same bloodline as the royal family, only your families split fifty generations ago. In that bloodline is a wild magic, an old magic, that some believe gave the powers to Queen Arianna and her brother Gift."

"Not the Fey?" Alex asked.

"The powers combined," Coulter said. "I suspect if you married a Fey, your children will have great powers as well."

Alex shuddered. Matt was intrigued. He had never heard that before. But then, why would he? The Fey were rarely discussed in his household except as evil things.

"Do you have this blood?" Matt asked, knowing that Coulter had great powers as well.

"No," Coulter said. "My powers come from a different source. Still Islander, but not the royal bloodline."

He peered at Alex. "If I agree to help you, you do things my way."

"My father—"

"I don't care about your father. I've coddled your father far too long." There was a fierceness in Coulter that Matt had never seen before. "Tell me, when did you last have one of these hallucinations?"

"This afternoon," Alex whispered.

Matt shot him a look. Matt had seen him in the throes of one that morning. "You had two today?"

Alex seemed to wilt. "I'm going crazy."

"No." Coulter sounded reflective. He frowned, looking toward the ceiling as if he could see through it to the sky. "What was the hallucination about?"

"It was jumbled," Alex said. "Like a dream. A really vivid dream."

"Both hallucinations were like that?" Matt asked.

"They always are," Alex said. "And when I come to, I sometimes can't remember where I am."

"Tell me what you remember," Coulter said.

Alex licked his lips, and for a moment, Matt thought he wasn't going to answer. Then he said, "I saw a throne made of darkness, and a Fey man with blue eyes touching it. Then the throne exploded in light."

There was silence for a moment, then Coulter said, "That's all?"

"No," Alex said. "That was just the first one. Early this morning, before dawn." He glanced at Matt. "I had three today, not two."

"What else?" Coulter asked.

Alex moved away from Matt. He walked toward the fire. It created a halo of light around him that made him seem larger than he was, but thinner too, and somehow vulnerable. Matt wanted to go to him, but knew if he did, he might ruin the moment.

"A woman," Alex said, slowly, almost brokenly. "A Fey woman, kissing an Islander." He glanced over his shoulder at Coulter. "I think it was you."

Coulter didn't move. He hardly seemed to be breathing.

"A baby, a different Fey woman, crying as she held it, and it played with her face." Alex looked away again. He clasped his hands behind his back. "Matt—real old— laughing, like Father does."

Matt felt his stomach tighten. His father didn't laugh. He cackled. Two days ago, he had come into the house, cackling. *The forces are gathering,* he had said.

"Me, surrounded by Fey. A woman, with an evil face, a Fey woman and a stone man who speaks with someone else's voice." Alex stopped, but sounded as if he had more to say.

"What else?" Coulter asked.

"My father—" Alex's voice broke "—searching for King Nicholas in the tunnels, and dying there. Without food. Without water. All alone."

This time Matt did go to his brother and put his arm around him.

"These are Visions from the future," Coulter said. "Sometimes they come true, sometimes we can avert them."

"The future?" Alex slipped out of Matt's grasp. "How do you know?"

"The Fey encourage such Visions. People with Vision become the Fey's leaders."

"Like the story," Matt said. Alexander became the leader, the one who had the royal blood. Matthias was the one who went insane. "You saw me. I was like Father."

"When you were very old," Alex said, as if that made it any better. "Your friend says that may not happen." But he didn't give Coulter time to elaborate on that. Instead, he asked, "How come they come to me?"

Coulter shrugged. "That's a philosophical question, not one I can give a real answer to. The Fey believe that you're born with your magical ability, like your blue eyes, and you get what you get. Some people get nothing, and some people, like me and your brother here, get too much."

"Do you believe that?"

Coulter hesitated slightly, just enough so that he couldn't hide his doubt. "I think magical ability can also be found."

"Found?"

Coulter shrugged. "I won't say any more at the moment. I'm like Scavenger. I've spent the last fifteen years studying all I can about magic." He waved a hand at all the books. "Unfortunately, the people who know the most about it, the Fey, never write anything down. I have to glean what I can from their stories, from things others have written, and from history."

"History," Matt said, thinking of his mother's tears. Which brought him back to the reason for their visit. "Can you help Alex?"

Coulter sighed. "I don't think I have a choice."

"What does that mean?" Alex put his hands on his hips. It was a tough stance that somehow only made him look younger.

"It means I started this school to help people like you, people who have nowhere else to turn. I just wish you weren't—" He stopped himself.

"What?" Alex asked. "You wish I wasn't what?"

"Your father's son," Coulter said. "I guess we all have prejudices we have to overcome."

Matt felt the words like blows. He had known that a lot of people didn't like his father, but he had never realized that Coulter, a man Matt secretly admired, hated his father. Had his father done all those things? Was that why his mind had left him?

Coulter straightened, as if he were drawing strength from inside. "If you want my help, you have to do things my way."

"What's your way?" Alex asked, not changing his stance.

"You have to study here every day. You will arrive when you're told and you will leave when you're told. You will study with the Fey when I tell you that you must, and believe me, with your magic skills, the Fey will teach you more than I ever could."

"No," Alex said.

"All right, then." Coulter turned away. "We're done."

"No," Matt said. He went up to Coulter. "Please help him."

"He doesn't want my help."

"He needs it."

"He has to make that choice," Coulter said. "A reluctant student doesn't learn."

"My father," Alex said. His voice broke again. That fear. Matt wondered what, exactly, was causing the fear. "Our father won't approve of any of this."

"Your father won't even know," Coulter said without turning around.

"You're saying we should lie to him?" Alex asked.

"Your father's mind is gone. He won't remember who you are in a year or so. He probably has little idea now."

"That will happen to us, won't it?" Matt asked. "Me and Alex?"

At that, Coulter did turn. His face, in the light, didn't have the anger that Matt expected. Instead it was even softer than it had been before. Compassionate. He raised a hand to Matt's face, tucked a curl behind his ear like Matt's father used to do when he was home more. When he was alive in his own eyes.

"You and I," Coulter said. "You and I run that risk much more than Alex does. We have the same kind of wild magic. The Fey call us Enchanters. We have the most powerful magic of all. But we're denied Vision, and without it, we cannot lead. And the price we pay for that magic, for that power, is that someday, we lose our minds."

"You haven't."

"Not yet." Coulter let his hand drop. "The Fey had Enchanters that lived for almost two hundred years before their minds went. How old is your father? Sixty?"

"I don't know," Matt said.

"Sixty-seven," Alex said.

"Too young, I think, to lose his mind so soon."

"Islanders don't live as long as Fey," Alex said.

"No," Coulter said. "But a two-hundred-year-old Fey is a very, very old Fey. Like a hundred-year-old Islander. It's only at the very end of their life that Fey Enchanters go mad. Your father could live another forty years like that."

Matt shuddered. He couldn't help himself.

"What's your point?" Alex asked.

Coulter looked at him as if he really didn't belong in this part of the conversation. "My point is simple. Fey Enchanters have been trained. They know how to control their magic. Your father didn't. Some of the damage he caused was because his magic leaked in ways that magic shouldn't be allowed to leak. I want to help you, Matt. If we train you, we might prevent the insanity that has gripped your father."

"What about me?" Alex asked.

"You turned down my help."

"You want me to train with Fey."

"You have Visions about them," Coulter said. "You might as well find out what those Visions mean."

"My father—" Alex started.

"Your mother allowed you to come here," Coulter said. "She has to know your father's opinions. She has to know what it means to have you here. Doesn't that sway you in any way?"

Matt held his breath. Alex looked at both of them. "I don't want to train with Fey," Alex said at last.

"Then you are not welcome here," Coulter said. "Good luck with your life and your future. You'll need it. Now leave me with your brother. I want to talk with him for a moment."

Alex opened his mouth, then closed it, then opened it again. "I'll be outside," he said to Matt.

"No," Coulter said. "Go home. I don't want you near this place."

Alex waited, apparently for Matt to defend him. Matt didn't know what to say. He had seen a side of his brother that completely shocked him, a side he hadn't realized existed. He thought his brother would get past his feelings toward the Fey, just as Matt had. But Alex didn't even try.

"I guess I'll see you at home, then, Matt," Alex said. He waited again, but Matt didn't turn. And finally, Alex left.

Coulter was watching Matt closely. "I didn't mean to cause a rift between you, but he worries me. I've seen that attitude toward Fey before, and it's always dangerous."

Matt wasn't going to talk to Coulter about his brother. "Why'd you want me to wait?"

"I want you to study with me."

"I have been," Matt said.

"I know," Coulter said, "but not in the all-involving way that most of my students do. I couldn't allow that, not without your parents' permission. I take your mother sending you here as tacit approval of the way I'm doing things. And I want to take advantage of that. I want to help you."

"Why?" Matt asked. He knew he was being sullen, but things hadn't worked out the way he had thought. He wasn't sure what was going to happen now.

"Because, Matt, you are a rare creature. There are very few Enchanters. There are three more on Blue Isle, besides you, me, and your father, and one or two in the rest of the Empire. That's it. With training—"

"I can be of use to the Fey?"

"No," Coulter said. "There's more to it than that. Every Visionary needs an Enchanter at his side. I don't think it's a coincidence that the two of you were born into the same family."

"You think I can help Alex?"

"And in helping Alex, maybe help the rest of us."

Matt felt dizzy. He sat in one of the wooden chairs. The wood was polished and warm, not rough like the wood in his home. "But I wouldn't be able to help him for years."

"It doesn't matter, as long as he gets help."

"He'll go to Father."

"I thought that's what you feared. I thought that's why you brought him here."

It was, but Matt no longer wanted to address that. "If I could help him, why didn't you? He would have worked with you."

"He needs a Shaman, not me. And the only Shaman are Fey. Most Visionaries are Fey. I believe in having my students trained by the best."

Matt nodded, not completely understanding. But Alex wasn't really the point anymore. If what his mother had said was true, if that old story was true, if what was happening to his father was a part of the kind of magic that Matt had, then he really had no choice. He had to get help. It was the only way to prevent that Vision his brother had.

"I'll let you train me," he said.

"The conditions will still apply," Coulter said.

"I don't care about the conditions," Matt said. And he didn't. What he cared about was Alex.

And Alex was gone.

CHAPTER SIX

ALEX GOT LOST in the corridors, wandering through the maze Matt called a school. There were Fey in the halls. They watched Alex as if they'd never seen anything like him, and when he wouldn't meet their gaze, he could still feel them staring at him, as if they would do something to him.

How could Matt believe these people could help him? How could Matt give up so easily? Their father had fought the Fey. He had helped the Queen to the throne because he knew she was at least part Islander, the lesser of two evils, not because he believed that her Fey ways would make Blue Isle better. His father had believed Blue Isle lost, and the only way to save it was to make some sort of peace with these people.

The fact that they shared powers, his father used to say, didn't make them like the Fey. It made them better than the Fey. The Islanders had always denied their powers, controlled them, held them in check. The Fey had used those powers to kill people and conquer half the world.

Now Matt, Alex's twin brother, the person he was closest to in the world, wanted him to be taught by Fey.

Finally Alex found that dining area. The two Fey girls that his brother had talked to were long gone, and the tables were now clean and polished. A lone torch still burned, as if left to give enough light for a transition from one room to the next.

Alex felt tension in his shoulders. That strange little Fey would be in the kitchen, and Alex didn't know any other way out. He would have to talk to the man.

He took a deep breath before opening the kitchen door. Another Fey, a girl he had never seen before, instantly covered her plate with her hands. She was his age, and her features were rounder than most Fey.

Was she part Islander?

"Who're you?" she asked. Her voice was soft, with the slight twang of Jahn in it.

"Nobody," he said. "Finish your meal."

Color flooded her cheeks, and that was when he realized her skin was as pale as his was. She had Fey features, but they had been tempered by her Islander heritage.

Slowly she uncovered her plate. Bits of sausage littered it along with a large hunk of cheese. He couldn't believe she would eat that much. She was very thin.

"You want some?" she asked in a tone that led him to believe she really didn't want to share.

"No," he said. "I was just leaving. Is that strange Fey outside?"

"Scavenger?" She nodded. "He usually is at night."

Alex felt his mouth grow dry. He really didn't want to see the little man again.

She seemed to sense his unease. The edges of her lips quirked in a half smile. "You want me to go with you?"

"No," he said.

"You running away?"

He supposed that was accurate. He was running from here, but not away. He didn't live here. This wasn't home. It wasn't like he was doing something wrong.

Was it?

Matt thought it was. That look in his brother's eyes had been one of hurt, not anger. Matt had brought Alex to this forbidden place so that he could get help, and Alex had refused. Couldn't Matt see that the way Islanders behaved was the only thing that made them different from the Fey? To learn how to behave from the Fey was wrong, and always had been.

He'd try to explain that to his brother later, but he had a hunch it would make no difference. Matt had made his choice long ago, and if Alex had known this was it, he wouldn't have lied for Matt. He would have told his mother exactly where Matt was.

Although her tears had confused him. Her tears and her willingness to send him here after discovering his hallucinations, his Vision, as Coulter called it. Maybe Matt had been right. Maybe Alex had needed to be here. Now he had learned what he needed to know: that such Visions were normal and that he had to learn how to live with them, how to use them. They were flashes of the future, and they could be changed.

The one that bothered him the most wasn't the one of himself surrounded by Fey. It was the one of Matt, cackling, his eyes empty, his mind gone.

Alex shuddered.

"All right," the girl said, returning to her food. "Don't answer me."

He had forgotten what the question was. He made himself smile at her as he slipped past her. "Sorry," he said.

This time, she shrugged, and didn't look at him. Her back was so thin he could see the outline of her shoulder blades and the ridges of her spine. Didn't they feed their students here? Was that why she was sneaking food? He'd have to warn Matt about that as well.

Alex pushed open the door, and felt a blast of cold night air. The door scraped against a wooden chair and it slid across the stone threshold. The little man appeared out of nowhere, grabbed the chair, and grinned at Alex.

"So," the man said, pushing the door closed. "Couldn't stay, could you?"

Alex was determined to move past him. This time, the man wouldn't make him angry, no matter what he said.

"Where's your brother?"

"Inside." Alex shoved his hands inside his coat pockets and bowed his head, hurrying across the yard. The little man kept up with him.

"Afraid of me?" he asked.

Alex didn't answer.

"Or are you afraid of yourself?"

Alex tightened his hands into fists.

"Just like your father, aren't you? Willing to deny everything you are because you can't face yourself."

Alex whirled. "My father is a good man."

"Your father has never been a good man," the Fey said. "But he has always been an interesting and complex one. I've seen him lately. It's sad what he's become."

"You don't understand it."

"I'm afraid I do." The little man was speaking softly now. "It's the one reason I'm happy I have no magic. I value my mind too much."

Tears touched Alex's eyes for the second time that night. He didn't like this place. He didn't like these people. He wanted them all to leave him alone.

Blindly, he turned and ran away from the school. But he didn't head home. Instead, he ran toward the center of town.

Most of the lights were out now, except for the torches that burned streetside. Those were a Fey custom, now adopted by Islanders, so that the streets were visible at night. Someone said it cut down on crime, but Alex's father said there had been no crime until the Fey arrived.

The houses were dark. Alex's footfalls on the dirt roads and his own ragged breathing were the only sounds he heard. The little Fey man hadn't followed him.

Alex was alone.

When he reached the plaza and its built-in stone booths, he stopped running. He had a stitch in his side, and he was tired on a level he didn't entirely understand.

He walked the rest of the way to the old meeting house, not seeing a soul, wondering if his mother had already been here to fetch his father. Alex suspected she hadn't. More and more, it seemed, she left his father on his own. It was as if she was disgusted with him, or frightened of him, or unable to deal with what he had become.

Alex pushed open the meeting-house door. The familiar musty smell overtook him. Old furniture was piled against the walls, and the candle, usually left by the door, was gone. It probably hadn't been there for a while. A lot of people had died in and near the meeting house during the battles for Constant in the last war, and no one wanted to come into this place any longer.

No one except his father.

Alex felt around, dust rising as he did so, his hands getting filthy as he searched for more candles and a flint. If Matt were with him, he would create one of those tiny flames on the tips of his fingers that lit everything so they could find a candle. But he had left Matt at that school.

It was the first real purposeful separation of their lives.

Finally Alex's fingers felt soft wax. He grabbed the candle, felt some flint beside it, and, after a few tries, managed to light it.

The mess in this place always looked worse in the dark, almost as if he could see the remains of the people who had died here in the year before he was born. He had heard the stories, how the Fey had become birds and rats and had attacked everyone, but he had never actually seen anything like it. Still, from the time he was a small boy, sudden sharp movements by small creatures terrified him. The stories had lodged deep within him and he knew, no matter what his brother said, that the Fey couldn't be trusted.

Shadows moved across the wall as the candle flickered. Alex swallowed, wondering if he should have come here at all. But he didn't want to go home. He didn't want to see his mother right now and have her ask questions, and he didn't want to see Matt. Matt would yell at him. Matt would try to change him. And there was no way that Matt could.

Alex had never realized how very different they were until tonight. They looked so much alike and they had been together almost every moment of their lives. When they were little, they even had their own language. Their mother had thought it cute, but their father was the one who had put a stop to it, insisting that they speak so that everyone could understand them.

Their father had been right, of course. In those days, he always was.

Alex crossed the dirty floor to the hidden door. He pressed the mechanism that opened it, heard the click, felt the rush of cooler air rise from below.

There were no lights. Maybe his mother had been here. "Father?" he yelled. He waited a moment, and heard nothing but the echo of his own voice.

He sighed and a bit of his breath hit the candle's flame. It guttered but did not go out. His heart started pounding. The last thing he wanted to do was go down those stairs and suddenly find himself in darkness.

Hot wax dripped on the back of his hand. This wouldn't work. He turned and searched until he found the remains of a torch. He used the candle to light it, then blew the candle out.

The wax had dried on the back of his hand. He wiped it against his pants, then went to the door again.

Taking a deep breath, he walked down the stairs, feeling them creak under his weight. They hadn't had care for years. He could remember coming down these stairs when he was little and thinking them wondrous, with their clean wood surface, their firmness despite their age. He, his brother, and his parents could stand on a step and it wouldn't make a sound of protest.

Things had changed. He knew that. But he still had hope that the answers to his new problem lay here, and not with the school. That even if his father couldn't assist him, the Words could. The Words and the trappings of the old religion. After all, that had been all that the first Alexander had had.

The stairs went down a long way ending in a wide corridor. It was built of the mountain stone, and filled with cobwebs and rotting wood. The smell of decay was strong here, and seemed to grow stronger every time he came down.

The stones were uneven and held in place with generations of mortar. Some had flaked off, and he could see the older material beneath. He had tried to touch it once, to see if the older material was the same as the newer, but his father had yelled at him as if he had touched something forbidden.

"Father?" Alex yelled again.

This time his voice sounded disembodied. There was no echo; there never had been in this portion of the corridor. It went on for a long way, and he sighed, realizing that he would have to go all the way to the Vault.

As he walked, the air got colder and damper, and bits of water glistened on some of the stone. It took a long time before he got to the section of the corridor that meant he was getting close to the Vault itself.

The floor had changed color. Earlier, it had been the gray of mountain stone after it had been cut away from the mountain. Now it was red like the mountains, like the mountain stone before it was cut away.

He was inside the Cliffs of Blood.

That thought always made him slightly uncomfortable. He envisioned the mountains rising to their incomparable height above him, and he always felt very small and fragile. In comparison to the natural beauty around him, he was nothing.

He had said that to his father once, and his father had laughed. A real laugh, not the cackle he so often used now. *Boy*, his father had said, *the beauty wouldn't exist without our eyes to appreciate it.*

His mother had laughed too, and called his father

self-centered. His father had put his arm around her and said, as he so often used to, that she was the best thing in his life.

Alex used to be jealous of that. Why weren't his sons the best thing? But now he missed it. Now he missed the father who gave them advice and sometimes played with them and instructed them. The father who loved their mother best of all and made no pretense at hiding it. Alex hadn't seen that man for a long, long time.

Maybe Coulter was right. Maybe Alex's father could no longer help him. But his father had always said, *If you can't find answers from the people around you, return to the Words.*

Alex was doing that, and returning to his father as well.

The corridor had stopped tilting downward and here he felt it, as he always did, stronger than usual. The pull of the mountain. He had felt it since he was an infant. His mother used to tell the story of Alex, reaching toward the sky. Once Alex asked about it and his mother said she hadn't known what he was reaching for. But his father had. He had looked at his mother with a grave expression and said, *Alex feels the Roca's Cave.*

His mother never told the story again.

The first time his father brought him down here, he held Alex's arm tightly. His mother held Matt. At this point in the corridor, both boys had felt the urge to run forward, to climb from the inside, to use the tunnels to take them to that mysterious place up the mountain, but their parents had held them fast. *See?* his father had said. *This is why I haven't brought you here before. I will only bring you if you resist that temptation. For up there is death.*

It was later that Alex heard how his father had nearly died there twice, fighting spirits that lived in the mountains, and that was where he had gotten the permanent bruise at the base of his neck. His father was horribly scarred from battles fought against the Fey. The worst scar ran along his face, puckering as he grew older, and knocking his features out of alignment.

Alex almost called for his father again, but did not. His father hadn't answered before. He probably wouldn't answer now.

If he was even here.

Alex's heart was pounding. The torch's heat was growing too much for his hand. The torch obviously had been discarded because it had grown too short. But it was all he had. He switched it to the other hand, and placed the hot hand on the nearest stone.

It felt cool to the touch. He loved the red in the stone, the way it looked hot and actually felt cold. This part of the corridor had once been polished by Islanders, but it hadn't been built by them. This was part of the mountain itself, the opening of a cave deep within the bowels of the mountain, a place that had been here before Islanders ever appeared in the area.

He loved the age, the history. He loved the way it felt here. He even loved the tug he had to struggle against, the way he had to resist the call of the mountain.

Finally, he rounded a corner. Before him was the large stone door. It had been carved of a single block of stone, and made to fit the area. Someone had left it open, the wooden bar that locked it was leaning up against the wall, the padlock on the ground beside it.

Keep this locked at all times, his father used to say. *You never know who might try to steal the Secrets.*

Alex sighed softly, then went through the door. It was dark in the main room. "Father?" he yelled again.

He thought he heard rustling, and despite himself, his heart started to race. Those Fey rats held his imagination, even now.

"Father?"

The rustling stopped. He suppressed a sigh. He turned to the side of the door, and used his torch to light the one on the left, then one on the right. The light flared off the deep red walls, illuminating the room.

As usual, it was hot down here. The chairs were askew and the table covered with the remains of a meal. The bed looked as if it had been slept in and not made. A faint odor, one that Alex hadn't smelled here before, floated on the air.

The smell of neglect.

Maybe his mother hadn't been down here in a long time. Usually, if his father disappeared for more than a day or two, his mother would come down here with a lot of food. She would clean the place, make sure his father ate, and then come home again, her lips in a tight line, her eyes sad.

Sometimes she sent the boys. But it had never been this bad, not when Alex had come. How long had his father been here this time? He couldn't remember. His father's erratic schedule had long since stopped being something Alex paid attention to.

Blankets were strewn over the couches as if a lot of people had slept in the room. It was large enough to hold several, although Alex didn't know anyone who came down here beside his family. Everyone else seemed to have forgotten about this place. Some people were actually afraid of it. Alex's father had once invited the Queen here, and she had refused, saying such a place was dangerous for one such as her.

His father had known that. He had laughed and said that she wasn't worthy of the throne.

A robe lay across one of the chairs. In the old days, before the Fey, the Wise Ones used to use this room for study. Now it had become his father's unofficial home away from home.

Near the bed, the small wooden door was also open, and light spilled out of the Vault. Alex sighed. His father had to be in there, waiting, wondering what was coming down here, what was going to get him this time.

Alex walked across the room. He put his torch in an empty holder. He knew he wouldn't need it in the Vault itself. Then he ducked through the door.

The light caught him, as always, the brightness of a room that should have been in complete darkness. The glow came from the white floor, the white walls, the white ceiling. It was an internal glow, almost as if someone had laid marble on a continual fire.

Alex blinked, waiting for his eyes to adjust. He could never get used to this room. It wasn't vast, even though it felt vast. The tapestries on the walls were askew. He checked the urge to straighten them. There would be time later, after he found his father. But Alex couldn't resist a glance at them.

He had always loved the tapestries. The strange light made the fabrics shine. The golds seemed golder, the reds vibrant, the greens as brilliant as damp grass on a sunny day. That had been his father's phrase, and Alex thought it accurate. The tapestries were hung evenly, like curtains, around the room, and ending only where the room branched off into a series of corridors.

Down one of those corridors, he felt the pull.

He ignored it, as he always did.

He glanced at the stone altar, rising out of the floor, the Words on top of it, the leather cover closed. He had half expected to see his father standing there, pondering the Words as he had done so many times, but he wasn't there. Although he was in the room. Alex could hear him breathe.

But Alex didn't step toward the altar, not yet. If he did so, he would ignite the jewels, and then the gold flare, and he wasn't ready to do that. His father, no matter how unbalanced he was, always responded when the jewels were ignited, and sometimes he responded as if the person who ignited them was a threat.

Instead, Alex checked the rest of the room, and was surprised to find it tidy. The table was still set up for the Feast of the Living, the silver bowls in the center of the table sparkling as if they had just been polished. Vials of holy water sat on freestanding shelves, and swords lay between them. Suspended from the ceiling in an arching pattern were the globes for the Lights of Midday. He felt as though if he touched one, it would flare into light.

Not that it had to.

He and Matt had been admonished all their lives not to touch these things, and they hadn't—or at least, Alex hadn't. Sometimes he wondered about his brother. Matt had been keeping secrets from him for a long time. At least, that was what Alex thought now. Now that he had seen his brother treat Fey as if he had spoken to them every day.

Several small dolls, made of handblown glass, sat on tiny chairs. Bottles lined one wall, and glowed redly as he looked at them. Skin drums hung from one pillar and Alex shuddered as he usually did when he looked at them. His father said the Wise Ones had believed the skin on the drums had been the skin of the Roca and the bones crossed in front of it, his bones. His father hadn't believed that, but he had forbidden them from touching the drums as well. Those were the only things in the room that Alex had never wanted to touch, so he hadn't minded that rule at all.

It relieved him, somehow, that all the Secrets hidden in the Vault were still in order. Perhaps that meant his father hadn't deteriorated as far as others had said. Alex always feared that his father would someday smash the dolls—the Soul Repositories, they were called—and pour the blood out of the bottles. Alex had no idea what would happen then, as the Secrets mixed on the white floor of the Vault, but he had a hunch it would be bad.

"Father?" he asked softly. He heard the rustling again. It came from behind the altar. He sighed yet again. If his father were leaning on the altar it would be glowing gold. So his father had to be hiding behind it, careful not to touch it. Thinking, perhaps, that Alex was the enemy.

Alex braced himself, then took a step forward. As he expected, his boot hit a ruby and it ignited all the jewels around him. The floor, which had been white, was now covered with jewels set about a foot apart from each other, and all the same size. To his right was an emerald that seemed to have a green glow as he looked at it. Beyond that, a sapphire, and farther along, a diamond that seemed like a clear hole in the floor. The jewels continued to form a large ring around the altar. To his left there were two stones he had no name for: a black stone that had a diamondlike brilliance and clarity, and a gray stone that also had a gem's brilliance. Then there was another diamond, and the pattern continued: ruby, emerald, sapphire, diamond, gray stone, black stone.

He took another step forward, and more jewels revealed themselves. Only the pattern had shifted slightly. This jewel, smaller and rounder, was an emerald. The ruby was to his left, the sapphire to his right. Another step, this time igniting a sapphire. The jewels that appeared closer and closer to the altar were smaller and smaller.

Everything worked its way out from the altar at the center.

He stepped on the black jewel, and then the gray jewel, and then he was at the altar itself. He peered behind it. Sure enough, his father was sprawled there, hands over his head. His hair was matted, and his fingernails were encrusted with dirt. Alex could smell his father from here, and it wasn't a pleasant odor: an unwashed body mixed with the stink of fear.

"Father," he said again.

"Demon spawn," his father whispered.

Alex hated this. He knew what his father referred to: the Wise Ones of Constant used to call anyone who was tall demon spawn because great height was usually—although not always—a sign of great magic. They had called his father this from the time he was a boy.

"Father," Alex said again. He walked around the altar and crouched beside his father, putting his hand gingerly on his father's back. His father's robe had a greasy feel, and Alex felt a sudden flare of anger at his mother who let his father go like this. "It's Alex."

"Alexander is dead," his father moaned. "Murdered by the heathen Fey."

"Not King Alexander," Alex said. "I'm your son. Alex. My mother's name is Marly."

As usual, the mention of his mother's name caught his father's attention. His head rose slowly, his twisted face looking hopeful. The scar's pucker seemed even worse than it had before, or perhaps that was the effect of the strange light and the dirt encrusting the old wound.

"Marly?" his father whispered.

"I can take you home to her," Alex said.

His father sat up and rubbed his eyes like a baby. Then he reached for Alex, catching his arm in a viselike grip. "You don't belong here," his father said.

"You're the one who first brought me here."

His father shook his head. "The forces are gathering. They saw us today. You cannot hide here."

"You do."

"I am lost." The words were plaintive, almost as if, in his madness, his father understood what was happening to him. "But you are not."

"I came to get guidance from the Words."

"They are a lie," his father whispered.

Alex had heard this before. "The real Words."

"They are not what I expected," his father said. "They are a letter. We have failed the Roca, and now evil is loosed upon the world. He brought it to us, and asked us to deny it, to keep it from spreading. But I have it. And I have given it to my children."

Alex's heart ached. He was beginning to wish this day would end. "I am your child," he said. "I came to you for help. I'm having Visions."

His father looked at him with the clarity that Alex had hoped for. It was as if his father were seeing him for the first time in a year.

"No, Alex," he whispered. "No."

"Mother cried when she heard," Alex said. "Matt took me to Coulter for help. But I wanted to come to you."

"I am lost," his father said.

"You can help me."

His father shook his head, the clarity gone.

"Please," Alex said. "Father, I came to you."

His father closed his eyes. His mouth moved as if in prayer. When he opened his eyes, that clarity was back, terrible somehow in its lucidness.

"Now I understand," he muttered, more to himself than to Alex, "how Nicholas felt. You protect your children no matter what they are."

Then, before Alex had a chance to move, his father grabbed his hand and shoved it against the altar. The stone was hot against his flesh, nearly burning it. Gold flared from him, enveloping them, wrapping them in its light. Alex felt blinded and warmed at the same time. He tried to struggle out of his father's grip. His father had warned them never to touch the altar and now he was forcing Alex to do so, and they would drown in the light—

"Your Visions are true ones," his father said, and he sounded sad. "The Roca's blood flows through you just as it flows through me. Perhaps stronger. Because of Marly."

The words echoed within the light, as if it trapped the sound and sent it back. Alex continued to struggle, but his father's grip simply grew tighter. Alex would be bruised if this continued.

Then his father let go. Alex leaned forward, nearly falling over. His father had tears in his eyes.

"I am lost," he said, but the clarity was still there. "My mind—it travels along the lines and corridors and boundaries of light, not of this world. I have few moments here any longer. The Roca was like this: that was why his own children refused to believe him when he returned. But he did return, in an attempt to save them."

His father leaned forward, so that their faces were only inches apart. His father's breath was sour with the smell of rotting teeth, the smell of a man who hadn't eaten in a long time. Alex tried to turn away, but his father grabbed his face, held it, so that Alex had to look him in the eye.

"The Roca's sons did not listen to him," his father said again, "but you must listen to me. You are so young . . ."

His voice trailed off, and for a moment, Alex thought he had lost him. Then his father blinked and said as if he were arguing with himself, "But Nicholas's children were young. And so was Nicholas. Youth sometimes cannot be enjoyed."

"Father, please," Alex said. It felt as if his cheeks were being pushed into his face. His father's filthy fingernails were scratching his skin.

His father nodded, as if Alex's plea was not for release but for more advice. "You are the one who can save us. You must read the Words, study the old religion. Learn the tapestries. You must take the foundation I have built, teach the Islanders and their half-breed children to repress the magic before it eats them as it has eaten me."

"But Coulter says it ate you because you repressed it."

His father shook his head. "Because I used it. Because I used all of it, until I was drained to nothing. It is in the Words. The Wise Ones misunderstood the Words. They thought the Words meant to kill those with magic, but that's wrong. The Roca wanted the magic suppressed, not used. That's why the tools hide in here, and in the Roca's Cave, so that they are *not* used. That's why they became Secrets. But the key to the Secrets must not be lost entirely. For if it is, someone will use them wrong and harm us all."

His father was ranting again. Alex tried to wrench his face away. His father moved closer. He didn't look as if he were gone. His eyes flashed like they used to.

"Remember," his father said. "A man with Vision and the Roca's blood has charisma, the ability to lead and to make others follow. It is a gift, my son. And you must use it. Become a Rocaan in the New Rocaanism. Set up the church in opposition to the evilness that the Fey have brought us. Do not let them control the power that is in this mountain. I have failed, but you cannot. Read the Words. Study the tapestries. Find someone who knows the old stories. It is all here."

"You know the old stories," Alex said.

His father's smile was sad. "Tomorrow I may not know who I am. I am lost, Alex, but you are not."

"Matt's gone to the Fey for help."

"Then you must bring him back," his father said. "They will teach him to use his magic, and he will become like me. Only you can prevent that. Only you."

Then his father released his face, and blinked, as if he hadn't known what he was doing. Alex had a sense, an odd sense, that his father had used energy from the golden light to give him clarity, and now the energy was gone.

"Father?" Alex asked.

His father shook his head. "I am a second son," he said. "I cannot have children. My life has been given to the Tabernacle."

He was gone. But he had been there for a brief moment, the moment Alex needed him. Alex brushed a hand over his father's face in affection, wishing he could do something and knowing he could not.

"I'll send Mother," he said softly.

"She does not deserve me," his father said with perfect lucidity, then moaned and lay on the floor again. And no matter what Alex could do, he could not rouse him.

Finally Alex rocked back on his heels. He was hot, shaken, and terrified. The image of his brother's face, as mad as his father's could be, was lodged in his mind.

Only you can prevent that, his father had said. *Only you.*

Was this why a man was given Vision? To prevent awful things from happening?

Alex didn't know. After a time, he stood, turned, and put his hand on the leather cover of the Words. He stared at it for a moment.

He had to lead now, whether he was ready or not. His father couldn't do it, and he knew it. His father was gone, his brother, misguided, and his mother, panicked.

It was all up to Alex, and the only help he had was in this strange room.

He opened the cover and stared at the cramped handwriting, at the Ancient Islander that his father had taught him to read along with Islander itself. Then Alex took a deep breath, and began his study of the Words.

EMERGENCE

One Week Later

CHAPTER SEVEN

$\mathcal{I}$T TOOK GIFT a week of argument to get the Shaman
to give him a hearing. After he returned to Protectors Village from the Black Throne, no one would speak to him.
The Shaman were having not-so-secret meetings, and he
suspected that they were trying to decide whether or not
to stop his apprentice training.

He went through his days tending the garden and
staring at the mountain itself. His hand ached from its
contact with the Black Throne, and at night he had dreams
about the light.

The dreams unnerved him. The light had a seeking
quality, a quality that he remembered vaguely from his
youth. Every being, he learned as a child, was Linked to
others, through love, through family ties, through some
strengthening and binding experience. Enchanters, Visionaries, and Shaman could actually see those Links as
golden ties connecting people. Sometimes those connections went from heart to heart, sometimes from mind to
mind, and sometimes from heart to mind to heart and

mind. But no matter how far apart the Linked couple's actual bodies were, the Link tied them together.

Enchanters, Visionaries, and Shaman could become beings of light, and travel across a Link. Their consciousness could enter someone else's mind. Gift had traveled the Links before he even knew what he was doing, and at the end of his travels, he had found Sebastian. They used to meet in Sebastian's mind when they were children, and Gift was able to watch his family—his real family—as if he were living with them.

But the most frightening experience he had ever had with his Links was the time his great-grandfather had discovered a Link that led him to Gift. His great-grandfather had entered Gift's mind, shoved Gift aside, and peered out through his eyes. In that moment, Gift had felt his great-grandfather's true self, old and complex and extremely strong.

Gift had never felt anything like it again until he touched the Black Throne.

Since touching the Throne, he hadn't been able to speak to anyone about it. Madot had forbidden him to. After they had left the throne room, she had told him to remain quiet. He had agreed—only if he could meet with the other Shaman and the apprentices so that they could all compare Visions.

He had a feeling something profound had happened that day, and he wanted their help in discovering what it was.

But no one would speak to him. Not even the other apprentices. It was as if the light from the Throne had encapsulated him, made him even more different than he had been before.

And now, Madot told him to report to the Hall of Gathering at twilight. The others, she had said, would be willing to grant his wish.

As he walked through the Protectors Village, he noted that no one else seemed to be moving about. If they were to meet him, they were already inside the Hall of Gathering. He felt a little prickle down his spine. He had spent the day in the garden, nursing the new young shoots, pulling weeds, and preparing the soil for the main planting. He hadn't watched any of the other Shaman; in fact, he had made certain that he would not look for anyone else. He didn't want to know what they were planning, what they were doing. He didn't trust this meeting. Since he had come back from the Throne, he felt as if he trusted nothing at all.

The air was cool as the sun set. Shadows spread through the valley, the huts huddled in the darkness. The Hall of Gathering was a traditional Fey structure, not a hut at all. Shaped like a U it had many rooms, some of which the apprentices were not allowed into. It was the oldest building in the village, made of a spelled wood no longer found in these parts. Some said it dated from the days the Fey had lived here, before they had begun their world conquest, and Gift believed that. Something about the Hall made him think of the Domicile in the place where he had grown up. The Domicile had been a long narrow building, filled with tiny rooms, mostly for the Domestics. But in one of the rooms lived the Shaman who had influenced his life. He had memories of going to see her when he was so tiny he could barely walk.

Those memories gave him comfort every time he walked into the Hall of Gathering. It smelled and looked different, of course, but it had a similar feeling, the feeling of magic just used for a good reason. It tingled in the air like a favorite scent just fading, and it always warmed him.

This time, as he pushed open the gray-brown door, he felt the same warmth, but with it, a trace of nerves that he knew were his. This meeting would be important. It might influence the rest of his life.

He was alone in the main hall. Fey lamps burned, the souls pressed against the glass, watching him. The wooden chairs, as old as the building, had been pushed against the wall and covered with Domestic-spelled woolen blankets. He could feel their comfort from here, along with the way they beckoned him to come, relax, rest. They promised to calm him before he went to his meeting.

He wondered if they had been set there as a distraction. He realized then that he had reverted to the way he had been during the Black King's invasion of Blue Isle: he trusted no one but himself.

Something had caused that reversion. He wasn't sure if it was actually touching the Throne, or because of the way Madot had treated him. She had been his mentor, and he had thought she had helped him because she trusted him. Then he learned it was because of a Vision, and she had been testing him all along.

The favor with which he had once viewed the village, looking at it as the most peaceful place in the Fey Empire, had changed at that moment. The interplay of personalities here was as important, if not more important, than anywhere else in the Empire.

And he had thought he was escaping all the politics by becoming a Shaman.

The Fey lamps illuminated the hallway to his left. The lamps hung on one side of the wall, and doors lined the other. He walked past all the closed doors, wondering if he should knock, and then finally saw one that was open.

It led into a room he had never seen before. The room was lit by candles, not Fey lamps, and smelled faintly of incense made by the Domestics to aid in Vision and Truth. There were no chairs. Instead, pillows covered the floor, and on each pillow sat a Shaman. The seven apprentices stood in the back, looking terrified and uncomfortable.

Madot sat in the middle. She rose when she saw him. "Gift," she said, extending her hands.

He didn't take them. He felt warmth suffuse his face. All of this attention on him. He hadn't expected it. He hadn't expected anything like this.

"Is this my meeting to discuss Visions?" he asked. "Or is it something else?"

Madot looked over her shoulder. Kerde, the Shaman who ran Protectors Village, stood. Her robe fell softly about her shoulders, shimmering in a way that no other Shaman's robe did. Her hair was so white that it was almost translucent. She was very, very old, and had been running Protectors Village as long as all the other Shaman could remember. She would not divulge her real age, but it was rumored among the apprentices that she had lived twice as long as any other Fey. Some said she had been here since the Shaman were assigned to protect the Place of Power, and they said she could not die.

Madot let her hands fall to her side. Her dark eyes had a look of disappointment in them, whether for Gift's rebuke or something else he could not tell.

"It was Foreseen long ago," Kerde said, more to the others than to him, "that the Black Family would reject the Black Throne."

Gift inhaled, caught by surprise. Was this all a test? Had they allowed him to come here so that they could test him and his heritage?

His great-grandfather's advisors had told him not to trust the Shaman, and his mother had once said the same thing.

"My family hasn't rejected it," he said. "My sister—"

"Is not the one the Throne accepted," Kerde said.

Gift looked at the others. In the semidarkness, he could only see part of their faces, making them look like people he had never met. "She has never had a chance," Gift said. "She didn't even know to come here."

"She was not raised Fey."

"I was," Gift said. "And I didn't know."

Kerde tilted her head. The thin light from the candles glistened through her thin hair. "That is because of the way the transfer happened. Information about the Throne was not passed from Rugad to his heir. Your family took control."

"I come from the Black Family," Gift said. He was getting angry now. They had no right to treat him this way. The future had been decided, and they were changing it. "We have been in control for hundreds of years."

"You come from the Black Family, yes," Kerde said. "And you come from the heirs to a wild magic."

"The Deniers," said a voice near the back. A male voice that Gift recognized but couldn't place. "They denied their magic, and believed denial gave them strength."

Kerde held up her hand for silence. "You have seen two Places of Power. It is your job, as Black King, to help us find the third."

"No," Gift said. "We will not locate the third Place of Power. My sister has decreed that conquest is over. We can live without the Triangle and whatever changes it will bring. We have so far."

"It is your job, as Black King," Kerde said.

"I am not the Black King," Gift said, the hair rising on the back of his neck. "I will not accept the Throne. Bring my sister here. She will take the Black Throne."

"It is too late," Kerde said. "She does not rule as a Fey. She has not even left her Island."

"She rules as a Fey. You say that because she is different, because you don't like her."

"The Throne wants you."

"The Throne would take whatever member of the Black Family stood before it." Gift was breathing hard. The incense disturbed him, making him slightly dizzy. He hated this. He hated the way they were trying to alter the way things had been for the past fifteen years.

"That is not true," Kerde said. "The Throne has rejected members of the Black Family before as not worthy."

"How do you know it will reject my sister?" Gift asked.

"It is too late," Kerde said. "It wants you."

He clenched his fist. "And if it cannot get me?"

"It will find someone else who will fulfill its mission."

"The Throne has a mission?" He looked at the other Shaman. They did not seem startled by this. What did they know that they weren't tell him, that they weren't telling anyone?

The apprentices in the back were pushed as far against the wall as possible. They said nothing, but Gift could not see their soft, furtive movements, the way they gathered themselves, and isolated themselves at the same time.

"The Throne seeks the Triangle. It is the way the world should be," Kerde said.

Gift was frowning. He had not learned that. "If that's the way the world should be," he said, "then why haven't the people near the other Places of Power tried? No one tried on Blue Isle, and there have to be people near the third Place of Power. Only the Fey use the Triangle as justification for their conquest."

"Blue Isle is full of Deniers," Kerde said.

"The Triangle will change the world. It may bring horrible magic on us."

"That's not what we have learned. It will *re-form* the world," Kerde said.

"And what does that mean? Your Place of Power re-formed the Fey into the magical creatures they are now. Did that make us better? Or simply more powerful?"

"The Triangle," Kerde said softly, "could make us gods."

"Or it could make us destroy the world we know." Gift looked at the others. They were watching silently. He wished someone else would speak up.

"We conquer," Kerde said. "We move toward the next place. The Triangle is within our grasp. We should take it."

He hated hearing Shaman argue for war. "The Shaman—" he said, and then cursed silently. He had never learned the name of the woman who had been his Shaman for the first eighteen years of his life— "The Shaman Rugad sent with Rugar, the Shaman who became my father's Shaman, she said the world needed peace, and the Fey needed to stop fighting."

"She was young," Kerde said.

Gift had never thought of her as young. "She died for that belief."

"And in so dying, saved a life who then helped your father defeat Rugad. If she had not done so, the Fey would be going to Leut now. We would know where the last Place of Power is, instead of being blocked."

"I agreed with my sister on that decision," Gift said.

He was shaking. Kerde hadn't moved. She still stood before him, slightly ahead of Madot. "I would have done the same. The Fey Empire is big enough. We do not need to expand."

"You learned that from your Shaman. She was wrong," Kerde said.

"She said you guarded the Place of Power, and prevented the Black Family from using it." Gift took a step forward. Some of the Shaman moved their hands to their knees and clenched their fists. The movement was uniform, as if it were planned, as if he were threatening them in some way. "Is that why you oppose me and my desire to be a Shaman? Because I am a member of the Black Family? Well, I have renounced the Throne. I am not going to search for the third Place of Power, and I believe the Fey have no business gaining control of the world. Why doesn't this reassure you?"

"Because it denies Fey magic," Madot said.

Gift turned to her. Her eyes were soft and were looking at him with warmth. He had not imagined it then, the affection she had felt for him. But he had expected too much from it. He had expected her to support him in all he did, as mentors should do with their apprentices.

"Fey magic," she said, taking his silence as a lack of understanding, "revives and transforms when mixed with new blood. Your family—your sister and you—have proven this beyond our greatest expectations. On your Isle, the magic is growing stronger, better. We have more Enchanters than we have ever had. Young Visionaries who might become some of the great leaders among the countries. New magics that we don't even have names for yet."

"And that's enough," Gift said.

She shook her head. "Someday, the fire between our lines will cool. The magics will dwindle or die. Magic was tame in your Isle before the Fey."

"No," Gift said. "We had two Enchanters."

"Two. And there are eight now, if we count the young children. The magic had dwindled. Most of your people had none, or had magic so small they did not notice it. Most of our people have some, and it has been that way as long as we have conquered other countries."

"You don't have to conquer people to form alliances with them."

"Were your people willing to ally with the Fey?" Madot asked.

His people. How strange this was. On the Isle, pure Islanders who talked to him of his people meant the Fey. Among the Fey, anyone who used the term "his people" meant the Islanders. "Obviously," he said, knowing this was not the answer she wanted, knowing that what he said was not entirely true, "if they didn't, Ari and I wouldn't have been born."

"Your father was always a special case."

"My father was never given the chance to ally with the Fey the way he wanted because you people were bent on conquest. It was the Fey who interfered with the alliance, the Fey who refused to live up to their promises."

"And so we always have," Kerde said, "because peace is not in our nature." She waved an arm around her. "Madot is right. Peace is contrary to Fey magic. Most of our magical abilities enable us to make war."

"Not the Domestics," Gift said. He heard a desperation in his own voice. Something he had believed since he was a boy was being challenged. "Not the Shaman. You can't kill. If you kill, you lose your powers."

"Think of how war is made, child," Kerde said. "It is all fighting and moving forward. There are defenses to be maintained, land to farm, people to heal. Our magics split, over the centuries, so that those who killed were not those who healed. It is efficient. And it is the way of things."

"The way of things can change," Gift said.

"Some things, perhaps," Kerde said. "But not all things."

He swallowed. No one else in the room spoke. It was almost as if no one else dared to breathe. Madot was watching him, some kind of plea in her eyes. The incense was flowing thicker now, making a gray smoke that swirled around the ceiling. He resisted the urge to sneeze.

"What do you want me to do?" he asked finally. "Accept the Throne and overturn my sister?"

"It would be best," Kerde said.

"What of Blood against Blood?"

"Your sister would defer to you."

They didn't know Arianna. She didn't defer to anyone. But she probably would give in to him, if she felt the choice were to let him have the Throne or create the chaos from the Blood against Blood.

"I cannot be a warrior leader," Gift said softly. "I cannot, and I will not. My sister is doing what I would do. I said that to Madot, and now I say it to you."

Kerde crossed her arms. "You don't know what you do."

"Do you?" he asked. "I asked a Madot a week ago if we could have a meeting, all of us, to discuss Visions, prophecies, and legends about the Black Throne. I come here, and you act as if I've done something wrong in acting my conscience. You act as if you know what is best for the Fey, for the Empire."

"We are the keepers of history. You should listen to us."

Gift crossed the room and pinched out the incense. Then he walked back to the door and opened it, letting the air move. "I asked to come here in good faith, as an apprentice, to train to be a Shaman. I have the right tools, and I have the best skills in generations. You took me, but you never planned to let me become a Shaman, did you?"

"Madot has told you her Vision," Kerde said.

"Is that a yes?" he asked.

Kerde inclined her head forward, like a queen granting a reluctant wish.

Gift clenched his hands so hard his knuckles hurt. "You cannot force me to lead."

"Shaman are leaders."

"You cannot force me," he said slowly, "to sit on the Black Throne."

"The Black Family cannot have access to the Place of Power. It is decreed," Kerde said.

Gift took a step forward. "Then why," he asked, "is the Black Throne here? That was clearly a palace that Madot took me into. The Black Family was here once. Madot said my great-grandfather visited here."

"And your grandfather," Kerde said. "The Throne rejected him."

She was changing the subject. "You haven't answered my question," he said.

"It was not your family's palace," she said. "It belonged to a Black line now gone."

"The Black King who went Blind?" he asked.

"You've heard of him?"

Gift made himself take a calming breath. "I was raised Fey."

All Fey Visionaries knew the story. It was a cautionary tale in some ways, a warning in others. After the Fey started spreading away from the Eccrasian Mountains, the Black King lost his Vision. He was a young man and had not yet fathered any children. He had false Visions, and led the Fey in circles. The Shaman tried to depose him, but there was no procedure for that. The Warders refused to develop new spells, and the Fey refused to follow him. They camped at the base of the mountains for almost a generation while he followed his false Vision, then went Blind. With his Blindness came a deep despair, and gradually he lost his mind, memory by memory until he was little more than a child.

"After him," said Kerde, "the Shaman and Warders tested the Visionaries—"

"I know," Gift said. "They tested the Visionaries until they found one who could see beyond the next battle. She became the first Black Queen, the one whose family was slaughtered a hundred years later and introduced us all to the power of Blood against Blood."

"After that," Kerde said, "the remaining Shaman and Warders, the survivors, again tested the Visionaries, and this time, they found your family. You are not of the direct line, Gift. You are from a branch of a branch of a branch."

"More than that," someone said in the back.

He waited. His throat was dry. It had to be the incense. He resisted the urge to lick his lips.

"The Shaman and the Warders tested, Gift. In us lies the power of the future," Kerde said.

"I see no Spell Warders here." Gift knew that the Spell Warders were not welcome in Protectors Village. The Warders were the only Fey, besides Enchanters, who had the power to do all Fey magics. Only with Warders, the power was very limited. It allowed them to test and develop new spells, but that was all. The nearest enclave of Warders was in Ghitlus, several days from the village.

"You did not ask how we tested the Visionaries," Kerde said as if he were a student in a private lecture.

"It was never part of the story."

"The parts left out are often the ones most important," she said. She tilted her head slightly. "Warders used to live in the village."

"I thought they weren't allowed here."

"They aren't, not any longer. They attempted to expand their own powers. They tried to make the Place of Power their own."

He narrowed his eyes. He hadn't heard that. "They failed."

"The Mysteries caused them to fail. It is a story that we do not tell unless you have become a Shaman." She ran a hand through her thin hair. "There are many such stories."

"And how you test Visionaries is one of those stories?"

"You had a Vision when you touched the Throne, did you not?" she asked.

He was beginning to understand her answer to the question she wanted him to ask, the question about testing. "Several. You know that. I wanted to compare."

"And so you shall, in a moment." She glanced at the others. Perdom, the main historian, stood.

He was thinner than most, and almost as old as Kerde.

He rarely spoke, but he listened often. The newest apprentices were assigned to him when they arrived in the village, and he made them spend their time talking about the history of their land, their people, their family. Gift spent an unusual amount of time with Perdom because he was the first from Blue Isle to come to the Eccrasian Mountains. Everything Gift knew about Blue Isle's history—which wasn't nearly as much as his sister knew—he told to Perdom.

"How many Visions?" Perdom's voice was as thin as he was. It sounded like a voice that was rarely used. But Gift knew that sound was deceptive. When he wanted to, Perdom could make his voice reverberate around the village, and fill it with the stories of old.

Gift shrugged. "I don't know."

"I don't ask idly, boy."

Gift swallowed, concentrated. "Seven," he said at last. "But I've had more Visions than that at one time. And some of these were things I've Seen before, things that are not possible."

"You do not know what is possible."

"They involve the dead," Gift said.

There was a momentary silence, then Perdom said, "Your mother is dead, is she not?"

"Yes," Gift said.

"Yet you have seen her, and spoken to her."

"Yes."

"And we know that the Mysteries are people who were murdered, as your mother was."

"Yes." Gift shifted slightly. Perdom had done this to him when he had first arrived, whenever Gift had made an assumption in the telling of the history of Blue Isle. Gift always felt dumb after these sessions as if he hadn't understood his own life, his own history, his own feelings.

"So you do not know if the dead you Saw—"

"I did not See him in a Place of Power," Gift said.

"Him?" Kerde asked.

But Perdom remained focused. "How do you know?"

"Water," Gift said. "I knew I had fallen into the sea between Blue Isle and Leut."

"And you Saw the dead there?" Perdom asked, his questioning now derailed.

"Yes," Gift said.

Perdom and Kerde exchanged glances. Then Kerde said, "It does not matter. What matters is that you had seven Visions—"

"I've had more," Gift said. "When my father attacked the Black King's forces outside of the palace in Jahn—"

"Those were Visions given to you at a shift in possible futures," Kerde said. "We are talking about Visions you received when you touched the Black Throne."

"You had seven," Perdom said.

"Yes," Gift said. "What is this all about?"

"Your great-grandfather had five. At that moment in our history, he had the most Visions while touching the Black Throne."

Gift swallowed. He had started to shake, and he wasn't sure why. "I wasn't touching the Throne any longer when the Visions came. I had them after I pulled away from the Throne."

"Seven," Perdom said as if he hadn't heard.

"After," Gift said.

"The light touched him," Madot said, "and passed me. It went nowhere near me. And as he fell, I saw his eyes change, roll back into Vision. He is telling the truth."

"Your sister," Kerde said as if Madot hadn't spoken. "Her Vision is not as great as yours."

"It came later," Gift said. "I had mine from childhood. She could Shift from childhood. Her Vision came when she was a teenager, like most Fey's."

"Yours is stronger."

"We don't know that."

Perdom nodded. "We know. The gift that comes in childhood is always stronger."

"Perhaps among your people," Gift said, putting a

sarcastic twist on the phrase they had been using against him. "But we don't know what's normal for Islanders. From what we can tell, Islander children get their powers in childhood. My friend Coulter had his when he was just a baby."

There was a pause. Then Kerde said to Perdom: "He has a point."

"I Saw my sister at the Black Throne," Gift said. "It was one of my Visions."

"But she would have no need if you took the Throne."

Gift nodded. "I know. But I will not take the Throne."

Perdom turned away from Gift and put his hands on Kerde's shoulders. The movement made the two of them a unit, as if they were the only two in the room. Everyone else watched them.

"This is not as simple as it seems," Perdom said to her. "The boy is right. We need to accept him as equal and tell him the things he wishes to know."

"He cannot be a Shaman," Kerde said. "He has blood on his hands."

"I do not!" Gift said. This he had made certain of. He came forward, was about to touch Perdom's arm, when Madot pulled him away. "I do not have blood on my hands. I saved lives. All my life, I have saved lives."

Kerde slipped out of Perdom's hold and took Gift's hands. They glowed, and as they did, blood dripped off them. Tears formed in Gift's eyes. "I haven't taken a life," he said. "I made certain—"

"On a hot afternoon fifteen years ago," Kerde said, "you hid in a hay bale with a Fey who had not come into her magic—"

"Leen," Gift said, not sure he wanted to remember that afternoon.

"—a Red Cap—"

"Scavenger." He felt the blood flow out of him, dripping into a large puddle on the floor. He wanted to make it stop, but couldn't.

"—an Enchanter—"

"Coulter."

"And a man with no power at all."

"Adrian." Gift swallowed. Adrian had had power. He had had warmth and love and affection. And courage. He had died protecting Gift and his family not long after.

"Your Enchanter started a fire in the bales after a Wisp found you. The Wisp grabbed you and you shoved it backward—"

"Breaking its bones, I know," Gift said. He could still hear the crunch of the fragile wings. Wisps had hollow bones, which was why they could fly. His adopted parents had been Wisps.

"And he could not fly. He could not rise. When the fire got too close, he could not escape it."

Gift's mouth dropped open. "No."

"On that same afternoon, your Golem took Bird Riders that had attacked your family, injured Bird Riders, and dropped them from a tower in the Jahn palace. The Golem shares your nature."

"Sebastian would never kill anything."

"If it threatened him or his loved ones, he would. As you would. You are right; you are willing to make the supreme sacrifice. You will give your life for the things you believe. But you will also defend that life if you must. You showed that years ago, and the blood still drips from your hands." She let his hands go. The dripping stopped.

There was no blood on the floor. There was nothing, except the feel, once again, of magic recently used. Had he been new to the village, he would have thought this a simple trick, but he knew it was not. He had seen potential apprentices subjected to the same thing if their desire to become a Shaman was in doubt. Sometimes the blood did not drip. It flowed.

"If you knew this," he said, "why did you let me live here for five years? Why did you give me hope that I could be a Shaman?"

"It took us a long time to find the source of your

stain," Perdom said. "We thought, perhaps, it was hereditary. Perhaps the Black Blood had so tainted you that its
violence dripped out of you anyway, even though you
had not killed."

"Then we found it," Kerde said. "Or Madot found it,
one afternoon as she worked with you."

"She felt the brush of pain, the remembered pain, and
found the taint. It is yours, Gift. It is buried deep within
you, but it is yours."

He looked at his hands. They were dry now, as if
nothing had happened. He hadn't remembered that. He
had put it all out of his mind. It had happened so quickly.
He and Coulter, Scavenger, Leen, and Adrian had been
running for their lives. They had left that farm and Coulter had had to use his powers to slaughter an entire army
of Fey. It had nearly destroyed him. In the trauma of that,
Gift had forgotten the swift push, the sound of breaking
bones, the knowledge that he had harmed that Wisp. He
remembered the fire, the smoke, the screams—

He closed his eyes and sank to the floor. "Now what
becomes of me?" he asked, more to himself than to them.

"The Black Throne—" Madot started.

"I do not want the Black Throne."

"What you want and what you must do are different
things," Kerde said. "In the beginning, no one wants the
Black Throne."

Gift shook his head. "I will not take it from my sister,
no matter what you do to me. Even if you leave me with
no choices, as you have done now."

"Then you will be a Leader with no followers, a threat
to your sister's Throne."

"Or a supporter of it." He rose slowly, and dusted
himself off. His heart ached. He wanted to be part of this
place, to practice, as the Shaman did, the art of peace.

Or so he had thought. But apparently he had been
wrong. He hadn't known all the stories.

He hadn't realized that in guarding the first Place of
Power, they also guarded the Black Throne. He hadn't

really understood that they had chosen two Black Families based on the power of their Vision and their need for conquest.

A need the Shaman said he had. A need he was denying.

They were watching him. All eyes, brown and intense, were staring at him with slightly veiled antipathy. He had not done as they wished. All along, he hadn't been what they wanted. And because of it, they wouldn't do what he wanted.

But he knew that wasn't entirely true. They wouldn't do what he wanted because they couldn't. Not under Fey magic. His hands were stained with blood.

He shuddered, once, and then squared his shoulders. "I want to compare Visions. I want to learn the legacy of the Throne. I want you to tell me the prophecies as you know them, and I want to know the history of the Throne itself."

"Some of this is not for the Black Family," Kerde said.

He no longer had anything to lose. He took a step toward her, then another, using his body to intimidate as he had once watched his grandfather do.

She backed away.

"You will tell me," he said. "You will tell me all. Or I will see to it that you are forced to leave this place."

"You cannot do that."

"No," he said. "But my sister can."

Kerde's eyes narrowed. She suddenly held her ground. "We will not go."

"You will fight the Black Family against all strictures?"

"It's been done before."

"It is the beginning of the chaos," Perdom said, taking Kerde's arm. "You cannot. It will not hurt to tell him."

"We have not told in the past."

"This is not the past. The light—"

She turned. The look she gave him was an order even Gift understood. It was an order to be silent.

"The light?" Gift asked.

"You have no right to know these things," Kerde said.

"And you have no reason to hide them." Gift hadn't

moved from his position. "Things are different now. You said so yourself."

Kerde bowed her head. Perdom put a hand on her shoulder. "The Throne already knows it's been rejected," he said. "The light seeks another. We are in a new place with new rules. The boy is right."

"And so ends a thousand years of orderly Fey rule," Kerde murmured.

"We do not know that," Madot said.

"We know," Kerde said. "The stories have always said the magic would seek its own."

"What does that mean?" Gift asked.

"It means that before we controlled the magic." Kerde leaned against Perdom as if she needed his support. "From now on, it will control us."

CHAPTER EIGHT

RIANNA CAME TO herself in the North Tower. She was standing before the windows facing north, looking over the rebuilt city of Jahn toward the mountains named the Eyes of the Roca. She had hidden in those mountains once, when the Black King controlled this palace. They were tall, taller than the mountains that ringed the rest of the Isle, and they had a power to them that still unnerved her.

She had no idea what she was doing here, what she was looking for, or why she was thinking of her past.

Her hands were clasped behind her back, her feet shoulder-width apart, her chin up, as if she were pausing in the middle of a discussion with her generals.

Her generals? She frowned. She had generals, but she had no need of discussions with them. She hadn't for years.

A shiver ran down her spine. Slowly she turned. The long gown she wore felt unfamiliar. Where were her pants? Her jerkin?

She shook the thought away. She hadn't worn pants

during her official duties in a long, long time. The Islanders preferred traditional clothes, and the Fey didn't care what she wore. She took a deep breath, making herself pause.

The room had been restored over the past decade: the broken windows repaired; the chairs pushed against the wall once more; the shattered furniture gone. The tower was as it had been, but she never came here. There were too many bad memories, too many fears, hidden in this room.

When she needed a tower to overlook her Isle, she went to one of the other two, and used the windows there.

This room had a slightly musty smell. It wasn't dirty— no place in the palace was—yet it had the feeling of neglect. Sunlight shone in the floor-to-ceiling windows that made it feel as if she were standing outside, and from here, she could see for miles.

Arianna put a hand to her head. What was happening to her?

She turned slightly, and saw Luke, the captain of her guards. He stood with his back against the door, as if he didn't want to be here, but had to be. He had been at her side, by Seger's orders, since that awful headache the week before, and Arianna had felt comforted by his presence.

But she had forgotten him too, until now.

He was watching her, his face impassive. Luke's face was rarely this guarded. He had round, open features of Islanders from the center of the country, and even though he was short, he was broad and muscular. He wore the light browns she had ordered for her Islander guards, a color that did not set off their fair skin and hair, and enabled them to have camouflage if they needed it, both within the city and without.

She had made that order fifteen years ago, and had almost forgotten the reason for it. There had been no war here, no battles, in all that time.

She was proud of that.

Wasn't she?

She felt something in her head. It wasn't quite a pain. It was more like a movement, as if something had slid from one part to the other. If she tried, she could hear rustling.

That shiver ran through her again. Luke was staring at her, blue eyes sharp.

She let her hand fall from her head, but her fingers clenched. There was a tension in her that she wasn't ready to acknowledge. She didn't even know where it came from.

Luke seemed tense as well. Obviously she wasn't behaving according to his expectations either.

But Seger had asked her to keep him at her side, and she knew she could trust Luke. He had been the most able assistant she had had among the Islanders. He had no religious prejudice that made him hate Fey, no desire to harm her because of her mixed heritage. Only a relief that she had taken the Throne and her relatives in the Empire had not. He had been happy to get work at the palace since Luke's farm had burned during the war.

"How long have I been here?" she asked.

He didn't seem surprised by the question. "Most of the day."

The shiver again. She clenched her other fist. "Doing what?"

"Staring out the windows."

"Did I say anything?"

His smile was small. It made the lines on his face deeper. "You mean after ordering me to get out?"

He seemed angry. She didn't remember any of this. "I guess."

"No."

She nodded. She glanced at the windows, wondering what she had been looking at. "Was I—rude?"

"Forceful," he said.

"Why did you stay then?"

"You told me to."

"Today?"

He shook his head. "When you and Seger discussed the headaches."

She remembered that. The conversation had been as open a conversation as she could have with anyone. He was never to leave her side, except at night, and even then they had brought a cot into the dressing area of her suite so that he could be there if she needed someone. He had sworn to protect her, and not to talk of this to anyone. He had vowed on his life to remain at her side.

"I ordered you to leave, and you did not," she said again.

He nodded.

"Then what did I do?"

"You grabbed me." His voice was calm, but his eyes were not. They had a smoldering anger in them. "And you threw me against the door and told me that I had to leave or you would make sure that I did."

"And then?"

"I reminded you of Seger's orders."

"Using her name?"

"Yes."

"And?"

"You grunted and turned away as if I hadn't said anything. I've been standing here ever since."

She beckoned him to come forward. He did, warily. "I'm sorry," she said softly.

He nodded, once, as if the apology meant nothing to him, but was something he had to acknowledge. "I have to tell Seger."

The rustling again. The near headache. Her lips were already forming the word "no" when she said, "Of course. We need to see what this is."

He didn't move. He continued to watch her as if he expected her to grab him at any moment.

"But you will not tell anyone else of this," she said. "That's an order."

"Permission to speak freely, Highness," he said.

She didn't want him to. He had been observing her all

week. She wasn't sure she wanted to hear what he had to say. But what she wanted wasn't as important as what she needed to know.

"All right," she said.

He swallowed. "This is not the first time you have treated me poorly during the week. Not," he said quickly, "that I expect you to treat me well. But you always have. This week, though, you have shown quick temper. You used words and phrases I've never heard from you before. You demanded things you have not ever mentioned."

Her eyes narrowed. She didn't remember demanding anything. "Such as?"

"Troop reports. You wanted to know where all the Infantry units were on Blue Isle. When I told you that I wasn't in charge of that, you smiled and said, 'Of course not. But you can get the information, can't you?' It wasn't so much what you said as how you said it. There was a sarcasm that you don't normally use."

She didn't remember the request. "What else?"

"You told Jair that there were too many Islanders in the palace. That it was a security risk. You told him you wanted more Fey Domestics and fewer Islanders working the kitchens. Then you stopped, and continued the discussion you'd been having before as if nothing had happened."

Her heart was pounding, hard. Of all the Fey to say that to, Jair was the worst. He headed the Infantry on Blue Isle and did tremendous work with it, but he also had spoken to her countless times about the Islander/Fey relationship. He believed that the Islanders had lost, even though they had killed the Black King. He believed as long as the Black Family was in power, then the Fey had won the battles they had been in. He saw the Islanders as a conquered people and hated that she treated them as equals.

But she kept Jair in his position as Infantry leader because he did not have to work with Islanders. She even kept him separate, most of the time, from Luke. Luke had only been present at that meeting because he had been shadowing her.

"What was Jair's response?" she asked.

"He smiled and said he would see what he could do. But since you hadn't given the order to anyone else, he couldn't do much. He has no control over who has access to the palace."

She got the feeling that Luke had warned her assistants about the order, and that they had prevented any action on Jair's part.

"Where's Seger now?" Arianna asked.

"Seeing to Sebastian," he said. "She thinks she might have found a way to loosen the voice."

Arianna got a feeling that Seger had told her that, but that she didn't remember it. "All right," Arianna said. She went back to the window, staring at the city below. It was a new city now. The Fey had burned it years ago, and the buildings that stood before her were mostly made of wood and river rocks. They had been rebuilt in the old Islander style: square, mostly, with windows and doors in the front and boxy rooms in the back, if they were houses; businesses had display windows up front, porches that provided good entry, and signs across the top.

But even though they had the Islander style, they did not have the Islander look. They were too new, and many were painted colors that the Fey had shown the Islanders—reds, blues, browns. Before, everything had been coated with white if it had been painted at all.

Beyond the city was the countryside and in the distance the bluish lines of the mountains. She put a hand on the wavy glass. She was giving orders that she didn't remember, losing track of time, doing things that she would never ever do. Perhaps she was losing her mind. But she had never Seen anything like that, hadn't known how to prepare for it.

The last time a Black King had lost his mind, the Fey were a tiny group. The Islanders never had a crazy leader. She rested her head against the window. The glass was cool and smooth. She knew the provisions, though. The best thing to do was to abdicate. But to whom? To Gift? He wasn't even here, and she wasn't sure he would take the Throne if she offered it to him. She had no children, and neither did he.

To her uncle, then? A man she had never met? Or to someone else?

And what of the things that Seger had said? It wasn't a coincidence that this was happening to Arianna at the same time that Rugad's voice had reappeared. Seger thought this all might be a magical attack, and who was Arianna to argue with her? It could very well be.

But it was working, that was the problem. And that threatened them all.

She had no one to confide in. Her father was long gone. Her mother's ghost had never appeared to her as it had to Gift. And Gift was in Vion, near the Eccrasian Mountains, as far from here as he could get.

"Send Seger to me," Arianna said, her breath making a small fog on the glass.

"She said I wasn't to leave you."

Arianna suppressed a curse. He was right. He hadn't left during her tantrum; he wouldn't leave now.

"All right," she said, and straightened. She took her hands away from the window. They left small palm-sized prints on the glass. Someone would have to clean that. Someone always cleaned up after her.

But no one would this time.

She felt a slight flutter in her stomach, and felt that faint rustling in her mind. *Who's there?* she thought. Something pushed against her skull from the inside. Pain, sharp and sudden, like fingernails digging into soft skin.

A tear formed in her left eye, and then fell, landing on her high cheekbone and rolling down her face. She must have taken a deep breath, because Luke had turned to her. The anger was gone from his eyes, replaced by worry.

She put the heel of her hand against her forehead, pushing against the pain. It was growing so bad that she was getting nauseous. She closed her eyes, and another tear fell down her cheek.

Who's there? she thought again, and this time, she heard a laugh. A familiar laugh, deep and warm and so pleased with itself.

She shivered, and fell to her knees. The pain had spread in a band around her skull. She bent over, clutching her head. *Stop this.*

She heard the laughter again, and with it came a deep, urgent need to Shift to a new form. *No*—she thought, but felt it happening anyway, her body changed, compacted, until it became a robin. She fluttered her wings, opened her beak as the dress she had worn fell on her head.

The pain was gone, though, and so was that feeling of being manipulated.

She didn't want to be a bird. She had had no thought of it until the Shift. She Shifted again, returning to her own form, feeling her legs grow, her wings turn into arms, her beak recede. Then she found herself on her hands and knees, wearing her dress like a tent.

"Sorry." Her voice sounded muffled inside the dress. She wondered what Luke was thinking, what he would say to Seger when he got the chance.

Adrianna flailed about for a moment, then found the sleeves and put her arms in them. After a bit more flailing, she found the neck, and slipped her head through it. She had to look a mess.

But the headache was gone.

In its place, a feeling of triumph that had nothing to do with rearranging her dress. She almost felt separate from the triumph, as if it were someone else's emotion, someone else's joy.

Luke was hunched beside her, his elbows resting on his knees. He looked concerned, almost frightened.

"Are you all right?" he asked.

She could have given him a thousand answers, none of them correct. Instead, she said, "The headache's gone." That was as much truth as she was willing to give him. If she said much more, she might reveal how scared she was.

Even when Rugad had invaded her mind years ago, he had not been able to force her to Shift. He had invaded her Link with Sebastian against Sebastian's will. Then Rugad had put his consciousness inside her brain, and held her prisoner in her own mind. But he had not been able to control her Shifting. She had Shifted to keep him off-balance, until she had, with Sebastian's help, shoved Rugad's consciousness out.

She had shut the doors to her Links years ago, blocking the connections with other people at the very source. She had done it voluntarily, so no one could cross into her brain from somewhere else. If she had been so attacked, she would have known. The feeling was familiar, and horrible, and this wasn't quite it.

Besides, an invader couldn't make her Shift if she didn't want to.

But something had.

Maybe she was losing her mind.

She stood, smoothed her skirt, and then smoothed her hair. Her hands were shaking, and there was an empty ache where the pain had been.

Luke rose with her. "What do you want to do now?"

"Find Seger," Arianna said as calmly as she could.

He took her arm as if she were an old woman. He had never done that before. She leaned on him. She felt weaker than she had ever been. And frightened. And uncertain what to do.

How had she gotten to this place, where she had no one to rely on, no one to help her? She had been a fool. In isolating herself, she was threatening her beloved Isle— and the Fey Empire. And if she wasn't careful, she might make a mistake that could injure them all.

CHAPTER NINE

NYEIAN SAILORS WROTE beautiful poems about
the sea. Lyndred could finally understand why. She had
never been at sea before—small sailing boats with friends
did not count—and she had never been on a ship like
this. This ship, *The Elizabeth*, had been built in Nye to
transport both people and cargo. It was not a warship as
most Fey ships were, and aside from the basic sailing spells
done to protect her family, it did not have any special
provisions for Fey. This ship was large, but elegant, as so
much of Nyeian work was. It was also comfortable—its
quarters twice the size of those on Fey ships.

Her father chose *The Elizabeth* not for comfort, but
to reassure the Black Queen that he was coming in peace.
His entourage included two more Nyeian vessels, one cargo
ship, and one Fey warship simply because he couldn't
stomach traveling without one. The ships sailed together,
the warship out front, the cargo ship bringing up the
rear, and the Nyeian vessels fanned out in the middle.

Gull Riders flew above, searching out troubles in the
waters ahead, and reporting back every few instances.

Weather Sprites sailed on this vessel to protect the Black Family from the fierce storms that sometimes hit the Infrin Sea, and two Navigators were aboard to talk with the underwater creatures and find out about treacheries within the water.

She didn't understand all the fine points. She only knew that no Fey fleet had ever run into trouble in the sea because of precautions like these. She listened as her father explained what he was doing, and she watched, knowing someday she might be responsible for a fleet of her own.

The idea made her stomach flutter. She was standing on the deck, her hands on the wooden railing. The wind was strong, filling the sails above her and blowing spray into her face. The spray felt like a light mist, cool and invigorating. The air here was the freshest she had ever smelled. It made Nye seem like a cesspool, filled with wretched odors. Sometimes, the ocean had a briny scent, but even that was better than the smells she had encountered on Nye.

They had been at sea for four days. Her father said the trip to Blue Isle would last a month or more, depending upon the weather. At first, she had been frightened by the time she would be trapped on this vessel. She had walked the ship with him before *The Elizabeth* sailed. The deck seemed small then, and her cabin, with its narrow built-in bed and single portal, claustrophobic. She wasn't sure how she would last a day on the vessel, let alone a month or two, all on the choppy water.

But she hadn't accounted for the fresh air, the wide and beautiful sea, and the clear sky. Sunlight seemed brighter here as it bounced off the white tops of the waves. Anytime she felt tired, she could stand at the railing and feel the spray against her face, invigorating her. And if she wanted work, there was plenty. The Nyeian sailors had been teaching her about knots, and she was hoping to learn how to make braided nets before the day was out.

Her father, of course, disapproved of this. He thought it beneath her. But she never saw learning as beneath her. It was something that improved her life, made her better at what she did, made her understand others. He worried that she spent too much time with Nyeians, thinking, she supposed, that she was more comfortable with them. He worried that she would engage herself to another like Rupert. What he didn't realize was that the sailors were completely different men from Rupert. Their hands had calluses, and their language could be coarse. They probably wrote the proper poetry for their potential mates, but the language wouldn't be as flowery as Rupert's had been.

Rupert had been a good man, and she could have been content with him for the rest of her life. But she hadn't been trying to marry him so that she could be content.

She had been trying to prevent this trip.

Her hands tightened on the railing. The wooden deck was slick beneath her feet. Her father hated to see her standing here. If he had his way, she would spend the entire trip in her cabin belowdecks, watching the sea go by through the porthole. Since he insisted that she come, though, she was going to see everything, be as much a part of everything as she could.

Live, as well as possible, because she had a hunch there was nothing but heartbreak awaiting her on Blue Isle.

No matter how tough her father sounded, no matter how much he claimed it to be the natural order of things, she did not want to lose him. He was still a young man in Fey terms, with half of his life ahead of him. The death she had Seen in her Vision, his death, had been a senseless one, a drowning. He had not even died in battle.

She shuddered. She hadn't Seen her death. The Shaman had asked her if she had. She had wondered how she would know. Most Fey Visionaries Foresaw their deaths, but they didn't understand the Vision. They Saw it up to the moment, and then believed that someone would rescue them, things would change. Or so she understood.

She hadn't Seen anything that would even come close. She had only Seen things that would harm her emotionally: the death of her father; the birth of a child that somehow broke her heart. A future that seemed bleak and cold and terrifying.

Her water repellent cloak was beaded. Her hair was wet, water dripping off her cheeks. Her special Domestic-spelled boots gripped the wet deck so that as the ship rose and fell with the waves, she didn't have to worry about losing her balance. She only held the railing because her father had insisted, and she didn't want to have him see her disobeying him.

A Gull Rider landed on the deck before her. It was in its Gull form: a full-sized white bird with what appeared to be a Fey riding its back. But when examined closely, it became clear that the Fey on the bird's back had no legs. The Fey's torso was attached to the bird itself.

This Gull Rider was male, his naked chest dark against his white bird plumage, his hair long, black, and falling free. He gripped his bird's neck with his strong hands, and both of his heads—bird and Fey—looked up as if he were surprised to see her.

"Off duty?" she asked, knowing he would have to either fly up to her ear level so that she could hear him, or that he would have to shout in order to respond.

He nodded.

She smiled, and took off her cloak, shaking the droplets off of it. Beneath it, she wore a Nyeian blouse that tied to her wrists and was open at the neck. Its thin material got soaked in the spray. She didn't care.

"Here," she said, putting the cloak on the deck. "I won't watch."

She put her hands over her eyes, but she kept her fingers slightly apart. She wanted to watch him change to his Fey form. She envied his kind of magic, the kind that had tangible results, the kind that could be controlled. Sometimes it felt as if hers controlled her—her Visions always struck unpredictably. Even if she tried to change them, she would never know if she was successful. Sometimes Visions that seemed to refer to an early part of a life really referred to a middle or later period. And sometimes trying to avert one Vision made another come true.

The Gull Rider stretched his arms and slowly grew. As he reached his full height, his stomach absorbed the bird's body. In full Fey form, he was as tall as Lyndred, trim and muscular. He looked as if he could fly on his own, without his gull wings. His black hair looked like feathers—even the hair on his chest that worked its way down his stomach. His nose was hooked, like a beak, and his eyes were darker than most, with that beady intensity so common to birds.

As soon as the transformation was complete, he took the cloak she had placed on the deck. "All right," he said. His voice was hoarse and full at the same time, with a lot of repressed power, like a caw.

She let her hands drop.

"Like what you saw?" he asked.

She felt a flush rise in her cheeks. She made herself shrug casually, as if nothing had happened.

He tied the cloak around him. Bird Riders—indeed, any kind of Beast Rider—weren't usually modest about their nakedness, but they had learned to treat the younger Fey, at least those who had been raised in Nye, differently from the rest. The basic Nyeian prudishness had found its way into Lyndred's generation—into Lyndred herself, if she was honest—and rather than fight it, the Fey simply looked on it as a quirk.

"You're Bridge's daughter," he said. He held out a hand in the Nyeian way. "I'm Graceful."

"Indeed," she said with a bit of a smile.

He smiled too, even though he had probably heard the joke a thousand times. "My friends call me Ace."

"Which is a much better name," she said, taking his hand. His skin was rougher than any she had ever felt, almost as if it were scaled, and his nails were sharp, like talons. "I'm Lyndred."

"The one who was going to marry the Nyeian poet." Ace hadn't let go of her hand.

"They're all poets," she said, keeping her voice light, wondering how he knew about her plans. "At least when they're in love."

"No," he said. "They all think they're poets, at least when they're in love."

She laughed. He had startled it out of her, catching her by surprise. She hadn't laughed that spontaneously since—when? And then her smile faded as she remembered. Since she got her Vision.

"Are you all right?" he asked.

"Yes," she said, reclaiming her hand. She ran it through her hair, noting that the strands were plastered against her head. "I must look a mess."

"Not really," he said, tucking a strand behind one of her ears.

She smiled. "You landed here to flirt with me?"

"I wish I could say yes." He turned his face toward the spray, closed his eyes, and tilted his head back. He was a magnificent man with a strong profile and an exotic face. The water beaded on it, accenting the planes and angles of his skull. She found that attractive somehow.

"But?" she asked.

"But I've been flying for the last day and a half," he said. "When I saw the ship, I simply came down. I need some rest."

"I thought you were only supposed to fly short distances."

He turned to her, opened those dark eyes. Water had gathered on his lashes, reflecting the sun like small diamonds. It made his eyes sparkle even though the twinkle came from without. "I thought I saw something."

"Did you?"

He nodded. "But it's something the Sprites can handle."

"A squall?"

"I think the storm is bigger than that."

"Then you need to report to them."

One of his eyebrows went up. "In your cloak?"

"I'm already soaked. Return it later."

He bowed to her in the Nyeian tradition; only his

dark eyes still meeting hers told her that he was mocking them both. She laughed again, and as he stood he gave her a grin that warmed her through. Then he walked away, her cloak flapping around him, looking somehow appropriate against his tall slender form.

She was glad he would bring it back to her. She was glad she would see him again. No one had made her laugh in a long time.

The water ran down her torso. Her pants were probably ruined. Her shirt needed to dry out, and probably needed the help of a Domestic to return the material to its normal wrinkle-free state. She waited until Ace had left the deck, and then she headed for her cabin.

The Nyeian sailors pretended not to see her, which told her that her clothes probably revealed more of her body than anyone except her personal maid had seen in a long time. She walked with her head up—she was Fey and not supposed to care about these things—even though her cheeks were flushed. She almost sprinted the last small distance toward the stairs. Grabbing the rope banister, she climbed down and walked through the narrow corridor to her cabin.

It had become a haven for her, even though she had hated it at first. Amazing how a short time at sea could change one's perspective. She had thought the room small on land. Here, it felt like a city, with its built-in wooden bed, the desk and chair both bolted to the floor, and the sea chest for her things.

She peeled off her wet clothes and tossed them on the wooden planking. Then she reached into the sea chest and removed a similar outfit—the soft blouse that tied at the wrists and the neck, black pants that gathered at the waist. Before she got dressed, she used a towel to dry her hair. Then she sat for a few moments on the edge of the bed, and wondered at the changes in herself.

She used to laugh like that. She used to value laughter above all else. But in the last two years, since the Visions arrived, she had become so serious. She would never have spent time with Rupert before that; he didn't know how to smile—and laughter would have been shocking to him. Nothing had value unless it was serious, and even then, its value was in its ability to wound, not its ability to please.

Maybe she wouldn't have been comfortable with him. But at least her father would have been safe.

She gathered her bare knees to her chest and hugged them, thinking of crawling under the blankets for warmth. Sooner or later, her father would come looking for her, and he would think her ill if he found her in bed at this time of day. There would be a meal soon in the mess, and maybe she would hear more about Ace's storm.

The storm didn't worry her overly much. It was the Weather Sprites' problem, just as he had said. They would either have to call up wind to keep the storm off their bow, or they would have to find spells to dissipate it. Maybe, if they had a target, they could send the storm elsewhere.

All of that would take a lot of casting, a lot of magic, but it was the main reason for Sprites on sea voyages. They kept the ships safe. If this were a war fleet, the Sprites would have other duties: they would create weather that attacked the enemy ships and even sank them. They would make optimal weather conditions for arriving at a destination in secret. Most of the Fey's seafaring war stories began with the Sprites creating rain or incredibly dark skies.

She had Seen nothing for this part of the voyage, and neither had the Shaman she consulted, nor did he know of any dire warnings about her family's journey to Blue Isle.

It was the Isle itself that scared her. Since she had spoken to her father, she had had two more Visions. In both of them, the Black Queen stared at her with empty eyes. A lisping male voice, breaking as if it could not finish a word without taking a breath, called weakly for help. And then her father, frowning as he looked at her, saying, *Perhaps I understand even less than I thought.*

She didn't know what any of this meant. She didn't know how the pieces went together and there was no one to tell her. Her father's Visions were weak—he always admitted that—and her uncles, whose Visions were not much stronger, hadn't come on this trip. The Infantry Leaders had a bit of Vision, a bit of insight, but not enough to consult them. And there were no Shaman here and none, so far as she knew, on Blue Isle.

The only other Visionaries with whom she could compare what she Saw were her cousins, Gift and Arianna. Lyndred shuddered. She couldn't imagine talking with the hard-eyed woman of her Vision or her brother who was said to be so like her as to be the male version of her.

Lyndred had to figure these Visions out on her own, and what she saw so far, she despised. Her father had told her to let them play out, but maybe, this afternoon, she had just been handed a different opportunity. Maybe, she had received a chance to stay away from the blond man who would, someday, father her child.

She put on the blouse and pants she had taken from her sea chest, then slipped on her boots. They were dry. She picked up her wet clothes. She would take them to the Domestics, and then she would find her father. She wouldn't discuss Visions or the future or anything so very obvious.

Instead, she would find out how he felt about a Gull Rider named Ace. This time, she would act with her father's approval. And this time, he wouldn't even know he was being manipulated.

CHAPTER TEN

GIFT STARED AT the Shaman. He felt even more distant from them than he had when he walked into this room. Most of them had not moved from their chairs. They sat with their fists clenched on their knees, and watched him. Only Perdom, Madot, and Kerde were standing beside him. The apprentices huddled in the back, clearly feeling out of their element.

The incense had cleared from the room, for which Gift was grateful. The door was open, and the light from the Fey lamps in the corridor seemed even stronger. The candles inside the room had burnt halfway down, their wax pooling in the base of their holders.

The Shaman had made it clear why he could not be part of their order. As angry as he was, as much as he wished they had told him sooner, he understood their reasons, and he was appalled he had not realized that he had killed someone, however inadvertently.

But things had changed—and more than in his status at Protectors Village. They had changed in the way the world felt around him, in what he understood about himself. He couldn't let his mixed and quite troubled emotions guided him. He had to take control of this meeting, and he had to do so with an authority he rarely used, an authority he had been denying since he had come here.

He had to do so as a member of the Black Family.

"The magic cannot control us if we understand it," he said, repeating and turning Kerde's words back to her. "That's the first rule any Fey child learns."

"Some magic is beyond us, and has always been," she said.

He turned and walked into the hall, half afraid they would close the door behind him. They did not, probably startled that he had treated their leader rudely. But he wasn't leaving.

He was right; the light from the Fey lamps had grown brighter. The souls trapped within had all moved within their little glass prison, crowding against the section closest to the meeting room. They were watching, trying to hear, and in so doing, shedding their light on the same area of floor.

He picked the nearest Fey lamp off its peg and brought it into the room. Kerde backed away from it. Perdom put his hands in front of himself as if to block the light. Madot shook her head, telling him without words that his action was incorrect.

"These souls," he said, "have given themselves over to another magic, one that we don't entirely understand. In here,"—and he waved his hand at the lamp—"are Shaman who believed their time was done, and in service to the rest of us, gave the last of their being to illuminate the world around us. You allow these lamps to burn for no reason at all, to light a corridor no one is using. You are wasting magic."

Kerde crossed her arms. "They cannot come in here while we meet."

"You have ceased meeting as Shaman to apprentice. You are now meeting with one of the heirs to the Black Throne." Gift made his voice sound powerful. He grabbed the lamp by its hook, and hung it on a peg. As he did so, he turned to the nearest Shaman. "Get the rest of the lamps. You," he said, pointing to another, "blow out the candles, and remove the incense holders."

They all looked at Kerde, as if waiting for her response. He didn't give her time to make one.

"You may stare at Kerde all you want," he said, "but the Fey follow simple rules. You are all subject to my family's authority. You heard Kerde. She believes I should be on the Black Throne. If that is the case, then you are not only disobeying the Black Heir, but the one who will, someday, take the Throne. Are you willing to risk that?"

It was a gamble. The argument was weak, especially given his denial earlier. But he was counting on the training, embedded early in all Fey, to do as the Black Family wanted and to avoid confrontation, since no one ever knew where such confrontation could lead.

Finally, the Shaman nearest him stood, and with a dip of her head as if she were trying to avoid Kerde's gaze, left the room. The other Shaman, the one Gift had told to put out the candles, rose as well, pinching the wicks with his wizened fingers. An apprentice in the back began to remove the incense holders. Another apprentice slipped to the front, and disappeared into the hallway, only to reappear with the first Fey lamps.

"Good," Gift said, in that new powerful voice. He stood as he had seen his Islander father stand, as his Fey grandfather used to stand, feet apart, arms at his side, braced, or so it felt, for anything that would come his way.

As more lamps came into the room, Gift could actually see faces, not as a uniform whole, but for who they were. He could put names on the Shaman before him, see how some of them had watched this entire proceeding with distaste and how others, mostly the older ones, had such impassive expressions on their faces that he knew they were hiding any emotion they felt.

They knew that the meeting was his now, that he had turned the tables on them in a way they didn't entirely understand, and that he would control what happened from now on. If they thought about it, they would realize that they had won. They had forever forbidden him from becoming a Shaman, and at this moment, his own future was, as Kerde said, in doubt.

But they would help him with that. He would not allow magic to control him or his family or the Empire that his sister ruled. He had felt like an apprentice going into that palace, and like a man controlled by magic when the blackness of the Throne swirled over his hand. But he would never forget the feeling of power he had at the moment in which he pulled away from the Throne.

The moment lasted long enough for him to note it, but barely longer than that, for he got slammed with the light and then the Visions, and lost that feeling of control, of victory that he had. But the moment had been enough.

He had learned from his father that nothing was impossible. No matter what Kerde said, no matter what the Shaman said, Gift knew that magic could be controlled. *All* magic. They just had to figure out how.

When the last of the Fey lamps had been brought into the room, it was as light as day. All of the tiny beings inside the lamps pressed against the glass, watching the proceedings. He pointed to another Shaman, a man who had never spoken to him, indeed had gone through the last five years with his face averted every time he crossed Gift's path.

Gift purposely did not use his name. "Tap the lamps. Warn them that they'll all burn out prematurely if they don't take turns resting."

The Shaman glared at him and for a moment Gift thought he would not do as Gift asked. Then he stood, so slowly that Gift thought he could hear the man's bones creak, and tapped on the lamp nearest him. Inside the lamp, half the beings sat down, their lights growing dim.

"All right," Gift said. "Now, we will do as I asked before. We will discuss *all* Visions that pertain to the Black Throne and the Black Family, as well as the history, all legends and all prophecies. I want to start with legends. Perdom."

Perdom didn't even look at Kerde for permission to go forward, which was good. Gift had taken such control of the meeting that Perdom probably didn't even think of turning to her.

"The Black Throne," Perdom said in his lecturer's voice, "has been in the custody of the Shaman for nearly a thousand years. The palace has been empty that long. Before the Shaman took it, the Black Family lived there. When the Fey started their expanse away from the Eccrasian Mountains, they abandoned the Throne."

"But not all at once," Gift said.

"No," Perdom said. "For the first several generations, a rejected family member guarded the Throne. Then, when the Black King went blind, the rush to the Throne by the other family members and those with Vision was so intense that people were killed—fortunately, there was no Black Blood against Black Blood at this point— and the Shaman intervened. Because we could not kill, we became the guardians of the Throne itself, determining who would and would not touch it, and whether or not they even knew it existed."

Gift had to restrain himself from taking a small, revealing breath. Some members of the Black Family weren't even allowed here. They had let him come not to study, but to wait until the appropriate moment so that they could take him up the mountain.

"From that moment on," Perdom continued, "we have controlled the Black Throne and the Place of Power. It has been the primary duty of the Shaman. For it is in this place that the Mysteries and Powers speak most clearly, and here where we get the most accurate Visions."

Gift had never heard that. He doubted that most Fey knew this. He wondered if the Black Family should have known.

The Shaman who was tapping the lamps had gotten halfway through the room. The intense brightness was decreasing, bringing the glare to tolerable levels. The other Shaman had removed their fists from their knees.

They were watching closely, but seemed more relaxed. Gift wasn't certain why.

"So," Gift said when it became clear that Perdom was not going to continue, "how is it that a member of the Black Family comes here?"

"Sometimes the member determines his own future, and comes on his own, as you did," Perdom said. "Other times, he is asked to come here. Every once in a while, a Black Ruler will request that a son or a daughter or a niece or a nephew be tested by the Throne and we usually accommodate."

"Then the Throne accepts or rejects," Gift said.

"Yes," Perdom said.

"And what happens after that?"

"Any potential ruler accepted by the Black Throne is assigned a Shaman."

"My great-grandfather did not have a Shaman," Gift said. At least not one that Gift knew of.

Perdom's chin raised slightly. "He did, once."

"The Shaman that became my father's Shaman?"

"No," Perdom said. "That Shaman, Chadn, was brought by Rugar to Blue Isle, not as the family's Shaman, but so that the troops would have someone to rely on in times of question. She was never to be a Shaman to the Black Family. She didn't have the training."

Gift started. "Training?"

"In interpreting a ruler's Vision."

"That interpretation," Gift asked, "is it an intuitive thing or does it follow certain rules?"

"He has no right to know that," Kerde said. Her voice seemed a little shrill.

"I think that we have already established that things are different," Gift said.

"Rules, of course," Perdom said, without looking at Kerde. It was as if he were trying to pretend she was no longer in the room. "It was the rules your great-grandfather objected to about his own Shaman, feeling she did not accurately reflect the Visions he was receiving, that she was not open to the wishes of the Mysteries so much as trying to control his actions."

"Perdom," Kerde whispered.

"So she was sent back here."

And Gift finally understood the undercurrent he was feeling. He looked at Kerde. "Did my great-grandfather dislike you that much, or didn't he trust you either?"

Her intake of breath was sharp. "You have no right to ask me such things."

"I have every right," he said. "You may have great powers, but beneath them all, you have a heart that beats just like the rest of us."

"Are you threatening me?" she asked with such shock that he almost wished he had been.

"No," he said. "I am saying that you love and hate and feel the same as any other Fey. My great-grandfather was a difficult man." Gift shuddered as he said that last, remembering how strong his great-grandfather had been when he had invaded Gift's mind. How strong, how intelligent, how resolute. A man like that would be difficult to like, and even more difficult to serve. "He had to have some reason for sending you back here. If a Fey ruler always has a Shaman beside him, then why didn't someone come back to take your place?"

"Because," she snapped, "he sent me back here to consult with the Powers about my behavior."

"Did you?"

"Of course not," she said. "That's not how the relationship works. But Rugad claimed that his five Visions when he touched the Black Throne made him the most powerful Visionary in all the Fey. He believed that gave him a reason to discount my interpretations."

Gift frowned. "Weren't you to compare Visions?"

"They were often the same," she said. "I believed they meant one thing, he another."

"But he was the Leader of the Fey. Wasn't it ultimately his decision?" Gift asked.

"You are as arrogant as he was," Kerde said.

Gift stiffened. The Shaman who was tapping the lamps

stopped on the next-to-last one and looked at Kerde with surprise.

"I was asking for clarification," Gift said. "As you mentioned earlier, no one in my branch of the family received instruction from the previous Black Ruler."

Kerde did not answer him. Apparently she still didn't like having her opinion challenged.

The Shaman tapping the lamps finished the last one, and snuck around the back of the room to return to his seat. The souls in the lights would come to the glass for a moment, press their see-through hands against the barrier, watch, and then exchange places with another soul in the lamp, who would then light up and go through the entire process. Gift watched that as everything else went on around him, realizing that in all the years of his life, he had never seen the souls in the Fey lamps behave like that.

"Most Black Rulers," Perdom said into the silence, "consulted and acted upon the advice they received from their Shaman."

But Rugad hadn't. And he had become the greatest warrior the Fey had ever known. Under his rule, the Fey conquered more territory than under the previous Black Rulers combined. Was that because the Shaman kept a clamp on the destruction? Limiting it, preventing too much, preventing precisely the revolt that Chadn, the Shaman he had known, had instigated?

Even though Gift thought about that, he said nothing. He didn't want to give anything to Kerde. Considering the mood that she was in, she might remember who she was and stop this proceeding at any time.

"So no one has governed from the Black Throne itself in a thousand years," Gift said.

"If they did before," Perdom said. "Just because something exists doesn't mean it is used in the way one would expect."

He didn't look at Gift as he said that last, and several of the souls in the lamps turned away as he spoke. The light in the room dimmed another notch.

A lie? Gift wasn't sure. If so, why would Perdom lie? Did sitting on the actual Throne do something, change something? Did ruling from that Throne mean more than ruling from any other Throne? Was that why the Shaman protected it?

They protected the Place of Power from the very Leaders they had chosen. They were afraid of something, something they weren't telling him.

"All right," he said. "Now tell me the legends."

Madot stepped forward. She had said nothing so far. "Gift," she said. "It would be best to discuss Visions and then have you leave this place."

"Perhaps," he said. "For you."

Kerde shook her head and walked to the wall. She leaned on it like an apprentice, taking herself out of the conversation.

Perdom watched her. "No one can agree on the legends," he finally said.

"So let me into the argument," Gift said.

The other Shaman did not move. They were eerily silent. If it weren't for their breathing, Gift wouldn't have even known they were there. The apprentices, on the other hand, squirmed and shifted and one of them slid down the wall to sit on the floor.

Perdom cleared his throat. "The only legend of the Black Throne that has survived unchanged through all the centuries is this: When the first Fey found the Place of Power, she stumbled into what is now the Black Palace. The Throne rose from the floor, created itself for her, and beckoned her. She went to it, sat, and was comfortable. Already changed by the Place of Power, she also gained the Throne's darkness so that she could rule the Fey."

"The Throne's darkness?" Gift asked.

Perdom looked at the others, but no one moved to help him. He sighed. "This is where the disputes begin. The Fey quest for blood, some say—"

"Who?" Gift asked.

Perdom again looked at the others. Finally Xihu stood.

She was one of the younger Shaman, her skin not as lined, her body a bit sturdier than most. She worked with a group of Shaman who studied the Place of Power. Gift had been warned, along with the other apprentices, not to approach those Shaman or question them about anything. He wasn't even sure he had heard her speak.

"We believe," she said, her throat husky, "that the Black Throne taints the magic from the Place of Power. There is a thirst for blood within the Throne itself, a thirst that becomes unquenchable in those of Black Blood. It is what leads them to conquer. That is why Chadn was allowed to join your mother when she left Nye on the warships for Blue Isle. Chadn had seen a Vision, confirmed by others in my sect, that the next great Black Ruler would be born on that Isle, and that Black Ruler would be untainted by the Throne."

Gift's eyes narrowed.

"But," Perdom said, "there are others who believe that once a bloodline has touched the Throne, it doesn't matter how many generations are removed from it. They will all be influenced by the Throne itself."

"So the Black Family has been corrupted by the Throne?" Gift asked. He clenched his fists so that his hands would not shake.

"About half of us believe that," Madot said. "The rest do not. We believe that the Throne is a necessary part of the magic provided by the mountain, the Powers, and the Mysteries, just as the Place of Power is."

"The belief we all hold in common is this," Perdom said. "We would not be Fey without the Throne."

"We would be like your pathetic people," Kerde said from her wall. "Island-bound, denying our magic, living a life that—"

"You have never been to Blue Isle, and you have no idea what kind of life existed there before the Fey arrived." Gift ran a hand through his dark hair. "Not even I know that. It's lost to all of us. We have no idea if it was better, worse, or simply different. I will wager that when we find the third Place of Power, the country that holds it will have completely different customs concerning its magic, no better and no worse than our own."

"The third Place of Power," Kerde said. "So you do intend to seek it."

When she spoke that softly and with such bitterness, he realized he had made a mistake. He swallowed, and considered his words carefully before he spoke.

"I believe," he said slowly, "that someday we will discover the third Place of Power. I also will do everything I can to prevent that day from happening. I don't believe we're ready to view the Triangle of Might. I don't believe we're good enough people to have that kind of power."

The souls in the lamps were coming forward again, their light getting brighter. Gift glanced at them. Finally, he couldn't take it any longer.

"What are they doing?" he asked.

Xihu was the one who followed his gaze. "Most of them guarded the Place of Power, and begged to live in the lamps after their bodies moved on. Some of us think that those in the lamps—those who volunteer to go—will have a place in the hierarchy of the afterlife. So what you say here, what you do about the Place of Power—what we all decide—has a bearing on their future as well. Only they can no longer speak to that future. They can only trust us to do what is best for them. For all of us."

The explanation made a shiver run down Gift's back. He hadn't expected that answer. He knew that the Islanders who had been placed in Fey lamps—murdered or newly dead and captured by Lamplighter Fey—sometimes did not know that their bodies had died. These Fey, these Shaman, knew it; they had a belief he did not understand, a sense of sacrifice alien to all that he had been taught by the Fey warriors who raised him.

He turned away from the lamps. "Tell me the other legends about the Throne."

Perdom glanced at Xihu. She opened her palms as if to say that he was the one who could tell the stories; she would be the one to correct him. Perdom shook his head slightly, then turned to Gift.

"One of the legends," Perdom said, "tells the story of a group of Shaman who tried to destroy the Throne after the Black Blood turned upon itself. They hit it with rocks, they got a powerful Enchanter to use all of his spells, they had the Warders devise method after method for destroying the Throne. But none succeeded. The stones broke, the spells were absorbed into the Throne itself, and many of the Warders died."

Gift threaded his fingers together. He thought of the fountain in the Place of Power on Blue Isle. The fountain grew out of the rock and seemed to be completely indestructible. But the Throne had a different sense to it: it seemed more like the giant swords that now blocked the entrance to Blue Isle's Place of Power. Each Place had symbols that were incorporated into the lives and the culture of the people who found the magical cave.

"That is why," Xihu said, "some believe the Throne is evil. It will kill to save itself."

"As will most creatures," Gift said.

Kerde made a soft sound of disgust from her place against the wall. She bowed her head as if Gift were not understanding what they were saying. He understood it; he just found the interpretation questionable.

Perhaps he was exhibiting the same arrogance that his great-grandfather had. Perhaps. But Gift's experience was different than most people's—Fey or Islander—and he knew some things that they did not. He knew that the symbols in Blue Isle's Place of Power, the swords, were not as they appeared. If used correctly, they provided the focus for all magic—all of Blue Isle's magic—and were quite powerful, and quite deadly.

But he had never thought of them as evil. Good or evil, those were choices made by the people who used the magic, not the magic itself.

"Have Shaman ever tried to sit on the Black Throne?"

Kerde's eyes narrowed. The souls in the lamp above

her looked down as if they were waiting for her response. Instead, Xihu said, "According to one legend, they did."

"And?" Gift asked.

"They died."

"They weren't rejected?"

"A few," said Perdom. "But a Shaman who sits on the Black Throne runs the risk of being absorbed into the Throne."

"Like the souls in the Fey lamp?" Gift asked.

"Only it seems—seemed," Perdom blinked as he stumbled over the word, glanced quickly at Kerde, and then continued, "it seemed as if the Shaman who were absorbed into the Throne were in a lot of pain."

"But they did it without the aid of someone like a Lamplighter, right?" Gift asked. Lamplighters collected the spirit of a person from the area in which it died, or they eased the movement from the body to the lamp. "There was no magical intermediary."

"None," Xihu said. "And we have never developed any. Perhaps because the magic is painful."

"The Fey have developed painful magic before," Gift said.

"But not of a kind used on Fey," Perdom said.

"Is there any reason you are defending the Throne?" Kerde's voice sounded powerful. She raised her head. Her dark eyes were flashing in the light.

"Is there any reason you take offense at an alternate interpretation?" Gift asked.

"We tell you how it is. You question. You should believe us."

"Maybe," Gift said. "But you told me at the beginning of this meeting that you have been leading me on for five years. Why should I trust anything you say?"

"If that's how you feel," Madot said from her place near the other Shaman, "then why ask the questions?"

"Because I don't want the magic to control us. I don't believe in listening to Kerde's pessimism. I believe that something about the Throne terrifies her, and because of that—and because she somehow failed my great-grandfather—she is unwilling to help the Fey or the Black Family." Gift turned to Kerde. "Am I wrong?"

"Of course," she said. "I have been around the Throne for centuries. You have just come here. You believe you know what is happening. You do not."

"Then tell me," he said. "Don't make me pry the information out of you."

Kerde rose slowly. The closer her thin hair got to the light, the more it seemed to glow. Her entire face had light on it, making her seem unreal somehow, as if she were something sent by the Powers instead of a living, breathing Shaman.

"The prophecies say the Black Family will reject the Black Throne. The Throne will then seek its new master, someone who will take it toward the Triangle of Might. Magic will guide us, instead of us guiding the magic."

"You already told me that," Gift said.

"The prophecies also say that the light the Throne sends, a band of light threaded in black, will revive all that should have been left dormant."

"What does that mean?" Gift asked.

"We have had scholars debate the prophecies for generations," Xihu said. "I believe—"

"We believe," Perdom said.

"—that we will not know what the prophecies mean until they come true."

"Then what is the point of a prophecy?" Gift asked. "The Mysteries and Powers give us the ability to See the future, and they provide us with prophecy. Isn't that to help us avoid the problems ahead?"

"Or is it to help us prepare for them?" Xihu asked.

"Now you understand why there is debate," Perdom said.

"The prophecy also says," Kerde said as if the others hadn't spoken, "that when the light shoots forth from the Throne, the Fey will no longer dominate the land."

"Who will?" Gift asked.

"Prophecies are not that simple," Xihu said. "If they were, we would understand them better."

"The Throne will belong to another, the prophecy says." Kerde made her voice carry over the other conversation. "One who shall lay down the Sword and abandon the Crown."

"Crown?" Gift asked.

"Scholars believe this means that the Throne wants us to turn away from our warlike ways," Xihu said, "as your sister has led us. And now you have turned away from the Crown, not accepting your proper rule."

"But you said the Throne already belongs to my family," Gift said. "The interpretation makes no sense."

"And we will not understand until it comes to pass," said Perdom.

"What are the other prophecies?" Gift asked.

"There are none," Kerde said, "except the Warning heard by Madot."

"Madot and the other three," Xihu said.

The Shaman turned toward Madot. She licked her lips, then said, "The hand that holds the scepter shall hold it no more, and the man behind the Throne shall reveal himself in all his glory."

"But this was not a Vision," Perdom said. "I do not trust it. I still believe you were wrong in taking the boy to the Throne on the basis of this Warning."

"She Saw him," Kerde said. "She Saw him receive the gift of the Throne from his sister."

"No," Gift said. "She did not See me. Tell them what you really Saw, Madot."

Madot glanced at Kerde, then closed her eyes, as if she didn't want to face what she was saying. "I Saw a Fey man with coal black hair. I Saw him from the back. I watched as Gift's sister handed the Throne to him."

"You told us this was Gift," Perdom said.

"When I Saw him, I thought it was." Madot swallowed so hard Gift saw her throat move. Then she opened her eyes. "But as he pointed out, I did not see the face. It could have been a Shifter—"

"There is only one Shifter in the Black Family and you saw her give the Throne to Gift."

"Now," Madot said. "There is only one now. I do not know how the Black Queen will look fifty years from now. She's a Shifter. She may keep her appearance unchanging."

Xihu sucked in her breath. Gift watched the other Shaman. They shifted in their seats for the first time since all of this began.

"You tell us you were in error?" Kerde said.

"I interpreted as I thought best," Madot said.

"But you took him to the Black Throne," Kerde said.

"At your direction. I fought it."

"And while I stood there," Gift said, deciding to throw more garbage into this mess, "she promised me she'd train me as a Shaman if I touched the Throne. Obviously that promise was a lie."

"I knew the Throne would want you," she said. "I thought I wouldn't have to fulfill."

Gift raised his eyebrows and said nothing. The rustling among the Shaman continued. Then Ylo, one of the kinder Shaman, stood. She worked in the garden with Gift quite often. She didn't say much, but when she spoke, he had learned to listen.

She said, "I too Saw the dark-haired Fey receive the Throne from Arianna."

"So did I."

"And I."

Two other Shaman stood. Gradually, six more stood as well, all confessing to Seeing the same Vision.

"But," Ylo said. "I did not See the man's face."

"Nor I."

"Nor I."

The remaining six hadn't seen the face as well. They continued to stand. Another Shaman, one of the old-timers who never spoke with Gift, stood.

"I did not See her give the Throne," the older Shaman said. "I Saw him take it."

"There can be that interpretation of my Vision as well," Ylo said.

"And when he did," the older Shaman said, "he spoke

of destroying Protectors Village so that he could discover the Triangle of Might."

Gift shuddered.

"It was a familiar voice I heard in my Vision," the older Shaman said.

"I have had the same Vision," another Shaman said. She had been sitting near the back. She stood as well. "I have Seen the Black King, his face in shadow, give an order to destroy the village, kill any Shaman who gets in the way, and take the Place of Power."

"I have Seen the troops come over the mountain, like ants," said a different Shaman as he stood.

"I have Seen all the old leaders, dead before the stairs," said an apprentice, her voice shaking.

"My Vision is of a young man, trained in Nye, apologizing as he pulls out his sword," Kerde said. "He is Fey and he knows he must kill me. We are standing before the stairs."

Gift had Seen none of these things, yet he felt shivers run through him. He had never heard the Shaman do anything like this, although he knew it happened. This was what he had come here for. This was what he needed.

"I have Seen the Black Queen standing before the Throne," Perdom said, "looking at it with such longing that I fear she shall devour it somehow."

"I have Seen that as well," Gift said. "The Black Queen, my sister. I Saw that after I touched the Throne. I also Saw her without a face calling my name."

"I have Seen you," Kerde said, "with a knife to the throat of a blond-haired man."

She spoke with such hatred that the room was silent for a moment. Then Gift said, "I have Seen two Shaman at the doors of the Places of Power, preparing to find the Triangle of Might."

"I have Seen that as well," said another apprentice.

"I have Seen the Blood against Blood," said Madot. "Just last night, I saw it, and it was Bridge's hand that tried to stop it."

"Bridge," Perdom said. "I have Seen him comforting his daughter on Blue Isle."

"I have Seen her look at the Black Queen with hatred," said another Shaman.

"I have Seen a Golem training infantry," said Xihu.

"Sebastian?" Gift asked, mostly because he could not stop himself. "Sebastian couldn't do that."

"In my Vision, he trains them with the comfort of one who has done so for a long, long time," Xihu said.

"I have Seen a fleet heading to Leut. A Fey fleet, with Nyeian and Islander ships. A war fleet," said Kerde.

"I have Seen a people who live in the mountains and decorate themselves in blood," said Perdom.

"I have Seen blood flowing like a river," said an apprentice.

"So have I," said another.

"And I," said a third.

"I have Seen Blood against Blood," said a Shaman in the back.

"And the chaos it brings," said another Shaman as she stood.

"I have Seen hands reaching for the Throne," said a third Shaman.

"And blood."

"And blood."

"And blood."

The voices ended up speaking in unison. Everyone in the room was standing. It had grown hot. All of the souls in the lamps were standing as well. Gift's heart was pounding hard. He felt a trickle of sweat run down one side of his face, even as another shiver ran down his back.

Gradually the voices stopped. Gift's mind was filled with images that he didn't know how to assemble. But he had one question, only one, that they had not answered.

"Has anyone else Seen my great-grandfather?" he asked.

"Have you?" Perdom asked.

"Is this the dead about whom you were referring?" Kerde asked.

"The first Vision I had after I touched the Throne," Gift said, "I Saw him sitting on Blue Isle's throne. And then again, I Saw him in a boat."

"But you had seen him on Blue Isle's throne when you were a boy," Kerde said.

Gift shook his head. "I never did. I never saw him in person. I wasn't in the palace until Rugad was dead. I have never seen him in a boat either. These were Visions, not memories."

The Shaman looked at each other. Finally, one said, "I have heard his voice, speaking as if he were still alive."

"I have Seen him kill a man with no tongue," said Xihu.

"I have Seen him touch the soil in Leut," said Madot, softly.

"Was it Rugad or was it one of his grandsons?" Kerde asked. "Bridge, it is said, looks more and more like him as he grows older."

"How can we know?" Xihu said. "We have not seen anyone other than Shaman for generations. We have met Rugad. The man I Saw looked like him, but Gift has some of him, in the set of the mouth, the shape of his nose. Only the eyes are different. Rugad's were so black that you could not see into them."

"There is no way to know," Perdom said, "without seeing Bridge and Rugat and Golden. And I, for one, do not want these sons of Rugar, grandsons of Rugad, here."

"Nor do I," said Kerde.

"They are not welcome here," said Madot, "especially after some of the Visions we've heard of Shamanic blood being spilled."

"We do not know when that will happen, and we cannot isolate ourselves more," said Xihu.

"We can do as we choose," said Kerde.

"We must do what is right for our people," said Perdom.

"The Fey?" Gift asked. "Or the other Shaman?"

"Or the rest of the world?" said Xihu.

Her words were greeted with silence. Slowly the other

Shaman sat down. The apprentices remained standing, bright-eyed for the first time since this began. Gift watched all of them, and then sighed. He had a headache caused, he thought, by too much information.

Kerde pushed her way back into the center of the room. She tilted her chin so that she could look Gift directly in the eye. "We no longer want you here, either. You will leave first thing in the morning."

"No," he said, startling himself as much as he startled her.

"No?"

"I have some things to finish here first. Then I'll go. I would like one of you to come with me." When he said that, he looked at Xihu.

"Why?" she asked.

"My family needs a Shaman. I had hoped to be that person, but it is clear I will not be. I need someone who will serve as advisor on this level, someone who'll be willing to work with me and my sister."

"That's not how it's done," Kerde said.

"You need two Shaman, then," Madot said. "I will come, if you'll still have me."

Gift looked at her. He still felt the sting of betrayal that had haunted him all week, ever since they had gone to the Throne. "One should do," he said. "Arianna and I have the same goals."

"Remember the Visions," Xihu said. "And remember that goals change."

"My sister is one of the strongest people I've ever met," Gift said. "She can hold her own."

"Even strong people can be changed," Xihu said. Already, Gift sensed, she was doing her job as Shaman to his family.

He turned to Madot. "I will think on it. I will tell you tomorrow."

"You will leave tomorrow," Kerde said.

"I will leave when I am ready," Gift said. "And not before."

He stepped away from her so that he could face the

other Shaman. They looked exhausted, as if everything that had passed in this room had nearly defeated them.

"Thank you," he said, bowing slightly in the Blue Isle manner, "for sharing things not normally shared with my family. For enabling me to hear all your Visions, and to hear the prophecies and legends about the Throne. If there is anything else you feel I need to know, but which you haven't said here, you can find me in my room. I will leave soon, but I want to make sure you all have your chance to be heard."

Then he turned and left the room without a second glance at anyone. In the corner of his eye, he saw Kerde frowning, and knew she would probably discourage more talk. It didn't matter. He'd heard what he needed. He knew now that something was happening, that his sister was in trouble, and the business with the Throne would somehow make things worse.

The corridor was dark. All of the lamps were in the room. It took a moment for his eyes to adjust, before he found the main room and the door.

He let himself outside. It was wonderfully cool here, and the air smelled of pine trees that covered the lower elevations. He took a deep shuddering breath, and as he did, he felt the familiar pull from the mountain.

He turned. The shimmer winked at him from above. He hadn't lied to the Shaman. He would leave. But not until he completed one more duty.

Not until he went to the Place of Power, and tried to summon the spirit of his mother, so that they could talk face-to-face.

CHAPTER ELEVEN

SEGER PLACED HER hands on Sebastian's throat. His skin was cool and smooth as stone, with jagged edges along the cracks. She wondered for the first time why she had never tried to repair the cracks. It would take some stone, the same stone she had used to put him back together, and a bit of time, and he would look as normal as a Golem could.

He stood perfectly still, staring at something over her shoulder. They were in his quarters, with their spectacular view of the garden. His bed was dented in the middle from the weight of his body, and through the doors she could see the chairs in the sitting room were also dented. He had had these rooms his whole life, and had never asked to change the furniture, had never asked to have anything brought to him or taken away. Even when his father reclaimed the palace from the Black King, Sebastian had taken nothing new, simply had his rooms restored to the way they had been.

The windows were open and a cool breeze was coming through, making Seger shudder. Between the unnatural touch of Sebastian's skin and the growing chill of evening, she would be very cold by the time she left here.

She had been searching for the place where the strange voice had taken root. So far, she felt nothing, no nodes, no bumps, nothing that would indicate a place where the voice lived. That worried her. It meant it had taken root inside of him instead of outside, and she wasn't sure if she had the magic to remove it.

She had consulted with several other Healers, as well as Domestics who specialized in creating Changelings. Sebastian had been a Changeling, a lump of rock that was molded to look like Gift when he was an infant, and placed in the crib to decoy Gift's parents while the Fey stole him. It was an ancient Fey practice, not used much, but one that had come in handy, especially when the Fey were a young people with little power. Most Domestics learned how to create Changelings but had never done so, and the Domestics who had created Sebastian were long dead.

Sebastian's shift from Changeling to Golem—Changelings usually lived a few weeks at most—was something no one had counted on. That he had shattered and reassembled three times at his own count was nothing short of miraculous. He had a strength that came to him from his formation, and a wisdom that she liked. He also was very childlike, and that concerned her, because it might mean that he wouldn't know what to fight if he needed to fight for survival.

Her fingers probed the cracks along his neck, hunting for nodes, for anything that didn't feel like stone. Everything felt right—as right as a Golem could be. She reached out with her magic, searching for the extra voice, the part of him that shouldn't be there, and finally saw it, threaded into each shattered piece, a strand of black in the gray.

Loosening it would be harder than she thought.

She dropped her hand. "Sebastian," she said.

"Yes . . . ?" He turned his head and looked at her. His

slate grey eyes had so much life. It was as if he were a vibrant, energetic being trapped in a body made of stone.

"Do you feel pain?"

"Here . . ." He tapped his heart.

"In your body?"

Slowly the stone face scrunched up into a frown of concentration. "Pain?"

"Yes. When you shattered, for instance. Did it hurt?"

"Here . . ." He tapped his heart again.

She put her hand on that spot. He didn't have a heart, not in the way that flesh-and-blood creatures did, but he had learned that his emotions lived in this place. She could feel a slight warmth on the stone.

"Anywhere else?"

He shook his head. One movement, very slow.

She took a deep breath and kept her hand on his stone chest. "Sebastian," she said carefully. "What I'm going to do is attempt to remove the new voice. It's threaded into all your stone. I don't believe this will hurt, but it will feel odd. Are you willing to let me try?"

"Please," he said.

His voice sounded steady, but his eyes held fear. She rubbed her hand on the warm spot of his chest, then smiled at him. "Ready?"

"Yes."

Seger moved her hand away from the warmth and, seeing with her magic, touched the blackness threading through the stone. She placed her index finger on it, then closed her eyes. The blackness felt harder, somehow, than the stone it was embedded in, but the blackness was thin, like a small band of material, barely thick enough to hold anything.

She slipped her fingernail beneath the blackness and tugged at it gently, like a seamstress would pull a bad stitch. Sebastian's body tightened, and he took a sharp breath. He could feel what she was doing. She slowed down her movements, careful to make them as gentle as possible.

Soon she was able to wrap some of the blackness around her index finger. She held it there for a moment, debating whether or nor she should cut it, when the blackness pulled back.

The pull was so hard that it slammed her finger against Sebastian's chest. She opened her eyes, lost the magic vision, saw her finger slipping into the stone. It took all of her concentration to look at it, not as it was but as the magic was, and see the blackness pulling small bits of color from her.

She slid her finger away. It ached. Bits of skin were gone and blood was welling from pinprick-sized holes.

Sebastian blinked at her, frowning. "It . . . is . . . tight."

"What is?" she asked, struggling to keep her voice calm. She didn't want him to know how uncomfortable the blackness made her feel.

"The . . . place . . . you . . . touched."

She almost put her hand on it, then thought better of it. Something else was going on here. Voices did not thread themselves through a body, although she wasn't sure how such things worked in Golems. They didn't have voice boxes like Fey did, nor did they have internal organs. Perhaps this was the only way the voice could attach.

Still, it should have come loose. It shouldn't have fought back. This was confirmation that the magic she feared was influencing what faced them.

She would need to return with a group of Healers, and when one failed, the other would have to try. If only they had an Enchanter here, or even a group of Spell Warders. The more power she had to fight this thing, the better she would feel.

"It didn't work this time," she said. "Can you stand the tightness?"

"It . . . is . . . eas-ing," he said.

"Good. I'm going to try again, but not today. Can you wait?"

"I . . . do . . . not . . . want . . . to, but . . . I . . . will."

She nodded. She took one more look at him through

her magic, saw that the blackness had gathered in that single spot as if it had pooled all its strength together. As she looked at it, her finger ached. She would need to have someone else look at that, to make sure she hadn't gotten tainted by the foreign magic.

A knock on the door made them both jump. The blackness dispersed along Sebastian's chest as if it hadn't gathered there at all. Seger took a step backward. As she did, the door to the sitting area opened, and Arianna swept in.

Her skin was an odd shade of gray, and there were shadows beneath her eyes. Luke followed her, his own expression carefully neutral. He shut the door behind them.

"I'm sorry to intrude," Arianna said. "Is it all right?"

Sebastian smiled. "I . . . am . . . hap-py . . . you . . . are . . . here."

"Did it work?" Luke asked Seger.

She shook her head. "We are facing some powerful magic." She almost showed them her finger, but did not, worried that they wouldn't understand.

"Yes," Luke said. He glanced at Arianna. Color filled her cheeks. She opened her mouth, then closed it, and then sighed.

"I—oh, Seger."

Seger held herself very still. "What is it?"

Arianna took a step forward. "I need to talk with you. Alone."

"She has been losing time," Luke said as if he didn't approve of the private conference. "She has said things she doesn't remember saying, and then, today, she got hit with another headache. Only this one was different, wasn't it?"

Arianna didn't say anything.

"This one caused her to Shift."

Arianna reddened even more. Sebastian put a hand on her arm. "Are . . . you . . . all . . . right?"

"For now," Arianna said. "Seger, please. Some time alone."

Seger nodded. It wasn't unreasonable for the Black

Queen to ask for a private consultation at a moment like this. "Luke," she said, "would you mind staying with Sebastian? I don't think he should be alone for a while."

"All right." Luke sounded frustrated. Seger had noticed that he never quite knew what to do around Sebastian. So many didn't. They saw only his slowness and didn't realize how intelligent the creature—the person—hidden by it was.

"Let's go to my suite," Arianna said.

It was just across the hall. Arianna led the way, moving quickly. Her gown flowed around her as she did so, making it seem as if she moved even faster than she was. When she opened the door to her suite, she walked through it as if to satisfy herself that it was empty. Then she closed her windows and the door before offering Seger a chair.

Seger sat, but Arianna did not. She paced in front of the fireplace, her fingertips brushing against the stone as if she were trying to dust it.

"What I tell you cannot leave this room, ever," Arianna said.

"It will not," Seger said.

"You will listen to me, and take only the action I want on this matter."

"As you wish," Seger said, not sure she was liking the direction this was taking.

Arianna turned, her gown whirling around her. She glanced at her fingertips, which were now blackened, and wiped them on her skirt. Then she sat in a chair.

Seger had never seen her look so forlorn. Before Arianna had always been in control of herself, always been extremely powerful, even when she was a young ruler learning everything.

Now she was uncertain, almost frightened. Her gaze met Seger's. "I think I'm losing my mind," she said.

Seger made herself listen to the words and not the emotions. That way, she could stay calm. "Let me diagnose."

"I have, apparently, said things I do not mean, given

orders I do not remember, and this afternoon I discovered myself in the North Tower, with no memory of getting there. Luke said I treated him badly, trying to throw him out, even though he would not go. I've asked for troop reports, and I have had thoughts that don't feel like my own." She swallowed. "And then I Shifted. Without planning to, without even wanting to, I Shifted into a robin. I had to make myself Shift back. It was hard."

Despite her resolution not to feel anything, chills ran through Seger. "Describe how you feel when you've lost time."

"Just confused," she said. "I don't even realize it's happened."

"And the strange thoughts?"

"As if someone other than me is thinking them."

"Then a Visionary has traveled your Links," Seger said. "You have been invaded."

Arianna shook her head. "I closed my Links fifteen years ago, and I haven't reopened them."

"Not even your Link to Sebastian?"

Arianna paused. "I don't know. Maybe. We're still close. I didn't consciously open it, if I did. But this doesn't feel like a Visionary has invaded me." She leaned forward. "My mind had been invaded once by Rugad when I was fifteen, and he couldn't control me. He couldn't make me Shift. He traveled along my Link to Sebastian, and Sebastian followed him into my mind, and saved me. But in doing so, I got lost." She blinked. "Are you following this?"

Seger shook her head. "I have heard of invasion, and I know that a powerful Visionary like Rugad can take over a mind. I did not know that he had been thrown out of yours, and I don't know how you could get lost."

"There was some kind of—explosion. Sebastian shattered, and the force of it sent me tumbling away from our Link," Arianna said. She held her hands apart. "I don't know any other word. I went tumbling back inside my own mind—it was like I was a little person inside my brain and I got sent into darkness and couldn't find my way out."

"So how did you?" Seger asked. This was all new to her. So many of the magics on Blue Isle were. She had never heard of anything like this.

"Coulter traveled across my father's Link and found me. He traced my trail in the darkness of my own brain, got me out, and told me to close the doors, the Links."

"Which explains," Seger said more to herself than to Arianna, "why you have not made friends or fallen in love since you have become Black Queen."

Arianna looked shocked. "What do you mean?"

"A Link is an opening, a vulnerability. You not only closed your current Links, you prevented any more from forming."

Arianna let out a small sigh. "That's bad, isn't it?"

"If someone is trying to cross your Links, no, it is not. But if you are under no threat, of course." Seger leaned forward, resting her elbows on her knees. "Arianna, if you had a child, or a loved one, you would not be feeling the fear you are now. You have only me to trust, and there is no bond between us. You simply know you can trust me because I am a Healer and I have done as I was bound, no more."

Arianna's nod was small, her eyes sad.

"This seems to me that you are suffering a magical attack, but unlike any I've ever known, which makes me wonder if an Islander hasn't provoked it." Seger frowned. "Unless you are leaving something out."

"There was a child." Arianna's voice sounded faint, as if she were having trouble remembering. "A baby—"

She gagged, and put her hands on her head. Then she wrapped her arms around her skull as if the pain were too much to bear.

Seger knelt beside her and touched Arianna, searching for magic. There were two active Links coming in from the outside of Arianna's body. One was faint, as if it were rarely used, and the other was thicker. Seger didn't have the magic to tell if either was being used. But she doubted it. The faint Link felt as if no one had used it in a long time. The other Link, the one she would have guessed attached Arianna to Sebastian, had a constant flow of energy through it, but the energy felt like it was part of Arianna, part of Sebastian, with nothing else.

There were no other active Links, no lines, no lights coming in from the outside of Arianna's body. And there should have been. There should have been countless Links.

And a magical attack would have left a trail of light.

Tears were streaming down Arianna's face. She made herself lift her head, her skin dark with the strain, her birthmark standing out against her chin.

"There was—a—baby," she said. Each word was clearly a struggle. She choked on the last. "In—my—mind."

She sounded so like Sebastian that it frightened Seger. Seger hadn't realized how close the two of them were until that moment.

"In your mind?" Seger asked.

Arianna nodded, the tears falling harder now, her mouth turned in a grimace. Seger could feel the pain radiating off her. Blood vessels on Arianna's forehead were standing out from the strain.

"When?" Seger asked.

"I—found—" Arianna closed her eyes, blinked, and then tried again.

"I—found—"

"You found the baby when?" Seger asked, afraid that the strain might actually harm Arianna. Seger could sense the struggle. She just didn't know where it was coming from.

"Moments—after—"

Seger took Arianna's hands. They felt like claws. This was clearly an important event, and something within Arianna didn't want Seger to know about it.

"After?"

"—Links—closed."

Arianna shut her eyes and leaned back. All the strength

seemed to disappear from her body. Her hands were limp and cold.

Then her eyes opened and the look in them was harsh, unyielding, and vaguely amused. "Satisfied now, Seger?" she asked in Fey.

In all the years Seger had known Arianna, she had never seen her like this. Arianna was right; this was a different person, someone alien. And someone familiar.

"Who are you?" Seger replied in the same language.

Arianna smiled. "Why, I'm Arianna, of course. Who did you think I was?"

But Arianna had never spoken like this. Her voice had never been so deep, so filled with wry contempt. Even the inflections were wrong. Arianna spoke Fey with an accent, the accent found in this, the central part of Blue Isle. She was fluent in the language, but had never—even though she had spoken it from childhood—completely adopted it as her own. She preferred to speak in Islander when she could. Fey was not her natural language.

"What do you want with Arianna?" Seger asked.

The woman's smile grew wider. "I am Arianna."

"Not the Arianna I know."

A single incline of the head, like a gracious ruler to a lower subject, again, something that Arianna had never done before. "I mean to change the way I do business."

Seger's chill grew. Arianna had sat up in the chair. Even her posture was different. It was rigid, more in control than Seger had ever seen her.

"Change how?" Seger asked.

"It's time to stop playing games, to stop 'learning and growing' into my role. It's time I become what I should have been from the start."

"And that is?" Seger asked.

"The best Black Queen the Empire has ever known."

Seger had to hold herself rigid to prevent a shudder. "How do you plan to do that?"

"You'll see." Arianna stood, took a step forward, and nearly tripped over the hem of her gown. Seger had to lean back to get out of her way. Arianna looked down as if she hadn't known what she was wearing; then, with the barely cleaned hand, she lifted her skirt and walked forward.

Then she wheeled around, unsteadily, and looked at herself as if she didn't know how she had gotten there. She dropped her skirt, leaving a dark handprint on it, her eyes wild. Her mouth opened, then closed, then opened. She looked completely like a woman at war with herself.

"Thought—"

She spoke brokenly in Islander, just as she had been doing before she slipped to Fey.

"—baby—"

Her mouth opened and closed again. The tears were back, tears of effort. Seger took a step toward her, but wasn't sure if touching Arianna would help her or hurt her.

"—Sebastian—"

She cursed in Fey, grabbed the skirt, and wiped off her face. Then she walked out of the room as if she had said nothing at all. Seger followed a few paces behind, only to see Arianna stumble and catch herself against the wall, hands on her head again.

Seger hurried toward her. Arianna slowly slid down the wall, and fell against the floor. She had passed out, her face gray, her birthmark red. She looked wan and ill. Seger crouched, then picked Arianna up. She was lighter and thinner than Seger had expected. It took almost no effort at all to carry Arianna to her bed.

Gently, Seger laid her down, and then stared at her. The entire thing had left Seger unnerved. She had never seen anything like it.

Seger didn't want to leave her, but she knew she had to, just to get some help. She ran to the hallway and crossed to Sebastian's suite.

"She's passed out," she said to Luke with no preamble. "She's in her bed. I want you to make sure she stays there until I can send a Healer to her."

"What about you?" Luke asked.

"I'll take care of her," Seger said. "But at the moment, you go."

"What if she wants to get up?"

"Tell her to wait for me," Seger said. Luke nodded crisply, then headed down the hall.

Seger turned to Sebastian. His fingers were threaded together, and his eyes were wide with fear. "All right," she said. "Tell me about the day Rugad used your Link to invade Arianna."

"It . . . will . . . take . . . time," Sebastian said.

"I don't care about that," Seger said. "Just tell me. And leave nothing out."

So he did.

CHAPTER TWELVE

COULTER THREADED HIS way through the five giant
swords outside the Place of Power. He put his hand on
the polished blade of one of them as he passed. The blade
was cool; it felt like a normal sword's blade, only finer. If
he wasn't careful it would slice his hand and absorb the
blood.

He'd seen that happen more than once when his people had cleaned the swords. The jewels were polished as
well, and they glinted in the fading light. It had been a
long time since he had been up here at twilight. It made
him think of the days when he was living in the cave with
Arianna, Adrian, King Nicholas, Gift, Scavenger, and
Leen, when they were the only thing that stood between
Rugad and his desire to conquer the world.

Coulter sighed. Those days were long gone, the unity
he had felt then was gone as well. He had failed them
when Adrian, who had been like a father to him, had
died—and even though Arianna had made it clear that
she wanted Coulter beside her, he had refused. He thought
she felt strongly about him because they had been through

so much together, because he had actually found her inside her own mind. That day, she had seen him as he saw himself, and she had still cared for him.

He valued that then, and he valued it now. His upbringing as an orphaned and unwanted Islander living with the Fey had left him with a loneliness that he couldn't articulate, a desire to be accepted that made him needier than he cared to think about. He was afraid, especially after his total devastation when Adrian died, to allow that neediness to come out again, afraid that he would make similar, very serious lapses in judgment.

Now it was his fear that was holding him back again. His fear for himself, and his fear for Arianna.

He could feel her at odd times as if she were in pain, as if part of her were trying to reach out, but unable to. Lately he had been dreaming about her as he had first seen her, a little Fey balanced at the border of adulthood, terrified because she was lost and yet unwilling to show it. She had been trying to save herself, and she probably would have done it without him. But she had allowed him to help her—she had allowed him to kiss her—and in his dreams, he felt that moment again and again.

She had been so beautiful, and she had looked at him with such trust. She did so in his dreams as well, looking at him with longing, and need, and with that same terrified plea in her eyes: *Help me.* She wouldn't say it—Arianna would never say that—but he could read it as clearly as he could read words on a page. *Help me.*

He would wake in a cold sweat, wondering if she were really reaching out to him, or if it was just his neediness showing itself again. He didn't know, and he had to know before he could make any kind of decision.

He stepped toward the mouth of the cave and stopped, as he always did when faced with the incredible light. The cave was always light. Some internal force made it glow inside. Gift used to say it was as if a small star had been captured and placed in a corner. Sleeping in here, Coulter remembered, had been like sleeping with the afternoon sun full on the face. His eyelids felt thin, and he could see shadows moving across them, and his dreams then had always been full of light.

Only the light was no longer white. On this level of the cave, the floor had turned blood red. Red light was what he saw now, and the change always startled him.

With the light came a dry heat that was welcoming. He stepped inside and let it embrace him as if he were an old friend.

There were no magic presences, at least not yet. He had hoped to feel one immediately. Instead he surveyed the cave to make sure no one had tampered with it.

The swords still gleamed on the walls. Some of them were damaged, and a few had been added by Scavenger when he brought his own personal arsenal here. They were on a separate side. The swords that belonged in the cave had been made with varin, a metal that was only found in the Cliffs of Blood. It was deadly to the touch, and could slice a man's arm off with no effort at all.

Coulter glanced behind him. The chalices were untouched, as they had been for centuries. There had never been any use for them, unlike the swords and the other items in the cave. Some of those items were ruined, used in the battle, and never replenished. No one knew how to make them. That magic was apparently lost forever.

The red light was an odd light, almost as if there were a dying fire under the floor. The walls were still white, but the upper stairs were not. The red had flowed into them. Even places like this, places that felt permanent, could change.

He was still alone. Whenever a Mystery appeared, he could sense it, even though he couldn't see it. He had always hoped for Adrian's appearance. Adrian had been slaughtered, but that had been in war, and apparently the Powers didn't think war a form of murder. Perhaps because it wasn't so personal. Perhaps it wasn't as easy to grant the soul who had died in war the power over his greatest enemy: most—maybe all—Mysteries chose the one who murdered him. And the one who had given the order to kill Adrian was dead.

Still, it would have been nice to see him again. Adrian was the closest thing to a father that Coulter had ever had, and sometimes, Coulter believed, Adrian had loved him more than he had loved his own son, Luke. That had caused a rift between Luke and Coulter that still existed. They hadn't seen each other since Coulter left Jahn, years ago.

The fountain below burbled as it always did. Coulter looked at it, at the bottom of the stairs, its water spilling into a basin. Nicholas had drunk that water, and had some sort of seizure. He had never told anyone what happened to him when he did that, and he had forbidden anyone else from doing the same thing.

Gift had continued to follow that command as if it were gospel. No one had tasted the water since Nicholas. Only Coulter knew that the magic in the cavern had spiked at that moment Nicholas drank. Coulter had told no one that, not even Nicholas.

Coulter had been outside, and he had come to the mouth of the cave, even though he hadn't been supposed to, and from there, he had felt the air fill with presences, with life that he could not see. He had felt drawn to it and repelled by it at the same time, knowing that it had not come for him, but wanting it, wanting it so badly . . .

Coulter sat down. The stone was warm against his legs. He looked down. The stairs went on for a long way. The fountain looked the same, and so did the table, rising out of the same white stone. The many tunnels leading off the cavern beckoned, as they always did. He wondered what made Nicholas finally go down one. Had he drunk more water? Had he been guided by all that magic? Or had he finally followed what was left of Jewel to his death?

The emptiness here was a tangible thing. Coulter felt like shouting out, but he knew it would do no good. He put his hands on his thighs and peered at the fountain. If he drank, would the presences come for him? Would they help him? Or would they see this as a trivial problem, one a simple mortal could solve?

Gift would be angry with him, and so would Leen. Because to drink from the fountain meant Coulter would be betraying the oath he had taken to protect this place. He had vowed to prevent anyone—including himself—from violating it. And Gift had been quite clear about what constituted a violation: taking anything from the cavern; using any part of the cavern for personal gain; and entering any of the tunnels. Drinking the water would violate two of those rules: Coulter would be taking something with him, provided the water stayed down, which it had not for Nicholas, and Coulter would be doing so for personal gain.

Personal gain. He closed his eyes. When had he started viewing his actions in connection with Arianna as personal? From the moment he had placed his hand on Nicholas's heart, and traveled through Nicholas's Link to save Arianna from dying because she was trapped inside herself? Or had it been after that, when they kissed in the garden beside the palace, the day he had left her for good?

"Arianna," he whispered. "What am I to do?"

He felt a slight magical swirling in the air around him. He raised his head, felt something like fingers brush his face.

"Help me," he said. "Show me what I'm supposed to do."

"Coulter?"

At first he thought the voice came from inside the cavern, and then he realized it came from outside. It was Leen, calling for him.

"Coulter?"

The fingers were gone, and so was the sense of the presence, gone as if it had never been. His heart twisted. So close . . .

Leen came inside, her shadow darkening the entrance. "Coulter?"

"Here," he said.

She walked up beside him, and sat on the stairs. She glanced at him. "What are you doing here?"

"Trying to make a decision," he said.

She frowned. "About what?"

"Arianna," he said.

"Has she contacted you?"

He shook his head. "Remember the day we saw that light?"

"You saw it."

"Yes," he said. "I've felt her since then. Off and on, as if she were in pain. As if she were in trouble."

Leen raised a single eyebrow, a look that made her seem all knowing and mysterious at the same time. "So you came here . . . ?"

"Hoping I'd get guidance. But I haven't."

"Well, maybe I can give you some advice," Leen said.

He looked at her, waiting, not certain if she could help him or not. She certainly knew him better than anyone else did. Not even Gift knew him this well. Maybe Gift never had. But Leen had been at Coulter's side ever since they'd met, and she had loved him, in her own calm way.

"All right," he said.

"I was raised traditionally, and so many customs of my people are gone."

Coulter straightened. Leen never talked about her family—slaughtered by Rugad when he came to Blue Isle—or her upbringing. She rarely spoke of her Feyness except as a fact, not as a way of life.

"When Arianna took on the role of Black Queen," Leen continued, "I think those of us who knew her, and who knew you, believed everything would be as it was before."

"I'm not following you. Ari and I had known each other only a short time when she became Black Queen."

"I'm not talking about how it was with the two of you before. I'm talking about Fey custom, Fey tradition."

His mouth had gone dry. He glanced at the fountain, wondering if his sudden thirst was a message to test the water, or if it was a physical reaction, a fear, of what Leen was going to say.

"Every Black Ruler has had an Enchanter at her side. Every Black King has used his Enchanter as a second in command, even though it's never stated that way. Even Rugad had Boteen, and used him until the day he died." Leen paused, and looked at the far wall as if she didn't want to see Coulter's face when she spoke. "I had always thought that you should be at Arianna's side, as her second. Her Enchanter. I would wager, even though I don't know, that her mother, the Mystery, believed the same, which was why she was willing to guide her daughter in the words she needed to take over the Fey."

"No one spoke of this."

Leen shrugged. "Arianna left this place and never returned. There were no major Fey advisors to her at first, and she wasn't inclined to listen to anyone anyway. She felt she had to establish herself on her own."

"She did that," Coulter said.

"She did," Leen said, "but maybe now she needs help. Maybe now she needs someone she can trust. And more than that. Maybe she needs someone whose magic complements hers."

Coulter shook his head. "I'm not trained."

Leen put her arm around him and rested her head on his shoulder. "I haven't heard you talk like that in a long time. Of course you're trained. And in control. You train others."

"Because they're like me. Islanders with magic."

"Because the Fey don't know whether to be afraid of them, or to teach them tricks they wouldn't otherwise know. Coulter, you're not the boy who lived in this cavern. Adrian's been gone a long time, and you've made sure you've never cared about anyone else since."

She sounded sad on that last. He knew she would have been beside him forever if he had only let her. But she needed more than a casual lover. She needed someone who adored her, and loved her more than anything. They both knew that.

"I'm sorry," he said.

"No, I wasn't saying that for me, but for you." She lifted her head off his shoulder. "This place inspires passion, Coulter. It exists because of some passions we don't understand. You fell in love here. I think Arianna did too."

"I lost the most precious person in my life here," Coulter said, remembering the pain of that, how it had pulled him apart, how it could still pull him apart, if he let it.

"Did you?" she asked. "We all lose our parents."

He turned to her. She had learned about the death of hers just before Adrian had died, and it hadn't shaken her like it had shaken Coulter.

"Losing your parents isn't supposed to end your life," Leen said. "It's just the beginning of your life as an adult. Adrian would hate the way you've lived. Without love, without any real drive."

"I have my students."

"Yes, and that's a good thing. But you do that only because it's something to keep you busy when you're not sitting here, staring at the site where you lost everything." Her arm remained around him the entire time she spoke.

He leaned into her. "I don't know, Leen. When I used my magic to help Gift, I alienated him forever. Then, to keep us all alive, I had to kill hundreds of Fey. I could feel something leaving me then. Something that made me care about lives. I don't want that to happen again."

"We're not at war, Coulter. There's no one to fight. I'm sitting beside you in the first country in the Fey Empire that the Fey failed to conquer. I'm beside you because we became allies, we became the same nation, with Arianna and Gift as our leaders. Our lives are different now because there was no conquest, because there was cooperation."

He frowned. Her argument made sense, but there was something wrong with it. "Then why do I think Ari's hurt? And what was that light?"

"I don't know," Leen said softly. "If I did, I would tell you what to do. But let me put it to you this way. What if you find out later that something happened to Ari, something you could have fixed, but you didn't? How would you feel then?"

His heart twisted. "And what if I'm wrong? What if I get there and she's fine?"

Leen looked up at him, and there were tears in her eyes. "Hug her for me. Tell her I miss her, and that if she ever needs anything, she knows where to find me."

"You wouldn't come with me?"

"No, Coulter. I don't belong there. I belong here, taking care of the students, watching this place for Gift."

Coulter sighed. "Do you think he'll ever come back?"

"When we're old, maybe. When he's a great Shaman and we're just people he once knew."

Coulter bowed his head. He and Gift had been closer than two people should have been for years, but time changed that. Time, and Coulter's fear, his quick response to Rugad's invasion of Gift's mind—even though it had been a correct response. And, strangely, Gift's unwillingness to share Coulter's friendship with Arianna.

"Funny," he said, "how you can lose everything by not doing anything."

"You haven't lost everything yet," Leen said. "You'll always have me."

Coulter wrapped her into a hug. She felt warm and strong and alive in his arms.

"You were wrong, you know," he whispered against her ear. "I have loved. I have let one person get close to me."

"But I was always a substitute," she said softly. "We both knew it."

"Maybe on one level," he said. "But not as my friend. I've never had a friend like you, who loved me and wanted nothing for herself. I was always the friend who acted that way."

"With Gift."

"For a long time, he was the only friend I had. And now you are. Are you sure you won't come with me?"

"I can't," Leen whispered. "It's hard enough letting you go on your own."

He leaned back out of the hug enough to kiss her on the lips, gently, in some ways the good-bye kiss they had never had. She kept her eyes open as he did so, the tears still lining the rims.

When he pulled away, he said, "You know, I asked for guidance, and I was disappointed no Mystery appeared to me. But I think they heard me anyway. They sent you."

Her smile was slow. "If I ever become a Mystery, I'll be one very angry Fey. I don't expect to die at someone else's hand."

He cupped her face. "I don't expect you to die."

"Because I'm hard to kill?" she asked playfully.

"Because you're the strongest person I've ever met." He stared at her for a moment. "The school will be a challenge."

"We have good instructors."

"For most," he said. "But I worry about Matt. His magic is stronger than anyone else's."

"Except yours."

"Perhaps."

"He's young. We can train him for a while. You'll be back before we need you."

"What if I have to stay at Arianna's side for good?"

Leen winced slightly before she covered it up. If Coulter didn't know her so well, he wouldn't have seen it. "We can always send Matt to you," she said calmly. "Maybe the big, bad city might tame him."

"Maybe," Coulter said. "But he has that same reckless streak his father had, that same disregard for the rules."

Leen smiled fondly at him. "I think it goes with the magic," she said. Then she stood and extended her hand. He took it and let her help him up. She put her arm around him again, and led him out of the cavern.

They stopped behind the swords. Darkness had settled over the mountains. Dash sat at the very edge of the platform, staring at the village below, his frame barely discernible.

"This isn't even a pretty place," Leen said. "It's stark and it's terrifying and it's dangerous."

"Filled with bad memories," Coulter said.

"And good ones," Leen said, pulling him closer.

"It's the only home I've ever chosen," Coulter said.

Leen was quiet for a moment, then she said, "You didn't choose this one. Gift asked you to stay."

Coulter let her words sink in. She was right. He had done as Gift asked, without thought to what he wanted. He had wanted to be at Arianna's side, but had thought it wrong for both of them—for her more than for him. In traditional Blue Isle, where women had never ruled, he thought it wrong for her to have a man beside her. The Islanders might have seen him as the real power, however wrong that would be. And he had thought he would fail her if pushed.

But that had been fifteen years ago. Since then, he had healed some, and Arianna had proven herself. The Islanders accepted her for who she was, and the Fey had given her no quarrel.

And his own words were haunting him: *Sometimes you could lose everything by not doing anything.*

It was time for him to start acting instead of reacting. It was time for him to go see the woman he had always loved.

CHAPTER THIRTEEN

*L*UKE HAD NEVER spent time in the Queen's bedroom before. He had seen it, of course, had even slept in
the adjacent dressing chamber, but he had never really
sat in the bedroom, and had time to contemplate it.

It was a lovely room, open, and filled with light. In the
summer, he supposed, it was filled with scents from the
garden filtering in through the open window. The bed
was big and covered with comforters, the chair he sat on
soft and welcoming. Only he didn't feel welcomed. He
sat on its edge like an intruder, a man who was out of
place in a world he had once known.

Arianna was sprawled across the bed, her gown and
fingers stained black, her face an odd gray. Her birthmark stood out red against her skin. Her eyes and mouth
twitched as if she were having a particularly bad dream.
She looked thinner than she had in years—not since he
met her had she been this thin. Then, though, she had
been gaunt from her days on the road, hiding from Rugad, the Black King.

Now she wasn't gaunt. Not yet. But the normally healthy look she had always had was gone. Her bones seemed more prominent, and somehow that made her look more Fey. The Islander in her was almost gone.

He shook his head, and stood. The bedroom door was closed, even though he knew, through protocol, that it shouldn't be. He would get in trouble for being alone with the Queen in her room, with the door closed, but he didn't care. At the moment, he didn't want to watch his back. He wanted to watch her.

Arianna hadn't been herself for a week, maybe more. And the woman she was becoming was a person he was afraid of. The glint in her blue eyes when she had demanded he leave the North Tower had a ruthlessness Luke hadn't ever seen in Arianna or Gift. Not even King Nicholas had had it.

But Jewel had. He remembered that, the way she had looked at him when she had captured him, years ago now. Luke had been a teenage boy playing at war. They had gone on a mission to destroy the Fey Shadowlands, and instead, Luke, his father, and another Islander had been captured. The Fey had killed the other Islander as an example, but they had set Luke free as a bargaining chip so that his father would teach the Fey about the Islander religion. Adrian had lived up to his end of the bargain; the Fey hadn't. They had placed some sort of spell on Luke so he would assassinate an Islander at the Fey's command. It had been a Charm spell, and they had placed other spells on him as well.

It had taken him years to get over that, and in those years, the memory of Jewel's eyes as she thought up this fake bargain had come to him in dreams. Cold, ruthless, mildly amused at herself for manipulating relationships in that way. Luke had never understood how King Nicholas had loved the woman, but he had, and through that alliance, Gift and Arianna had been born.

Luke had always felt it lucky that the children had taken after their father, not their mother.

Now, perhaps, that was ending. Now, perhaps, Arianna's Feyness was breaking through, destroying all that was worthy within her.

But that didn't explain the look of concern on her face—no, that fleeting moment of fear—when she realized she had been giving orders, walking around, and interacting with people, and she didn't remember any of it.

Luke stood and clasped his hands behind his back. He walked around the bed and studied her. She looked older in repose, lines crinkling around her eyes, the edges of her mouth. He could almost see what she would look like as an old woman.

She still twitched, her eyelids flicking, her hands moving. He couldn't believe that Seger had left her alone. Seger, who had looked frightened. And worried. And horrified.

Maybe he was looking at this all wrong. Maybe it wasn't Arianna's "Feyness" coming to the surface. Maybe it was something else.

He walked to the window and looked into the garden. The trees had little buds on their branches, the bulbs near their base beginning to sprout. The gardeners had turned the dirt, so that it looked black and soft, ready for planting.

Beyond the garden's wall, the city sprawled, Fey and Islanders doing business together as they had for the last fifteen years, first uncomfortably, and now as if they had always done it. Someday, perhaps, his people and the Fey would be one people, with skin not too light or too dark, eyes either brown or blue, and features that were a comfortable mix of both. Maybe someday, people like him, who remembered what it was like to hate the other and who had to overcome that hatred each and every day, would be gone.

He wasn't being fair to her. Of all people, he should understand what she was going through, what she *had* gone through. What it was like to wake, as if out of sleep, and find you had done something you would never normally do.

He had tried to kill the Rocaan, and he never would have done anything like that, not in his entire life. He had been a devout Rocaanist then, churchgoing and religious. He would never have killed the leader of that religion, wouldn't even have known how, except under someone else's influence.

Under magical influence.

He turned. Arianna's headaches and strange behavior, Sebastian using a voice not his own. The Black King's voice. Seger seemed to think these events were tied together. Perhaps Luke should as well.

If Arianna were under magical attack, who would do it? His understanding of the Fey Empire was that no one ever attacked the Black Ruler. It was forbidden in a thousand different ways. And no one with interest in the Throne itself could attack her either, for that would bring the Blood against Blood on the land, a concept he didn't wholly understand, but one he knew the Fey feared above all else.

Who and why? Those were the real questions. Seger was doing what she could to protect Arianna, and Luke was guarding her from the outside. But that would do no good if the threat came from within. He was a simple Islander with no magical powers. He couldn't fight magic.

She needed someone who could. Someone who could defend her against magic Luke didn't even understand. He walked back to his chair and sank into it.

If something happened to Arianna, there was only one other person in all of the world who could rule both Blue Isle and the Fey Empire, one other person who would have the same goals, and the same beliefs as Arianna.

Her brother, Gift.

But Gift had renounced power, renounced the idea of ruling, and had done the Fey equivalent of joining the Tabernacle. Gift had gone to learn the gentler side. He probably wouldn't come back here.

But he might if he knew his sister was in trouble.

Luke threaded his fingers together. He was taking matters into his own hands, but he knew that no one else would do this. He also knew that Arianna had no advisors who would even consider bringing Gift back. All of them saw Gift as a threat, not understanding that the man truly had given up something he did not want.

But Gift was halfway around the world. There was no easy way to get a message to him. Luke could send a member of his guard, but the man would have to take ships and find ways to cross two continents before he ever got to Vion, not to mention the trek into the mountains. It could take half a year, and by then it might be too late.

Arianna's hand clenched into a fist, and then unclenched. Her mouth moved and she turned slightly. Luke watched her, feeling almost guilty for his thoughts.

The only way Luke could get a quick message to Gift was to use the Fey. He would have to ask a Gull Rider to take a verbal message—a simple one: that Arianna needed Gift—and a written one as well, a message in Islander (which most Fey could not read) from Luke, begging for Gift's help. But the Gull Rider would want to know on whose authority Luke acted, and Luke had no authority with the Fey. He was merely captain of Arianna's guards, and one of her more trusted Islander companions. Nothing more.

He touched her hand, again clenched into a fist. The muscles seemed taut as if she were fighting within herself.

He would have to lie. He would have to claim he was acting on her authority, and he would have to do so without her knowledge. For he wouldn't know, if he asked her permission, if he was asking permission of Arianna or the thing that sometimes controlled her brain.

And, if he was honest, he wasn't sure either one of them would want him to send for Gift.

But someone had to. Because Gift was the only one who could save them if Arianna fell.

And if Gift was causing this—

Luke shuddered at the thought.

If Gift was causing this, then perhaps he was no

longer the man that Luke remembered, no longer the gentle soul dragged into a conflict beyond his ken.

Luke had to trust what he knew, what he believed, and what he had experienced. He knew Arianna was a good leader. But he had experienced how magic could force people to do something they didn't want to do. He believed that Gift had the same goals as Arianna.

Luke hoped he was right in all three things, because if he wasn't, then sending for Gift was wrong. But if Gift was causing this, he would come to Blue Isle anyway. Luke's message just might hasten the process.

He had to take a risk, but he had taken them before. Risks provided opportunity, even in the face of something overwhelming and impossible to understand.

He let go of Arianna's hand. He hoped she would forgive him for usurping her authority. And somehow he knew that this act, which could be construed as treason, was the least of his worries. For if something got to Arianna, if something destroyed or changed her, then the balance so precariously achieved on Blue Isle would vanish forever. And everything he loved would be gone for good.

CHAPTER FOURTEEN

SEGER HURRIED ACROSS the courtyard to the Domicile. The courtyard was empty except for the dogs rooting in piles of hay. The flagstones were dirty and slippery beneath her feet. She was walking faster than she had ever done. Usually she moved with deliberation. This time, she was nearly running.

Her heart was pounding, and she knew it wasn't because of her exertion. Sebastian's story had frightened her.

It had taken her a long time to get the story out of him. He even offered once to use the Black King's voice, and she had said no so loudly that it had startled him. Then she had forbidden him from using that voice ever again.

She had to pull the voice out of him and she had to do so quickly. Time was running out, and she hadn't even realized it until this afternoon.

The steps of the Domicile were clean, bright, and welcoming. She took them two at a time. The Domicile had once been the barracks for the Blue Isle's guards, but Luke didn't like the location. He wanted the guards stationed all over the city, with access to the palace through the maze of tunnels that ran beneath Jahn. He felt if there was an emergency, it would be better—and easier—to guard the entire city if his people knew how to get from one end to the other underground.

So the Fey Domestics had taken over the building. It was U-shaped and filled with small rooms, just as most Domiciles were. But it had no magic. The Domestics had to purge the place of the violence of its former occupants, and then they had cleaned it, inside and out. The violence had permeated all parts of the building, and for years the Domestics did a special airing every spring and every fall. In the last few years, the airings had become annual and soon, some felt, they could disappear altogether.

She stepped into the narrow hallway and stopped to catch her breath. No need to bring in all the fear she had felt in the palace. It would be better for her to be balanced, to be strong. She stepped into the main room. Spinners sat at their chairs, the work on their wheels glowing softly, bits of thread falling around them like brightly lit rain. Weavers worked the looms, one weaving the material, the other spelling it. In the kitchen, she heard the clang of pots and laughter as others experimented with food recipes. A group of Healers sat near the door, winding bandages and investing them with healing energy.

All the work slowly stopped as the other Domestics realized she had arrived. Apparently she hadn't been able to calm herself as much as she thought.

"I need the oldest Domestics here," she said, "and all the Healers. We need to speak now."

Thimble, one of the seamstresses, who was spelling the material, stood. "We have Charged this room. Can you use the hospital wing? We have no patients."

Seger nodded, turned, and headed down the hallway. The only thing they hadn't changed in all their years of residence was the darkness of this area. It discouraged the casual visitor, some said, and others liked the reminder that they were not in a Fey-built Domicile. Here they kept the rough wood planks on the floor and didn't paint the walls as they had everywhere else. It did give the illusion of being not-Fey, and right now Seger found comfort in that.

She pushed open the door to the hospital wing. The cots lay side by side in uniform precision, healing blankets folded neatly on top of them. Bandages lined one wall, herbs and potions lined the other two. There was the faint smell of springtime in here, the way that the outdoors smelled just before everything bloomed. It was a healthy, life-giving smell, and sometimes, Seger believed, that alone was enough to heal the sick.

Perhaps it was appropriate they meet here. She moved the healing blankets aside so that everyone could sit on cots. As she did, five Healers entered, and six other Domestics followed. She watched them: a Spinner, a Seamstress, an Embroiderer, a Baker, an Herb Gardener, and a Nanny. All of them friends, all of them familiar, none of them possessing great magic. She needed them for their memories. She also needed them for their calm.

"Please sit," she said, "and close the door."

The last, Lero, shut the door carefully, the touch of his hand against the wood gentle. That was the hallmark of a Nanny: the gentleness, the extreme care, the warmth. He looked at her with narrowed eyes, his lined face as calm and reassuring as if he had been her Nanny.

"What is it, Seger?" he asked.

There was no backing into it. She had to tell them directly. "Rugad is back."

Drucilla, one of the Healers, a young one born on Nye, shook her head. "That's impossible."

She was shushed by Comfort, another Healer. He was sitting beside her, his arm around her.

"How do you know?" he asked Seger.

She held out her hands. They were shaking. She was not calm. She probably wouldn't be calm until they had a solution. "What I say cannot leave here. You must take an oath to keep this quiet. Do you swear?"

As a unit, they agreed. Somehow it didn't make her calmer.

"Fifteen years ago, Rugad invaded Arianna's mind. He left a construct there. A baby. I am guessing she thought it was Sebastian."

"How is that possible?" Drucilla asked. "How could she mistake the Black King for a Golem?"

"It made sense with the events going on around them," Seger said.

"I thought constructs could only be formed in lesser minds," said Annabella, another young Healer, again from Nye. She had come to Blue Isle with Drucilla to complete her training with the best Healers of the Fey. Rugad's former Healers. Seger's people.

"I thought constructs didn't last," Drucilla said. "I mean, not fifteen years."

"There is a theory," Lero said, "that the great Golem who outlived Rugark wasn't really an independent creature, but Rugark himself who lived inside the Golem after his own body died."

Rugark was Rugad's grandfather, known, until Rugad took the Throne, as one of the best of the Black Kings.

"Rugark," Galerno, the Baker, said. He was sitting on the bed nearest Seger. He was twice as old as she was, perhaps the oldest in the room. His dark face was sprinkled lightly with flour, making the lines in his skin look as if they had been painted white.

"What about him?" Seger asked.

"He did not want his son to inherit the Black Throne," said Galerno. "He died just after his family's trip to the Eccrasian Mountains."

"But, in those days, Rugad was too young to rule," Lero said, as if remembering.

"And the Golem lived throughout the reign of Rugo, surviving five attempts to destroy it," said Galerno.

"So you're saying this has happened before, only to a Golem?" Seger asked.

Galerno shook his head. "I'm saying it could have happened. I'm saying that some among the Domestics, particularly Rugark's Healer, believed she saw Rugark in the Golem's eyes."

"Why would that occur?" Drucilla asked.

"Wouldn't destroying the Golem then have meant Blood against Blood?" Annabella asked.

Good questions all. Seger felt herself spinning. She sat on the edge of one of the cots.

Galerno gave her a sharp glance, then said, "No, destroying a Golem wouldn't mean Blood against Blood because a Golem can always be re-formed. And if it's not, who's to say what was destroyed was the real Rugark or only a distant part of him? Apparently the magic doesn't believe that's a crime that invites chaos."

"Actually, we don't know that," Lero said. "Since the Golem disappeared shortly after Rugad became Black King."

"What does this have to do with now?" Drucilla asked.

"I think your first question was better," Seger said. "Why would a Black King create a construct of himself?"

"And why would it come out now?" Annabella asked.

"It grew up," Lero said.

Annabella frowned. "We aren't taught about constructs."

"Not at your stage," Seger said. She stood. Lero was right. Constructs grew the way that any living beings grew, and this one had been a baby when Arianna found it. She had kept it inside herself, and it had grown to a teenager, with all the memories of the former Black King. Rugad, the most ruthless man ever to lead the Fey.

"How can you be sure this is Rugad?" asked Sistance.

"I spoke to the Golem," Seger said. "This is complicated, so let me talk for a moment."

The others settled in, leaning forward, concentration evident on their faces. She sighed, knowing she could tell them what she had learned from Sebastian, but not what she learned from Arianna. In fact, she had come

perilously close to breaking that confidence a few moments ago.

"Sebastian had been captured by Rugad. Rugad discovered that Sebastian had a strong Link to Arianna, and Rugad crossed that Link. The Golem followed, and, with Arianna's help, got Rugad out of Arianna's mind. Sebastian then waited until Rugad was trapped in the Link, trapped outside of any body, and Sebastian shattered, hoping that Rugad wouldn't be able to find his way to his own body. But he did somehow."

Seger paused. All of them were watching her closely.

"I treated Rugad after that shattering. It made him destroy the jar that had been holding his voice, which the Golem then captured. It also meant he got stabbed with shards from the Golem's stones. He was infected with the Golem's magic, and it made him vulnerable to attack. I removed the shards, and in fact, they became the basis for rebuilding Sebastian."

"So the Golem could have left part of himself in her, knowing he was going to shatter," Sistance said.

"He could have, if he had been a normal Golem and raised Fey. When I spoke to him today, he knew nothin about constructs."

"Not possible," said the oldest Healer, Uhce. Golem is a construct. He would have known from own creation."

"His own creation was haphazard, done by accio when Gift was a baby trying to get home. Neithe them had awareness at the time. Gift's frequent vis the body of his Changeling caused bits of himself t left behind, bits that eventually formed into Sebas He didn't know that such a thing could be done del ately." Seger sighed. "I wish he did."

They were all silent for a moment.

"Perhaps Sebastian left the construct by accide Lero asked after a moment.

Seger shook her head. "He didn't have time. Thi deliberate creature. He does one thing at a time. He thinking only of saving Arianna, and he did tha

wouldn't have left a construct. It took too much thought, too much energy."

"Was anyone else there? Anyone else that she shared her mind with?"

"The Enchanter," Seger said. "Coulter. Another Islander."

"But he's been to their Place of Power. He would know how to make a construct."

"After," Seger said. "Besides, I saw the creature inside Arianna briefly. It spoke Fey, and it knew me quite well. It was Rugad."

Galerno stood, crossing his arms over his chest. "We need a Shaman. This is not ground any of us knows how to explore."

"If it's a construct, we could remove it," Uhce said.

"How?" Seger asked. "We can't shatter Arianna."

"But it's not fully formed," Uhce said. "It may not be completely integrated. We might be able to move it to the Golem."

"If we can move it," Drucilla said, "why don't we simply take it out?"

She was young, Seger knew, and not very well trained, but very talented. Her work had always been with the true illnesses, the physical kind, not with the magical kind.

"Because it isn't something we can hold," Seger said. "It's something we have to capture. We lure it to Sebastian. That would be easier than trying to remove it ourselves. We don't have the skill. But it might cross the Link to Sebastian, if we do this right."

"Then what?" Drucilla asked.

"Then we shatter it," Seger said.

"Destroying the Golem," Drucilla said.

"Maybe," Seger said. "It has survived three shatterings. I was thinking of shattering it to remove the voice."

"No," Comfort said. "If we leave the voice, the construct might not object to the move."

"If we leave the voice, we run the risk of letting Sebastian become Rugad," Seger said.

"It's not as bad as having Arianna lose herself to him," Uhce said.

Seger looked at her. Uhce shrugged. "If she loses herself to Rugad, we cannot prove it. There is no magical diagnosis for this. She is the Black Queen, and she remains so. She would simply get rid of us, and bring in a new healing team, saying we were the problem. And really, she would be right."

"How's that?" Annabella asked.

"Rugad ruled us for most of his life. It is only recently that his rule has been questioned, that his abilities were seen as a problem rather than something good for the Fey. He has every right to rule us, just as she does."

"But he's dead," Drucilla said.

"Is he?" Uhce said. "We do not know if a construct is real or not."

"You just said it wasn't." Drucilla looked at Seger.

"I said we couldn't hold it." Seger's heart was pounding hard again. She had worked with Rugad, and she had thought him a necessary evil. But in the end, she had disobeyed him by keeping the Golem's shards. She had thought Rugad wrong, and she had acted contrary to all her training. She had disobeyed a Black King. No one else knew that. Just her and Rugad.

"Then shouldn't we let this alone?" Drucilla asked.

"If we left it alone, wouldn't it be Blood against Blood?" Annabella asked.

"Rugad doesn't have to kill Arianna," Comfort said. "He just has to control her. And that should be hard. She's a Shifter. He wasn't."

Seger ran a hand through her long hair. "He has made her Shift against her will. He's only done this once, but that means this construct knows the magic."

"It also means the construct might be close to total control. We have to act fast," Uhce said.

"We have to explain this to Sebastian," Seger said.

"What's to explain?" Comfort asked. "He's a Golem."

"There is some debate as to whose Golem he is,"

Seger said. "Gift formed him, but some say that Jewel—who is a Mystery—is the one who kept him alive."

"A Golem controlled by a Mystery?" Annabella asked.

"Held by a Mystery," Seger said. "There's a difference."

"What is it?" Drucilla asked.

Seger looked at her. "The difference is that a Golem held by a Mystery could be considered alive."

"Alive? But it can reassemble after it shatters," Drucilla said. "Living creatures don't do that."

"Yes," Seger said. "But I don't mean that it lives and breathes and eats. I mean that it has its own existence, and there is value in that existence. This has to be his choice."

"Can he make it?" Comfort asked. "I mean, if he has Rugad's voice, perhaps he is already owned by Rugad."

"Perhaps," Seger said. "And if that's true, then logically the Golem would want the construct."

"Logically," Sistance said, "the Golem would want the construct to stay where it is."

"This is a delicate procedure," Comfort said. "Something that is nearly beyond a Healer's skill. We need a Shaman, just like Galerno said."

"There are no Shaman on Blue Isle. The nearest one is in Nye. It would take months to get him here." Seger threaded her fingers together.

"We may not have months," Sistance said.

"Would it hurt to try?" Drucilla asked. "And if we fail—"

"Then it knows that we are aware of its existence," Seger said. "It might take control quicker."

"If it can," Comfort said.

"What about an Enchanter?" Lero asked. "Couldn't an Enchanter cross a Link and remove the construct?"

"I believe Arianna's Links are closed," Seger said. She couldn't say any more, not even about the faded Link, the one that hadn't been used in a long time.

"Even if they weren't, it would be a risk," Comfort said. "The Enchanter would have to know what he's doing."

"And the only Enchanter of worth on Blue Isle," Lero said, "is Coulter, who is not Fey-trained."

"He is trained," Seger said. "He made a point of learning. He might have other ideas on how to help Arianna."

"Where is he?" Uhce asked.

"I believe in the Cliffs of Blood. We would have to send for him," Seger said.

"Again, it would take time," Comfort said, "time we may not have."

Seger shook her head. "I wish we had another Visionary."

"We have Infantry Leaders," said Annabella. The entire group looked at her as if she had made a mistake. She shrugged. "They have Vision."

"But not enough," Seger said. Somehow this discussion frustrated her more than she had expected. She had hoped, with the assembled age and history and healing knowledge in the room, that they would come up with a better solution.

"You look discouraged," Lero said to her softly.

She looked at him, then sighed. "If she has integrated the construct so much that it can make her Shift without her wanting to, I'm not sure we can separate it. The voice is threaded throughout Sebastian's stone. I'm afraid the construct has done the same with Arianna."

"We could still separate it," Uhce said. "It would take time and patience—"

"During all of which the construct would be trying to fight us. Don't forget," Seger said, "we're not dealing with any construct. We're dealing with Rugad."

"So you believe," Comfort said. "I still think it could be an accidental dropping from the Golem."

Seger rose and rubbed her hands together. "You wouldn't believe that if you had seen the way it looked out of her eyes. It was Rugad. I knew it the moment I heard her—the Golem's story. It was Rugad, and it knows what he knew. Only once it consolidates, once it makes her flesh its own, it'll be more powerful than it ever was."

"How do you know that?" Annabella asked softly.

"A great ruler's mind," Seger said, clasping her hands behind her back and pacing forward, "the mind of a man who has lived for ninety-two years, in the body of a young female Shifter. The physical power would be immense."

"Won't we lose our Visionary Leader?" Drucilla asked. "I mean, can a construct have Vision?"

Seger turned to her. She didn't know the answer to that. Strong constructs were a mystery because they were so rare.

"Arianna will still have her Vision," Comfort said.

"But she'll be trapped inside her own mind," Seger said. "She might not be willing—or able—to share what she Sees."

"So if the construct takes her over, he runs the risk of ruling without Vision," Drucilla said.

"Perhaps," Uhce said. "But we are taught that Visions are gifts from the Powers and Mysteries. Do they send that gift to a particular body, or to a particular soul?"

"Body," Comfort said. "Magic all originates in the body."

"You sound so certain," Seger said. "Yet when we treat magic we treat it throughout the person, not as if it was lodged in a single spot, like the heart."

"But some magics are specific to the body," Comfort said. "Shifting is, for example. The body has to be able to make that transition. The same applies to Bird and Beast Riders, and Wisps."

"Yes," Seger said. "But did they train their bodies into that ability because their personality had the gift for that kind of magic or did the body give them that magic?"

"The question is beyond us," Sistance said. "And not something we can answer." He stood too, placing his hand on the edge of the cot, as if for support. "Here's what I believe. I believe we need to act fast. I believe we need to do what we can, and if we fail, we ask for outside help."

"No," Seger said. "We send for the help. We send for Coulter, we send for the nearest Shaman. We should probably send for Gift."

"I don't think that's wise," Uhce said, her voice somber.

"Why not?"

"Because if you're right, and Arianna has been over-taken by her great-grandfather, the man her father—who was not of Black Blood—killed, then how will Gift re-act?" Uhce took a deep breath. "He will make it his goal to get rid of Rugad and to bring his sister back."

"It could accidentally spark Blood against Blood," Galerno said, as if he hadn't thought of it before.

"Yes," Uhce said, "and Gift would believe he was in the right. If we fail now, all that will happen will be that we will once again live beneath Rugad's rule. We did that for years. We can survive it."

"If the Powers allow it," Lero said.

Seger nodded. "I had forgotten that. If the Powers feel this is a perversion of all that we are, they might help us."

"Or they might let us flounder," said Galerno. "The old stories are not clear on how much the Powers inter-fere and how much they simply watch."

Seger clasped her hands behind her back and looked at the others. They didn't know Arianna, at least not well. She did. She had to make one final plea.

"Arianna is a good woman," Seger said. "She has kept a fragile peace among a warrior people through the sheer strength of her personality. She has made the Empire richer, not by conquering another country, but by improv-ing and concentrating on the lands we already have. If Ru-gad takes over, we go back to conquering. Most of us here will go back to trying to save lives that are, in some way, ruined by violence and death. The Empire will grow richer not because we are growing things, and making things better, but because we are acquiring. Someday that fragile thread, the thread between holdings, will break. It almost did when Rugad died. It might if he goes on to Leut."

"Do you think he would?" Drucilla asked softly.

Galerno looked at her. "The third Place of Power lies in the lands we have not yet seen."

Annabella closed her eyes. Uhce let out a small hiss of breath. Clearly none of them had thought of that.

Seger watched them, realizing that they were now feeling the same fears, the same frustrations, that she was. "Uhce's right. We act now, and we do the best we can. At the same time, we send for Coulter, and not one but all the Shaman we can think of. Some may not yet have the talent we need, and if we fail, we will need a lot of talent."

"If the construct takes over Arianna, and we try to dislodge him," Uhce said, "he will see that as treason."

Seger shuddered. She had seen what Rugad had done to those he felt had disobeyed him. Some he slaughtered. Others he left alive, so gravely damaged that they would have rather died.

The entire room was silent for a moment. They were all watching her. Some of the other Domestics, the non-Healers, hadn't said a word. They looked frightened and out of their depth, and now that Uhce had reminded them what Rugad was like when crossed, they seemed almost paralyzed.

Seger swallowed hard. She was the one who had worked as Rugad's personal Healer. She was the one who knew the inner workings of the Black Family better than any of them. The others would listen to her because of that authority alone.

"We work to support life," she said. "As Domestics, that is our mandate. To heal, to grow, to move forward. Rugad died fifteen years ago. His life has ended. Arianna's continues. It seems to me that we continue our work. We support life."

"And if we fail?" Comfort asked softly.

"Then we go to those more powerful than we are, the Shaman and the Enchanters, just as we planned."

"And if they fail?"

Seger closed her eyes. "It becomes a matter for the Mysteries and Powers."

"If they'll interfere," Galerno said.

Seger nodded. She opened her eyes. "You do not have to help me with this. Any of you who wants to back out, can do so now, as long as you say nothing about this meeting."

No one moved. No one spoke. They would all stand behind her. That, at least, was good. Saving Arianna would have been impossible alone.

CHAPTER FIFTEEN

*I*T WAS BARELY dawn when Gift slipped out of his bed. He dressed in the chill silence, pulling on his apprentice robes even though he no longer held that position. He made the bed, as all apprentices had to, with such precision that an inspection later would find the sheet crisp, the blanket folded, the pillow fluffed. He doubted he would sleep here again, but he saw no reason not to adhere to the rules.

He hadn't really slept here the night before. He had tried. But his door had opened countless times: Shaman coming in to report things they didn't feel they could say in the meeting. Some had Visions of Kerde dying at the hands of a Fey with dark hair trailing down his back; others had Visions of the Triangle of Might forming across the land; and still others had Visions of Blood against Blood, instigated when Gift again set foot on Blue Isle.

But those Visions were somehow expected. They didn't disturb him like some of the legends did, the legends no one wanted to speak of before the other Shaman.

Those who reported the legends insisted he not get out of bed, he not look at them. Many of them wanted to pretend as if they were speaking to someone who wasn't really there. He let them. He wanted to hear what they had to say, not know who felt they had to hide their identity while speaking.

So the whispers came to him, like Warnings:

". . . the Throne consumes its standard . . ."

". . . the Black Ruler is the opposite of Shaman . . ."

". . . Anyone who touches the Throne loses his heart . . ."

Gift heard those over and over, but they weren't the ones that chilled him. The one that chilled him was just as simple, but even more terrifying:

". . . The Throne feeds on blood . . ."

He heard variations of that all night:

". . . The Throne was created by blood . . ."

". . . The Throne constantly seeks new blood . . ."

". . . The Throne will not be satisfied until the land is covered in blood . . ."

And the one that made him wonder about all the others:

". . . The Throne strives for Blood against Blood . . ."

After that, he hadn't been able to sleep, even though most of his visitors appeared in the early part of the night. When he did close his eyes, he saw the floor of the cavern, Blue Isle's Place of Power, the floor that had once been white. In his father's hand was a shiny black stone, created by the joining of his hand with the hand of his enemy, created when the dripping power from their joint magic changed the floor to the color of blood.

Gift hadn't seen the magic—he and Arianna had hidden from it, afraid that its effects might kill them as well—but he had been told the story and he had seen the floor. He knew that there was power in this world that he did not understand, power that the Fey, for all their mastery of magic, did not understand either.

He hoped to gain some understanding that day.

He pulled on boots despite the discomfort. He was no longer an apprentice, and he didn't have to follow Shamanic practices anymore. Then he left his room.

He walked through the kitchen, took some bread left by the Domestics the night before, and drank water until he felt bloated. He didn't know when he would get a chance to drink again.

When he was done, he let himself out into the growing light.

The sun hadn't risen over the mountains yet, but glowed behind them, coloring the sky a pale orange. It would be a beautiful day.

He hurried through the village and saw no one. Not even the master gardeners were out this early. The individual huts looked as if their occupants were still asleep. Only the joint quarters for the Shaman still too young to go off on their own looked as if anyone were moving inside. He avoided the windows and jogged toward the mountain.

When he reached the stairs, he hesitated. He had been forbidden to go up here alone. But that had been when he was an apprentice, when he swore he would let the Shaman control his life. As an apprentice, he was the lowliest of the low, and he had allowed that. He had been true to his promise, even if the Shaman hadn't been true to theirs. They had never seen him as an apprentice, probably always afraid he would usurp their authority as a member of the Black Family.

Doing so, however, hadn't crossed his mind. Until yesterday. Now he would leave here, as they wanted him to do, but he would do so on his own terms.

He started up the stairs. They felt the same as they had the week before, making each step he took seem easy and light. He had been afraid that some sort of magic would block him, would prevent him from climbing at all. Perhaps prevention magic was built into the stairs, but it didn't affect him. In fact, he didn't have to regulate his pace this time. He wasn't with Madot, and she wasn't trying to slow him down. This time, he was alone, and the faster he reached the top the better.

The shimmer from the Place of Power drew him like

the Place of Power on Blue Isle had. It was a pull that seemed to wrap itself around him and lift him. He let it. He jogged up the steps, feeling no sense of exertion at all.

The sun rose and broke through the mountain peaks, shedding golden light on the stairs, making them gleam. Grass was poking through the dirt where there had been none a week before, and the air had a fresh scent to it.

It seemed to take him only a few moments to reach the first plateau, although he knew it had taken him longer than that. The sun was past the peaks now, and when he turned and looked down, he saw Shaman like small ants moving through the village, going about their daily tasks. None of them seemed to notice him. None of them seemed to know that he was breaking all of their rules.

They would figure it out soon enough.

He made himself eat part of the bread on the platform, and take some deep breaths there too, even though he didn't want to do either. What he really wanted to do was to push everything and everyone aside so that he could get to the Place of Power, so that he could answer the call of that shimmer.

Part of the reason he took his time here was to make sure that he was in control of himself. After his speech the day before, the last thing he wanted was to have the magic control him.

A slight wind had picked up. It was cool. He felt it ruffle his hair, blow some of the crumbs from his hand. He pocketed the rest of the bread and started up the stairs again.

He was getting warm, despite the breeze. He still ran these last few steps, but he paced himself, making sure that he didn't go too fast, so that he was exhausted when he reached the top. When he got there, he knew, he would have to face the Shaman Protectors. And he might have to do things to get past them that he hadn't considered doing in years.

The idea made his breath come a little shorter. He

didn't want to think about what might happen at the top. He only wanted to get there. He needed advice, and the Place of Power was the only place he could get it.

He made himself slow down as he got closer to the top. The sun had risen even higher now, and shadows fell across his path. The long trek had seemed as if it had only taken a heartbeat, but he had spent time at it. The steep steps helped him breathe, rest, keep a measured pace.

When he neared, a staff hit the polished stone platform in front of his face. He looked up. He wasn't entirely to the top; he still had a few feet to go.

It looked as if he might not make it the rest of the way. Pelô and two other Protectors, a man and a woman, blocked his way.

They all wore the robes that blended in with the mountain, and they all plunked their staves before him, creating a barrier to the rest of his climb. The polished stone platform looked like something he could easily fall off.

The shimmer from the cave, though, felt like a pull, reminding him of his goal.

"You have no place here," Pelô said.

"Says who?" Gift asked. He pulled himself up another step, careful to keep his hands away from their staves.

"We guard this place," Pelô said as if Gift were a stranger to him.

"For my family," Gift said.

"For the Fey," said another of the Protectors, a woman. She looked like most other Shaman, her white hair exploding around her face, her skin wrinkled and dark. Gift did not recognize her or the third guardian, and that did not surprise him. The Protectors kept to themselves.

"I am Fey," Gift said.

"Half Fey," Pelô said.

"Fey," Gift said. "If you count blood, then you should always count blood. Most Fey have the blood of other races running through their veins."

He climbed another step. Now his torso rose above

the platform. If they wanted to push him backward, he had nothing to hang on to.

Pelô lifted his staff. Obviously he was thinking just that.

Gift smiled. It felt like a cold smile. He didn't mean anything by it except a showing of teeth. "Push me off," he said, "and I will fall a very long way. If I hit my head and die, you have not only killed someone, which will make you lose your power, you will have also killed the closest heir to the Black Throne. Don't think my family won't investigate that."

"I will make certain you're only injured," Pelô said, lifting his staff higher.

"And if you injure me, I'll make sure my sister pulls all the Shaman from Protectors Village. This place will be ours," Gift said. "You will have no rights."

Pelô stopped, holding his staff slightly off the ground. The other Protectors looked at him, worry on their faces.

"If you let me go by with no questions asked," Gift said, "you can continue your business here as if nothing has changed."

"To let you by would be to fail in our duty," Pelô said.

"To let me by, or to let anyone by?" Gift asked.

"You," the woman whispered. Pelô shot her an angry look. She shrugged. "You have been to the other Place of Power."

"Your people control it," the third Protector said. "What will stop you from finding the Triangle?"

"Why you, of course," Gift said with as much sarcasm as he could muster. The third Protector looked surprised. "Or should I say, the Shaman from the village?"

"Are they coming for you?" Pelô asked.

Gift shrugged. "It doesn't matter. I'm not going in to find the Triangle. I wouldn't know how if I wanted to, and I wouldn't know how to coordinate my efforts with anyone on Blue Isle. I'm going to see my mother."

"Your mother?" Pelô asked.

"She's a Mystery. I can't see her anywhere except a Place of Power."

Pelô frowned. He had clearly not expected that.

"You may come with me if you want," Gift said. "All of you can. I swear I won't touch anything, nor will I remove anything. I'm just going in the mouth until I can see if my mother will show up."

"You think she will?" Pelô asked.

"You think she will not?" the third Protector asked at the same time.

"I haven't seen her since my father disappeared," Gift said. "Except that I got a sense of her just before I touched the Black Throne. I want to know if it was really her I felt, or something else."

Pelô set his staff down gently. It no longer seemed like a threat. "We could forbid you."

"You could," Gift said. "But you can't enforce it. If I choose to use violence to go around you, I can. The only people you prevent from using the cave are those who don't know the limits of your powers. You might want to think about that in the future when you choose your Protectors."

Pelô narrowed his eyes, but he stood back. At his cue, the others did as well. Gift took the remaining stairs and stepped onto the platform. As before, he suddenly felt the effects of his exertion. His legs were tired, his hands ached, and he was thirsty.

He reached into the pocket of his robe, and pulled out the half-eaten loaf of bread. "I'll share," he said, "if you have water."

The female Protector disappeared behind a rock. The male Protector took some bread, then looked at Pelô as if asking permission. Pelô nodded once, a small movement that seemed grudging.

The woman came back with a stone mug filled with water. Gift lifted it to his mouth, and then said, "This isn't from the cavern itself, is it?"

"No," the woman said as if he had shocked her.

Gift held out the mug to her. "You first."

She took it and drank, something she wouldn't have

done if the water had come from inside the cavern. Then she offered the mug to Gift.

He took it and drank. The water was cool, and slightly brackish, just like the water in the village below. It tasted fine, though, considering how thirsty he was. He took a bit of bread and gave them the rest. Then he turned to Pelô. "Are you coming with me?"

Pelô nodded.

Gift wasn't surprised. If he had been doing Pelô's job, he would have had the same response.

"You two remain here," Pelô said to his companions. "Make sure he has come alone."

The woman nodded. The man looked down the stairs, as if he could see the friends that had come with Gift. Gift shook his head slightly. As if he had any friends here. He had people who feared him, and people who feared him less. Plus a handful who believed he was doing something he shouldn't be doing, and another handful who believed he needed to be the next Black King.

At that thought, he glanced at the stairs leading to the Black Throne. A shudder ran through him. He did not want to go down there again. Instead, he walked past the polished bench.

The mouth of the cave was recessed into the reddish stone. It looked like the mouth to any ordinary cave: nothing marked it as separate, unlike the Place of Power on Blue Isle. There the swords stood as testament to the religion founded after the cave had been discovered. But the Fey had no real religion. They had accepted the magic as magic, not as a gift from God. They had treated it with no reverence at all, and that was reflected in their cave.

The stone platform, though, remained polished all the way to the cave's mouth. Gift walked toward it slowly, followed by Pelô a half step behind him. At the mouth, Gift again felt the tug of the cave's magic, a visceral thing, as if the entire area longed for him to be inside it.

His hands were shaking. This cave felt different from the one at home. This one felt older, more powerful, and not as benign. Perhaps that was because the other Place of Power had, in some ways, been his. It had also been untouched for centuries. This one had Shaman coming to it all the time.

As he grew closer to the mouth, he heard water burbling. It sounded louder than the fountain in Blue Isle's Place of Power. He glanced at Pelô, who tilted his head slightly when his gaze met Gift's. It was a mocking look, a look that challenged, although Gift wasn't exactly sure what the challenge was.

The cavern looked dark from the outside. Gift took a step through the mouth, and felt warmth. A warm dry breeze that smelled faintly of cinnamon, and beneath it, crisp, fresh water.

The floor here glowed red, a red so dark it was almost black. The color was halfway between the red on the floor of Blue Isle's Place of Power, and the black stone his father had shown him. Gift shuddered. Was that how the Throne turned black? So much power spilled that it had fallen into the floor, the walls, the very ground itself, and from that ground arose the Throne?

He didn't want to speculate. Instead he looked.

The walls here were red, a light red, adding to the glow. The ceiling was still white. All of the stone was polished and shone in the unnatural light.

There was nothing on the walls. No swords, no globes, no tapestries. The walls were sheer, as if time had polished them smooth.

But there were stairs in the center of the cavern. A long flight of stairs, as dark a red as the floor. Gift stepped inside, felt the warmth envelop him like an old friend. The sound of burbling water grew louder. He peered over the stairs, expecting to see a table and a fountain, just as there was in Blue Isle.

Instead, he saw a stream that cascaded down a far wall and bubbled through the large polished stone at the bottom of the stairs, then disappeared into a hole beneath the stairs themselves. The water looked powerful, almost angry, a violent mixture of froth and movement.

He backed away. Pelô was watching him. Gift felt the hair rise on his arms, the back of his neck. He turned.

"It is not as you expect?" Pelô asked.

Gift wasn't going to answer. He wasn't going to give Pelô the satisfaction. "The tunnels leading off the stream, have all of them been explored?"

"Some," Pelô said. "And some of the explorers never returned."

Gift nodded. He knew how those tunnels felt, if they were anything like the ones in the Place of Power at home. He'd gone into one without his father's permission. There was a sensation of time slowing, and the feeling that if he took any branch, he would end up somewhere else. He had gotten a sense of this place in one of Blue Isle's tunnels, and the sense of another place too. He supposed here, he would sense Blue Isle's Place of Power and that third, as yet undiscovered place. But he could not go there. That took the help of another, just as he had said.

He took a deep breath. He hadn't come in here to see the cave. He came here to see if his mother would appear to him again. "Give me some room," he said.

Pelô bowed slightly, another mocking gesture. "As you wish." He retreated to the cave's mouth and stood there like a sentry, holding his staff as if it were a spear.

Gift walked to the stairs and sat on the top step. The stone here felt unnaturally smooth, and too warm. The redness seemed to swirl inside it, coming up against him and then moving away like water. It almost seemed to him as if the redness wanted to touch him and in touching him, was satisfied and left.

"Mother?" he whispered. "If that was you I saw by the Black Throne, please talk to me."

His whisper echoed faintly down the stairs and toward the water where it seemed to bounce along the top of the froth. He could almost see his words.

Why should she appear to him? Why would she? She had disappeared with his father, her one true love, into one of the tunnels off the Place of Power in Blue Isle. She didn't need Gift anymore. She had fulfilled her purpose.

Or had she? Her enemy still lived. Matthias, the one she hated the most, was the last Gift heard, still alive in Constant, attempting to restart the religion of Rocaanism.

"Mother?" he whispered again.

He felt a hand on his back. He turned, about to tell Pelô to back away, when he saw himself looking into a familiar face.

Arianna's face, only more Fey, harsher and wiser at the same time.

His mother.

Jewel.

She held out her arms and he slid into them, letting her hug him. He hadn't seen her in a long time and he thought he had lost this need for her, a feeling that had grown in him at the other Place of Power, when he had seen her almost every day.

Over her shoulder, he saw Pelô frown. Gift's movement must have looked strange. Only three people could see Gift's mother. To everyone else, she was invisible, something they couldn't even hear or sense. Pelô knew this, of course, but he probably hadn't seen it before. Most Fey hadn't.

Slowly Gift pulled back and studied her. She looked the same. She could choose how she wanted to look and she always chose how she looked on the day she first saw his father. She had been a young woman, a teenager, her long black hair in a braid down her back, an old-fashioned Fey leather jerkin covering dark breeches. Once she had seemed impossibly old to him. Now she looked like a child with an old woman's eyes.

"You didn't hear my Warning," she said.

"In the Throne room?" he asked.

She nodded.

"I saw you for a moment, and that was it."

She closed her eyes and bowed her head. Her hair turned silver along its roots, and then went back to black. "I was afraid of that," she said. "It's my fault. I should have Warned you before you came here. But I lost track of time."

She raised her head, her eyes open, and put her finger beneath his chin. "So much time has passed."

"Yes," he said.

"You haven't married."

"No."

"You haven't even loved."

He flinched. "No."

"Arianna has no children." His mother shook her head. "You must, Gift. You must or Bridge's children will inherit. They will lose all that we have won."

"Is that what you wanted to Warn me about?" he asked.

"It's too late now." Her words were soft. "What I wanted to stop you from doing you have already done. A Warning now is wasted."

He swallowed. "You didn't want me to touch the Throne."

The finger beneath his chin slid into a caress. "It's voracious, Gift. It triggers dark magic. It will devour all that is good about the Fey, all that is good about the world."

"Why didn't it devour me?"

Her smile was small. "It tried. But you have your father within you. His strength. And he has none of the blackness that I brought to you. You are the first member of my family to resist the Throne. I'm proud of that."

"I hear some reservations, though," Gift said.

She nodded. "It couldn't take you, and Arianna has the same strengths you do. So it released a Searchlight."

"Which is what caught me? That light?"

"Yes," she said. "It sought dark magic, or Black Blood that would fulfill the Throne's mandate. It wants the Triangle, and then the world."

"The Throne is a thing," Gift said. "It can't control the world."

Her gaze flattened as if he had failed an important

test. "It can control the person who controls the world," she said. "That is the same thing."

"But you already said it cannot control Arianna."

"Not as she is," his mother said. "But she is becoming what it needs."

He frowned. "What do you mean?"

His mother let her hand fall. Lines formed in the corner of her mouth. "She has been infected with dark magic." She looked down the stairs, toward the burbling water. "And there is the possibility that you have too."

"Possibility?" Gift asked. "You mean you don't know?"

His mother shook her head. "Some things are hidden from me."

"Why?"

She sighed, ran her hands along her face, then bowed her head. For a long moment, she didn't answer him. It was as if she was trying to think of the proper way to respond. Finally she shook her head slightly as if rejecting the very thought she'd had, and then she said, "There are factions in the Powers. Some believe that the Throne will do what it will; others believe the light will prevail. They forbid the Mysteries from interfering in this battle. The Powers prefer to watch, to see how this all will unfold. Because they cannot agree, they prefer to let events take their course."

Gift's hands felt moist. He rubbed them on his robe. "Do the Powers usually interfere that much?"

"They guide," she said. "They let us provide Visions and Warnings and they have their favorites. Sometimes they allow things to happen that shouldn't, and sometimes they throw something new into the mix just to see what it will change."

"You seem like you don't approve."

She shrugged. "I'm a lowly Mystery. I take myself out of the politics most of the time. There isn't much I can do to change the Powers. So I enjoy what's been given to me, and I survive as best I can."

"But you disobeyed them," Gift said. "You tried to Warn me when I approached the Throne."

"I should have been able to Warn you," Jewel said. "The Black Palace is in this Place of Power. You should have been able to see me. The Powers blocked it. They let you make your choice."

"And I chose wrong."

She turned, her dark eyes flashing. "You let a Shaman trick you," she said, and there was fire behind her words. "You, a Black Heir, let a Shaman treat you as if you were nothing, and you allowed it."

"I was trying to become a Shaman."

"That is a lowly aspiration for a man like you."

"Is it?" Gift asked. "The Shaman control the Places of Power."

"Do they?" Jewel asked. "They share the same skills as Visionaries."

"They have other skills."

"They have developed and trained the other skills. There is nothing to say that someone else with Vision can't use the Places of Power. Your father, a man who lacks Vision, managed to use his to save Blue Isle."

Gift hadn't thought of that. He had been raised within the Fey traditions, and apparently he hadn't thought outside of them. He shook his head slightly, frowned, felt the discomfort that an idea like that placed in him.

His parents had defied convention in so many ways: through their agreement, their marriage, their children. Gift had been raised by Wisps who believed in following rules and not asking questions. His grandfather, a man who had made the rules, had seemed terrifying, and his great-grandfather, a man who embodied the rules, even more so. Gift never thought of questioning them, never thought of defying the rules.

The only time he had ever disobeyed something important had been with the encouragement of his father. Gift hadn't wanted the Black Throne. He hadn't wanted to rule. And Arianna was better suited to it. No one seemed to care that she ruled as long as Gift didn't care. It didn't feel so much like defiance as the right thing to do.

And the other right thing, it seemed, was to become a Shaman. The Shaman ran the Place of Power, and on Blue Isle, the Place of Power had once been controlled by the religious. It seemed the same thing to him. Now that both were in the Fey Empire, it seemed logical that the Shaman would control them, and what better place for him to be than among the Shaman?

"You have seen the Shaman now," his mother said. "You know what they are. They have failings like the rest of us. You cannot let your memories of one guide your actions toward another."

He nodded, but he wasn't really listening, not to that part. He had already learned that. He had learned it all too well, in fact, and probably at great cost.

"You said something is happening to Ari." He used his sister's nickname on purpose, hoping that Pelô wouldn't catch it, and even if he did, that he wouldn't understand it.

Gift's mother stood. She was wringing her hands together and her dark hair had turned half-silver. She looked as she would have looked now if she had lived: a woman in her fifties who had been through a lot.

She opened her mouth, faded until she was nearly invisible, and then re-formed, her fist clenched. "This is what I cannot say. I am forbidden to say."

Her voice sounded strangled.

Gift watched her. "It has something to do with the Searchlight I released from the Black Throne?"

"You did not release it," his mother said. "It left after you rejected the Throne. You cannot take responsibility for that. It would have happened one day no matter what. You or your sister would have had the same reaction. The question was only in the timing."

"What's it doing?" Gift asked.

"I told you all I can," his mother said.

"But what should I do?"

She crouched beside him. The web of fine lines on her face made her seem wiser than she ever had. And sadder.

"Guard your Place of Power," she said. And then she touched his face. "And make an heir to the Throne—both thrones—as quickly as you can. Bring a child untouched by the past into this mix. It is the only way."

"What about going to Jahn?" he asked, a quick glance at Pelô to see if he was listening. Pelô stood in the same position beside the mouth. Gift couldn't tell if he was listening or not.

His mother caught that glance, seemed to understand Gift's caution. "I fear for you if you go there," she said. "Sometimes dark magic triggers other dark magic."

"But Ari needs my support," Gift said.

"It will take you months to reach her." His mother's voice was sad. "And by then she will be gone."

"Dead?" Gift asked.

His mother's gaze met his. "I chose my words carefully, Gift. I have to now."

He felt cold, despite the warmth of the stone floor. "So you're saying that I should avoid the palace? But if I do, and something happens, who will have the Throne?"

At that, Pelô did turn. Gift's mother sighed. She kissed Gift lightly on the head, and then held his cheeks with her hands. "I cannot tell you any more. I have to go."

"But if Ari's gone," Gift said, "then who—?"

His mother put a finger against his lips. "All I can tell you is this: You must be vigilant. You must do all you can to avoid Blood against Blood."

Then she pulled him up and hugged him. He hugged her back, startled as always at her solidness. She seemed like a living person to him, even though others couldn't see her. Even though to everyone else except Gift's father and Matthias, she was dead.

"Remember the children, Gift," she said. "They are your future."

And then she disappeared.

He staggered forward, hating that. He had always hated that, the way she could just vanish as if she had never been. It made him feel as alone as he had before he met her, before he realized that he was special to someone.

Pelô watched him as if Gift had suddenly lost his mind. Gift stopped moving and forced himself to sit. Pelô wouldn't know that she was gone. He would think Gift was still conferring with her.

And Gift needed time to recover. His mother had said many things he didn't completely understand—dark magic, rules among the Powers—but the one thing he had understood chilled him completely.

Arianna was in trouble. By the time he got back, she might be gone. Not dead, necessarily. Gone. The distinction chilled him and his mother's concern for the future chilled him as well. It was as if she had already given up on Gift and Arianna. Something had tainted them, something had made them unworthy of his parents' goals, and the only way to set everything right was to have children, new heirs.

That would take a minimum of fifteen years, probably more. Did that mean he gave up on his sister until then?

Guard Blue Isle's Place of Power, his mother had said, and avoid Arianna. Dark magic might be catching. But he might already have it.

He had to leave, just as he had realized earlier. He had to leave, but he wasn't sure where he would go. Home. That much was certain. He would return to the Isle. But he wanted to go to Arianna's side, and his mother said that was the worst thing he could do.

He ran a hand through his hair. Of the seven Visions he had had when he touched the Black Throne, three had been of his sister. And they had run in a progression. If he closed his eyes, he could still See them:

Arianna was standing before the Black Throne, looking at it with such longing that it frightened him. He wanted to warn her, to tell her to stand back, but it was almost as if he didn't recognize her or the look on her face. He took a step toward her—

Arianna, her face gone as if someone had drawn it and then wiped it away, calling his name—

Arianna, screaming—

How could he abandon her to that, no matter what

the risk? He shivered once, felt a coldness run through him that had more to do with the future than with anything else. His future. His choices had just narrowed. Some of the dreams he'd had for himself, he had to now put away. He needed to do things that were right for generations to come.

He had to assume the mantle of a leadership he didn't want, a leadership he might not take, but one he had to protect at all costs. He had tried to run away from it, he had refused it, and still it kept coming to him. His mother had said this was inevitable, and he was beginning to realize that she was right.

Sometimes choice was an illusion. Sometimes it was a dangerous illusion, one that other people could take advantage of, one that could keep a man blind to the realities around him.

He bowed his head. His eyes were open now, his future set. He could accept it, fight it, or make the best of it.

And all the while he would hope that his mother was wrong.

CHAPTER SIXTEEN

BREAKFAST WAS TWO slices of yesterday's bread, a bit of cheese left over from the wheel his mother had bought a month before, and some root tea. Matt ate it slowly, feeling conspicuously alone at the table. His mother was still asleep, sprawled across the bed as if she had fallen there in exhaustion, her clothes and boots still on.

Alex hadn't come home last night, just as he hadn't come home either of the two nights before that. He had said he was with their father, but Matt wasn't sure that was all Alex was doing. Alex wasn't saying how he spent his days.

He wasn't saying much to Matt at all anymore.

Matt broke off a hunk of bread and ate it, letting its heavy texture fill his mouth. His family had been precarious for a long time, but he didn't know how it had managed to fall apart so badly in the last week. No matter what he did, no matter what he said, Alex would no longer talk to him. Sometimes Alex looked at him with cold eyes, as if Matt had been the one who had done something wrong.

All Matt had done was try to help them both.

Coulter, at least, provided warmth and help. Coulter was beginning to explain the types of magic that the Islanders and the Fey knew about, and in that explanation, Matt had learned some important things.

He had learned that magic drains its user. He had learned that magic always exacts a price. He also learned that someone who had an abundance of magic must use his powers to benefit those who have none.

Those were the rules he could understand. They made sense. But the one he did not understand, the one that frightened him, was the one that Scavenger believed Matt should have been thrilled about.

Matt learned about Enchanters. Enchanters, like him, had all the powers of the Fey except Vision. Even then, Enchanters shared some of the powers of a Visionary. What the Enchanter lacked was the ability to See the future. An Enchanter could use any magic that had been altered, invented, or designed, not as well as those who specialized only in that magic, but a bit nonetheless. Few Enchanters tried Shape-Shifting spells, for example, and even fewer tried to pick a permanent shape like the Fey Beast Riders. But Coulter had told Matt that anything he could imagine, he could do.

Scavenger said that made Matt more powerful than most people in the world. But it was a power that raised several questions in Matt's mind: why did he get it, and what did he need it for? So far, all it had done was terrify his family and make his brother hate him. And Alex had never hated him before.

Matt had asked Coulter why Alex didn't have the same powers. They were twins. They looked exactly alike, but their abilities differed. Coulter had looked uneasy about this, and when Matt pressed him, had finally mentioned what Matt's mother had: that the entire Islander system was based on the idea of two brothers, one to lead the country and the other to lead the religion. Only in the past, Coulter said, it had been the Enchanter involved in the religion and the one with Vision who led the country. He didn't know what it meant to have those roles reversed in Matt's family.

It wasn't until Matt got home that day that he found himself wondering why Coulter had accepted the importance of Matt's family so easily.

He planned to ask Coulter about that later today. He also planned to ask his help with Alex, again. Coulter had said he wouldn't help, but maybe if Matt explained how close they had once been, Coulter would relent.

He finished the last bit of cheese and checked on his mother. She looked exhausted, sprawled across the bed, snoring softly. Not even sleep made those circles beneath her eyes disappear. He knew she had been staying up late, making herb baskets and poultices, ointments and other healing potions she could sell or trade for food. He also knew that, in the last week, she had twice gone searching for his father and both times she had come home, locked herself in her room, and sobbed.

What his father had become scared him so much he didn't even want to think about it. Especially after Alex had told him of his Vision of Matt in the exact same condition.

Matt gently closed the door to his mother's room, then went outside. No Alex on the road, no Alex resting by the front door. Matt gazed at the mountains, glowing red in the predawn light. He and Alex used to say, when they were separated for even a short time, that the mountains could always see them both.

Well, Matt hoped the mountains could see Alex. He certainly couldn't. And he missed him, more than he could say.

He sighed, and started up the road, deciding to avoid the usual paths. If he saw Alex in the mood he was in, he might say something he would later regret. He wanted to get closer to his brother, not farther from him. Speaking harsh words wouldn't help.

The morning was crisp and colder than he had expected. He hadn't worn a coat. The thought made him a bit sad. Usually his mother knew what the weather would be. Usually she kept track of him. But she hadn't been keeping track of much this week. She felt the loss of Alex as much as he did.

Matt took a shortcut, a dirt path he and Alex had found a long time ago, when they had been fairly little. They had gotten strapped for walking on it by their father, who said the Fey used that road and it was dangerous. Matt hadn't used it again, but since there was no one to monitor him, he would try it.

Walking along the narrow path made his heart pound. Twice he looked over his shoulder. When he had been little, he believed his father could see everything. Sometimes, he imagined, his father would approve of what he saw, and sometimes, he knew, his father would hate what Matt did.

These days, his father would hate what Matt did.

Just as Alex hated it.

Matt shivered. He wished he had the coat. The sunlight wouldn't warm the day for hours yet.

The path wound down toward a branch of the Cardidas River. Most of the townspeople used this branch to bring extra water to their homes and, in the summer, some of them used it to bathe. The water here was as red as it was in the river proper, but it wasn't wild. It was almost placid and it had no undertow. No one had ever drowned here—at least not to Matt's knowledge—though people drowned all the time in the main part of the Cardidas. They slipped off rocks or overestimated the depth of the water. Here, the bottom was visible through the calm surface, and no one misjudged anything.

The river had an odor that carried to this part, the odor of freshness mixed with marshy grass and mud. He loved that smell. It meant home to him. He walked past it, breathing deep, when he noticed a movement in some reeds.

He hadn't expected to see anyone. People stayed away

from this part of the river in the spring—mostly because the water was still icy cold from the winter thaw. If people did come here, it was to get drinking or cooking water, and they usually waited until midday so that their hands wouldn't freeze when they dipped their buckets.

His breath was coming quicker than he wanted, and he stepped off the path onto the grass so that his feet wouldn't make any noise as he walked. The reeds rustled again, and he frowned at the movement. It didn't seem like someone who was trying to hide. The closer Matt got, the more he realized that the person in the reeds hadn't even heard him come.

It was a tall man, obviously Fey, who faced the water. In his hands, he held a pole. He wore boots that went to the tops of his thighs. His hair was braided in a fashion Matt had never seen before—thin braids, and a lot of them, that fell across his face and back. He had the sleeves of an old and dirty shirt pushed up to his elbows, revealing forearms covered with scars. The scars appeared to have a pattern to them.

Matt was going to walk past, but the Fey man looked so unusual that Matt slowed. In that moment, the man backed up, knocking the reeds again, nearly falling backward, his pole bent and the line taut.

The strain was evident, both in the line and on the man's face. He was too thin—he obviously didn't eat well and hadn't for a long time—and the concentration with which he fought the fish seemed out of place to the result. Matt had seen the fish that had come out of this part of the river; they were small at best, meager most of the time, and they tasted oily and foul. No one should have to eat those.

Still, the man probably would eat anything he could. Matt had seen Fey like that before, former warriors who didn't know how to live off the land, and who no longer had a purpose within the Empire. They certainly didn't have a purpose on Blue Isle. Most of them didn't even have homes here, and they had been fighting so long, they had no homes to go back to.

What had Coulter said? Use power to help those with none?

Matt flicked a wrist, raised it, and strengthened the line with his finger. As the man pulled the pole, a fish emerged from the water, as scrawny as Matt expected. He made the fish larger, and placed on it a wish for better taste.

The fish, now the size of a man's foot, rose dripping and fighting, splashing as it did. The man made not a sound as he fought it, and slowly worked it toward shore. Eventually, he grabbed the line and brought the fish home.

Matt smiled and walked on. He almost whistled, but he didn't want to call attention to himself. He had reached a bend in the path when he felt a hand on his arm.

He looked down, saw the long dark brown fingers of the man he had helped. Up close, the scarring was white and red and clearly deliberate. Little choppy lines decorated the skin, and looked as if some were fresh. It seemed as if they failed to heal in the manner someone wanted them to, so they were cut open to heal again.

Matt had no idea Fey did such a thing.

The smell of fresh fish was strong now, and so was the odor of the river, musty and overpowering. Beneath it was the scent of dirt and of clothes that were cleaned haphazardly.

Matt looked up from the hand to the face of the man who had stopped him. The man had delicate features, a few lines on his skin, and silver near his temples. He was at least as old as Matt's mother, maybe older.

When Matt met his gaze, the man looked at him with soft brown eyes and smiled. Matt smiled back. The man bowed slightly as an acknowledgment, then pointed at the reeds. Behind the reeds, in a secluded area that Matt hadn't been able to see when he walked up from the other direction, was a clear spot covered with brush and sticks for a fire. A canvas sack leaned against a rock, and on the ground beside it was an iron skillet and a shiny metal mug.

Matt smiled, a bit uncertainly. Then the man pinched his forefinger and thumb together and brought them to his lips, miming eating. He swept his free hand open again as if inviting Matt to join him.

The man couldn't speak. Matt had never met anyone like that before, at least not anyone Fey. His father said the Fey didn't like deformities, couldn't accept anyone who wasn't completely whole. But Coulter had told Matt that the Fey could heal most serious problems, and when they couldn't, the Fey chose to die to serve their people either in Fey lamps or to allow their bodies to be used for magic.

"It looks like it's been a long time since you've had a good meal," Matt said. "Why don't you bring your stuff and come with me? I know some people who'll feed you."

The man shook his head rather wildly. He pointed to the river.

"Bring your fish," Matt said. "Then you'll be sharing with them as they share with you."

The man looked uncertain for a moment. Then he smiled and bowed again. He held up one finger, signaling that Matt should wait, then hurried to his camp.

He put the skillet and cup in his bag, and began picking up other things, things Matt couldn't see. Matt came over to help him. The man nodded and pointed to a small pile of knives beside the makeshift fireplace.

They were knives of varying shapes and sizes— whittling knives, carving knives, hunting knives. One still had bits of wood on it, showing that it had been used to help this man find his fuel. Another had fish scales all along its scarred blade. A hand-carved wooden box sat beside the knives, and Matt opened it. More knives were inside. It was, apparently, how the man stored them.

The man had clearly been on the road for a very long time. Matt put the knives away, amazed that the man would trust him with them. Apparently the man didn't want Matt to have any surprises.

Matt picked up the box, and walked toward the man.

He was taking the string and hook off his fishing pole. He put it and the box in his canvas bag, then pulled the cord around the bag's mouth closed. He hoisted the bag over his shoulder as if he had done so all his life. With an elaborate sweep of the hand, he indicated that Matt should lead the way.

Matt did. The walk to Coulter's was long, but each time Matt offered to help with the sack, the man shook his head. Matt found it odd; because the man couldn't talk, Matt felt no need to. They walked in silence until they reached the school itself.

The magic yard was empty. It was still too early for many people to be around. Usually Coulter didn't allow use of the magic yard until afternoon anyway. Near the main door, Leen was feeding a small collection of cats and two dogs that had been strays but now somehow belonged to the school.

Cats were rare in all parts of Blue Isle but this one, or so Matt's father had once said. King Alexander had ordered all the cats slaughtered when the Fey first came and he had learned that some Fey could shift into that form. Matt thought that a shame. If he had been one of the students who needed to live on-site, he would have offered to feed the cats himself.

"Hey, Leen!" Matt shouted.

She jumped as if she had been caught at doing something bad. The cats didn't even look up, but one of the dogs barked deep in its throat. Leen petted it as if to calm it, and then looked at Matt.

"Who's that?" she asked.

Matt turned to his companion. The man mimed writing on his hand. "I don't know," Matt said. "He can't talk."

Leen's face eased into a small frown, so short that it almost seemed as if Matt imagined it.

"I think he hasn't been eating well. But he caught a nice-sized fish this morning and is willing to share it. I told him he could share it with all of us, and we'd give him a proper meal."

Leen nodded her head. She was studying the man as if she had never seen a Fey before. She wiped her hands on her pants and walked over to him.

She spoke to him in Fey.

He held a hand out as if in apology, then he touched his fingers to his mouth and shook his head.

She asked him another question.

He shrugged.

Matt looked from one to the other, wishing they would speak Islander so that he could follow them. Enough of learning how to control magic. Next he would ask Coulter to teach him Fey so that no one could have a conversation in front of him that he didn't understand.

Then Leen took the man's arm and led him toward the kitchen. The cats had finished their tidbits and obviously smelled fish. They circled the man, mewling piteously as if they had never been fed. The man smiled, and Matt laughed. The creatures were shameless.

"Let's give the fish to Tink," Leen said to Matt. "She's cooking this morning. Then let's get this man to the Domestics to get him cleaned up. Maybe later we'll get a Healer to look at his mouth."

The man put a hand over his mouth and shook his head slightly. No Healer? If Matt couldn't talk, and he knew someone could fix it, he would want the help. Why didn't the man?

"Well," Leen said as if that were some kind of answer, "we are going to get you cleaned up. And some fresh clothes. How long have you been wandering?"

The man flashed his right hand three times.

"Fifteen days?" Leen asked.

The man shook his head.

"Fifteen weeks?"

He shook his head again. Then mouthed something.

"Years?" Leen asked, and this time it wasn't so much a question for information as the sound of shocked disbelief.

The man nodded once.

"Here on Blue Isle or have you come from Galinas?"

The man pointed to the ground. Here, then. Matt was as shocked as Leen. This man had been wandering for the entire length of Matt's life.

"And you haven't lived anywhere?"

The man shrugged. The question was clearly too complicated to be answered as a simple yes or no.

"Well, " Leen said. "You'll get a chance to tell us, I guess. Let's go in." She opened the door and led him inside, taking him through the kitchen quickly and toward a side door. The man stopped, beckoned Matt forward, and handed him the fish.

It was slimy and scaly and smelled oily. Matt felt his stomach lurch. But he made himself smile and the man smiled back. Smiles—small, large, and everything in between—seemed to be his language. Leen tugged the man's arm, and together they left the kitchen.

Tink watched it all from the hearth. She was slender and she seemed to be getting taller by the day. Her brown hair was caught in a braid around the top of her head, and her skin, the color of weak tea, looked clearer than usual this morning. She had slate gray eyes, and a narrow mouth with Fey cheekbones that gave her entire face a foxlike appearance. But she was no beauty, unlike pure Fey girls. She looked too cunning for that.

She walked over to Matt and looked at his hands. Her mouth curled up when she saw the fish. "What am I supposed to do with that?"

"Cook it," he said.

"How?"

He shrugged. He'd never cooked a fish before either. His mother made a great fish stew, but she bought the fish or got it in trade, and it was usually in pieces already.

She made a face at him, as if the fish were his fault. "Put it on that plate, and get Scavenger. He'll know what to do."

Matt put the fish on the platter she pointed to, then

held out his scaly hands. She dipped a bowl into the cistern, put the water on the table, and a towel beside it. He cleaned off his hands and asked, "Where is Scavenger?"

"Outside, doing his meditations, like usual."

Usual? Matt had no idea Scavenger did anything except annoy people. "All right," he said, and let himself out.

Scavenger wasn't in the magic yard, and so Matt went around the building. Scavenger was sitting on a bench a previous group of students had carved—Matt, as a very little boy, had watched them with envy—and he was staring at the mountains, much like Matt had done that morning. Scavenger had his head tilted back, and for the first time since Matt had ever met him, looked vulnerable.

Matt cleared his throat.

Scavenger snapped to attention, the vulnerable look gone. "What do you want?"

"Sorry," Matt said. "We have some fresh fish inside and Tink thought you'd know how to clean it."

Scavenger made a sour face. "Once a Red Cap, always a Red Cap," he said.

"What?" Matt asked, not understanding.

"They think when you used to work carving up the dead for magic, you're an expert at skinning anything." Scavenger stood. He was shorter than Matt, and sturdier. "Lucky for you, she's right. Besides, I like fish."

He walked beside Matt, around the building and back into the magic yard. "So," Scavenger asked, "what's teacher's pet going to do now that teacher is gone?"

"Huh?" Matt asked. He hated talking to Scavenger. The man loved taunts and he loved talking in riddles.

Scavenger raised his slanted eyebrows. "You don't know? Coulter left yesterday."

Matt felt cold. Why was everyone leaving him? "Where'd he go?"

"Jahn." Scavenger leaned forward, lowering his tone. "He may not be coming back."

"That's a lie!" Matt said, moving away. "If he was going away, he'd tell me."

Scavenger shrugged and walked across the dirt to the

door. "Believe what you want," he said as he pulled it open and disappeared inside.

Matt stayed in the magic yard, staring after Scavenger. It couldn't be true. Coulter couldn't have left without telling him. Without talking to him. He thought Coulter cared about him. He knew Coulter did.

The cats started circling Matt, mewling again. Either he still smelled of fish or they hadn't forgotten that he had been with the man who carried it. One of the cats put a paw on Matt's leg and licked his finger, its tongue scratchy against his skin. Matt moved his hand away.

Scavenger had to be lying. He had to be. Matt pushed through the cats and pulled open the door.

The entire kitchen smelled of fish. The cats meowed, and Matt had to push them away with his foot to keep them from coming inside. He closed the door. Scavenger was sitting at the table. The spine and head of the fish were on a separate plate, and a pile of scales and tiny white bones were beginning to surround them.

Tink had her back turned. She was stirring something in the pot over the hearth.

Matt went over to her. "Is Coulter gone?"

She shot him a glance, then looked at Scavenger with something like anger. "He left last night."

"Why?"

"Leen says the Black Queen needed him. It was an emergency."

An emergency. Matt sighed. If he had lived here, Coulter would have told him. But in an emergency, a man didn't run all over town telling people he was leaving. He just left.

"How'd he go?"

"He took our only carriage and Dash to handle the horses."

"I didn't know Dash knew anything about horses."

"His father was a groom at the palace, I guess," Tink said. She kept her head bowed. "Not a lot of people know yet. Leen's going to make an announcement later."

"How come you know?"

She looked up. "I watched him leave. He looked—"

"Scared," Scavenger said. "And he's a damn fool."

Scavenger wiped his hands on a towel. Tink winced as he did so. Then he pushed the fish fillet toward her. She picked it up and stared at it as if she had never seen fish before.

"I can make a stew if you want," Matt said. "For lunch."

He hoped, anyway. He'd watched his mother do it, but had never done it himself.

"All right," she said, wrinkling her nose.

Matt pushed up his sleeves and took some water from the cistern. He would have to ask where the flour was, and he wondered if the school had enough money to buy butter from one of the local farmers. He hoped so. He'd never made a roux without it. Unlike most people in the area, his mother considered butter a staple, not a luxury.

Scavenger picked up the towel by one end and threw it on a pile that the kitchen staff set aside for the Domestics. Matt hoped he would take it out of there, or the kitchen would stink of fish all day.

Scavenger met his gaze. Matt knew that Scavenger wanted him to ask more about Coulter, but he wouldn't. He would wait until Leen made her announcement. The word "emergency" had soothed him. He didn't want Scavenger to get him upset again.

After a moment, Scavenger shrugged. "Need me for anything else?"

"No," Tink said. "You've been a great help."

At that moment, the kitchen door opened and Leen came in, followed by the strange man. He looked different with his face scrubbed clean and wearing traditional Fey clothes. His braids seemed as exotic as before, but his scars weren't quite as frightening.

"I'm going to make the fish," Matt said. "But for lunch because . . ."

His voice trailed off when he realized that Scavenger was staring at the newcomer as if he had seen a ghost. The strange man was staring back, a challenge in his eyes. For the first time since Matt met him, the strange man looked powerful.

Scavenger's gaze went from the man to Leen. "Where'd you find him?" Scavenger asked in a low tone.

"I found him," Matt said. "By the river. He caught the fish you cleaned."

"I thought you were dead," Scavenger said. He sounded bitter and angry, and almost frightened.

The strange man's smile was small, apologetic. Matt found the language of the man's smiles so easy to understand. He wondered if the others did.

The man touched his mouth.

Matt was getting cold. This man had something to do with Rugad then? With the battle fifteen years ago?

The man shook his head and touched his mouth again.

"He can't talk," Matt said.

"Don't be a fool," Scavenger snapped. "Of course he can talk. Talk is the basis of his magic."

The man's smile had disappeared. He shook his head and touched his mouth again, as if to say that he couldn't.

"This is Rugad's Charmer." Scavenger said this last as if it were the worst thing in the world. "His name is Wisdom."

The man nodded, and Matt whirled. This man had once served the famous Black King?

"He was Rugad's second in command, the one who carried out all his orders. He had to do it because he could Charm anyone into doing anything he wanted." Scavenger crossed his arms and gave Matt an intense look. "Is that what he did to you, boy? Charmed you?"

"Even if he had tried, it wouldn't have worked," Leen said. "Matt has Enchanter's magic."

"He's an Islander. The magic bends here," Scavenger said. "And I don't think we dare risk the most talented Charmer in Rugad's arsenal on this motley crew."

The man—Wisdom?—touched his mouth again and shook his head.

"As if I believe that," Scavenger said. "All you would need is a sympathetic Healer and you could talk again."

Wisdom looked pained. Finally, he sank to his knees, opened his mouth, and pointed.

Scavenger frowned. He leaned forward, looked, and then turned away in disgust.

Matt couldn't help himself. He looked too. The man had no tongue. What was there looked as if it had been ripped away. The scar was old, but brownish black as if it were still a wound.

"What happened to you?" Matt whispered.

"He crossed Rugad," Scavenger said. He seemed to have control over himself again. "Apparently before Rugad died, and in some particularly horrible way, because it was usually Rugad's method to kill his detractors. Instead, he made it impossible for Wisdom to practice his magic."

"We have Healers who can probably repair you," Leen said.

Wisdom shook his head vehemently.

Scavenger looked slightly amused. "Did Rugad curse you as well?"

Wisdom shrugged.

Scavenger rolled his eyes. "Rugad is long dead. His curses mean nothing."

"We don't know that," Leen said.

"Of course we do," Scavenger said. "He was a Visionary, not an Enchanter. His curses can't linger past his death. Didn't you know that, Charmer? Repair him, Leen, and send him on his way."

Wisdom rose slowly, as if his knees bothered him. Matt helped him. "Do you want to be fixed?" Matt whispered.

Wisdom bit his lower lip, shook his head, then nodded, and then closed his eyes. Finally he shrugged.

Leen put a hand on his arm. "It's your choice. But Scavenger is right. Rugad has been dead a long time. I don't think anyone should still be punished for things that Rugad deemed crimes. You probably didn't do anything wrong."

Wisdom opened his eyes. They were sad. He shook his

head. When she frowned at him, he touched his heart and shook his head again.

"He did do something wrong," Matt said. "That's what he's trying to say. He deserved the punishment."

"Is it a crime you'll commit again?" Leen asked.

Wisdom's smile was small. He shook his head.

"Then I'm taking you back to the Domestics. Our Healers should be able to repair this."

Scavenger caught her arm. "Only if he promises to leave."

She looked at him as if measuring what he had to say.

"We can't have a Charmer here. We don't have anyone to counteract him."

"What counteracts a Charmer?" Matt asked. "You mentioned Enchanters."

"Sometimes," Scavenger said. "But mostly Visionaries."

"Like my brother."

"Your brother wouldn't help us," Scavenger said. "Your father taught him to be afraid of everything."

"But I'll help," Matt said.

"Why are you asking for him to stay?" Scavenger asked.

Matt stopped. He didn't know why. Because Coulter had left? Because Wisdom had nowhere else to go? Because Matt understood how it felt to be unwanted?

"Maybe he knows stuff we don't," Matt said. "Stuff we can learn from."

"He probably does," Scavenger said. "But that doesn't offset the dangers of having a Charmer in this place."

He walked over to Wisdom and stood in front of him, his chest out, as if by doing that he could make himself taller.

"Promise you'll leave and we'll help you. Promise."

"After we feed him," Matt said.

"He'll stay longer than a few hours," Leen said. "I suspect the Healers will want to monitor his progress."

"Promise," Scavenger said.

Wisdom touched his mouth and shook his head. Then he walked past Leen and Scavenger, and went outside.

Matt stared at all of them for a moment. They looked as surprised as he felt.

"Maybe he's too scared to be fixed," Matt said. "Maybe he doesn't want it. Maybe he's had other opportunities and he's turned them down."

"And maybe he's playing with us," Scavenger said.

"Why?" Matt asked. "He's clearly starving."

"He is that," Leen said. "Go get him, Matt. We promised to feed him. It's the least we can do."

With an angry glance at Scavenger, Matt ran to the door. He pushed it open in time to see Wisdom hoist his canvas bag over his shoulder and start toward the path.

"Wait!" Matt shouted.

Wisdom stopped, but didn't turn. Matt ran to him.

"We promised—I promised—to feed you, and we have your fish. You don't have to do what we want. You don't have to say a word. You can stay as long as you want. Scavenger's just afraid of what you'll do if you can talk."

Wisdom bowed his head, but not before Matt saw a tiny, rueful smile. Was Scavenger the only one who was afraid of what Wisdom would do if he could talk? Or was Wisdom afraid of that too?

Matt took Wisdom's arm. Wisdom looked down at him. "Come on," Matt said.

Wisdom took a deep breath, looked at the path with a mixture of longing and regret, and then turned around. He put a hand on Matt's shoulder as they walked.

It had been a long time since anyone had touched Matt in such a friendly way. Not even Coulter had done it. Coulter, who had left after promising Matt he would take care of him. Matt hoped that Leen would give him a special message from Coulter after she had told the others that he left.

But Matt doubted it. She could have done so already, but she had said nothing. Some things, apparently, were more important than Matt. He had learned that his whole life.

He straightened a little under Wisdom's friendly touch.

Coulter would be back soon. This was his school. It was his dream, his love. Scavenger was just being bitter because Scavenger was always bitter.

But, Matt knew, even when Scavenger was bitter, he always told the truth.

CHAPTER SEVENTEEN

"N O WAY," his father mumbled. "No way for a man to live."

Alex leaned against the stone altar. Golden light bathed the room. He was trying to concentrate on the Ancient Islander text. He could read it, but he certainly couldn't understand it. He wished he had some sort of context to place this information in.

"No way," his father said, voice rising. "Matt!"

"Alex," Alex said, not letting go of the altar. The ability to tell the difference between his sons was one of the first skills his father lost.

Alex didn't know exactly where his father was—he suspected he was beneath the table—but he didn't want to look for him. His father had proven to be the most difficult part of Alex's new resolution to use the old texts to discover how to control his own Visions. If, of course, Coulter was right.

What startled Alex was not the magical instructions, but the way certain names kept recurring in this text.

Alexander and Matthias were the original sons of the Roca, whose real name had been Coulter.

Maybe his father had been mad from the beginning. Maybe his father really saw himself as the Roca returned, as some people charged. Or maybe something else was going on. All this magic that everyone had been talking about, all of this energy that had taints and purities and light, maybe it recurred after a certain number of generations, and it took a specific kind of ability to set it right.

Maybe.

"Not living," his father said. "Matt!"

"Alex," Alex said between gritted teeth.

His father smelled bad and couldn't be convinced to wash. He rarely ate, and he urinated into a jar. Sometimes he remembered to empty the jar outside, and sometimes he didn't. The times he didn't, he also forgot to clean up any spills.

Alex wished his old father would come back, the man who could answer any question about the history of Blue Isle. The man who claimed he didn't believe in God, but that he should learn how. The man who said that God was visible in the mountains, in the magic, in the power he gave his people. The man who wondered what happened to that God long ago, and whether that God had been a man, just like the rest of them.

Alex remembered the questions. He just didn't remember the answers. And he didn't understand what he was studying. He knew the Words, the original Words that he was looking at, were a letter the Roca had written to his sons, Alexander and Matthias, after the Roca had been somehow reborn.

The Roca had been trapped in this cave, unable to leave, because the moment he stepped outside, he vanished. But he wrote this letter and sent copies of it to his sons, asking them to give up the magic he had discovered, the magic that grew in them like weeds in a flower garden, and telling them how they could control the magic that had slipped out of their grasp. He spent the rest of his days developing weapons that could destroy magic or capture it, and he filled the cavern with them.

In this part of the letter, the part Alex was trying to read, the Roca explained how the items were to be used. Something in the Words about aiming, about choosing a target, and unleashing. But he couldn't concentrate, and the language was familiar enough to be confusing, unfamiliar enough to make understanding difficult.

"Matt!" his father yelled.

"Alex," Alex said and closed his fist on the stone. The altar was the strangest thing of all. Whenever he touched it, it glowed. His father had laughed the first time he saw that, and said, "They hate it, those Wise Ones. We have the Roca running through our veins."

His father appeared in the doorway, his hair matted and tangled, his face dirty. His robe was ripped and stained, but he wouldn't take it off to put on the new robe that Alex had brought for him that morning. In his left hand, he clutched a necklace, a filigree sword. The sword used to be the symbol of Rocaanism. His father had wanted to change that; when he developed New Rocaanism, he wanted the symbol to be something that didn't suggest war. Only he couldn't think of anything.

"Matt?" he asked softly.

"Alex." This time Alex spoke firmly. "I'm Alex."

His father frowned. "You should be Matt."

"Sorry," Alex said.

His father's eyes seemed clear. A frown made all the lines on his face deeper. "The second son takes to religion."

"Not in this family," Alex said. "The second son learns magic from the Fey."

His father closed his eyes and leaned his head against the wall. Then he slammed his skull against the stone so hard that the sound echoed.

"Dad!" Alex said. "Stop!"

His father opened his eyes. They still seemed clear. "How long?" he asked.

"How long has Matt been studying with the Fey?"

"How long since the last time I spoke with you?"

"You've been talking off and on for days, Dad."

"No." His father's voice shook. "Since you came here, speaking of Visions."

His father was back, if only for a brief time. Somehow that made Alex sad. "A week."

"Has your mother been here?"

"Every day," Alex said. "She made me bring you a new robe."

His father took the skirts of the robe and looked at it, brushing his fingers along the stains.

"You wouldn't put it on."

His father raised his head. "This is no way for a man to live," he said.

"No," Alex said. "It isn't. You should go home."

"I keep waiting for her to come and take me."

"She's been here every day. You won't go."

"Not your mother." His father's voice was harsh. "Her."

"Who, Father?" Alex asked, but his father didn't seem to hear him. He was looking at the carved ceiling of the Vault as if he hadn't seen it before.

"I always thought she should be able to come here. The Roca could be visible here. Why couldn't she? Or did she show respect? I kept expecting her to take me."

"Who, Dad?"

His father looked at him, eyes still clear. "Get your mother for me."

"Are you going to go home with her?"

His father shook his head. "I need to speak with her, now, while I still can. Hurry."

His father had tried this before and it hadn't worked. The last time, Matt had been the one to run for their mother. When they got back, Alex's father had been sobbing in a corner, and completely unable to speak. He hadn't asked for anyone since.

Alex almost reminded him of that time, then realized it would do no good. The only thing he could do was what his father asked of him.

Alex closed the Words, then left the altar. He walked

through the Vault—it was such a place of reverence, he didn't feel as if he could hurry, and then, when he got to the outer room, he ran.

The outer corridor felt strange to him. He had never run through it before. He noticed how it curved and went uphill, his feet slipping beneath him as he tried to go faster. He reached the steps quicker than he ever thought possible, and as he started up them, the door above opened.

His mother stared down at him.

"Mom!" he shouted, excited now. "Dad's calling for you. He's himself! Hurry!"

She came down the stairs faster than he'd ever seen her move. She had a basket over her arm that she dropped at the foot of the stairs. Then she took his hand and together they ran back the way he had come.

The doors were still open, and the faint smell of sweat and urine filled the hall. But as they came in, Alex was startled to see the father he remembered, not the one he had just left.

His father was wearing the new robe, and he had used the water that Alex had been bringing to clean his face and wet his hair. He seemed older, but his eyes had life in them for the first time in a long, long time.

His mother made a small cry and let go of Alex's hand. She ran to his father, and wrapped her arms around him, holding him tight. Alex had never seen her do that. Until that moment, he hadn't realized how hard it was on his mother, seeing his father that way. He wished Matt were here, so that he could be part of this, but Matt was probably with his Fey friends. Alex knew there was no time to find him.

After a moment, his father pulled out of the embrace. He stroked his mother's hair, and then kissed her. It seemed like such a private moment that Alex looked away.

When he looked back it seemed as if they had forgotten him. They were staring into each other's eyes with so much intensity that Alex finally understood how such different people as his parents had gotten together. Finally, his father kissed his mother's forehead, and said, "It's time, Marly."

"No," she said. "Ye come home with me. 'Twill be all right, I'll make sure a that."

He shook his head. "I was hoping that if I stayed here, I'd find a magic to reverse this. But the curse the Roca saw really does exist. I'm not going to get better. If Alex is to be believed, I'm worse. I certainly looked worse. If I don't take care of things now, I'll be less than a child by the end of the year."

"Matthias—"

He put a finger on her lips. "Marly, please, I don't know how long this clarity will last. Let me say my bit."

Alex was biting his own lip, waiting. He could barely remember when his father was in this much control. Usually the clarity flashed in and out, and then disappeared at the very last moment.

"I figured if I couldn't cure myself here, maybe Jewel would come for me. But she hasn't. I'm not sure she can get into this part of the Roca's Cave, and even if she could, I'm not sure she will. The soul repositories—"

"Ye dinna need her. She'll kill you, Matthias. Ye know that. Come home." His mother sounded almost desperate. "Please. The boys and I, we need ye. More than anything here ever could."

He kissed her again. Alex was twisting his own hands together, half wishing, half praying this father would stay, and knowing, deep down, that he could not.

"I know she'll kill me, Marly," his father said. He was holding her by the shoulders as if to make sure she wouldn't break away from him. "I know. I want her to."

"No. 'Tis na right 'n ye know it. Come home, Matthias."

"It is right," Matthias said. "We have an old score. And besides, maybe she'll leave after she takes care of me. Then the boys are free to live the life that we planned for them. Take care of them, Marly. They need you."

" 'Tis you they need," she said. "I canna do it alone, Matthias."

"Yes, you can," he said. "The last thing you need is a

crazy husband who'll be little more than an infant soon. I could live for another forty years. If I do that and get worse, as I have been, then what? You'll have no life."

"I have no life without ye," she said. "Matthias, please."

He kissed her again. "Let me go, Marly." His words were soft. "Tell me you understand. Please. I know you do."

She bowed her head. Tears dripped off her face. Alex was squeezing his own hands so hard that his fingers ached.

"I canna convince ye," she said. "I never could. Ye'd always been the man ye said ye were, and ye always were fair with me." She took a deep breath and stood up straight. Alex had never realized before that his parents were of a height. "Well, then. Ye gave me the best years of me life, Matthias."

"And some of the worst," he said with a smile.

" 'N I wouldna trade em for the world. Go with God, then, and if somethin' heals ye in the Roca's Cave, come back to me."

Alex's father caressed her face. "I never knew what I did to deserve you," he said. "But I'm thankful for it, every day of my life."

Then he looked over her head at Alex. "Tell your brother to remember what I taught him." His gaze softened. "And you, take care of your mother. She needs you."

Then he bent his head, kissed Alex's mother one last time, and turned away from both of them. Without a look back, he walked into the Vault.

"Where's he going?" Alex asked.

" 'Tis a small tunnel, hidden, in the back a that room," his mother said. "He dinna want me to tell ye about it. He dinna want anaone to know. But 'tis too late for that now. The tunnel leads into the mountain. He's gone there before."

"When he killed the Black King."

His mother nodded, her eyes filled with tears. " 'Tis ye 'n Matt he's doin' this for."

"No," Alex said. "We have nothing to do with it. He doesn't want to be crazy anymore."

His mother didn't seem to hear him. She walked to the small wooden door that led into the Vault. She put her hand on the frame and stared inside.

"Go with God," she whispered again. "Go with God."

CHAPTER EIGHTEEN

*I*T FELT AS if she were climbing out of a long dark tunnel. Arianna kept her eyes closed for a moment, feeling an exhaustion that she had never felt before. It was as if she had been struggling for days, fighting against a giant hand determined to hold her down, keep her in a dark place where she couldn't see, couldn't breathe, couldn't even think.

The giant hand had relaxed for a moment, and she leaped past it. The breath in her lungs was her own. Her body lay at an odd angle, and her left arm was asleep. Her right leg had an ache in the knee; she had been in this position too long.

She didn't want to open her eyes—so much of her wanted to sink back into that exhaustion—but she did.

She was on her bed. Sunlight was falling across it. She had been talking to Seger, she thought, telling her about the awful day Rugad had taken her mind, the day Sebastian had saved her and then shattered, the day she had met Coulter. What had changed?

Arianna had a vague memory of struggling, fighting to get out words. Words about—

Her brain skittered over the thought, and she felt a lancing pain, as if someone had stuck a pin in a sensitive portion of her mind. She winced and forced herself to sit up.

Something was very wrong with her.

She put a hand to her head and moaned just a little. A rustle beside her made her stop. Luke had been standing by the window, looking into the garden. Apparently he hadn't realized she was awake until she made a sound.

He looked awkward and uncomfortable, as if he had been caught doing something wrong. He came over to the side of the bed and sat in a chair that hadn't been there before, a chair someone had placed there.

"Seger asked me to stay with you," he said. He reached out toward her with his blunt, scarred fingers, then pulled his hand back as if there was something improper in his compassion. "How are you?"

Arianna let her own hand fall to her side. The pain inside her mind—it wasn't a headache so much as something that stabbed her from within—was easing now.

"I did it again, didn't I? I lost time."

He nodded.

"What did I do to you this time?"

"Nothing," he said. "Seger got me. Talking with you helped her realize what was happening. Apparently you told her something—"

The baby. The thought came unbidden, and right on its heels, another stabbing pain. She had to close her eyes. It felt as if the needle that was piercing her would come out of her eyeballs if she didn't protect them somehow. She held back a moan, and made herself concentrate.

The baby. She could picture him now, a little boy no more than a few hours old. He had been crying. She had picked—

Another stab. She had to bite the inside of her cheek to prevent herself from crying out. *Concentrate. Concentrate.*

—picked him up and cradled him to herself, carrying him with her—

The pain was getting so bad that she was going to black out if she continued doing this, continued remembering it. Luke was still speaking to her, and even though she heard his voice, she wasn't sure what he was saying.

Concentrate.

—carrying him with her to the center part of herself, the place where she dwelt, where she ran everything—

Black spots danced before her eyes. She clenched her right fist and felt the fingernails dig into her skin. Tears were running down her cheeks and she concentrated on their wetness as a way of avoiding the pain.

—carrying him with her to the center part of herself—

Another stab.

Concentrate.

—and she never saw him again.

The pain released her, and she fell back against the pillow. The sharpness was gone, but there was still an echo of it, a feeling that if she tried to think again, the pain would be back, and it would be worse. How could she concentrate on something without hurting herself? Obviously this was an important memory, something that held the key to everything that was happening to her.

She opened her eyes. Luke was standing beside her—hovering was a better word—holding a linen handkerchief, and obviously trying to decide to wipe her face with it. She solved his problem; she wiped the tears off her cheeks and chin with the back of her hand.

"What happened?" he asked.

She had never seen him look so unnerved. His pale face was even paler, his blue eyes seemed almost glassy, and he had bitten through his lower lip. She felt a moment of compassion for him: people used to taking action felt so helpless when faced with illness, something internal, something they couldn't bludgeon or threaten or beat up.

"Pain," she whispered, her voice a mere croak.

"Do you want me to send for Seger?"

"Yes," she said. "You go."

"I can't," he said. "I'm under orders not to leave you alone."

"Hers or mine?" Arianna asked.

"Both, if you'll remember."

If you'll remember. She gave that order before, but had she given it again? These blackouts made her question herself and that wasn't good.

In fact, it was the worst thing a ruler could do.

That thought came in Fey, in another voice, almost like someone else was speaking inside her head. Still, she looked about the room, just to see if there was another speaker.

The bedroom door was closed. She and Luke were alone. No wonder he had looked so uncomfortable when she woke.

"What just happened?" he asked.

She couldn't answer that. She couldn't answer anything. Could Sebastian handle the day-to-day business of the Isle until Gift returned? She didn't know. Seger had been worried about him too, with that mysterious voice.

Rugad's voice.

Another stab of pain, this one not with a needle but with a knife. She hunched over, clutched her head, bit back a scream.

Get out of me, she thought. *Someone please get him out.*

A laugh, this one inside her head once more, echoing as if it were in an empty room. *You invited me in, little girl,* the voice said in Fey, and now she knew it for what it was. Rugad's voice. Rugad. He had left a part of himself in her mind.

Very good, he thought. *Very, very good. It only took you fifteen years to figure that out.*

Get out of my mind, she thought.

I couldn't if I wanted to. He sounded wryly amused. She closed her eyes, actually saw him, a lanky teenage Fey boy with long dark hair and a handsome face. Rugad's face—the old man's face—had not been handsome.

It had been a strong face, with its high cheekbones and dramatic eyebrows, but it had been an unkind face, the sort of face that no one would turn to for romance or comfort. This boyish face held promises that it would never fulfill—the promise of love, the promise of hope, the promise of a life well lived. It held the promise, as well, of the face that Arianna remembered, but she found it fascinating that he could have chosen another way.

Stared long enough? he asked.

I didn't expect to see you, she said.

Of course not. You have an amazing gift for forgetting the unpleasant.

She didn't forget how he had felt in her mind the first time, a whirlwind determined to destroy her, to bend her to his own will.

And I will achieve that, he said.

She gasped, felt the air run through her body, as well as heard the reaction in her mind. Luke actually touched her shoulder. She wanted to shake him off, to warn him—

I'm not interested in that man, Rugad said. *I already have you.*

She crossed her arms. She found she existed in two places: within her mind as a small being that could stand and fight and move around, and within her body as she had always known it. When she crossed her arms, the small being crossed hers while the large body did as well.

You lost the last time you faced me in here. I Shifted until I could control you.

He smiled. It was a beautiful smile. Early on, then, in his rule, he had combined the natural leadership abilities of a Fey Visionary with the charisma of a handsome man. It surprised her. She had always thought him the embodiment of evil.

She suppressed a sigh. He had probably heard that too.

Of course, he said. *You are drawn to me because I am part of you. You cannot throw me out this time, neither you nor your Golem. You willingly took me to the part of you that controls everything and I grew there. I am you now. I can Shift you at will, make you say what I want, do as I say.*

If that's true, she said, *then why haven't you taken complete control?*

She felt a whisper then, a moment when he didn't control, a bit of an answer floating by her. So that was what her thoughts felt like to him. Only he knew how to control his.

His smile grew wider. *I am a trained Visionary, with ninety-two years of life in my own body, and fifteen more years of life in yours. I know the edges and corners of the magic, things you never bothered to learn, and things you can't even imagine.*

He held out his hands to her, and there was something warm about him, something about his energy that made him draw her to him.

Together, he said, *we would be the most formidable team the Fey have ever known. We would take the Triangle, and no one would know until it was done. You and I would lead our people to greatness.*

No, she said. *I don't believe in making war. I've seen what it does. It destroys everything.*

It is necessary to our way of life.

To yours, she said. *Not mine. I am retraining the Empire, teaching them how to grow with what they have. The expansion would eventually destroy it.*

His eyes narrowed and his hands dropped. The warm feeling of welcome was gone. *You have no understanding of what we are.*

It was her turn to smile. *I do. You have no idea of what you had become.*

We are a warrior people. Take that away from us, and we will turn upon each other. I am preventing that.

And when there are no more lands to conquer? Arianna asked. *What then?*

We will have the Triangle, he said. *The power that comes from it is unimaginable.*

How does anyone know if no one has seen it?

His dark eyes narrowed, as if he were contemplating telling her. Then he said, *I have had Visions of it.*

Is that all?

So have others. It is the destiny of our family. I will not let you or your poorly trained brother interfere with that.

You didn't answer me, she said. *If you have control, why haven't you taken it?*

Again, that fleeting thought and this time, she caught it. He didn't have full control yet. He didn't know all the corners and angles of her. He would have it soon, but he wasn't ready.

Something changed, she said softly. *You weren't going to do this for another ten years. Something woke you.*

For a moment, he looked confused, as if he didn't know why he was awake either. And then she caught his next thought.

A shiver ran down her back.

If he had awakened in ten years, as he planned, he would have been inside her for twenty-five years, and he would have completely integrated into her. Gradually, he would have taken over—no pain in the head, no quick movement to control. Bit by bit, she would have become him, or he would have become her, and no one would have been the wiser.

This is a mistake, isn't it? Her heart started to beat harder. She felt a small bit of hope, the first she'd felt for days. *You weren't ready. You're trying to do this all fast.*

I have done all I needed to, he said.

(Except one thing.)

That thought, suddenly and loud, made both of them stare at each other. He hadn't planned to let her hear it, and yet she had. She had.

Now all she had to do was find that one thing.

He shook his head. *You'd need a knowledge of the magic to do that.*

Share it with me.

His smile was back. She had made some sort of tactical error. *I can tell you this,* he said, *and perhaps you will use this technique someday. I created a construct of my-*

self, and left a bit of my personality in it, enough of that personality to build the one you face. I also left all of my memories with it, all of my dreams, and all of my desires.

You knew you were going to die, she said.

He shook his head. *It was a precaution, one my family has often used. Sometimes the personality is left in Golems, sometimes in heirs who are not as talented as their predecessor. If Bridge had followed me, as it had seemed he would, then I would have done this to him. But your mother prevented it by giving birth to Gift, and I Saw the birth. Saw how talented he would be. Then, a few years later, I Saw you.*

If you planned this from the beginning, Arianna said, *why didn't you come when we were babies?*

His smile grew. *You do not know the history of your own people. We do not wage war constantly. We take over a country, consolidate and annex it, mate with its people, and make it ours. Then we move on to the next place. I was finishing with Galinas, making certain that the entire continent would remain a happy and healthy part of the Empire when you were born. I figured I could take care of you and your brother at any time. And I was right.*

You did this to Gift too?

He didn't answer her. She got a sense that he was amused by the question, as if he were hoping she was going to ask it.

He held out his hand again. *Work with me on this. You have a brilliant and incisive mind. An instinctive understanding of the Islanders, and a ruthlessness that is matched only by a compassion I barely understand. Together we can build on that, be greater than we are separately.*

If you're so in control, she said, *why do you need me?*

I don't. But he didn't sound as confident as he should have, and again she felt the brush of a thought not her own. She controlled something that he could not touch. But what?

Perhaps he had lied. Perhaps she believed something she shouldn't have. She reached even deeper inside of herself, to the part that Shifted and began the process that would change her into a robin.

She felt her face shorten, feathers grow on her arms, and then, as suddenly as the process started, it stopped.

Wrong guess, he said.

And she lunged for him. No practice, no thought. She just ran, thinking she could shove him so far into her brain that he would get lost just as she had. The moment before she hit him, he stepped aside and she had to catch herself before she went too far, remembering that what she saw here was merely an illusion and not subject to physical laws.

He was laughing, as if he had played a wonderful trick on her. She whirled, angrier than she had ever been.

I have beaten you before, she said. *I will beat you again.*

You have never beaten me without your Golem, he said. *And I own him now, just like I own you.*

And then he vanished, as if he never was. She didn't relax. She wasn't sure where he had gone, what he would do to her. It felt as if he were really gone. But he couldn't be. He had integrated himself into her. They were, in many ways, the same person.

Only he wasn't fully formed. He hadn't taken over some parts. She just had to find them.

She opened her eyes. Luke was crouched on the edge of the bed. The door was open, and so was the door to the suite itself. He must have called for help, but for the moment, it was only the two of them.

"Arianna?" he whispered.

She was half crouching, still bent over as she had been when the pain first hit her mind. One arm clutched her stomach, the other still had a single feather on it—a gray one, a robin's feather, just like she had planned.

A single feather.

There wasn't one part of her he had failed to take. He hadn't completed taking any part of her. She just had to find the holes in his conquest.

Like this one.

She tugged the feather, felt the same pinprick of pain she would feel if she had tugged a hair on her arm. Then she Shifted that single feather back to what it had been. Her skin and hair returned.

So the commands she sent went through, and he didn't counter them. He overlaid them. Strange. It was as if her body had two masters, and did the bidding of the stronger.

"Arianna?" Luke asked.

She raised her eyes to his. How could she tell him what was going on? How could she tell any of them?

"Where's Seger? I have to talk with her."

"I sent for her," he said.

"Is there anyone outside?"

He shook his head. "I sent the extra guard."

"Good," she said. She pulled him close, so close that he looked terrified. "I may not be able to tell her this. You'll have to remember what I say, repeat it word for word. Can you do that?"

He nodded, a small frown line appearing between his eyes.

"Tell her—" Arianna paused. If she told the truth, word would spread, and any enemies she had would use this information to bring her down, even if she defeated Rugad. After all, who could prove that he had left?

She waited for an echo of laughter and heard none. For the moment, he was gone. Tired? Or was he doing something even worse?

"Tell her the baby awakened early. It didn't finish its task, but it's close. Tell her that it's in everything, but there are holes."

Luke's frown grew. "Will she understand that?"

"I hope so," Arianna said.

"You can explain it to her."

"I may not be able to," Arianna said. "But tell her one more thing. Tell her it won't destroy me. It'll just bury me."

"Bury you?"

She nodded, waiting for the pain to come. It hadn't. Was she being manipulated? Or was he really giving her this chance to save herself? Or had something else gone wrong? Had she taken some control that she didn't realize she had?

"You'll remember this?"

"You can trust me," Luke said.

"Good," she said, and closed her eyes. The exhaustion was there, deep and heavy. "It's nice to know I can trust someone."

Especially when she could no longer trust herself.

CHAPTER NINETEEN

SEGER FOUND SEBASTIAN in the courtyard on the far side of the palace. He was leaning against the stone wall, one leg bent and the other crossed at the ankle, his arms folded across his stomach. Seger had never seen Sebastian stand so casually, as if his body were made of flesh instead of stone.

He seemed impervious to the cool spring air, and the sunlight only heightened the darkness in the cracks on his skin. The doors to nearby buildings were closed, and the dogs had left the area. But Sebastian wasn't alone.

He was watching twenty Infantry—the palace unit that served as exterior guards—practice their sword fighting. Their movements were deft and sure. How many times had she seen just this sight, and in how many countries? The only difference here was that the Infantry was using the wider Islander blades—practicing with the heavier and, in some ways, deadlier weapons. The clangs of metal blades against each other echoed through the courtyard.

Sebastian didn't move as she approached. In fact, she

would have thought he didn't see her at all, until he turned his head and grinned at her.

She wasn't sure she had ever seen Sebastian grin before. It made her feel cold.

"Aren't they magnificent, Seger?" he asked in Rugad's voice. The sound of it made her shiver. He saw the movement and his grin widened. He looked like a maniacal version of himself. "I've been thinking of ways to improve their performance. Do you think they'll take orders from me or should I go to Arianna?"

Was there a code in what he said? It certainly felt as if he were layering some innuendo, but she couldn't tell what.

"You're speaking well, Sebastian," she said, careful to keep her voice neutral.

"I am, aren't I?" He leaned his head against the wall. His skin color and the stone seemed to blend together—and suddenly she understood part of his magic. Sebastian's magic, not Rugad's. The Domestics who made him had used, as their base, clay from Blue Isle. Once upon a time, Golems had been made from clay found in the Eccrasian Mountains. Those Golems had special powers as well.

She worked to keep the realization off her face. No one else needed to know this, not yet. She would figure out how to use the information someday.

"It only took me thirty-three years," he said, and then chuckled. The chuckle didn't sound natural coming from him.

She looked at him in confusion, then understood what he had been referring to. Using the voice. Time. But Sebastian wasn't using Rugad's voice. Rugad's voice was using Sebastian's body. And the voice was speaking in Fey.

"Well," she said. "Sometimes it takes a while for the magics to come together."

He looked at her then, sharp gray eyes set in a cracked face. Eyes that had no warmth at all. Rugad's eyes. How could he be here? Sebastian had barely used the voice, and when she had felt the thread of the voice the day before, Rugad had not been a part of him.

She wished there were a Shaman here, someone she could consult with. Healing magic hadn't prepared her for this.

"You know," she said in Islander. "Arianna has forbidden you from using this voice."

He opened his mouth, and a breathy sound came out, followed by: "Help . . . me . . ." in Sebastian's normal tones. Then he cleared his throat and said, "Help me figure out a way to work with the Infantry. I really don't want to consult with my sister."

He said that in Fey again. The Islander was a trigger, but only a small one. The pathetic sound that Sebastian had uttered made her chill even worse.

"I'm afraid that working on improving war methods is not what I do," she said, pretending she hadn't heard Sebastian at all, pretending she was fooled by this charade. She couldn't tell if he believed her. Those sharp gray eyes watched everything with a sort of grim amusement.

The sounds of sword fighting had stopped. She turned to the Infantry. A few members, women all, were standing in the center of the fighting field, sweat pouring down them, swords out. But the men seemed tired and ready to move on. The women turned to each other, and began work again. This time, the blades moved quickly, each thrust and parry so fast that she barely had time to register it.

"You know, improving war methods doesn't seem to be what anyone's working on these days. And if we want to move to Leut, we need to work our troops. This group doesn't even know what battle is like." He extended a hand. Such a rapid movement seemed unnatural coming from Sebastian. "Look how organized this fight is. What they need is someone to wade into the middle of it and throw it into chaos."

He was right, of course, but she hadn't been able to see it until she watched for a moment. Her chill grew even deeper. Sebastian wouldn't have known anything about fighting. He despised it. Sometimes he covered his eyes and left the area, saying it brought up old memories, memories he would rather forget.

Sebastian was so childlike. There was no innocence in those eyes now. No child left in that face.

What had happened to him? And how had it happened so very quickly?

"I assume you came to see me for a reason," he said.

His comment jolted her back to herself. By the Powers, she couldn't talk to him now. She might not ever be able to talk with him about this, not with Rugad dominating him. The plan she and the other Healers had devised would fail if she told him of it. She only hoped Sebastian would think of shattering all by himself.

How could she trigger it without tipping her hand to Rugad? She didn't know.

"Seger?" he said, sounding so much like the Rugad who had been her commander for years that when she looked at him, she almost expected to see the craggy imperial face.

She swallowed. "I had heard you were using Rugad's voice." She made herself sound calm, gave her own voice that slight patronizing tone so many people used with Sebastian. She was hoping he wouldn't realize she knew that Rugad was completely in charge of the Golem. "I wanted to warn you about it, remind you about its dangers, and then to tell you that if you don't stop, I will have to tell your sister."

He laughed, a deep throaty sound that carried across the courtyard. Several of the Infantry looked over at him, with startled expressions on their faces. The Infantry Leader, a woman who had served with Rugad, actually looked frightened for a moment before she could control her expression.

"What would Arianna do?" he asked. "Send me to my room without supper?"

Lies always created trouble. Seger licked her lips.

They were dry and cracked. She hadn't noticed before. "She would probably make me remove the voice."

"I thought you were going to do that anyway."

"Is this your last fling with it, then?"

He smiled, but turned his face away from her, as if he didn't want her to see his expression. She had never seen this sort of change in a Golem, but she had seen it in creatures that Shifters changed into. A bird that was really a Shifter would sometimes get a very Fey expression on its face. It would move in ways that a Fey moved, not the way that bird moved. That was because its main form was Fey, and it sometimes forgot that other creatures moved differently. Rugad was so used to fluid movement that it bent Sebastian's stone body in all sorts of forms the body had never used before. Seger wondered if that would harm the Golem. She wasn't sure.

"I've been thinking," she said when he didn't respond to her last comment, "that perhaps removing the voice is the worst thing I can do."

This got his attention. He stood up straighter. Sebastian was slightly taller than she was. She had never realized it before. "Why?"

"It's so integrated into your stone, I figure the only way to rid you of it is to shatter you, and I'm not sure you can survive another shattering."

"It's certainly not something I look forward to," he said. "That last shattering was difficult enough."

For Rugad. For Sebastian it had been the same. But it had nearly killed Rugad, and it had caused him to lose his voice in the first place.

It was confirmation that she wasn't dealing with Sebastian. Very subtle confirmation that went with all the rest.

The clang of swords began again. She turned toward the fighters, just because she didn't want to look at the Golem anymore. The men were in the ring now, fighting each other with measured movements. He had been right; it looked more like dance than war.

She watched. The men moved together. Even the parries came at the same angle, and almost at the same time.

The older Fey would be happy to have Rugad back in the form of Arianna or they would think she had simply come to her senses. The younger Fey wouldn't know what to do, how to behave. Already some of the old ways were being lost.

He was watching her, a wry and vaguely amused expression on his face. It surprised her that Sebastian's cracked skin could have such a range of movements, such a repertoire of expression. Sebastian had none.

What surprised her even more was that she could read Rugad as well as she always could. That had been the secret to her healing him—knowing when he really needed help and when he didn't. He would never tell her, of course. He expected to fight through everything. But sometimes he would listen to her—those times when he was the most damaged, and needed the most care.

He raised his eyebrows in an unspoken question. He wanted to know what she was thinking. Fortunately, she hadn't lost her ability to hide from him either.

"I had forgotten how beautiful fighting could be," she said, knowing it was what he wanted to hear.

He smiled. It was Sebastian's smile, with a cruel edge to it. "Beautiful," he said, "and profitable."

She nodded once. To say any more would raise his suspicions. Then, with a single last glance at the Infantry practice, she said, "Be careful with that voice."

"Yes, ma'am," he said and saluted her in the Islander fashion.

She smiled. She had to. It was supposed to be a joke. But she couldn't suppress a shudder as she walked away. She only hoped he didn't see it.

The clang of swords followed her as she crossed the flagstones. She could almost predict when she would hear the sound. Cross, scrape, clang. Repeat. So orderly. So un-Fey-like.

The Fey had been a perfect warrior people under Rugad. They had conquered half the world, stopped only by the unexpected wild magic of Blue Isle. She had been raised in the warrior culture, raised as a Healer whose work depended on a constant stream of injured. When she had been young, she had appreciated the challenge—always something new, always something impossible to attempt—but now that she was older she hated it. She saw the waste, saw too many lives cut short. Even the impossible hadn't been able to save some of her favorite people.

She had been burning out when she was approached by Rugad to be his personal Healer and she had taken the opportunity. The work was easy most of the time, and when it wasn't, it was so challenging that she created new frontiers in Healer magic. How to save a Black King, over and over again, and yet allow him to maintain his power, maintain his rule? When he had been stabbed in the throat, his head nearly severed from his body, she had kept him alive using techniques Healers had only discussed. He was back on his feet within a few weeks, as strong as ever.

The logical thing to do would be to turn her back on what she saw. Sebastian was gone. Rugad had the Golem's body, and Rugad would rule the Fey again, in one way or another. It would only be a matter of time before he had Arianna under his complete control.

Seger wondered if he had known—or somehow divined—her plan, the plan that would not work now. She couldn't put the construct into the Golem, not with part of Rugad already there, and active. He might know ways to cover the cracks in the skin. It had been years since anyone had seen Gift. All it would take would be some simple maneuvering, and Rugad could transform the Golem into his template. Rugad would rule through a stone body, pretending to be Gift.

When she reached the wooden door leading into the Fey wing of the palace, she pulled it open and stepped inside. The doorway was cool and dark and empty. She closed the door behind her and leaned against it.

The logical thing. She sighed. Her heart didn't want

her to do the logical thing. She had liked Arianna, liked the way that the Fey were learning to live within their own Empire. They could be warrior people, Arianna had once said, tough people, whom no one invaded, no one picked fights with, no one conquered. The difference was that they didn't have to do any of those things to anyone else either.

Seger had heard sense in that. She saw no need in taking over the entire world. She saw only loss in it. And there had been no uprising within the ranks of Fey, as she had expected initially, no complaints about the new policy.

Could a people grow tired of movement and conquest as well? Or had they simply needed another rest?

She didn't know. What she did know was that Arianna, with her lack of Fey training, her lack of a traditional Fey government, had left herself vulnerable to a kind of magic so rarely used that Seger hadn't paid much attention to it.

If she was going to save Arianna, if she was going to save the new future of the Fey—the one that meant fewer deaths and richer lives—then she had to find a way to fight Rugad's construct. She had to find a way to stop the magic that was re-creating the most ruthless Black King the Fey had ever known.

She would need help, and she wasn't sure she had time to find it. She needed to act with stealth. So far Rugad didn't suspect that she knew as much as she did. But once he knew, he would make certain she would never come near him again.

Seger stood, straightened her shoulders, and headed deeper into the Fey quarters. She needed to send Gull Riders and Wisps over half the world, and she had to do so without the knowledge of Arianna—or Rugad. It would be tricky. And whatever help came first was the help she had to use.

She would only get one chance at this. She had to do everything right. For all their sakes.

And for the sake of the world.

THE BLACK QUEEN

THE RESCUE

Three Days Later

CHAPTER TWENTY

THE SKY WAS a brilliant blue. The ocean itself picked up the vibrant blue, and mixed it with its own natural grays and greens, making it seem as if they were sailing on a majestic woven carpet made especially for them. The breeze was light, but enough to fill their sails, and the temperatures had grown warmer. The storm that threatened three days before had been a small one, easily dissipated by Bridge's Weather Sprites, much to the surprise of the Nyeian crew. Nothing serious loomed ahead, but Bridge's Navigators told him that this balmy section of ocean—called the Evil Warmth by most sailors— would disappear shortly, and then they would hit an area of the sea that all dreaded for its unpredictable weather. More ships had been lost in the upcoming section of ocean, his Navigators told him, than in any other part of the Infrin Sea.

That didn't worry him, not yet. Besides, part of the problem was that non-Fey vessels were lulled into a kind of contentment in the Evil Warmth, and would then come upon the treacherous waters unprepared. Bridge's ships were prepared, and there were Bird Riders ahead, scouting the area, ready to warn them about anything unusual.

Bird Riders. Normally he liked them, but one particular Bird Rider was setting his teeth on edge. Bridge was standing on the deck near the captain's area—he never could remember nautical terms—watching his daughter flirt with Ace. Ace was young and talented and smart, everything Bridge wanted in a Gull Rider. But not what he wanted in a son-in-law.

What was it about Lyndred that made her so needy? She was a beautiful girl with a glorious future. The last thing she needed was to be bound to a Bird Rider whose entire life would be one of service.

At least she wasn't flirting with the Nyeian crew. Bridge had been afraid of that, but she had surprised him with this Rider.

Ace was hanging on to the railing as he spoke to her. She was leaning against the railing herself, but not paying much attention to how she was grounded. A sudden swell would knock her into the water. Apparently Ace noticed that too, for he kept one hand behind her at all times.

The boy was cautious, if nothing else. Cautious and infatuated with Bridge's daughter.

Lyndred had tried to be coy about the whole thing. A few days ago, when Ace had brought news of the storm, Lyndred had come to Bridge, ostensibly to find out what such news meant. Actually, she watched him from the corner of her eye as she talked about Ace, trying to see if Bridge approved.

He approved of Ace. He didn't approve of a union with Ace and his daughter. And he didn't know how to tell her that, but he would have to.

Or he would have to forbid the boy from getting near her. That, of course, would make things worse. Kids their age thought it romantic to be denied each other's company—he certainly had with his first wife. That was a match he would regret for the rest of his life, if it weren't for the fact that it gave him Rugan. The boy didn't have Vision like Lyndred but he did have sense, which she somehow lacked.

His second wife, whom Bridge married after his father died, had been a gem. By then, though, Bridge had known who he was and what he wanted. Lyndred was too young to know any of that.

But if he told her that, she would get angry. He loved this child, his youngest—more than any of the others, truth be told—but she exasperated him. His only girl, and his hope for the future, and she was determined to screw it up.

Bridge sighed. He wished he were as clever as his father or as manipulative as his grandfather. Then he would know how to handle this daughter of his. But he didn't. And so he watched, in complete frustration, knowing one day she would take it too far, and he would have another fight with her, like he had over that silly Nyeian poet with the ridiculous name.

Something white against the blueness above caught the corner of his eye. He turned, saw a Gull Rider spinning out of control, attempting a dive toward the deck and failing. Instead, it landed in the water, still in Gull form. He didn't hear a splash. If he hadn't seen it, he wouldn't have known that it landed.

He ran to the railing, and so did one of the Nyeian sailors. The Gull Rider was floating on the surface, wings spread, beak down. Only its tiny Fey body remained out of the water. Its small head was back, and its arms dangled. It was going to drown.

Bridge stepped onto the rail when the Nyeian sailor put a hand on his chest, holding him back. Instead, another Nyeian stripped, tossed his ruffled sailing clothes against the deck, and dove, completely naked, into the sea.

By this time, Lyndred and Ace had come to the railing to see what happened. His daughter stepped beside him, watching. Ace was behind her, looking uncomfortable now that he realized Bridge was there.

"Who is that?" Lyndred asked Ace.

"I don't know. I don't recognize her."

Until that moment, Bridge hadn't even noticed that the Gull Rider was female. He was more concerned with the way that her bird's body listed, the way the tail feathers were starting to go under. The Nyeian sailor swam with broad, easy strokes, covering the distance quickly.

When he reached the Gull Rider, he picked her out of the water, and stared at her for a moment. Bridge could almost see the thought running through the man's head: *Now what do I do with it?* Then, as if in answer, he rolled on his back, placed the Gull Rider on his chest, and swam toward the ship.

His backstroke was powerful, and fortunately the sea was calm. No waves took him, and nothing knocked the Gull Rider off him. When he reached the side of the ship, another Nyeian met him. Bridge hadn't even seen that Nyeian climb down the rope ladder. The second Nyeian grabbed the Gull Rider, and carried her up to the deck.

"Get a Healer," Bridge said to Ace, wondering why he hadn't thought of that sooner. He had probably thought that the Gull Rider was going to drown in full view of all of them. Ace didn't have to wait for a second instruction. He hurried below decks.

The rescuer grabbed the rope ladder, flung his long wet hair out of his face, and began to climb up. Bridge wanted to pull his daughter back, but he had the sneaking suspicion she had already seen a naked Nyeian male before.

The Nyeian carrying the Gull Rider made it to the deck. Bridge met him, and took the Rider from him.

She was tinier than most Gull Riders, but her form was compact, built for speed. He could feel her heart beating in her avian breast. The gull's head was limp, eyes open and unseeing. He wondered if the bird form could die, and the Fey form still live.

He didn't know.

The Rider herself was tiny as well. Her naked torso was sun- and windburned, her eyes closed, her breathing shallow. Her features were etched sharply against her skin. He had seen other Bird Riders look like this—decades ago, in the middle of the Nye campaign. His grandfather and his father both used Bird Riders as messengers in that campaign, sometimes demanding that the Riders perform miraculous feats in order to get a message somewhere on time.

He carried her as if a false movement would break her. There was shade near the stairs. He brought her there.

Lyndred was peering at the form in his hands. "Who is she?"

"I don't recognize her," he said, but that didn't mean anything. He didn't know every Bird Rider.

But he knew all the ones he had brought on this trip.

She had come from somewhere else, and it didn't seem as if she had come from the same direction they had. His heart was beating rapidly. If she came from anywhere else, it had to be Blue Isle.

Why would Arianna send a Bird Rider at a killing pace back to Galinas? She had never done so before.

Ace came up beside him, and crouched. "I have a Healer," he said. He bent over the Gull Rider, and frowned.

"Who is she?" Lyndred asked again.

He shook his head. "I've never seen her before." He brushed the hair off her tiny forehead. "But she nearly flew herself to death."

"She missed her landing," Bridge said. "She was trying for the deck."

"With the last of her strength, I'll wager," Ace said. "I'm not sure how she could fly like this. Look." He delicately touched part of her wing. "Most of her feathers are gone. That doesn't happen to real gulls. Only to Riders who push themselves too hard."

The Healer had finally come above decks. She was an elderly woman with a compassionate face. Her name was Kir, and she had accompanied Bridge everywhere. He trusted her more than he trusted members of his family.

She bent down as well. "By the Powers, this child is in terrible shape."

"Child?" Bridge asked.

Kir nodded as she moved the Rider's arms, checked beneath her wings, adjusted her gull's head. "I don't think she's much older than Lyndred, and certainly not trained for this sort of thing."

Bridge frowned. "So you think she's on an urgent mission too?"

Kir lifted the bird head slightly, revealing a pouch. "She's a long way from anywhere. If we hadn't been here, I don't know what would have happened to her."

"She probably saw us from far away," Ace said. "And let her guard down. That was enough to interrupt her flight."

"She's still lucky." Kir picked her up. "I'm taking her below decks." Then she raised her head and looked at Bridge. "You might have to spare one of your own Bird Riders."

"I'd already thought of that," he said. "Let me know when she wakes."

"We'll wake her shortly," Kir said. "It's our duty to find out how urgent her mission is, as well."

Bridge nodded. Kir carried the Gull Rider below decks. Ace started to follow but Lyndred held him back.

"No," Bridge said. "Let him go."

Lyndred flashed him an angry look, but let go of Ace's arm. Ace followed Kir down the stairs, disappearing into the darkness.

Lyndred crossed her arms. "You were spying on us."

"You were hard to miss."

"And now you're going to give me that 'he's not good enough for you' lecture."

Actually Bridge was, but her words stopped him. "No," he lied. "I wanted to ask you something."

He put his arm around her and led her away from the stairs. They walked to a more secluded section of railing. There were no ropes here, only the wooden sides and the rail above.

The ship created a white wake in the blue-green-gray

sea. The spray was warm, the breeze still gentle. Kir was right. The Gull Rider had been lucky. Lucky to land here, lucky to find them, lucky that the sea was warm.

He pulled his daughter close. Perhaps he was the problem. Perhaps his coolness toward her had made her seek out other men.

"Daddy?" she asked, sounding younger than usual. "Will that Rider be all right?"

"I hope so," he said.

"I wonder who sent her."

"Me too." He leaned his head against his daughter's. Once upon a time, he could rest his cheek on the top of her head, but no longer. There was even a possibility that she would grow taller than he. Some Fey hit the last of their growth in their twenties.

She slipped her arm around him. He didn't want to lose the moment, but he knew he had to, knew they had to talk.

"Lyndred," he said softly. "You said, when you wanted to marry that Nyeian, that you did so because you wanted to prevent your Visions. Is that what's happening with Ace?"

"No!" She let go of him as if his touch burned her. "Of course not."

"Lyndred, I don't mean to question your emotions. If you feel something for him, fine. I just want to know what you're thinking."

She glanced at Bridge, then looked away. He remembered that movement from her babyhood. It was a way of checking his mood before doing something, trying to make sure that he wouldn't yell. He suspected the motivations were more sophisticated now, but not much. She was still Lyndred, after all.

"I like him," she said.

"I know that," he replied, and then stopped himself from adding, *You liked the Nyeian too*.

"It's harmless," she said.

"Is it?" he asked. "You said that on Blue Isle there's a

blond man who will give you a child you do not want. Did you mean that you will bear his child? Or did you mean an actual child, someone else's child, that he will give you custody of?"

She bit her lower lip. "It'll be my child," she said sadly.

"Is that what you're trying to prevent?"

She gripped the railing with both hands. The spray touched her face like a thousand tiny tears. He wanted to put his hand on her shoulder, but he knew better than to touch her now.

"It'll break my heart, Daddy," she said.

The tone of her voice almost broke his. It sounded as if the event had already happened, as if it had damaged her in some way, even now, months, maybe years, before the event.

He took a step closer to her, still not touching her, even though he wanted to take her in his arms and hold her like he used to do when she was a little girl. When did a man stop wanting to protect his children from harm? It seemed as if his own father had found that point. Bridge wasn't sure he ever would.

"Have you ever thought," he asked slowly, "that perhaps it breaks your heart because you already love someone else? That by trying to prevent this Vision, you may actually create it?"

She whirled so fast he had to take a step backward. The beaded water had run down her face and stained her Nyeian-style tunic. "Do you think that could happen?" she asked.

"Yes," he said. "Visions are tricky things. They can be deceptive. They can lure you to the place that you're trying to prevent just as easily as they can guide you toward that prevention."

"Why?"

Always, his Lyndred needed a reason. She had from the moment she could speak. Fortunately, he had an answer to this one, even though the answer was not his own.

"A Shaman once told me that the Powers send us Visions, but the Mysteries control the Visions. And the Mysteries are still tied to this world. So sometimes, the Mysteries only give us part of the Vision, to influence the outcome as best they can."

"Do you believe that?" she asked.

He shrugged. "It's the best explanation I've ever heard. I've always wondered why Visions come in pieces, why we can't See the whole thing."

She turned back toward the sea. Her hands gripped the railing so tightly that her knuckles were turning white. "Have you ever Seen your own death?"

"I'm not sure," he said. "They say one of the earliest Visions is of death, but a lot of times we don't recognize it. You think you've Seen my death."

"Yes."

"And you're convinced it'll happen while we're on Blue Isle."

"Yes."

He placed a hand on her shoulder. "Lyndred, you cannot go through life being afraid of what may come. You have to live now."

She bowed her head. "I don't want anything to change. I didn't want to leave Nye. I didn't want to come here. I don't want any of those Visions to come true."

"Some will," he said. "And some won't. You know that's the way of things. Sometimes you can change them just by acknowledging them."

She sighed, then rested her cheek on his hand. Her skin was warm, and damp from the spray. "What if I love Ace?"

"Do you?" Bridge asked, hoping she would say no.

"I don't know."

"Then wait until you do know, and talk to me."

"Would you approve of my match with a Gull Rider?"

He sighed, and gave her the answer he had to give. "We're Fey, not Nyeians. I don't have to approve your match, at least not within our own people. Outside of our people, I do, and maybe even the Black Queen does, because it might represent the wrong kind of alliance. So you could marry a Red Cap if you wanted, and I wouldn't say a word."

She lifted her head, wrinkling her nose in a delicate expression of disgust. "A Red Cap? Daddy! Yuck!"

He grinned, and so did she.

"You know," she said, "you would probably forbid me from marrying a Red Cap."

"Probably," he said. "But a Red Cap is Fey. You would still be able to do what you wanted."

She giggled. "Imagine me with someone who has no magic and dirty fingernails."

"Well," Bridge said, "there was this Nyeian . . ."

She made herself look serious. "His fingernails were clean."

"But he had no magic."

"Not the kind you're referring to," she said and paused for a long moment. "But there was a certain—charm—to his poetry."

Bridge laughed, and as he did so, he felt a hand on his shoulder. He turned. One of the Domestics stood behind him. "You're wanted belowdecks," she said.

He nodded, feeling serious. He squeezed Lyndred's waist and let go of her, following the Domestic down the stairs to the area that he had assigned them. The corridors were narrow down here, and the Fey lamps swayed with the movement of the ship. He heard footsteps behind him, and realized that Lyndred had come too.

The Domestics had made the largest quarters on this deck into a sickroom. They had had the usual cases, a bit of seasickness, some reaction to bad meat, a few injuries among the Nyeian crew. But nothing like this.

Bridge let himself be led into the sickroom. The room was actually a bit smaller than his own compartment, but the Domestics had managed to add several short bunks and a few hammocks into the space. The bunks were attached to the floor by some method he couldn't see, and the hammocks swung like the Fey lamps. The Gull Rider lay on the bed built into the wall. She was on the pillow, looking small and lost among all the blankets and folds. She still hadn't reverted to her Fey form.

Ace sat on a nearby bed, his fingers laced together. He was watching her. He barely looked up as Lyndred entered. Bridge found that interesting.

Kir stood near the door. She took Bridge's arm. "You need to speak with her alone, but do not tire her. Her name is Cassandra. She was born on Nye, but her parents took her to Blue Isle with Rugad's fleet. She's been there ever since."

So she was from Blue Isle. He felt an excitement in his belly. Something was happening.

"Did she say why Arianna sent her?"

Kir shook her head. "There's something strange about that, I would say. But she won't talk to me. I told her she needed to talk with you, that you're Black Family, and she has to do as you say. Don't tire her. She flew beyond her breaking point and she's devastated about failing her mission."

"Well, she hasn't failed yet," he said. "Clear the room for me."

"Not too much time," Kir cautioned.

"I promise," he said.

She took Ace's arm and got him up. When he finally saw Lyndred, he smiled. She smiled too, but her eyes were for the Gull Rider on the bed. Kir spoke to Lyndred softly. Lyndred looked at her father, an appeal to stay all over her face. He shook his head slightly, and she sighed. Then she followed Ace out of the room. The other Domestic left as well.

"Will you stay?" he asked Kir.

"I'll be right outside the door." And then she, too, left.

He walked over to the built-in bed. It was shaped like his, long and fairly narrow, but with a deep area for a mattress. It was one of the most comfortable beds he had ever slept in; its three walls and small ceiling made him feel as if he were in a cave, and the rocking of the ship soothed him.

Cassandra did not look soothed. She looked terrified. Her bird's eyes were still closed, the wings immobile, but she had propped her Fey torso up by her elbows, even though it clearly took effort. She wore a small shirt that someone had dug up, or had made quickly, and her hair—now dry—spilled about her shoulders. Her eyes were sunken with exhaustion, and her lips were still an odd shade of blue.

He sat on the main part of the bed, not too close to the pillow. "Hi," he said, making sure he spoke very gently. "My name is Bridge. I'm Rugar's son, and Arianna's uncle."

"Cassandra," she said in a small voice. He had to strain to hear her. "I need some help. I need to leave. I have a mission—"

"I gathered that," he said. "But you're very far from land, and you're not going to make it to Nye without help. We're heading to Blue Isle, and we can't turn around. If I knew what your mission was, perhaps then—"

She was shaking her head long before he finished. "I swore I'd go. I promised."

"You'll die, then," he said. "You aren't trained for this sort of work. You're lucky you found us."

She eased off her elbows and lay back on the pillow. Her small face had gone an alarming shade of gray. She closed her eyes, and he was about to call for Kir when he saw a tear slide down Cassandra's cheek.

"I promised," she said.

"I know." He spoke to her as gently as he once spoke to Lyndred, when she was young and disappointed and in over her depth. "But there are ways to fulfill your promise, even now."

Her eyes opened and she sat up, only to moan and lay back down, a hand on her forehead.

"We can give your assignment to one of our Gull Riders who'll complete it for you. You'll have to promise to serve in that Rider's place, and do that Rider's duties once you're well."

Her sigh was small. "I have a written message and a

verbal one. I promised I'd be the one to give the messages, and no one else would touch them."

"The other Rider," he said, "would, in effect, become you. I don't have to know the message if it's that secret."

But he wanted to. His father, he knew, would have found out, and so would his grandfather. But Bridge had always been a different sort of man, not as cunning and not as ruthless. The Rider's distress wouldn't have affected his father. It bothered Bridge.

"It's a long mission," she said. "I've only just started."

And she fell, exhausted already. "When did you leave the Isle?"

"Five days ago."

"You made excellent time." And that, he knew, was part of the problem. She had gone too fast too soon, not knowing that the long-distance fliers paced themselves. Someone would have to train her. What was happening on the Isle that not even the Bird Riders knew how to use their best skills?

She plumped up a small section of her pillow. "I can't even move the gull parts," she said. "And your Healer—"

"Kir."

"Kir said that I won't be able to take Fey form for several days. I didn't mean to have this happen. I'm not sure how it did. I have to get to Vion."

"I know," he said. "We'll get your message there. I promise."

There was such sadness on her face. He knew what it was like to fail. He had done so more often than he cared to think about, so often that his father had told him he was worthless.

"Thank you," she said.

He nodded. "You're welcome." Then he stood. "I'll have Kir come back."

"Um, sir? Bridge?" In the formality he heard a bit of Blue Isle. The Fey never gave each other titles of respect.

"Yes?"

She propped herself on the pillow so that she was higher. He crouched anyway.

"Are you going to Blue Isle?"

"Yes," he said.

"Were you summoned?"

What an odd question. He shook his head. "I just decided it was time to see Arianna."

And even odder that he answered it. But he felt a kinship with this girl, something tied to her failure, he supposed, or her deep regret.

"Why do you ask?" he said.

Her small lips pursed. "I think it's good that someone from the Black Family go to Blue Isle."

"Is there a problem?"

"Nothing they've told me." Her dark gaze met his. Without revealing her message, she was telling him something important. She was giving it to him for his kindness to her. "But I've heard things."

"What sort of things?"

"The Black Queen is ill. She collapsed outside a meeting, and when I left, no one had seen her for over a day."

He felt a discomfort at that. Arianna was still a young woman, about the age of his oldest son. "Are you sure it's illness?"

"No," Cassandra said. "But I think it's important. Especially since they're sending me to Vion."

Vion. That was what she was trying to tell him. The Eccrasian Mountains were in Vion, and he had heard that young Gift went there years ago to become a Shaman. Bridge had thought that odd; no member of the Black Family had ever become a Shaman before.

"To find Gift?" he asked, knowing that she wouldn't answer. "He's the heir, isn't he?"

"I don't know affairs of state," she said. "All I know is the gossip from the Isle. And I think it's good to have the Black Family close. I've been worried."

Which was why she flew so hard, why she nearly killed herself out in the middle of nowhere.

He brushed a thumb against her small forehead. "Thank you," he said. "Rest now."

"I will." She eased back onto the pillow and closed her eyes, the expression of pain still on her face.

He walked past the bunks to the door. Kir was outside of it. "She's resting," he said as he passed.

Kir smiled at him, asked no questions, and disappeared inside the room.

The only other person in the narrow corridor was his daughter. She was sitting on the wooden stairs, her head against the banister. He didn't want to see her right now. He had to take care of his promise to Cassandra.

Lyndred patted the stair beside her. He didn't sit. "Lyndred," he said. "I need to—"

"Talk to me first," she said. "It'll only take a moment."

He sighed. "What?"

"That Gull Rider, she has a mission to finish, right?"

He felt himself grow cold. Sometimes his daughter was too smart by half. "Right."

"And she can't do it."

"That's right."

"So you're going to send Ace."

Caught. It had seemed an elegant solution to his problem. Besides, Ace was good at his work, properly trained, and trustworthy. "Yes."

Lyndred stood. With the help of the stair, she was taller than he was. "I suppose it'll do no good to ask you to send someone else. You'll just do what you want."

"Is there a reason he shouldn't go?" Bridge asked.

"You mean besides the fact that I want him to stay?" Lyndred shook her head. "You just want him out of here so that he'll leave me alone."

"No," he said. "This is what Bird Riders do. They go on missions for their commanders. They're gone for weeks, months, sometimes years at a time."

"So you're trying to teach me a lesson."

"In part, maybe," he said. "But the lesson is different from the one you're expecting."

"What is it, then?" There was a hint of anger to her tone, a hint of I-will-not-listen-no-matter-what-you-say.

"It's this," he said. "If you truly feel something for him, and he truly feels something for you, then those feelings will still be there when he gets back."

Her lips thinned, and she shook her head. She obviously knew that the argument was too logical to fight, but she wanted to. She took a breath. "If I hadn't brought him to your attention, would you have sent him?"

"I don't know," Bridge said honestly. "Maybe not. But he's one of the youngest Gull Riders I have and he's strong. He needs to go to Vion for this mission, and that's a long way from here. I need a good Gull Rider, and I need one I can trust. Ace fits that. And I learned that thanks to you."

Color filled her cheeks. "It's not fair, you know. We had a good talk on deck about my future and now you screw it up."

"No," he said. "I'm living my life, just as I told you to live yours. Now, I need to find Ace because he has to leave. This matter nearly killed one Gull Rider. I think we should honor her and make sure her message gets delivered."

Lyndred tilted her head slightly. That last had clearly gotten through to her. "You know what the message is?"

"She didn't tell me," Bridge said. "But she gave me enough sideways information that I can guess. They're calling Gift home. It seems Arianna is ill. It's good that we're going to Blue Isle."

Lyndred's eyes narrowed. For the first time ever, he saw her great-grandfather in her face. It wasn't in her looks, but in that slight expression of cunning that passed across her features before she could cover the look up.

"So why deliver the message? Maybe we should be the ones who're there."

He met her gaze, his heart pounding. "Are you willing to take the Black Throne by deception, Lynnie?" He purposely used her childhood name, trying to remind her just how young she was. "Are you able to keep Gift away and prevent the Blood against Blood? Are you strong enough, smart enough, and cunning enough to do that? Because if you are, I'll stop the message from leaving this ship."

"Would you help me?" she asked.

He took a deep breath. Would he? Opportunities like this came very rarely. "Of course," he said. "But let me give you your first lesson in cunning. My grandfather always said the only way to make sure that the Blood remained calm was to make certain you never got the blame for family matters."

"What does that mean?" she asked.

"It means," he said, "that we send Ace. We make sure he finds Gift and delivers the message. And while he does, we double our pace to Blue Isle. Even if Gift moves quickly, even if he has help, he cannot get to Blue Isle before us."

"But what if she dies after he arrives?"

Good question. These were the nuances of manipulation that he always screwed up.

"Maybe we should send an older Gull Rider," she said, "one not as good, one who might not make it. Then, if the Rider fails, no one will blame us."

She learned fast. It had taken him years to begin to understand the deviousness that motivated the rest of his family. His father had been long dead when she was born, and his grandfather left when she was small. Perhaps a select handful in his family were just born that way, devious and brilliant in equal measures.

"It's a great plan," he said, "but we don't have any Riders like that. I saw no point in bringing them."

She sighed. "Then we don't send anyone."

He shook his head. "Cassandra will know."

His daughter's gaze met his. The look in her eyes chilled him.

"Even if she doesn't live," he said, "others will remember her. Word will get out. No. We send Ace, just as we planned. We do everything correctly. And then, when he's gone, we head to Blue Isle as fast as these ships will take us. No more leisure cruise. We will get there in half the time."

Lyndred smiled, then she reached over and kissed him on the cheek. "You're more devious than you give yourself credit for, Daddy."

He shook his head. "I'm not devious enough. Your grandfather would have made more of this, somehow."

"No," she said. "He would know more. He had greater Vision, that's all."

Something in her words made him stop. "You saw the Black Queen in your Vision."

She nodded.

"Was she in poor health?"

Lyndred shrugged. "All I saw was her face."

"And it wasn't yours."

She laughed. "I would have known that, Daddy."

"So Arianna will be alive when we get to Blue Isle." He was silent for a moment. "We're basing all of this on the supposition that the illness is fatal."

"Why else would she send for her brother?" Lyndred asked.

Rugad had thought Arianna and Gift worthy successors to the Black Throne, which meant they thought like Lyndred. Bridge, on the other hand, was unimaginative and rather straightforward.

"We could be wrong," he said. "She may need him for some other reason."

Lyndred nodded. "I'd already thought of that," she said, "and if she does, and he's not there, she'll have to turn to her family, won't she? And that will be us."

There was a coldness in the center of her, a self-interest that Bridge had tried not to notice. That was why she could forget Rupert the poet so easily, why she was trying to lure Ace under her spell. She was protecting herself, just as her great-grandfather used to do. She looked at the world with a coldness that made everything clear. Was that what frightened her about the Vision of the child? Because her heart would be broken, which meant that somewhere, somehow, her heart would be engaged?

He made himself smile and kiss her before he went up the stairs to find Ace. "I think Blue Isle will be the most interesting place we'll have gone in years."

"Oh, Daddy," she said, "I know it will."

CHAPTER TWENTY-ONE

THE CARRIAGE STOPPED inside the courtyard near the stables. The smells of hay and manure coming in through the open window were pungent and vaguely familiar. Coulter had forgotten that this was the main entrance to the palace.

His entire body was still bumping. He wondered who had come up with this singularly uncomfortable form of travel. He had half a hundred bruises, all from mud holes or the carriage lurching right when he expected it to go left. He had tried to sleep on the long trip, but the back of his head kept bouncing on the wooden seat. Somehow he had managed naps, but they had been shallow, uncomfortable things, filling his dreams with driving and bumping and narrow, winding corners.

The last thing he wanted to do was see Arianna now. He had to look as bad as he felt with several days growth of beard, and clothes he had been wearing since he left Constant. This was not as he imagined.

Nor had the reception at the palace gates been anything like he had imagined either. He had thought he

would have to explain himself to the guard. He hadn't
been here in years. He didn't expect them to know his
name. Yet one guard had acted as if Coulter were visiting
royalty, and two others had disappeared into the courtyard ahead of him with news of his arrival.

The door to the carriage opened and Dash peered in.
His face was windburned, his blond hair tousled, but his
blue eyes were lively, despite the long trip. Every morning, he had let Coulter drive the carriage while he slept,
and somehow Dash had no trouble snoring his way
through the most treacherous roads. They'd had to get
fresh horses at some village along the way, and Coulter
suspected he got the worse of the trade. But not even the
horses looked as bad as he felt.

"You gonna stay in here all day? I'm starving. I hope
they'll feed us here."

That had been Dash's comment at every stop. Coulter
sighed and grabbed the door frame, pulling himself out
of the carriage. "They'll feed us," he said, "if only to get
rid of us."

He stepped down the single step as the carriage rocked
lightly. The flagstones looked familiar, and so did the
stone wall, but it still seemed odd to him to see all the Fey
faces milling about, from Domestics to Infantry. They
looked like they belonged.

When he had last been here—when Nicholas had
asked him to live here—the mixture of Islander and Fey
in this place wasn't nearly so easy.

Several grooms surrounded the horses and were getting ready to move the carriage somewhere less obtru-
sive. Dash was watching the flurry of people, his mouth
open slightly. Coulter had forgotten that, while Dash's
father had worked at the stables, Dash had never been to
the palace.

"This place is huge," Dash said in an awed voice. He
was staring at the palace itself. Coulter remembered having the same thought the first time he saw it, with its
three towers and its high stone walls. Clearly it had once
had four towers, but one had been removed to make way

for a modern kitchen with a high ceiling and ventilation in the roof. Sometimes Coulter thought of the towers as the eyes of the palace. The round rooms with floor-to-ceiling windows at the towers' top allowed anyone to stare down at him, but it didn't feel as if anyone were staring at him now.

"Yes," Coulter said. "It is huge." And he suddenly felt silly. He had come all this way because of what—a worry? How would he explain that to Arianna? He wasn't even sure he would get to see her. He wasn't sure if he wanted to. What would she think of him after all these years? She had taken control of an entire Empire. He had created a school.

"Coulter!"

The voice that called him was familiar, but he couldn't place it. He turned, saw a Fey woman in Domestic's robes running across the courtyard. She held up her skirts with one hand and was waving at him with another.

She was a Healer, and her name was—Seger. She had saved the life, if you wanted to call it that, of Sebastian by keeping his pieces when Rugad had ordered her not to. For that, Arianna had deemed her trustworthy.

Why had Arianna sent her?

Dash stepped back slightly and Seger stopped beside him. "I'm so glad you're here," she said, sounding breathless. Apparently she wasn't used to running. "You made good time."

Coulter frowned. He remembered her as a Healer. Had he been wrong? Was she some sort of minor Visionary or was he confusing her with someone else? "You knew I was coming?"

She stepped back slightly and tilted her head. "You didn't get my message?"

"No," he said.

"Then what—?" She stopped herself, and glanced at Dash. "Is this a friend of yours?"

"Dash, this is Seger." Coulter watched as Dash bowed slightly, hands behind his back. The movement made him look courtly. "Dash handles horses better than I do, so he drove the carriage here."

"Coulter underestimates himself. He just wanted company," Dash said.

Seger didn't look interested. Something made her mouth tight, and even though she smiled in the proper places, the smile didn't reach her eyes. "Forgive me," she said, "but I need to speak to Coulter alone."

Dash shrugged, trying to look casual but managing to look lost instead. "Certainly. I, um—"

"He's hungry," Coulter said. "Do you think someone in the kitchen could be persuaded to feed him?"

"I don't think that would be a problem. We'll go in that way." Seger threaded her arm through Coulter's as if she expected him to disappear. She led him to the wooden kitchen door, propped open despite the day's chill. A waft of heat billowed out, along with the smell of fresh bread. They stepped inside.

This area was as he remembered it. Fires burned in the great fireplaces, and pots with stews hung from iron racks. Stoves, with their own internal fires, were also hot, and chefs stood before them, working on the evening meal. The bakers had the brick-lined ovens working, and rows of fresh baked bread already stood on the warming tables behind them.

Coulter's mouth watered. He was hungry too.

No one seemed to notice them as they passed through, but Dash gave a longing glance at the bread. Seger led them past it to the pantry. There a table stood, along with several chairs. The day-old bread and baked goods stood on one shelf, as did the sausage ends and cheese curds. This was where the servants ate, where the servants had always eaten. Coulter had never taken a meal here, but he had seen it more than once.

Seger pulled back a chair for Dash. "Eat as much as you want," she said. "When you're done, wait here. I'll send someone for you after I've spoken to Coulter."

Dash looked at Coulter for confirmation. He nodded,

then let Seger lead him out of the pantry. The next area was the buttery, and he could hear low conversation as men worked the churns. Seger opened a door, and they found themselves in the Hall, with its great arched windows and the swords that covered the inner wall.

Light filtered in, revealing dust motes floating in the air. Seger went to the inner wall and, with her fingertips, opened a hidden door. Coulter never would have noticed it if she hadn't pulled it open.

She beckoned. He followed. The area was dark, and he nearly fell down a flight of stairs that began at the door. There had been no landing. The interior here smelled musty. Below him, Seger lit a torch.

"Close the door," she said.

He shoved it closed, and realized that the door was as hidden on this side as it was on the other. It was part of the maze of tunnels that ran below the entire city. He had heard of them, but he had never seen them.

Seger led him through a long corridor, and finally she stopped at a place where the corridor intersected another. She lit three more torches and placed them in holders down the passageways, so that they could see if someone was coming.

He doubted anyone would. The corridors were lined with spiderwebs—albeit fairly new ones. There wasn't much dust, so someone cleaned these tunnels regularly, but they looked and smelled as if cleaning was all that happened here.

"If you didn't get my message," Seger said, "what are you doing here?"

"I felt it was time to come," he said, which was not a lie, but which was as much truth as he was willing to tell for now.

She nodded as if that didn't surprise her. "I sent a Wisp for you three days ago. I sent her to Constant."

"I left five days ago. Four and a half, if you want me to be accurate." He waited. He wasn't going to say anything more.

Seger glanced down the corridors. "You can feel if anyone approaches, can't you?"

"If you want me to," he said. "I can get a sense of anyone, as long as they have some magic. Usually, I don't do that."

"I want you to," she said.

"Who are you afraid of?"

Seger sighed and bit her lower lip. "I need an Enchanter, Coulter. This is too big for me."

"What is?"

"Arianna," she said. "And Sebastian. Both."

He felt cold. "What's happened to them?"

"Rugad has them."

"Rugad?" He wasn't sure he'd heard that right. "Rugad is dead."

"No," she said. "His body is dead. His personality and his memories live on. They're taking over Arianna, and I think they may have Sebastian."

"How—?"

"Arianna sent me a message yesterday. She said something triggered the takeover early. It was supposed to happen ten years from now, and there would have been no reversing it. But she believes that Rugad doesn't have his full powers yet, and we can dislodge him."

Coulter's head was reeling. Rugad, alive? Coulter had only seen him once, and that through Gift's eyes. Literally. Rugad had taken over Gift, and Coulter had known it, had seen the stranger—the malevolent stranger—looking out of Gift's eyes. Without thinking, Coulter had crossed Gift's Links, gone inside Gift's mind, and thrown Rugad out, closing all the Link doors behind him. That action had caused a rift in his friendship with Gift that had never entirely healed. Gift had believed that Coulter's action put Sebastian in jeopardy, and Gift had been angry at Coulter for taking control of Gift's body without his permission. Coulter always felt as if, for the second time since they had known each other, he had saved Gift's life.

But he still remembered how Rugad had felt in pure energy form: strong and old and so very powerful. The only reason Coulter had defeated him that day had been because Coulter had caught him by surprise.

And now Seger was saying he was back.

"When?" Coulter asked. "When did this all start?"

"I don't know when it started," Seger said. "We noticed it almost two weeks ago. Arianna was getting headaches . . ."

She went on speaking but Coulter wasn't listening to the details. Almost two weeks ago, he had first sensed something wrong.

"So the light went through here first," he said, interrupting Seger.

"The light?" She frowned. "What light?"

"A strong magic stream, a white light, threaded with black. Didn't you—?" This time, he stopped himself. He knew a lot about Fey magic, but not enough. Apparently Healers couldn't see such things either.

"Threaded with black." She leaned against the dusty stone wall. "A light, filled with magic. And threaded with black."

"That means something to you?" he asked.

"You saw this about two weeks ago?"

"Yes," he said. "And from that point on, I had a sense that Arianna was in trouble."

Seger put her hand on his arm. "Thank you," she said. "Arianna had mentioned a light, and so had Sebastian, but I didn't know what kind it was. Now I do. The black awakened Rugad early."

"You call it Rugad, but is it?"

She shrugged. "It's a construct, with his memories and his personality. As far as I can tell, it's him."

Coulter was silent for a moment. Then he said, "You have a way you want me to help?"

"I want you to remove it. Can you?"

He didn't know. He supposed he could. According to Scavenger, Enchanters could do anything any other Fey could. But Coulter didn't know if any other Fey could remove this thing.

"I can try," he said, beginning to get a picture of what he could do. "But I'll need a place to put the construct, someplace away from Arianna so that when I destroy it, it won't go back to her."

"Will Sebastian do?"

"No," Coulter said. "She's Linked to him. Maybe a Fey lamp would do it. I'd need the help of a Lamplighter."

"Of course," Seger said.

"And we need to do something about Sebastian. You said you can remove the voice. I think it would be best if you worked on him, while I worked on her. That way, if information does cross their Link, Rugad will not know that we're coming for him in both places until it's too late."

Seger looked relieved. "I was wondering how to get around that."

Coulter closed his eyes. He could imagine this, and if he could imagine it, he could do it. "Sebastian will have to shatter as you remove that voice. It's the only way to get the threads out of his stone. Can you put him back together?"

"Yes," she said, "I know someone who has done it twice. He should be able to do it again."

"Good," Coulter said. "Let's not tell Ari I'm here. That might tip off Rugad. Let's just pick a point and do this."

"I'll be ready tonight," Seger said. "How about you?"

Coulter nodded. "That gives me a chance to sleep and think about it." He took a deep breath. "If we fail—"

"Then we'll have to think of something else." She squeezed his arm. "It's always better to expect success."

"Perhaps," Coulter said. But he had learned a long time ago that Rugad was a master at turning success into failure. Only Rugad wasn't ready this time. He wasn't prepared to meet with opposition. Surprise usually defeated the Fey. Coulter hoped it would this time too.

CHAPTER TWENTY-TWO

CON STOOD OUTSIDE the remains of the Tabernacle, staring at the once magnificent towers. They were hollow wrecks now, damaged by a fire decades ago, then looted and finally destroyed by squatters. During Rugad's brief reign as ruler of Blue Isle, the Fey had completely defaced the building, destroying everything except its outer shell.

The magnificence of the shell remained. From a distance it was still possible to see how the Tabernacle had once been the twin to the palace across the bridge. Twin seats of power, separated by the Cardidas.

Those days were gone, and Con knew they couldn't come back, not now that the Blue Isle's royal family had Fey blood in it. But the Tabernacle shouldn't be a ruined husk. It could still be a center for New Rocaanism, or so Con had argued to Queen Arianna not three months before.

He had had similar meetings with her countless times, and every time she had been gracious as she refused him. This time he had brought his secret weapon, Sebastian. Sebastian, in his halting voice, had reminded her how much they owed Con and how trustworthy he was.

Con could never be the kind of Rocaanist he wanted, not any longer. He had killed too many people—in battle, true enough, but still, it went against all he had ever been taught. And he had gone on a pilgrimage to Constant—a town that, like him, had been named for King Constantine. There he had been permitted to go into the Vault and read the Words. He didn't know if they had inspired or disillusioned him. What they had shown him was how linked Rocaanism and Fey magic was. They were two sides of the same coin.

He had accepted that. He had accepted many things. He even wore Fey clothing now, the breeches and jerkin instead of his Aud's robes. The old trappings of the religion were gone. They had to create new symbols, and new ways of doing things. The only thing he kept was the small filigree sword around his neck. He wore it constantly, to remind himself of who he was and what he believed.

Con had used the changes when he spoke with Arianna this last time. He had pointed out that Rocaanism would never die, and that Arianna—as the hereditary leader of Blue Isle, with the blood of its religious leader, the Roca, running through her veins—should control the direction Rocaanism was taking, that she could prevent the use of the Secrets that killed not just Fey, but could, in the wrong hands, be turned against anyone with magical powers. And then he reminded her that the mastermind behind New Rocaanism was Matthias, the man who had killed her mother. Wouldn't it be better, Con had asked, if the people who revived Rocaanism were her people, people she could trust, people who understood the link between Fey and Islander?

Sebastian had then spoken up, reminding Arianna of the times Con had saved his life. Arianna had seemed irritated at that as if she didn't need to be reminded (and, in all fairness, she probably didn't), and for the first time had appeared to consider Con's suggestions. When she asked him how he would prevent Rocaanism from turning into a Fey-hating religion, he had said simply, "We allow Fey to join."

She had looked at him as if he had found the key to all the world's mysteries, and then she had smiled at him. "If you swear to me that the Fey will be involved in all levels of the religion, including the upper levels, that one day a Fey—or someone like me—can become Rocaan, then I will help you."

He swore that to her, and he meant to make good on it. It was, in all truthfulness, the only way he believed the religion could work. Belief in God was not limited to a single race. Any race could believe and, Con thought, if any race could believe, then any race could worship as well.

And she had given him permission to rebuild the Tabernacle. She hadn't provided funds or workers, telling him that the church had to provide. And he believed it would.

He had begun the difficult process of raising funds, and found that he needed more than that. What he was learning was that a lot of Islanders had little money to give, but they had time and skills. He needed the money to get the materials, but one of his assistants, another former Aud, decided they could barter for materials as well. Con liked that. It meant that one day this project would get done.

But right now, it seemed overwhelming. He was standing on what had once been a beautiful tile courtyard, filled with images from the religion's history. Most of the tiles were gone, destroyed by time or weather or thieves. The outer walls remained, but everything, from the torch holders to the door, were gone. Over the years, plants had crept up the walls and along the demolished tile. Their branches were budding now, and if he didn't clear them away soon, they might completely block the entrance.

He still couldn't bear to go inside. He had done so once, saw the magnificent staircase that now led nowhere, the blackened crumble that had been the walls to the audience room, the corridor where he used to stare at the portraits of all the Rocaans, now gone. So many people had died here, hideously, and there were still remnants of that as well, a bit of cloth here, a half-burned copy of the Words there.

Looters had been through the place countless times, and nothing of worth was left. Just the memories, and the overwhelming feeling that even with all the help he was gathering, he would never be able to rebuild.

"Are you Con?" a voice asked behind him.

He jumped. He couldn't help himself. He turned, and saw a Fey in Domestic's robes standing at the edge of the courtyard, looking at the destroyed tile with distaste. She was young. Con wasn't even sure she knew what this place had been.

"Yes," he said.

"You're wanted at the palace."

He sighed. So Arianna had changed her mind. She had probably gotten reports that he was here—which was why he had put off coming here in the first place—and she wanted to tell him she had talked to her advisors and they had told her it wasn't a good idea after all.

"Tell Arianna that I still plan to go through with this."

The Fey put her hands behind her back. The expression on her narrow face was one of barely contained disdain. "The Black Queen did not send for you."

That surprised him. Now the Fey had his full attention. He turned, mimicking her posture, with his hands behind his back. He stood straight, even though he was considerably shorter than she was. He found, in dealing with Fey, that standing with his shoulders back at least got their attention. They still saw shortness as a sign of inferiority, and he always had to work against that.

"Then who wants me?" he asked. Sebastian had never summoned him, and Sebastian seemed to be the only other person in the palace who would need to contact him. Sebastian always came to him.

"An Islander named Coulter and a Healer named Seger. They ask on behalf of Sebastian."

Coulter? The boy who had traveled with Arianna, and then left the palace so suddenly all those years ago? Con barely remembered him, remembered only that Sebastian had treated him like a brother, and Coulter had been cold to him. Only Coulter wouldn't be a boy now. He was older than Con, significantly older. Con hadn't seen him in a long, long time.

And Con knew Seger well. She always went out of her way to greet him when he did come to the palace. She had never forgotten the way he had treated Sebastian. And even though she needed a verbal reminder now and then, Arianna hadn't either.

"What's this about?" Con asked.

"It is a matter of some urgency," she said. "They tell me I cannot bring you without your sword."

He felt a chill. He hadn't picked up that sword in a long time. He had plucked it off the wall in the palace when he was fighting the Fey, and discovered that the sword had the ability to slice through anything quickly and with complete precision. It had other powers as well, and had, more than once, saved Sebastian's life. Arianna had given the sword to Con after she became Black Queen, saying that it belonged in his hand and at his side. He kept it in a prominent place, but never carried it, seeing it as a symbol of his religion's failure to do things as the Roca had wanted, through peaceful means instead of warlike ones.

"What's happened?" he asked.

"I cannot tell you. I must simply escort you to the palace, and make sure you have your sword."

He nodded. "The sword is in my quarters," he said.

"Then we shall go there." She looked at the Tabernacle and wrinkled her long nose. Con turned, and saw it as she did, a ruined hulk dominating the city's south side.

"I'm going to rebuild it," he said.

"You should tear it down," she said. "Not even the walls will hold up under new construction. There is nothing of worth left."

"It has history," he said.

"But is it a worthwhile history?" She turned and walked back to the road, waiting for him there.

He stared at the Tabernacle again. Perhaps she was right. After all he had learned about his religion, all the misunderstandings and miscalculations, perhaps what he would be saving would be the memory of something that nearly caused the destruction of Blue Isle.

Maybe. Or maybe he was saving a part of his own people's identity, their need to believe.

Whatever he was doing, it would wait. Seger and Sebastian needed him. And his sword. He shuddered. He knew from that small detail that whatever they needed him for wasn't good.

CHAPTER TWENTY-THREE

ONLY THE SHAMAN knew the quickest ways in and out of the Eccrasian Mountains. It had taken Gift and his party nearly a week to get to Protectors Village five years before; now it took him and Xihu three days to get out.

They had traveled through a crack in the mountains—not a valley, really, but a place that looked as if one giant mountain had split down the middle. Perhaps it had. Gift didn't know the entire history of this place. Over the years, Shaman had worn a path through the area, complete with stairs in the trickier parts. The trek was short partly because of the Domestic spells that enabled travelers to walk quickly without getting exhausted.

Gift and Xihu covered more ground rapidly than he had ever covered in his life, and he had once walked half the width of Blue Isle. The weather had cooperated. It was as if the mountains approved of his departure.

He didn't. His entire body longed to return to the Place of Power and, if he could admit it to himself, the Black Throne. The longing increased the farther away he got until, on their short rest stops, he dreamed of it.

The dreams were not of the Throne as he had experienced it. They were of a place filled with Fey, a place that was warm and inviting and beautiful. The Throne itself was a glittering obsidian, and it beckoned him, inviting him to sit, to be part of it, to be part of the excitement that filled the room. In each dream, he drew closer to the Throne, and in each dream, his hesitations about sitting there grew fainter and fainter.

When he was awake, the dreams horrified him, but he longed for them as well. He wasn't certain what was happening to him. He could only hope that once he was out of the mountains, the longing would disappear.

Xihu had been an excellent traveling companion. She hadn't spoken unless she had something to say, and she knew the road. She didn't ask him about his dreams, even though it was clear she knew of them and they disturbed her.

He learned a bit about her as well. She was young for a Shaman, and was part of the generation that included Chadn, the Shaman he had grown up with. They had similarities—a certain calmness, a willingness to question, and a dedication to all that was best for the Fey, however they saw that. He had thought, before he came to Protectors Village, that these were things all Shaman had in common. He was sad to learn that he had been wrong.

Madot had confronted him before he left, asking him again to take her with him. But he couldn't. He couldn't get past her betrayal, and he had an odd feeling in the base of his stomach that she was going not because of him but because some other Shaman had ordered it. If she accompanied him, he felt that she would betray him again, and in a way that he would not be able to survive.

So he and Xihu traveled mostly in silence, eating the provisions the more sympathetic Shaman had given them, and concentrating on working their way down the mountains. Toward the end of the third day, when the sun was flirting with the tips of the mountains, they reached a hidden plateau. This plateau had been carved near the path, and was clearly man-made. Its front was a facade made of stone that went higher than most buildings. It was the only part of the mountain that hadn't been cut away when the plateau had been made. Small viewing slits were carved into the rock at eye level.

Xihu went to them before Gift even saw them. She was peering through them, crouching just a little so that she could see. He joined her.

The rock framed his vision, narrowed it slightly, and gave him no choices about what he saw. He recognized the view. It was of the main road, the one he had taken when he went to Protectors Village, the one that his guides had brought him on. Right now the setting sun covered the red stone with an orange light, making it glow. No one was on the path in any direction.

Xihu took his arm. "We're clear," she said.

He finally understood what they were doing. No one but the Shaman knew this plateau was here, and no one but the Shaman knew to even look for it. If someone suddenly appeared on the path from nowhere, then others would be alerted to look for this place.

Xihu slipped through a crack between the facade and the mountain. It had been carved into a place that was always in darkness, where piles of rocks stood, and where bits of stone rose beside the mountain itself, like saplings aspiring to be trees. The crack looked like a natural feature, not a hidden entryway.

He hadn't realized until now what a closely guarded secret the Shaman's road was.

"Aren't you worried that I'll let others know about this path?" he asked.

"No." Xihu gathered her robe in one hand and stepped daintily over some rocks.

"But anyone in Domestic-made clothing could walk this way."

"If they know the right Domestics," she said with a smile. "The ones that are also Shaman in the village."

So that was the trick. "What happens if they're not?"

"Exhaustion," she said. "Exhaustion so great that they get perhaps a day up the trail and have to turn back."

"What about those that are too stubborn to turn back?"

She gave him a measuring look. "They encounter a sheer cliff about halfway up. Beside it, an avalanche has taken away an entire mountainside, destroying path and stairs. An impenetrable barrier."

"I saw nothing like that."

"Because it does not exist," she said, "except in the minds of those who should not be on this path."

He nodded, amazed at the levels of magic he continually encountered. Xihu squeezed through the crack, her back perfectly straight against the mountain, her hands braced against the rock face. The ground beneath her wasn't solid; it was covered with pebbles and went down to a sheer point. It took a bit of maneuvering for her to work her way through, and even then, her robe caught on one of the rocks. Gift had to work the material free.

Then he handed her the packs, and followed her through. The stone was cold through his cloak, the pebbles sharp beneath his boots. Even though he had the properly spelled clothing, this part wasn't easy.

Finally he squeezed through. Xihu already had her pack over her shoulders. She was standing on the edge of the road, peering down. He joined her.

They weren't very far up the road. In fact, this part of the road was in Ghitlus, an old country, the first place the Fey had conquered. The story went that the Fey had ridden down from the Eccrasian Mountains, killing or conquering all the nomadic peoples who lived and traveled that rough terrain. But when the Fey encountered the swords of the Ghitlan, the Fey learned how to die at someone else's hand. They retreated up the mountains, fashioned their own swords, and the Infantry was born.

The Ghitlan were the first people conquered by the Fey using most of the methods that Rugad had used in conquering Nye. The country remained Ghitlan in custom and the people became part of the Fey Empire. Some believed that the original Fey were Ghitlan, but there was no way of knowing since the cultures had intermingled for so long. The Ghitlan people were dark-skinned like the Fey, but a Ghitlan with no Fey blood was shorter, had arching eyebrows and eyes that seemed like slits in a wide forehead ridge. They spoke a tonal language composed of similar sounds, and Gift, in his years in the village, had only been able to learn a few words. Even those, he was told, he said incorrectly—using a high tone when he should use a low one.

He was glad to have Xihu along. She had mastered all of the languages of the Fey Empire except the recent ones: Nyeian and Islander. Gift spoke both of those.

The edge of the road was slick and the exhaustion he hadn't felt on the climb down was catching up with him here. There was always a price to magic, even the benign and helpful kind like that practiced by Domestics.

The city of Dzaan stood below them, a short walk away. It was the oldest city in Ghitlus. It was built around a hill at the base of the mountains. A stone wall, so ancient that no one knew when it had been built, surrounded the entire city. No new buildings were allowed outside the wall, and new construction only happened when an older building was allowed to be torn down. The Ghitlan loved their heritage, and wanted no one to tamper with it.

At the top of the hill was a great fortress that had once been a home to the Black Family. Before that, some said, it was run by Ghitlan chieftains, but no one knew that for certain. Gift suspected it was true though, because the view from above showed that the city and the walls protected the fortress, not the other way around. Over the centuries, people had added to the fortress. The buttresses and towers all had differing styles, but Gift suspected if he went inside the fortress's oldest section, he would find the same crumbling stone as there was on the lower parts of the city's wall.

Beside him, Xihu took a deep breath, as if she were

preparing herself for the hike down. He glanced at her. She was biting her lower lip. He had forgotten that she had spent decades in the village, protecting the Place of Power. She hadn't been off the mountains in years.

He put a hand on her back, the first time he had ever touched her voluntarily. "It'll be all right," he said.

Her smile was small, an attempt, he knew, to reassure him. Shaman did not show weakness if they could help it. He imagined that her fear of this trip was greater than she'd ever admit, even to herself.

He adjusted the pack on his back, and started down the road. She caught up to him.

"Do we need a story?" she asked him. It was rare for Shaman to come off the mountain.

"The truth is good enough," he said.

"You want them to know who you are?"

He glanced at the city. The first time he had come here, he had kept his identity a secret. He wanted to move among the Fey unencumbered by his heritage. Through all three continents, Vion, Etanien, and Galinas, he had observed his own people, saw how the different cultures they had adopted had changed the Fey who remained, and had been incorporated into the ones he had known. His mother's people had an identity of their own—it was fierce, independent, and strong—but it was fluid and adaptable, something he hadn't seen in any other culture.

"Yes," he said. "They have to know who I am. It's the only way we'll get the help we need."

Xihu looked at him. "Help?"

"I have to get home fast, and we don't have enough coin—Ghitlan or otherwise—to get me there. We're going to have to use my status as heir to do so." He sounded as reluctant as he felt. He had never done this, never used who he was to an advantage. It felt foreign to him. But, for the first time in his life, it was necessary.

"The people of Dzaan know the Black Throne is up here." She was matching his pace, but for the first time since they'd started on this trip, she sounded winded. They both were feeling the effects of the loss of magic. They would have to rest in Dzaan.

"So?" he asked.

"So, they may think you are planning to overthrow your sister."

"And that will prevent them from helping me?"

"Of course," she said.

He sighed. They didn't have far to the base of the mountains. "Then we tell them that Arianna summoned me. That's not too far from the truth. Those Visions I've had were like a call."

Xihu glanced at him. He had not told her all of his Visions, nor had he said much about his conversation with his mother. He wanted to keep those private, for now.

"And we tell them that I was studying to be a Shaman. That's also true."

"They won't believe it. A member of the Black Family never does that."

He grinned at her. "The Black Family didn't have blue eyes until they came to Blue Isle either. If they've heard of the Isle at all, they've heard of it as the small home of a strange religion. The religious impulse, you'll tell them, is strong in Islanders."

"How many lies must I tell for you?" she asked.

"What makes you think that's a lie?"

She nodded. "I see your point."

The road leveled onto a barren plain. There were trees inside the city's walls, but not outside. The trees had been brought, centuries ago, by traders seeking to gain entry into Dzaan. The Dzaanies took the trees, but did not allow the traders into the city. Some said their bones could still be found on the plains outside Dzaan.

Gift had learned many of the Dzaan stories in the week he spent in the city, waiting for guides to take him to Protectors Village. He had asked a thousand questions, as he had done in each place he visited, and gained an appreciation for the richness of the Empire. Arianna had been right in insisting that the Fey look to the greatness of the parts of the world they already inhabited. None of them seemed to understand how unusual these places were.

The walk to the city's gates was longer than it looked from above. Gift and Xihu had to stop twice, once to eat and once to rest, before they reached the eastern gate.

The guardians of the gate were Fey Infantry. They were both young men, and one of them was very tall, suggesting he hadn't come into his magic yet. They wore the Ghitlan coats over their jerkins and breeches, and fur boots on their feet. Even though spring was coming to this part of the mountains, and even though Dzaan was lower than Protectors Village, it still got very cold here the moment the sun went down.

Xihu bowed to them, her hands pressed together. She spoke slowly, each tone clear and warm. Gift couldn't understand a word of what she said, but he watched her gesture toward him at least once. He had been planning to speak to them in Fey before Xihu took over. Obviously, she felt that Ghitlan would be more appropriate.

One of the guards spoke to her, and she again indicated Gift. Then the guard turned to Gift and said in singsong, heavily accented Fey, "We have not heard of your pending visit."

"It was a surprise to me," he replied in the same language. "I have been summoned back to Blue Isle. It seems to be an emergency."

"No messenger came through here," the guard said.

And they would know. The entire city would know. Its population was kept constant. Only a certain number of visitors were allowed in the city at any one time. The populace had to follow other regulations as well—only two children per couple, and then only at approved times. If a couple wanted to start a family before that, they had to leave the city.

Gift nodded in acknowledgment. "They came a nontraditional route."

The guards looked at each other. "We must get approval for your entry."

Gift made himself look amused. "You deny entry to the Black Heir?"

"We have no proof of who you are," the guard said. "No one from the Black Family has stayed in Dzaan for at least sixty years."

"I did," Gift said. "Five years ago."

"We would know," the guard said.

"I used my given name, Gift. Talk to others. You don't often see Fey with blue eyes."

"Evil eyes," the other guard said in Fey so heavily accented that Gift almost didn't understand him.

Gift let his mouth widen in amusement even though he hated that phrase. He had heard it a lot that week in Dzaan. Most Dzaanies had never seen blue eyes before.

"Yes," he said. "Some of your people called them that."

"I remember you," the second guard said. "My wife, she would not let me look at you on the street."

Gift raised his eyebrows at the first guard.

"That is not proof," the first guard said. "That is merely acknowledgment that you stayed here before."

"There was talk," the second guard said, "that this evil eye, it came from far away. That there were evil eyes in the Black Family now. My wife, she thought maybe you were the Black Heir. You had the name and the look."

"Your wife was right," Gift said. "I didn't want anyone to know then. It was five years ago. Now I must get home in a hurry, and I need some help doing so."

"Help you get in Dzaan?" the second guard asked.

Gift wasn't certain how to respond to that, wasn't sure what would be good and what wouldn't according to these two. So he opted for the truth.

"If possible," he said. "If not, just a good night's sleep and some directions out of here."

The second guard smiled. "We can do this." With his gloved hand, he pulled open the wooden gate. "You are welcome here."

Gift smiled in return. "Thank you," he said.

"You must go to the place of visitors," the first guard said.

"I remember," Gift said.

Xihu spoke to them in rapid Ghitlan and then bowed again. They didn't seem to acknowledge her, but the second guard bowed to Gift. He wasn't sure of the protocol, so he didn't bow, thinking it probably wasn't appropriate for a Black Heir to act obsequious if, indeed, that's what the bowing was.

Inside the gate, it felt as if he had entered a different world. No horses were allowed within the walls, so all carriages were small things, which could be pulled by a single person. There were several on the road ahead of him. Women carried a stick across their shoulders, a basket on either end, infants tied to their chests in small sacks with only the heads peeking out. Men carried large items on their backs, and sometimes, four men carried a palanquin with another person inside.

The trees hadn't gotten their leaves yet, but their branches were decorated with multicolored string in the winter tradition. The streets looked as if they were part of a tapestry. This part of the city had two-story stone buildings, the homes of the rich. Banners with Ghitlan words and sayings written vertically on them hung from the second-floor windows. Gift couldn't read the banners, but he remembered them from before. The only difference was that, this time, the windows were shuttered—glass was rare here—and the shutters had a familial scene painted on the outside. The scene usually enhanced the look of the banner.

The wealthier women wore headdresses decorated with beads and charms and small bells that rang as they walked. The sound was delicate, mixing with the bells from the other women. The air smelled remarkably fresh considering what close quarters the people had, and Gift thought, as he had before, that he wished Jahn, the main city on Blue Isle, smelled this good.

He was the one who had been to the city most recently, so he was the one who had to find the visitors center through the maze of streets. There was no central market, like there was in Blue Isle and in many of the cities on Galinas. There were booths that lined the roads all the way through the city, and outside the walls were other areas where people sold goods. Mostly, though, families grew their own produce in their gardens. They kept a single goat, and a few chickens, and took care of their own needs. It was a strange arrangement, and made visiting even more uncomfortable.

The center was at the base of the city's main hill. Above it, the fortress loomed like an angry warrior. Gift went into the center, Xihu at his side. He had awful memories of this place: his guide the last time hadn't known the language well, and the confusion had almost gotten them evicted from Dzaan.

This time, Xihu knew all the customs. She bowed, pressed her hands together, and spoke softly. The officials, both women—both short and dressed in the traditional sheepskin gown with the high collar and long sleeves—had aprons that encircled them with colors as vibrant as the string on the trees. Instead of elaborate headdresses, they wore their hair in tiny braids, hundreds of them, as a function of the Ghitlan religion. They were not Fey, or at least they were not full Fey. But when Xihu nodded toward Gift, obviously mentioning who he was, both women bowed immediately and pressed their hands in his direction.

He nodded in acknowledgment, assuming that Xihu would tell him if he was doing something wrong. She continued her discussion with the women, who pointed frantically after the introduction. Xihu shook her head several times, but the women seemed adamant.

Finally, Xihu sighed. "They will be putting us up in the fortress," she said. "They claim it belongs to your family, and that no one lives there. It sits empty waiting for the Black Family to return."

"Wonderful," Gift said.

"Yes," one of the women said in broken Fey. "Wonderful."

She had misunderstood his sarcasm, which was probably good. "Is it livable?" he asked.

"They assure me it is. It's not fair to say no one lives there," Xihu said. "Servants do. There is no leader in residence. You have to go there, and they're going to try to make you stay."

"Tell them about our urgent business," he said. "Ask if they know of guides who can get us out of Ghitlus fast."

"I have," Xihu said. "Someone will join us first thing in the morning."

Gift nodded. He really didn't want to climb any more today, but he knew there was no choice. The women spoke again, indicating some freshly brewed green tea and some biscuits beside it. Gift knew enough of the customs to understand this one. They were honored by his presence and would be insulted if he didn't share from the bounty of their table.

He suppressed a sigh. He was hungry, but what he really wanted was rest. He smiled at them, and swept a hand toward the small stone table with its clay cups. The women giggled and bowed at him again. One of them pulled a chair out. He sat. Xihu looked as annoyed as he felt.

The other woman served them, and Gift drank the warm tea. The biscuits were sweet and brittle, just like they were supposed to be, a perfect complement to the tea. The entire ritual happened in silence as it had the other times Gift had experienced it. The only difference was that the second woman did not stay for the tea. She disappeared out a side door.

Xihu noted that as well and raised her eyebrows at Gift. It was, apparently, her way of acknowledging strange events. She didn't say anything either, and once she started sipping tea, she kept her back to him, just as she was supposed to.

When they had finished, the woman bowed to them,

took the tea, and pressed her hands together. She looked at Gift as she spoke to Xihu.

"It would honor them if you stayed in the city for at least a week," Xihu translated.

"Please remind her that we have to leave immediately, that it's an emergency, and tell her I would be forever in her debt if she sent me the guide I requested."

Xihu repeated the phrase. The woman argued with her a bit more, but Xihu's voice grew firm. Finally, Gift told Xihu to thank the woman and ask her how they get up to the fortress.

Xihu shook her head just a little, but clearly did what he asked. To his surprise, the woman grinned and walked to the door. She opened it.

Gift followed her, expecting her to point to a road or to give Xihu instructions on how to get to the fortress. Instead, a palanquin stood outside, with the four men who were going to carry it standing at attention beside it.

"No," Gift said. "I won't—"

"You will," Xihu said. "It's an honor."

"But I can walk up there just as easily—"

"Maybe," Xihu said. "But you would disgrace the entire city if you did so."

He looked at her, trying to plead only with his eyes so that he wouldn't offend the Dzaanies. "Please. Get me out of this."

A slight smile touched Xihu's mouth. "You're the one who wanted to let people know who you are."

She was right, of course. And he hated it. But there was no turning back now. He couldn't use some parts of his heritage and be upset when others wanted to honor it.

"All right," he said. In very bad Ghitlan, he said thank you to the woman, then walked to the palanquin. There was a silk banner with words that he could not read covering the door and windows. Inside were cushions of silk and fur.

He sat down gingerly, leaning on the fur-lined walls.

There was room for him, Xihu, and their packs. She climbed in after him.

"Oh, this will be interesting," she said with a grin. "I've never traveled in such style before."

Neither had he. Pomp and circumstance were part of Blue Isle's royal tradition, not the Fey tradition, and he had been raised Fey. Still, it felt good to sit down. He was exhausted. Maybe this would be comfortable after all.

He closed his eyes and started to relax when the palanquin swayed underneath him. The men had lifted it. Gift opened his eyes and met Xihu's startled gaze. Then her lips turned up, and she stifled a giggle. She seemed just like a young girl, laughing when she wasn't supposed to. Gift grinned too.

The men handling the palanquin did so with complete precision, but Gift had never felt movement like this. He found small handholds and wrapped his fingers around them.

It would be a long trip up the hillside.

CHAPTER TWENTY-FOUR

$\mathcal{F}$OR THE FOURTH morning in a row, Matt fixed his own breakfast in the morning chill. He didn't start the hearth fire because it would need to be dampened around midday, and he wasn't sure anyone would be around to do it. His mother had slept late each day. He was getting worried about her. She wasn't awake when he came home either. It seemed to him that something was very wrong with her, and he wanted to talk to someone else about it, but he couldn't.

Alex hadn't been home the last three nights either.

It seemed like everyone had left him. Coulter had gone without warning, his mother was sleeping too much, and his brother was beginning to spend his nights with their father, in the Vault. At least Coulter had left Matt a message, delivered later on the day he left by Leen.

The message was a short one: *While I'm gone, focus on limits and control. With the help of the others, learn your limits—exactly what your magic can and cannot do. Then learn how to control your magic so that it doesn't leak and it does what you want when you want.*

It sounded so simple, but it wasn't. Matt wasn't sure about his limits. Scavenger promised to help him try various spells by remembering what other Enchanters could do. The Domestics stood by while he tried, so that they could put out accidental fires. The old Enchanter, the one who had taught Coulter, wouldn't come out of his room, so it was the younger Enchanters—some as small as three years old—who watched as well. They weren't learning from him. They were supposed to teach him.

Five of them, freaks all, and Matt the oldest and the least experienced. It made him feel uncomfortable to be told by an eight-year-old how to hold his hands in a fire spell. All the other children were half-Fey, half-Islander. Matt was the only full Islander among the Enchanters.

Leen told him that was one of the reasons Coulter had taken special interest in him. Coulter was all Islander too—born before the Fey came to Blue Isle—and his powers were greater than any completely Fey Enchanter. Matt suspected even the half-Fey, half-Islander Enchanters weren't as powerful as Coulter was.

Coulter expected Matt to be just as powerful. And that was why, Leen said, Coulter was very sorry he couldn't be here to start Matt's formal training. The emergency took precedence. He had to go to Jahn.

In all of Matt's years, he'd never heard of Coulter leaving Constant, let alone going to Jahn. The more he thought about it, the more important it had to be.

The others agreed as well. They didn't remember Coulter leaving before either, and he had had a lot of opportunities.

So Matt knew that Coulter didn't leave because of him. Whatever was wrong, Coulter would take care of, and then things would be better.

Matt wasn't so certain of that with his mother.

He knew she got up every day because things were moved in the house when he returned at night. His breakfast dishes, which he meticulously scrubbed and left out to dry as she had taught him, would be put away. There would be stew still in its pot above the coals of the hearth fire. His mother would be asleep, in a different position than what she had been in before he left, and sometimes in different clothing, but such a sound sleep that she wouldn't hear him softly call her name.

If she wasn't up this morning after he finished eating, he would shake her awake and ask her if she felt well. Maybe she needed him to stay home and take care of her. Maybe something was wrong with her that he could fix.

He hadn't done this before because he had been too afraid that she had changed her mind, that she didn't want him to go to Coulter's school. If she discovered where he spent his days, she might not approve. But his fear of her disapproval had vanished almost a day ago, and now he simply wanted to see her awake and smiling.

If only Alex were here. But he wasn't. For all Matt could tell, Alex hadn't been here since the day he ran from the school. Matt knew he had gone to the Vault—his mother had told him before she began her long sleep—but that didn't excuse this sort of behavior. Their father could do it because their father was crazy. But Alex wasn't. At least, not yet.

Matt ate pieces from the day-old bread he had brought home from the school the night before, worried that there would be no food in the house, and drank the cool water he had drawn from their well. When he finished, he scraped off the dish and mug he'd used, then wiped the crumbs from the table. Once that table had been filled with people—not just him and his brother, but his father and his friends. There was Denl, a warm man with a limp, and Tri, another survivor of the Fey wars, badly scarred, but nice just the same. They still came sometimes, but not nearly as often as they had when Matt was little. He was alone here, and he didn't know how to change that.

He stood for a long moment in the empty kitchen, shivering slightly. No matter what he did, his hands got cold without the fire going. He could, he knew, start his own small fire magically, and put it out the same way, but all the Fey teachers at the school stressed conservation of magic. They said that the powers were to be treated as special things, not everyday things, and they insisted that he not waste what he was given.

That was easy for him. He hadn't used his powers much around home because they unnerved his mother and alarmed his father. His father used to look at Matt whenever Matt created something magically, from a little lick of fire to a bit of water, and say, "In that lies madness." His mother shushed his father, but the words stayed with Matt anyway.

Matt took a deep breath. He had no idea how his mother would react to being awakened. But he was going to do it anyway. He had never felt as strange as at this moment.

Then he heard the front door open. He went into the hallway, and saw Alex letting himself in.

Alex glanced up at him in surprise. In that moment, Matt knew that his brother had been coming home every day, but he had been doing so when he knew he wouldn't see Matt.

Matt didn't say anything, and neither did Alex. Any greeting felt false.

"How's Mother?" Alex asked. So he too knew that something was wrong with their mother.

"Sleeping," Matt said. "Like she always has been lately. I was just going to wake her up so that I could find out what's wrong."

Irritation and something else crossed Alex's face. "She hasn't told you?"

"I haven't seen her awake for three days."

Alex closed his eyes. Something was different about his brother as well. He seemed thinner, and older, as if the short time he had spent away had aged him somehow.

"What's going on, Alex?" Matt asked.

"Let her sleep," he said. "She'll be all right."

But he didn't look as certain as he sounded. With the intuition that had always bound them, Matt knew his brother was extremely sad and very scared.

"What happened, Alex?" Matt asked again. "Is it Dad?"

Alex flushed. He pushed past Matt. "Is there anything to eat here?"

And with that question, Matt suddenly had a revelation. His mother hadn't been cleaning and cooking during the day. His brother had.

"Alex." Matt followed him into the kitchen. "I'm going to keep asking until you tell me."

"I thought you had to go learn how to be Fey." Alex crouched before the hearth fire. He took some wood out of the bin and laid it in the ashes from yesterday's fire.

Matt was not going to listen to the taunt. "Is she dying?" he asked softly.

"No," Alex said, then rocked back on his heels. "By the sword, Matt, will you just go?"

"When did I stop being a member of this family?"

The words had just slipped out, but he felt them, all the way down. His voice shook by the end of the sentence.

Alex bowed his head, then stood, placing his hand on the hearthstones as if for balance. He started to speak, and then stopped. "Three days ago," he said finally, "Dad came back."

"Here?" The emotions Matt felt were so jumbled and so sudden that he had trouble separating them. "He came home?"

"No," Alex said. "But he was lucid. He had me get Mother, but she must have already known because she was on her way into the Vault."

Matt's coldness grew. He gripped the back of a chair for support.

"Father knew what was happening to him."

"He always did when he was lucid," Matt said.

"And he knew how bad it's been getting." Alex swallowed. His eyes were filled with tears. "He decided to go into the mountain."

"He can't!" Matt said. "The Fey Powers, they'll kill him."

"He knew," Alex said. "He was waiting for them to come into the Vault. He said they could. But they never did. So he went to them."

"And you didn't get me? He was himself, he made this choice, and you didn't give me a chance to talk him out of it?"

"He didn't want to be talked out of it," Alex said. "Believe me, I tried."

"I could have done it." Matt was raising his voice and he couldn't stop himself. "We're more alike than you are. I understand him."

"No," Alex said, "you don't. None of us did."

He sounded very tired.

"Surely Mother tried to stop him?"

"In her own way." Alex grabbed the tinderbox off the mantel. "But she couldn't either, and I think she understood."

"We have to get him," Matt said. "We have to go in after him and save him."

The look Alex gave Matt was so condescending, so full of pity, that Matt took a step back. "It was three days ago, Matt. Even if he survived one of those days, he wouldn't have survived the others. Mother told me the full story. The first time he went to the Roca's Cave, he nearly died immediately. The second time, he captured the evil spirit, but she would have killed him right away that time too. He's dead. I don't think we can doubt that. And all we would do if we went after him would be to die too."

"You don't know that," Matt said.

"That's what Dad said." Alex lowered his voice. "Matt, please. Let it go."

"Let it go? My father walked off to die three days ago, no one bothered to tell me, and you say let it go?"

"Yes," Alex said. "He's better off dead."

"Who're you to decide that?" Matt asked.

"I didn't," Alex said. "Dad did."

"Boys."

Matt turned. His mother stood behind him, her hair

sleep-tousled, her eyes swollen. He finally understood why she was sleeping so much. She was mourning his father in the only way she knew how.

"Dinna fight," his mother said. "Yer da wouldna a wanted it."

"Just like he didn't want to see me before he chose to die," Matt said. "We should always do what Dad said, even now that he's gone. He didn't want me because I wouldn't have let him go. You both didn't care about him."

"You cared about him?" Alex asked. "You didn't even know he was gone. When was the last time you saw him? Two weeks ago? I saw him every day before he died."

Matt sucked in a breath. The comment hit home. He hadn't seen his father because he couldn't face what his father had become.

"Boys." Their mother's voice was raspy.

"You think we should have found you? I think you should have known the time was coming. Mother did." Alex took a step forward. "And maybe I did too. Maybe—"

"My magic," Matt said, deliberately using the word that wasn't allowed in this household, "is different from yours, Alex. I don't See things like you do. I couldn't have known. And no one bothered to tell me. No one even sought me out."

Alex had stopped moving, his face pale now in the morning light. He knew he had been wrong. Matt recognized the expression. Alex knew it, and regretted it.

But he didn't say so, and that made Matt even angrier.

"You were always afraid of me, always wanting me to be something different. I couldn't be myself in this family because of what I might become. And now you tell me that I wasn't even worth finding when you knew my father was going away." He turned to his mother. "You could have found me. I would have stopped him."

"I know," his mother said. " 'Tis why I dinna. He wanted ta go."

"He could still be alive in there."

"No," his mother said. "He went to a place where he knew death'd find him. He's gone, Matty. Ye have ta accept that."

"Maybe I could if I'd had a chance to say good-bye to him like you did," he snapped. "But you didn't think me worth it, either of you."

He had his fists clenched so hard his fingers ached. Alex was watching him warily. His mother just looked overwhelmed.

"Well," he said when neither of them spoke. "You couldn't have made it more clear about how I fit into this family. You don't want another burden like Father. Fine. You won't have one. I have a place to go, a place where people are willing to help me and to treat me with respect. I don't need either of you."

He pushed past his mother and headed to the front door. She called his name. He didn't stop.

"I guess you don't want to know the message he left for you," Alex called.

Matt silently cursed his twin, who always knew how to reach him. Matt held the door open, without turning, but waiting to hear.

"He knew," Alex said, sounding closer than he had a moment ago, "that he might not be lucid for very long, so he said his good-byes then. There was no time to get you, Matt."

Matt was silent. They had already had part of this argument.

"So he gave me a message for you."

Matt waited. He wasn't going to turn. He wasn't going to look at either of them again. Ever.

"He said that you should remember what he taught you."

Matt bowed his head. "Remember that I should be ashamed of who I am? Remember that he taught me to hate half the population of Blue Isle?" He kept his voice low. "I'll remember that. Believe me. And I'll make sure I'm a better man than he ever was."

Then Matt stepped outside the door and slammed it shut. He stood there for a moment, catching his breath, feeling a weight so heavy that it felt as if it would crush him.

Neither his twin brother nor his mother came after him. Why would they? They hadn't shown any consideration for him before. And even if they did, he wouldn't go back inside with them. He was done with them, done with the whole family.

He would be like the unwanted kids at the school, hidden away because he was different. Only it took his family fifteen years to shove him out. Maybe it would have been easier if he had been like those kids, dropped off as soon as their magic grew uncontrollable. Maybe it wouldn't have hurt as much.

He shook himself, then walked toward the road. There was nothing for him here. His future lay elsewhere, in a place that taught him to see how strong he was, and how to control that strength. A place where he could be what he was meant to be. A place where people appreciated him for who he was.

CHAPTER TWENTY-FIVE

ALEX LET OUT the breath he had been holding. He was shaking. He wanted to go to the door, throw it open, and pull his brother back inside.

But he wouldn't. Matt had to come back on his own. Maybe after he cooled down, he would realize that Alex had told him the truth: there hadn't been time to get him, and both Alex and his mother were afraid that Matt, good old impulsive Matt, would go into those tunnels too, and bring their father back.

It was clear to both of them that his father wanted to go. Alex hated it, but he understood it. Who would want to live as his father had lived? How could a man knowingly survive the gradual loss of his mind?

His mother was still standing in the hall, a hand over her mouth. She didn't have anything left. That was so clear to Alex. He wasn't even sure if she knew how hurt Matt was.

In a few days, Alex would go after him and bring him back. By then, Matt would know that he didn't fit in with those Fey. By then, he would want to come home.

Alex turned and put his arm around his mother. In three days, she had gone from being a strong woman who stood tall and ordered her sons around to an old woman, hunched and broken, whose eyes barely saw anything. He and Matt had been arguing for a long time before she showed up, and Alex wasn't sure if she had come in because their voices woke her up or if she was actually trying to stop the discord between them.

He led her into the kitchen and sat her at a chair. Then he went back to starting the hearth fire.

"Alex," she said softly. "Dinna let Matty go."

"He'll be all right, Mother," Alex said. He had finally got the fire lit. It would take a few moments, but then it would warm the room.

"Yer da, he dinna want ye ta be apart."

Alex said nothing. He didn't really want to go after Matt. He wanted Matt to see the mistakes of his ways and return home. Otherwise, Matt would take Alex back to that place, where the Fey walked freely and the leader, Coulter, had eyes that could see right through him.

The more Alex studied the Words, the more leery he became of Coulter. The Roca had originally been named Coulter, but this Coulter had none of the Roca's blood like Alex's family did. There were dark hints in the Words of a split, not just between the Roca's sons, but of another, a more insidious one, one that nearly tore the Isle apart. And it had happened between the Roca and the others who had discovered the cave with him. They were trapped, or so the Words said, in some of the soul repositories, trapped and unable to influence the Isle in any way.

Alex had a sense that history was repeating itself. Only this time, his father was the Roca, he and Matt were the sons who would eventually lead the Isle, and the man named Coulter was the one who had to be destroyed. Alex just didn't know how to tell his brother that. Matt would think he was lying, think that he was trying to get Matt away from that school where they were taking over his mind.

Maybe if Alex went there, armed with some of the Secrets from the Vault, maybe then Matt would see the people he was associating with for what they really were.

"Are ye all right?" his mother asked.

Alex realized he was still crouching. He got up, and found some bread on the counter. His brother must have brought it. For a moment, Alex felt a pang. Matt had to have felt very alone the last few days. Even now, he had to feel alone.

But he wouldn't realize how much he needed his family if Alex came running after him.

"Alex?" his mother asked.

"I'm fine," he said. He turned, smiling, even though he hadn't felt like smiling for days. He looked at her, saw that she was clearer than she had been. Her face was puffy and her eyes red.

"I was wondering," he said. "Maybe we should have some kind of service for Dad."

" 'Twould need a Rocaanist, an Aud maybe or a Danite," his mother said.

"What about Denl?"

"Perhaps." His mother leaned her chin on the palm of her hand.

"It would be a good way to get Matt to come home again."

"Maybe." His mother was frowning slightly. "But I dinna think yer da would want it. He dinna die the normal way. His body may be gone, but he's of the Roca, ye know. Part of him, the important part, may still be in the mountain."

"I know," Alex said gently. He had already thought of that. Why hadn't he told Matt that? Matt didn't know as much about Rocaanism as Alex did. Maybe Matt would find the same kind of comfort in that thought as Alex had.

" 'N ye know how powerful words are," his mother said. "If ye have a service, ye may call that part of him away from where he should be. It may na be good for any of us."

Alex sighed. She could be right. "Or maybe," he said, "it's precisely what Father needs."

She shook her head. " 'Tis na the way of the Rocaanists ta do a service with na body. 'N I willna let you or Matt go in that cave. Ye may na come out agin. I dinna like the way ye spend yer time in the Vault."

"I have to learn," Alex said.

"There're other ways," his mother said. "There're others who know the religion."

"But the Words are there," Alex said. "And that's where I'll find my answers."

His mother sighed. "The Words. They dinna help yer da."

"Sure they did," Alex said. "They helped him save us all."

Her lower lip trembled. " 'N at what cost?"

Alex was silent for a moment. "I don't know," he said. "All of that happened before I was born. Maybe the cost wasn't as great as you think, Mother. Maybe if he hadn't done it, Matt and I wouldn't have had a father at all. Maybe none of us would be here. There are warnings of that in the Words, discussion of the great power that lies hidden in the caves all over the world. Maybe the Fey would have found that, and destroyed us."

"Maybe," she said. But she sounded like she didn't believe him. " 'Tis na either-or in this world, Alex. Best ye learn that now. Sometimes, 'tis a bit a this and a bit a that, and none of it what ye want."

"We're talking about Matt again, aren't we?" Alex said.

" 'N you too," his mother said. "What ye both share is na good. Ye share an ability to see the world in only two ways: yer way 'n the wrong way. 'Tis na good, especially now, when ye dinna agree. Yer brother is hurt—"

"And so am I," Alex said. "I lost my father too."

"But ye got to see him. Matt dinna."

"So you apologize," Alex said. "You were there too."

His mother stood, very slowly, as if it took all her strength. Then she wiped a hand across her face, turned away from him, and disappeared down the hall.

He knew where she was going. She was going back to

bed. He knew better than to challenge her like that. She was only pushing him to do something she felt she wasn't strong enough to do herself.

But the rift between him and Matt went deeper than this last meeting with their father. It went to the very core of who they were. Matt had been going to the Fey for years, and he wouldn't accept that they were evil. Alex knew they were, and now that he had learned why his brother had been slowly changing, he knew that their ways were making his brother evil too.

Alex would try to save Matt, but only when he was ready. Only when he discovered, through the Words and through meditation, the best thing to do.

Matt would have to wait until then. It would all have to wait. Because the last thing Alex wanted to do was to make anything worse.

CHAPTER TWENTY-SIX

*T*HE FORTRESS WAS huge and, as the Dzaanies said, empty. Gift stood outside the two-story wooden doors and stared at the walls. They went so far up he had to crane his neck to see the top. The front of the fortress served as a second wall, another barrier to the interior, just like the city and its wall served as a barrier. This place was so highly fortified that nothing could get inside without someone seeing or preventing it.

The men who bore the palanquin watched Gift as if they were uncertain what to do next. Xihu had already told them to go, but apparently they were to take no instructions from anyone except the Black Heir.

He turned to them and thanked them in his awful Ghitlan, his mind still on the fortifications he saw. The men picked up the palanquin and headed back down the hillside. They moved easily, as if this was nothing to them and perhaps it wasn't, but the ride had tired Gift even more, and he hadn't been carrying anything at all.

"Magnificent, isn't it?" Xihu asked. She sounded awed. She was looking up as well. Just behind the front of the fortress, the towers of the main building were visible, disappearing into low clouds.

"I've never seen anything like it," Gift said. "This thing was costly to build. Look at those doors. There's no wood like that here."

"It's esada wood," Xihu said.

Gift looked at her. "There are Shaman here, then?"

She shook her head. "It must be very old. See how it has grayed on the edges? We have wood in Protectors Village that is centuries old and doesn't have that grayness."

A half-dozen Fey Domestics had come out side entrances. They stood at attention, watching Gift and Xihu. Gift got the sense there were no pure Ghitlans up here, only Fey and those of mixed heritage. He wondered if his sister even knew this place existed—and how many other fortresses and palaces there were across all three continents that were being kept empty like this, just waiting for members of his family to arrive.

One of the Domestics came toward him. She was heavyset, which was unusual among the Fey—at least in Gift's experience—and her upswept eyes were surrounded by laugh lines. Her generous mouth was upturned naturally, even though he got the sense she was trying to look somber. She wore traditional Fey Domestic's robes, but they were trimmed with fur along the cuffs and collar. In her fur-lined belt, she had a small clear glass stick tied in place by blue ribbons.

She put her hands together and was about to bow when she remembered that such a greeting was not customary among the Fey. So they did entertain Ghitlan dignitaries up here as well. Somehow that made him feel better.

"Sir," she said, using the customary greeting when she hadn't been granted permission to use his given name. "We have rooms for you and your companion. We've also put together a dinner for you. It is not as elaborate as we would have liked, but it is what we could do at the last moment."

Gift smiled and inclined his head toward her. "I'm sure it will be fine."

"I am Jalung, Head of the Household on Black Mountain."

The name of the mountain startled him. He hadn't expected the fortress to have a name associated with his family. He expected its designation to be Ghitlan in origin, just like Jalung's name.

"I am Gift," he said, granting her the permission she needed to talk to him as a near equal. He had met his first Head of Household on his trip to the Eccrasian Mountains, and after one social gaffe, he was told that Heads of Households were some of the most important people among Domestics who did not travel with a military group. But no one was completely equal to the Black Family, and no matter how he tried to change that, it would never happen. "And my companion is Xihu."

"You are welcome here," Jalung said to Xihu. "If there are lapses you see, please tell us so that we can improve the Mountain."

Xihu's smile was gracious. "I'm sure everything will be fine."

"Let me take you through the Mountain," Jalung said, "and then to your rooms."

"Actually," Gift said, "the tour can wait. I would like to rest in my room first. I would also like to meet with a guide, so if you could send for one from Dzaan, I would appreciate it."

"A guide awaits you," Jalung said. "Would you like to see her after your rest? She was instructed to wait until morning."

Gift smiled. Much as he wanted to get some rest, he also wanted to make sure the guide was what they needed. "I'll see her first."

Jalung clapped her hands together. From those same side doors, some Ghitlan boys appeared. So Gift had been wrong. There were full Ghitlans here, but they were the servants of the Fey. Despite the early evening chill, the boys wore nothing but short pants. Their feet were bare.

The boys bowed, their muscled backs glistening with

sweat. They had been working on something difficult inside, something that took a great deal of effort.

"The *slivans* will take your belongings," Jalung said. She clapped her hands again, and one boy took Gift's pack while another took Xihu's.

Gift asked under his breath, *"Slivan?"*

"Leased servants," Xihu answered as softly, "usually given in repayment of a debt. In this case probably the parents'."

Gift shuddered. The boy who took his pack led his group back inside. The boy with Xihu's pack led a different group through the other door. Gift had the odd sense that they would continue the procession all the way to the rooms.

"Follow me," Jalung said, as if nothing unusual were happening. Which, to her, nothing was.

She untied her glass stick, and rapped it once against the door. A blue spark flew off the door, stopped in front of Gift as if it were inspecting him, and then rose slowly into the air. The air smelled faintly of sulfur.

Jalung was watching this. "The Mountain recognizes you," she said with approval.

Gift knew better than to question the magic, but it still made him uneasy. He had never been here. He didn't know how he could be recognized.

The doors swung open revealing a large, well-lit hall.

"Please take Xihu's arm, or she will not be allowed to enter with you," Jalung said.

Gift did as he was instructed. Xihu looked slightly amused. They walked inside. Gift half expected the door to close tightly behind him, but it did not.

The hall smelled faintly of sandalwood. Banners hung from the ceiling in the Ghitlan tradition, but the words on these banners were Fey. "Protect" and "Serve" altered with each other, surrounding a large banner in the middle that held the same symbol as the one he had seen above the Black Throne: two hearts pierced by a single sword.

"It does belong to your family," Xihu said softly. "The banners bear your crest."

"My family's crest is two swords crossed over a single heart," Gift said.

"No," Xihu said. "Not the crest of your Islander family. The crest of the Black Family."

He squinted at it as if the multicolored silk appliqué would explain the puzzlement he felt. What was the likelihood of two families, living halfway across the world from each other, having similar crests? Inverted crests, in some way. On Blue Isle, two swords cross in front of a heart, protecting it. Here, a single sword pierces two hearts, harming them. Was that the intended symbolism? Or did it mean that the swords drew them together?

"You've never seen the crest before?" Xihu asked.

"I saw it once," Gift said, "near the Throne. I didn't know it was my family's crest."

Xihu smiled. "You'll see it all over Ghitlus. I doubt it's as prevalent anywhere else. Your family seemed to lose the need for something as obvious as a crest."

Gift nodded. He stared at it for a moment longer, wondering why it made him so uneasy, and then he let Jalung lead him forward. As she did, he glanced on either side of him. The mud-brick walls separated into several corridors leading to rooms. The corridor on the building's exterior had arrow slits, which surprised him. Arrows were not the weapon of choice for the Fey.

Jalung saw his glance. "The Ghitlan are and always were a warrior people. It took the Fey a long time to conquer this place. It still bears the scars."

Gift nodded in acknowledgment of her words. The history of this place was phenomenal. He had trouble seeing the conquerors of half the world as a nomadic tribe descending on a small city, attempting to take it over. He was so used to the way the Fey simply conquered whatever they faced that the idea of a loss in battle—at least in Vion—seemed strange to him.

He continued to walk forward, amazed at how big this section of the fortress was. The ceilings were low, indicating that there were three stories on this part of the building instead of the two that he had assumed. This section also had a feeling of very great age.

Two *slivans* were replastering a crack off to his left. To his right, heat blew at him, and he smelled the iron scent of metal work. No wonder the *slivans* wore no shirts. Their work kept them warm enough.

Then Jalung opened two more wooden doors—these made of pine—and stepped outside. Gift and Xihu followed. They found themselves in a massive courtyard— if that was the proper phrase. It was like a small city in itself. There were trees in the center, and a vegetable garden to the right. A well sat off to the left, and beyond that a small shrine that he recognized as part of the Ghitlan's major religion. He assumed it was for the Ghitlan: most Fey had no religion at all.

Stone paths wove throughout the dirt, all leading to different doors in the exterior walls.

"We'll have grass and flowers soon," Jalung said. "In the summer, we have so many different kinds of flowers that the hummingbirds come, even though it is said they prefer warmer climates."

"It must be beautiful," Xihu said.

Jalung smiled. "It is my favorite time." She led them along a side path. The stones were flat and even, and Gift could see places in the dirt where someone had worked to make certain that a stone fit into its place after the winter snows. It took him a moment to notice that this part of the yard was filled with people, most of them in plain brown robes, most of them on their hands and knees tending the plants.

He felt his amazement grow. His family hadn't lived here in hundreds of years. The last member of his family to visit had probably been his great-grandfather, Rugad, decades ago, and still this place was tended as if the Black Family would return at any moment. He had done that, he supposed. He was taking advantage of a system that had been set up so long ago that to disturb it would probably disturb all the rituals of the city below.

The far side of the courtyard had built-in areas for outdoor work. Several firepits lined the front, and beyond them was a large pool. It was deep and the water clear. It wasn't a reflecting pool then, but one that was used for cleanliness and perhaps drinking water at times when the well wasn't working.

Just beyond that was the building he had seen from outside. Up close, it was even more spectacular: straight, high, mud-brick walls that disappeared into the clouds. The windows were blocked with woven shutters and, higher up, with very expensive glass. Halfway up the building were more multicolored strings, and at their bases, small bells that jingled in the wind. It sounded like a small bell choir above, with the tones chosen at random.

Jalung did not stop. Instead, she led him across a small footbridge that arched over the pool and into the fortress proper. The ceilings were high here, and the sense of space incredible. There were frescoes on the walls and ceilings, most of them of battles fought on horseback. The people on the horses were clearly Fey; their victims had Ghitlan features, but were shorter and squarer. Surprisingly, the Fey were extremely pale-skinned in the frescoes. It was the Ghitlan who had the dark skin that most cultures associated with the Fey.

Jalung saw him staring at that. "The Ghitlan gave us many gifts," she said. "They gave us color. And they taught us how important it was to be ruthless."

He looked at her, startled.

She shrugged. "They defeated us for years before we began to refine our magic. Don't you know the stories?"

He did, but only in the simple phrases—one-sentence aphorisms about each country conquered by the Fey. *When they encountered the swords of the Ghitlan, the Fey learned how to die at someone else's hand.* How inadequate those aphorisms were.

The main hall had several fireplaces and sitting areas all around them. Big furs draped the walls and floors. The entire place looked comfortable.

But Jalung did not lead him there. She turned down a

side corridor and led him under an archway. The room had dozens of arched alcoves and a large fireplace on one wall. The furs were thick across the floor, and several more covered the benches that encircled the room. In the center was a large thronelike chair, with lamps around it and a huge table at its side.

It wasn't until Gift walked in farther that he realized the alcoves were all filled with books. The musty scent was welcoming. He hadn't spent enough time with books since he had come to Vion, but he had, in the years before that, learned to love the feel of leather under his hands.

Jalung saw his expression. "The Ghitlan have a long literary history, and all of their books are illustrated. We have several other books from Vion cultures, and Fey war histories as well. When you return to your home, we would appreciate it if you send us some books from Blue Isle. We're trying to complete our collection. We would like books from every country in the Empire."

"It looks like you're close," Gift said.

Jalung shook her head. "We have almost no books from Galinas, and only half of what we need from Etanien. So many countries want more than another book in trade, not realizing that information is a valuable thing."

This woman was consistently proving herself to be sharper than he expected. He started to go deeper into the room, but she stopped him.

"It is our tradition to remove our boots before walking on the rugs." She indicated a small bench beside the door. "We have slippers if you want to keep your feet covered."

"We're waiting here for the guide?" Xihu asked. She hadn't said a word through the walk, as if absorbing things were more than enough for her.

"Yes," Jalung said. "I will make certain you have refreshments while you wait."

Gift sat on the bench and leaned his head against the whitewashed section of wall. Xihu sat beside him.

"I never realized," he said, "despite that week I spent in Dzaan, that anything like this was possible."

"You were not raised like the other members of the Black Family." Xihu bent over and untied her boots. She slipped off the first and then rooted beneath the bench. She came up with a pair of fleece slippers and put one on. It came up to her ankle and looked strange with her robes.

"They would know about this?" Gift bent over to untie his boots as well. He could fall asleep in this position— he could fall asleep in any position at the moment—and so he made himself concentrate on the very simple task before him.

"If they didn't know," Xihu said, "they would demand something like it, even if it meant taking the best house in the city."

Gift whistled softly. His adoptive parents raised him to be unassuming, even though they knew who he was. Perhaps they had done that on purpose.

He pulled off the other boot and found some slippers for himself. They were soft and warm and unlike any shoe he had ever worn. It took him a moment to realize that they probably had been Domestic-spelled for comfort.

While Xihu put on her remaining slipper, Gift stood and walked into the center of the room. The fur rugs were even softer—it felt as if he were walking on cushions. He hadn't felt luxury like this since he left Blue Isle— and even what he remembered of his life there hadn't been this comfortable.

A man could get used to this. A man could grow to love it.

Two Domestics came in the main door and set down a tray with brick tea, more sweet biscuits, and some fruit he didn't recognize. He picked up a mug of tea. It had been flavored with soda, butter, and salt, making it rich and filling, nothing like the ritual green tea. He sank into the thronelike chair and closed his eyes.

It seemed like only a moment later that Xihu touched his shoulder.

"I fell asleep," he said groggily.

"Well, wake up." Xihu's whisper was crisp. "I heard Jalung down the hall with your guide."

Gift blinked, then rubbed his eyes. He heard something too—the jingle of many bells. He ran a hand over his face, then made himself stand and stretch. The short nap had helped him. He didn't feel refreshed, but he also didn't feel as if he would fall asleep at a moment's notice.

Jalung came through the arched doors. She wasn't wearing any bells and she hadn't changed clothes. The sound Xihu had awakened him for must have come from the guide, who remained outside.

"Gift," Jalung said in a very formal tone, "I bring you the best guide in all of Ghitlus, Skya."

Jalung stepped aside, and a woman came out of the shadows in the hallway. She was Fey, which surprised Gift. He had been expecting, for some reason, a pure Ghitlan. She was also quite tall, suggesting she had strong magic.

Gift took a step forward. He couldn't help it. Her dark eyes were powerful, her narrow face angled so that it looked as if someone had carefully formed the bones into a perfect Fey face. She wore her black hair in a bun around the crown of her head, but strands fell alongside her face, softening it. Around her neck, she wore a small collar of bells. Her robes were not Ghitlan nor were they Fey: they were made of purple, red, and gold silk, and covered her in layers. She had a sword tied around her waist, and a knife in a hilt strapped under her left arm.

He knew he should say something, but he felt as if the power of speech had left him. He had never seen a woman like this, and knew he probably never would again.

Skya crossed her arms. Apparently she wasn't going to speak until he did.

It was Xihu who saved him. "We are honored," she said softly. "Thank you for making the trip to the Mountain."

"I wouldn't have missed seeing the Black Heir for anything." Skya's voice was low and musical.

Her slightly sarcastic comment broke the moment. Gift felt a surge of irritation. He was beginning to hate being called the Black Heir. "Call me Gift," he said.

"Hmm." Her eyebrows raised, making the amusement on her face even clearer. "A L'Nacin name. And I thought you were born on Blue Isle."

He wasn't going to defend himself or his name. "I didn't expect to see a Fey, especially one with magic."

"Yes, I know," she said. "We don't have 'guiding' magic, more's the pity. It would have been easier."

"Than?"

"Answering this question every time a Fey party wants to hire me." She crossed her arms. "I was born in Co to an Infantry soldier whose Vision was so slight he never transferred out, and a DreamRider mother. I am by nature a Spell Warder, but I can think of no drearier way to spend my time than thinking up spells for other Fey to cast on their great adventures."

"Warders are rare," Gift said. "You were given dispensation?"

Her gaze went up and down his Shamanic garb. "Black Family members are rare. Were you given dispensation to leave your warrior heritage and attempt Domestic magic?"

She was more defensive than he would have expected. "I was asking about you," he said calmly.

"And I answered you long before you asked the question," she said. "I did not mention dispensation. Dispensation is for people who care."

True enough. He almost grinned, but he felt that would be inappropriate. "I need to get to Blue Isle as quickly as possible, which means I need to cross Ghitlus fast, and then find a guide who will get me to Nye so that I can find the fastest boat to take me across the Infrin Sea."

"Why don't you send for some Beast Riders and make them take you home?" she asked.

"Because it would take them time to get me, they would tire, and I would need more. Besides, Beast Riders—especially Horse Riders—resent passengers. Is this a test to see if a blue-eyed man is really Fey or is this the way you greet all of your customers?"

To his surprise, she smiled. The smile softened the angles on her face and turned the rigid perfection into a welcoming beauty. "It's the way I treat members of the Black Family."

"You've guided others then."

"No," she said. "You're my first."

He smiled in return. He liked her honesty and her directness. He hadn't had enough of that all day. In fact, he hadn't had enough directness since he'd come to the Eccrasian Mountains.

"So," he said, "now that the preliminaries are out of the way and you've heard my route and my needs, can you help me?"

"No."

Jalung looked at Skya as if she had committed an unpardonable sin. Gift almost laughed at Jalung's expression, but managed, somehow, to keep the laughter inside. He suspected it escaped through his eyes anyway.

"No?" he asked.

"It's silly to hire a second guide, and it's even sillier to go all the way to Nye by land. I propose we go to Btsan and sail to Tashco. You should be able to find a ship from there that will take you to Blue Isle."

"I have never been to Tashco," Gift said. "Do the Tashil have ships that can handle a sustained ocean voyage?"

For the first time since she entered the room, she looked at him with surprise. He felt a flush warm his cheeks. Apparently he had asked a stupid question—stupid, at least, for a member of the Black Family, who should know everything about the Fey Empire.

"The Tashil," she said, "are the major shipbuilders in Galinas. The Nyeians run a distant second. In fact, I suspect many of the Nyeian ships are Tashil in design, with a redecorated interior."

This woman would be useful in more ways than one. "How much time would this save me?" Gift asked.

"The trip from Btsan to Tashco by sea will save you one month alone. I have no idea how much time it will save from your trip to Blue Isle, but if the maps I've seen are even slightly accurate, Tashco is closer to the Isle than any port in Nye, and that portion of the trip has the added benefit of keeping you out of hostile territory."

"Hostile?" he asked, and at the look on her face, stopped before adding, *I thought everything was part of the Empire.*

"How long were you hiding among the Shaman?" she asked.

"I was studying," he said, "for five years."

That wasn't a good enough answer. He could see it in her face. She was beginning to think him an idiot. "The Co have always hated the Fey, and lately they've been more aggressive about it. They would love to have the Black Heir in their territory. Your sister would get a message from them with a bit of your ear, maybe, or a finger, demanding ransom—if they decided to let you live. They might kill you and see what happened from there."

"I take it the Co aren't the only ones?"

"Is this a game?" she asked. "Or a test? Because I hate tests."

"It's neither," he said. He may as well admit to her now how little he knew. She would learn it on the journey anyway. "I was raised on Blue Isle, outside of the Black Family. When my sister took control, she took it after Rugad's death without his prior training. While she spent time studying the Empire, my training hasn't been that formal. I've only picked up what I've learned in my travels."

"And obviously the Shaman taught you nothing."

His smile was bitter. "They taught me less than nothing. But they did manage to introduce me to some things that surprised me."

Skya looked pointly at Xihu. "Yet you travel with one."

"Xihu has volunteered to serve as Shaman to my

family. We've been without Domestic Vision for a long time."

"So she will be traveling with us."

Gift clasped his hands behind his back. "Do you object to that?"

"I don't like Shaman. They get in the way with their Visions and their pronouncements and their rules."

Her words hung in the air for a moment, then Gift said, as calmly as he could, "You'll be traveling with two Visionaries. And you'll have to listen to my pronouncements, and follow my rules."

This time her cheeks flushed. "I didn't mean—"

"Yes, you did," he said. "And I'm beginning to understand why you don't Ward." The Spell Warders had more rules about behavior than any other group of Fey.

She jutted out her pointed chin. "Do you still want me?"

Gift's mouth opened slightly. Want her? He warmed at the possibility. But he answered the question the way she meant it. "Jalung says you're the best guide in Ghitlus. You've already saved me a month, maybe more. Of course I want you."

There was more warmth in his voice than he intended. The double entendre caught them both.

Her flush deepened. "We haven't talked payment."

"We haven't decided how far you'll guide us."

"I can take you to Tashco, and find you a good Navigator and several Sailors for the ship."

"You claim to have seen maps," Gift said. "I don't know of any Fey maps that include Blue Isle, and the Nyeian maps only go from Blue Isle to Nye."

She licked her lips, a clearly nervous gesture. "They're not Fey maps."

"I believe I just said that."

She was breathing hard now. "They're from Dorovich."

"I don't believe I've ever heard of Dorovich," Gift said.

She glanced at Jalung, who looked as confused as Gift felt, and Xihu, who seemed slightly worried. "Dorovich," Skya said. "It's not part of the Empire."

Gift felt the hair on the back of his neck rise. "Really? Is it a city or a country?"

"A continent."

"And why do they have accurate maps of Galinas and Blue Isle?"

She shrugged. "I just saw the maps. I didn't draw them."

"Have you been to Dorovich?"

"No," she said. "I haven't been out of the Empire."

"Then where did you see the maps?"

"Tashco," she said. "A Co trader had them."

"Co," Gift said. "The people who so dislike the Fey."

"Yes."

"And how recently was this?"

She shrugged. "A year ago, maybe more."

He stared at her for a moment. She no longer thought him an idiot, that much was clear. None of them did. For the first time in a long time, he didn't feel like an imposter. He felt like a man who was close to the Throne.

A man who wasn't happy with what he was hearing.

"You expect me to base my travels on a foreign map made by people who are not native to this region?"

"Yes," she said.

At least she didn't try to justify it. She wasn't trying to justify anything.

"How do you know the map is accurate?"

"Because it is in other parts."

"So you've met people from Dorovich?"

"No," she said. "But I have the map."

"Here?"

"No," she said. "But we can pick it up along the way. If you still want me."

Again that phrase. This time, he answered her. "I want you," he said, his voice deliberately husky.

Her eyes widened, and she ducked her head. She had apparently thought she had misunderstood him the last time. There was no mistaking him now.

He was a bit surprised at himself. He had never spoken to a woman this way, never felt this instant attraction, or this instant challenge.

"I will be your guide, and that's it," she said.

He feigned surprise. "Isn't that what we're discussing?"

She took in a sharp breath. "Do you expect me to guard you as well as guide you or will you be hiring someone else for that?"

"I can take care of myself," he said.

"Forgive me," she said, not sounding contrite at all, "but you have Domestic training, not warrior training, and while I'm good, I can't be everywhere. A Shaman is worthless in some of the areas we're going to. You kill first and ask questions later."

"I can take care of myself," Gift said again.

"I don't want to get blamed for your death," Skya said.

"Believe me," Gift said. "No one will even know you're with the Black Heir."

"Of course they'll know," she said. "You come in here, announce yourself, make everyone bow to you. That kind of behavior is not common."

He let himself smile. "That's a good thing, considering my family are the only ones who should be behaving like that."

"That's not what I meant," she said.

Gift ignored that. "If you're as good a guide as Jalung says, then we don't need to tell anyone who I am, at least, not until we get to Tashco."

She sighed. "If we do that, I can't get you the proper accommodations. They're just not available to the average traveler."

"I don't care about the accommodations," he said. "All I want to do is get home as quickly as possible."

Something crossed her face, some flicker of suspicion? anger? He wasn't sure. She turned to Jalung. "Would you leave us for a moment, and close the door?"

Jalung inclined her head, as if she felt uncomfortable not bowing, and then left. After a moment, the wooden door closed, its bang echoing in the room.

Skya walked toward him until she was an arm's length away from him. "I cannot be party," she said, "to the overthrow of the Black Queen, no matter who you are, no matter what your reasons."

"What makes you assume I want to overthrow my sister?" Gift asked.

"You didn't come to study Shamanism. You came to visit the Black Throne, and now that you have its approval, you want to put yourself on that Throne."

"Interesting assumption," Gift said. "And how would you see yourself helping in this illegal overthrow?"

"By getting you there quickly, before your sister knows what you've done."

"I see." Out of the corner of his eye, Gift could see Xihu. She was sitting on one of the benches, legs out, as if she was enjoying the show. "I admire your ethics. I don't see ethics like that very often."

Skya's face went completely blank. "Making fun of me won't—"

"I'm not making fun of you." Gift took her arm. The silk of her robe was soft, the layers thick. He couldn't actually feel her arm through the fabric. He pulled her closer, until their faces nearly touched. She didn't flinch. He had thought she would.

Her eyes were a dark brown, her skin flawless. He wanted to rub the back of his hand along her cheek.

"I admire your concern," he said so softly that he doubted Xihu could hear him. "I wasn't making fun of you. I was complimenting you. I have told you the truth— or as much of it as I know. I did study Shamanism, and now I have a family emergency that I must tend to."

"Something happened to the Throne," she said.

He tried not to let his surprise show. "What makes you say that?"

"I am still a Warder, even if I choose not to practice in the acceptable methods. I felt a ripple and so I pinpointed its source." She blinked once, her long lashes just brushing the tops of her cheeks. "Warders are the only Fey who can do that, you know. Identify the source of a magic."

He put his other hand on her other arm, mostly to stop himself from touching that magnificent face. "I do know something about the Fey."

"I wasn't certain. I—"

He put a finger on her lips. They were generous and warm. He could feel her breath against his skin. "I touched the Throne and rejected it. That's what you felt. The violent reaction the Throne had to my rejection."

She removed his finger from her lips. But she didn't let go of his hand. Instead, she wrapped it inside her own, and held it against her shoulder. The gesture was intimate, and Gift didn't move for fear of destroying the moment.

"You're a Visionary," she said, and it was clear to him she was finally beginning to understand. "You're hurrying to Blue Isle because of something you Saw."

"Yes."

"And you won't tell me what that is?"

He let out a small breath. She was Charming him, and it nearly worked because she was not a Charmer but a Warder, with tiny bits of all magic. Most Charmers angered Visionaries; the Charmer's magic never worked on true Leaders. But apparently Charm itself did.

He leaned forward and kissed her. She tasted sweet as she kissed him back, apparently thinking he was still under her Charm. He left his free hand slip into her hair, taking it from its bun and setting it loose down her back. He wondered how far she would take this to find out what he knew, who he really was, what he needed from her.

Then he ended the kiss, and pressed his forehead against hers. "Mmm," he said. "You're very good."

His hand was still wrapped around her own. She tilted her head toward him, apparently willing to Charm him further. He was tempted to let her do so, but he didn't. He needed her at his side—she had already proven invaluable—and he didn't want her too angry at him.

He slid his other hand from her hair to caress her cheek. Out of the corner of his eye, he saw Xihu stand.

He would wager she knew what was going on, and that she was getting ready to put an end to it.

"Very good," he whispered. "But a little bit of Charm in the hands of a talented Warder doesn't match my Vision. It's nice to know you have this ability, though. We'll be able to use it."

She disengaged herself from him so fast that he almost lost his balance. Then she cursed him in three different languages, her dark eyes flashing.

Xihu sat down. Gift laughed. Skya stopped swearing and stood, legs spread, arms crossed. "You had no right—"

"No right?" Gift asked, his laughter fading. "If you had tried that trick on my grandfather Rugar, he would have had you killed. I shudder to think what my great-grandfather would have done."

"So you're going to punish me?"

"Depends," Gift said. "If you consider traveling with me and Xihu punishment, then yes, I will. If you look forward to the trip, it won't be punishment at all."

"You're not what I expected," she said.

"And neither are you."

"I had a right to know what you were asking me to do," she said.

"I told you exactly what I wanted." Gift's hands were still tingling from the touch of her skin. This reaction wasn't simple Charm. It was more. It was a real reaction to her. "You could accept or decline my offer to hire you. And that's as far as this transaction had to go."

"You touched the Black Throne."

"Indeed, I did," he said. "Unwillingly, at the urging of another. And then I rejected the Throne. And it released some sort of power in the form of light."

"You're going to warn your sister of that?"

Gift stared at her for a moment. Then he sighed. "This interview is done. We will not require your services."

Her eyes narrowed. "But I'm the best."

"And the nosiest. We can make do without you. You've already told us the route."

"You can't accomplish it without me."

"I was told I can't do many things, and I've done them all. Thank you for your time, Skya. You are dismissed." He turned his back on her. Xihu was watching him, face impassive. But he thought he detected a twinkle in her eyes.

"You could have simply said no questions," Skya said.

Gift walked to one of the alcoves. All of the books in it were bound in the same kind of leather.

"He asked you to leave," Xihu said.

"We're not done," Skya said.

"Yes," Xihu said. "You are."

"You won't find anyone else like me," Skya said.

Gift agreed with that. In thirty-three years, he hadn't met anyone else like her. His heart twisted at the thought of letting her go.

"You are not the unique one here," Xihu said. "There is one Black Ruler and one worthy heir, and you are being asked to guide that heir to his home. In asking questions and in playing games, you not only disgrace yourself, you threaten the Empire."

"Big words," Skya said.

"True words," Xihu said. "It is better for us to have one guide who is not as good as you than have one whose knowledge of things she should not know threatens us and our travels."

Gift bit his lower lip to prevent himself from turning around. He wanted her to stay. He wanted to ask her himself, to do this entire meeting over again, to charm her—not with magic—but with his own personality.

"Either you do things our way and listen to us," Xihu said, "or you do not guide us. Is that clear?"

There was a long silence. Gift held his breath. Finally, Skya spoke.

"I understand."

He wanted to turn, he wanted to ask her if she was going to stay, but he didn't. He waited.

"Will you serve us as we ask?" Xihu emphasized the word "serve."

"Yes."

"Will you cease playing games?"

"Are you afraid I'll finally succeed?" Skya asked.

"Against the greatest Visionary the Fey have ever known? No. I am afraid you will play the wrong game in front of the wrong people at the wrong time."

"I'm careful."

"Are you?" Xihu said. "Is that why you played your game in front of Jalung? Do you know who she is?"

"I have known her for a decade."

"And you know where her loyalties are."

"Of course. She's taken care of this place her whole life."

"So she has a stake in what happens to it."

"Yes." Skya sounded annoyed. Gift frowned. He wasn't sure where Xihu was taking this either.

"And if Gift decided he wanted to stay here, and to put his own staff here, displacing Jalung and her staff, she would not mind that."

"Of course she'd mind. She's put her heart into this place."

"Then she is not to be trusted around the Black Family, is she?" Xihu's voice was soft. Gift suppressed a smile. He had made a good choice with Xihu. "And you know her. Imagine how you might misjudge someone you do not know."

"I'm good with people."

"Yes," Xihu said. "I saw that in the way you handled Gift."

That was enough. Gift turned. Skya's face was flushed, her eyes bright with shame. She hadn't changed her posture yet. She was still standing defiantly.

Her gaze met his. That got Xihu's attention, and she turned as well.

"It's your decision," Xihu said. "But I believe we should get a different guide."

Gift hadn't taken his gaze off Skya. "If I hire you," he said, "I will hire you for your knowledge and your advice. But you will do as I say, even if it goes counter to everything you believe. I will fire you if you violate this even once. If you can work under those conditions, you have a job."

There was a wildness in her, despite her subdued posture and the embarrassment on her face, that could not be tamed. He recognized it as the same quality his sister had once had, and he suspected his mother had once had it as well. The quality had its uses—and its dangers.

"I will see your ship off in Tashco," she said. "And I will get you there faster than anyone can without resorting to magic."

"That's all I can ask," he said and somehow—although he wasn't sure how—he knew that he lied.

CHAPTER TWENTY-SEVEN

XET'N, THE LAMPLIGHTER, was so old that he looked like he shouldn't be able to move as well as he did. His body had shrunken into a question mark, and his skin was so wrinkled that his eyes were nearly hidden in the folds. It had taken Coulter a moment to realize that those eyes held a great and mobile intelligence, and they were what kept that decrepit body alive.

Lamplighting was one magic Coulter didn't entirely understand—the art of capturing a soul even after it had escaped a body, placing it in a lamp, and getting the soul to convert itself to light. Because he didn't understand it, he felt that he couldn't do it, not as well as he needed to.

Xet'n wasn't sure if a construct had a soul, but when Coulter told him that the construct had a dead person's memories, a dead person's personality, and that person's soul had not been captured, Xet'n sucked in a long breath.

"Then it is likely," Xet'n said, "the soul lives in the construct." Xet'n raised those intelligent eyes to Coulter's. "It would take Enchantment or Vision to manage such a thing. Great Vision."

Coulter did not reply. Xet'n continued to stare at him for a long moment.

"Very few have such Vision, and those who do rarely have access to one such as the Black Queen."

"What are you saying?" Coulter asked.

"That we must be cautious. Such a soul would be difficult to capture under normal circumstances. These circumstances are not normal."

Coulter agreed with that. These circumstances were anything but normal.

His heart was pounding hard as he climbed the stairs to the living quarters of the palace. He hadn't been to these rooms in years, not since he had left to go to Constant. Arianna was here, unconscious, locked in what Seger had called a struggle to protect her own self from Rugad's construct. Seger checked her before sending Coulter and Xet'n to Arianna's suite.

"I don't know if she'll know you're there," Seger said. "This work is unlike any I've done before."

Seger was across the hall, in Sebastian's rooms. She and Con, whom Coulter had remembered as a wide-eyed, scrawny boy and who had grown into a slender ascetic man, were in those rooms together. Con carried a dirty, battered sword that still bore traces of old blood.

This entire procedure terrified Coulter. It was the most important thing he had ever done, and there was no way to test it, no way to think it through.

The family portraits were as he remembered them: rows of blond-hair, blue-eyed people until they reached Jewel, who looked so out of place that hers was the first portrait he noticed. Not even Arianna's was as startling. Coulter paused before hers, looking at the familiar face with its blue eyes, rounded cheekbones, and upswept eyebrows. The artist had captured her wild spirit and, for some reason, had downplayed the birthmark on her chin, the very thing that showed her to be a Shifter.

Xet'n had passed Coulter and was waiting near the railing. "I thought we were in a hurry," Xet'n said.

Coulter pulled himself away from the portrait. Would she even know he was here? Would she be happy to see him if she did? He had promised he would be her Enchanter. He had promised he would always be there for her. He had promised he would see her again.

He had done none of those things.

But he was here now, and that was what mattered.

He followed Xet'n, who was carrying a small bag, to Arianna's suite, and stopped in surprise. Luke stood outside, his arms crossed over his chest. He wore the uniform of the guards, and when he saw Coulter, he did not smile.

By the time Coulter had moved in with Luke's father, Adrian, Luke already had a home of his own. Adrian had adopted Coulter, mostly because no one else wanted him, but Luke never saw it that way. He had always seen Coulter as a rival for Adrian's affections, even though Adrian had given up his freedom—and had been willing to give up his entire life—for Luke.

Coulter and Luke hadn't seen each other in a long time, probably as long as it had been since Coulter had seen Arianna.

"I didn't know you were here," Coulter said softly.

"One of us has to follow through," Luke said.

Coulter looked away. "You know what we're doing."

Luke nodded. "You only get one chance at this."

"I know," Coulter said.

"Don't freeze up."

Coulter felt a pang. Everyone knew how he had failed years ago in the Roca's Cave. "Don't worry," he said with a confidence he didn't feel.

Luke reached down and opened the door. With his right hand, Coulter indicated that Xet'n should go in first. Before he did, Xet'n stopped.

"Don't open this door until I tell you," Xet'n said. "No matter what you hear."

Luke didn't look at him, but at Coulter instead. "You're asking a lot."

"You can come in with us," Xet'n said. "But it's important for my work that no door or window is open until I say it can be."

Luke continued to stare at Coulter. Coulter felt the tension grow in his shoulders and arms. Was Luke expecting Coulter to forbid him to enter? Coulter wouldn't. It didn't matter who was there. What mattered was what he could do for Arianna.

"I'll make sure no one goes in," Luke said at last. "The window over the garden is open. You might want to close that."

Xet'n nodded and went inside. Coulter hesitated for a moment. "Luke—"

"Whatever you're going to say, I don't want to hear it," Luke said. "We have our own lives now. That they intersect here means nothing."

Coulter closed his mouth. He wasn't quite certain what he had been planning to say—something conciliatory, probably, something about being raised by the same man who had loved them both and wanted them to care for each other. Or maybe something simple about burying the past—but the moment was gone. Luke was right. They had their own lives now.

Maybe, if Coulter was successful, they could go back to those lives.

Coulter went through the door, and Luke closed it behind him.

Coulter had never been in these rooms. The door opened into a large sitting room, with a huge fireplace. Through a door on the other side, he saw a dressing room, and behind that, a bed.

His heart was pounding even harder. Arianna was in there.

From the room came the sound of shutters closing. Xet'n had explained the logic of this to Coulter earlier. Souls never saw themselves as beings of light or energy or air. They remembered having a body, and they acted upon that remembrance. They were often stopped by closed doors or windows, not knowing how to get through them. Even the savvy souls, the ones who knew they had no bodies, still hesitated before going through a wall, or penetrating a closed door.

Coulter walked through the dressing room and into the bedroom, pulling all the doors closed behind him.

Arianna lay across the bed, her arms at her side. Someone had placed her here, he realized. She would never have lain that rigidly on her own.

He slipped into the chair beside the bed. It wasn't fair to say she hadn't changed. The last time he saw her, she had been fifteen years old, all spit and fire. Her body had filled out, and her face had narrowed. She looked more Fey than she had as a girl. Part of that was the fact her eyes were closed. They, and her skin that was darker than his but lighter than most Fey's, made her look different. There were laugh lines at the corners of her eyes, and a single strand of hair on the side of her head had turned silver.

It had been too long.

He had told her on that long-ago day that he had loved her. He had also told her that he was not worthy of her. And when she didn't accept that, which was the truth, he had made up a lie:

We're not ready to be together. You have to figure out what kind of ruler you'll be. And I need to heal. Maybe when I'm better and you're established, we can try again.

And then he snuck out of that garden, and out of her life, never intending to return. She hadn't needed him then. Now she did.

Xet'n had taken a small lamp from his bag and set it on the nightstand. Then he sat in the chair opposite Coulter's. His gaze met Coulter's and he nodded, ever so slowly.

Time to begin.

Seger was probably already under way.

Coulter took a deep breath and touched Arianna's

left temple with his forefinger, and her birthmark with his thumb. The birthmark was rigid against his skin, throbbing, as if it lived on its own. She had said she loved him that day, which meant there had to be a Link between them, even if she had closed the door, as he had instructed. If the door were truly closed, he would have to try something else, but he suspected it wasn't. The Link between them had formed after he had told her to close the doors. She might never have thought of closing this one.

He shut his eyes, and used his second sight. There were a lot of disconnected Links floating about her, none of them tying to the others. There was also a blackness threading through her entire body, and a golden light that seemed to envelop her. Neither of those looked familiar. They were magics he had never seen before.

He put his other forefinger on her right temple and his thumbs brushed on her chin. That would hold them together, no matter what.

He touched one active Link before he realized it was not the one that connected her to him. Then he found his own Link to her, closed off on his side, the door slammed the day he walked out of the garden. He opened the door, and stepped into the light.

The light extended the short distance between them, existing only in the air beyond their physical bodies. The doors that Coulter saw actually existed inside their minds, but the Link was an actual road of light that connected them.

As he stepped out, he saw, as he had hoped, an open door. He slipped inside and he was inside her mind.

He had been here before, years ago, when she had been lost and he had had to find her. Then it had been a wild, unformed place, damaged by the recent fight. Now it was rigidly divided, and he had no sense of her at all.

But he should. He should feel her in here. Her presence should be all around them. He walked through a narrow pathway, lined with black—all the walls and paths were lined with black—and went to her eyes. They were closed. If he tried, he could feel his own fingers against her temple. The birthmark throbbed beneath his thumbs, but he couldn't feel the throbbing from in here, and it should be a dominant feeling.

"An Islander who looks Fey," said a male voice. It echoed around him and spoke in both Fey and Islander at the same time.

Coulter felt himself grow cold, even though he had no body in here. Only an imaginary body, the body he envisioned within himself. It manifested as a tall Islander, with blond hair, blue eyes that slanted up, blond eyebrows, and slanted ears. An Islander who looked Fey.

Slowly he turned away from Arianna's shuttered eyes. Coulter took his time, assessing what he had heard. Someone who had enough mastery to speak two languages at once, to know such a thing was possible within this place, and then to use it.

What he saw surprised him: a teenage Fey boy with Gift's face. No. The face was slightly wrong. It was too narrow, and the eyes were so brown they seemed black. But the expression of wry amusement was Gift's and so were the set of the chin, the way the brows moved when he spoke, the slight upturned edges of the mouth.

The boy was lanky with the suggestion of great strength to come in the shoulders and legs.

"I don't believe we've met," the boy said in both languages. "I'm Rugad."

Coulter felt that chill again, in his nonexistent body. He hadn't expected a young Rugad, and he hadn't expected the young Rugad to look so much like Gift at the same age.

"And you're the Islander Enchanter, the one I searched for, the one my son raised from an infant. It's pathetic how much you want to be Fey. Is that why you're in love with my great-granddaughter? Or is it because she's the female version of my great-grandson, the one you're Bound to?"

The words were intended to make Coulter mad. He

knew that. And they worked. But he held back. He wouldn't lose his temper here. He had Arianna to think of.

"My name is Coulter." He made sure he spoke Islander and Fey as well.

"Coulter." Rugad spoke softly. "Coulter. You have come to save your precious Arianna. But it's too late. I've already built my encampment here."

"I see that," Coulter said.

"It's permanent."

"Really?" Coulter asked. "Then why aren't you in control of her body yet?"

A violent shudder nearly knocked him off his feet. The shudder came from Arianna's body. He didn't know if she intended it, or if Rugad had done it to throw him off.

Coulter had to remember that nothing he felt in here was real. Nothing could hurt him. To remind himself, he floated a few feet off the surface he had been standing on.

"I shut the door to the Link," Rugad said, "and we're both trapped in here."

"I don't think you want to keep it closed," Coulter said. "You'd be stuck with me, and I'd side with Arianna."

"You'd die without your body."

"You didn't," Coulter said. "And I learn quickly."

"It's not part of your magic."

"Everything is part of my magic." As he spoke, Coulter realized he was making a mistake. Rugad was trying to distract him. Nothing was as it seemed here. The rules did not apply in the same way. Just as Coulter could speak two languages at the same time, he could be in more than one place at once.

He split part of himself off, made it invisible, and sent it in search of Arianna. As it floated away, he felt something niggle at him from Rugad's words.

"Then I could go to your body," Rugad said. He clearly didn't know that Coulter had separated part of himself. "Imagine what I could do with an Enchanter's powers."

"Nothing," Coulter said. "You wouldn't know how to use them."

The second part of himself saw lines and walls and divisions everywhere. They were all established by Rugad. Arianna did not like or believe in walls. They were all threaded with black, and they looked as unnatural as buildings erected in a cave. He did not see or feel Arianna in any of them.

"Ah, but I would figure it out," Rugad said.

He was still trying to distract Coulter. Why? There was something he didn't want Coulter to see. It had something to do with a mention Rugad had made earlier.

"Where's Arianna?" Coulter asked.

"Here, of course," Rugad said. "Did you think I'd harm her?"

"You can't harm her," Coulter said. "If you did, she'd die and then you'd have no body."

That was it. The body and the Links. Rugad had said he could go to Coulter's body. Seger had said she had conversed with Rugad in Sebastian's body. Sebastian and Arianna were Linked.

"Are you so sure that her death wouldn't mean that I controlled this body?" Rugad asked.

Coulter was sure. That was one bit of magic that Coulter did understand. It was common to all constructs. They needed a form maintained by someone else in order to survive. That was why Golems were so perfect. The form was created by someone else, and could be maintained by the construct.

But Coulter decided to play along. "You couldn't," he said, making himself sound panicked. "You'd do that blood thing."

Rugad laughed. "Black Blood against Black Blood? It only refers to physical blood. It's very literal. And you've even seen how the blood creates itself."

He had? He decided not to think on that now. His second self still hadn't found Arianna. And he needed a third self.

"Are you sure?" Coulter asked. "If you're wrong, you destroy everything."

"I'm sure," Rugad said. "As long as I don't cause death to the physical body."

Slowly, gently, Coulter separated half of his remaining self, and made sure it too was invisible. Then he sent it toward his own Link door. If Arianna kept her Links like Gift kept his, all the doors would be in one place.

"But," Coulter said. "If you destroy her soul, her body will die."

"Not if someone else controls it, keeps the heart beating, the blood pumping, and the air moving."

That sounded right. The panic Coulter feigned filled him briefly. He pushed it away.

"You forget," Rugad said. "I am not an invader like you. She took me into herself. I am part of her now."

Coulter's third self had found the Link doors. All of them were closed except his. He was about to turn away when he saw—

"I own her," Rugad said.

—a door slightly open. He went to it, and touched the Link, and felt a presence as cold as stone, yet with a warmth that was sweet and innocent. He recognized it immediately.

Sebastian.

Suddenly he felt a presence beside him. Rugad somehow knew what he was doing. Coulter slammed the Sebastian door closed and locked it with one of his own locks. A personal lock could only be broken by the person who established it.

Rugad grabbed Coulter's third self and slammed him against the door, trying to shove him toward his own Link and out. Coulter fought hard, but Rugad was three times stronger than he was, and younger—

—and a construct who knew he had no physical presence. Coulter turned himself into water and slipped away, then called back his missing parts. He hurried to his own Link door and locked it.

"I'm not leaving here until I find Arianna," he said.

Rugad laughed. The sound was a live thing all around him. "Then you're not leaving," he said.

"As long as I'm here," Coulter said, leaning on his door, "you'll never get to exercise any power. You'll have to fight me for the rest of your life."

"The rest of *my* life?" Rugad rose up, crossed his legs and arms, and floated. He looked very relaxed. "Actually, I'll only have to fight you for the rest of yours."

Coulter suppressed a curse. Rugad was right, of course. Rugad was a construct, with no body. He was designed for this. Coulter had his own body that, in days, would fade away and die. He had to be in it to get it to eat and drink. Without either food or water, he wouldn't live long. He doubted Seger would be able to help him. His time in here was limited, whether he liked it or not. And he had to consider that, because if he left when his body was too badly weakened, he wouldn't be able to help Arianna.

"Hadn't thought of that, had you?" Rugad asked. "I have all the time in the world. I will eventually become this body. You are the intruder here, not me."

"We both are," Coulter said.

"I was welcomed." Rugad spread out his arms. "And I must say, this is a fantastic body. It has powers that I never did have."

Coulter had to separate again, had to start searching for Arianna, but he was reluctant. He didn't know what Rugad would do, and now that he was here, he wasn't sure how to fight him. Arianna had to know that Coulter was here. She had to hear their voices, feel the doors close, know that something was going on.

She had to.

Or was she near death already?

"You have no Vision here," Coulter said. "That magic belongs to Arianna, and you have no body of your own. You can't appropriate her Sight."

Rugad's arms dropped and his dark gaze grew cool. So that was the problem, the problem that Rugad had thought he would solve before taking over. If he never solved it—and being awakened early, as Seger said, may have interfered with that—he would need Arianna for the rest of her life.

That, at least, was good news.

"I don't have to appropriate her Sight," Rugad said. "She shares it with me. She shares everything with me. Are you jealous of that, Islander?"

She shared everything, and not willingly. No wonder she couldn't fight him. If he could hear her thoughts, she couldn't plan. She couldn't do anything.

Coulter had hoped that, once he found her, he would have her help. But that wouldn't work. Rugad would then know what they were going to do.

Coulter had to take care of Rugad himself, and then he had to find Arianna. Two different tasks. And the first one was the hardest because Coulter had no idea what to do.

CHAPTER TWENTY-EIGHT

*S*EBASTIAN STOOD NEAR the closed window, just as Seger instructed him to. His arms were at his side, his gray eyes staring straight ahead. He wore only a cloth wrapped around his middle. Seger would have preferred him nude, but Sebastian insisted. He was modest on top of everything else. That was the only one of her instructions he did not follow. Otherwise he did everything else she asked. He had an amazing ability to stand immobile, and it made him look like a cracked and ruined statue of Gift.

Con sat on the edge of the bed. He was wearing Fey clothes, but the small filigree sword he wore around his neck rested on top of his jerkin. His real sword, the one that they needed, lay across his thighs. The sword was old and battered, with dried blood from other battles on its blade. Con had told Seger he was afraid to clean the blade, afraid he would hurt himself, and afraid he would destroy the sword's power.

She wasn't going to touch it. She remembered how badly it had injured Fey, years ago, when Con and the sword had fought their way through more than twenty more experienced warriors. She had cleaned the wounds of the warriors who had survived, and she had seen how cleanly the sword had cut through them, as if they were made of butter instead of flesh and bone.

Con was so much older now, his adult face covered with care lines, the boyishness gone. When he had come in, he had hugged Sebastian, and Sebastian had returned the hug, as slowly as Sebastian always did.

That was how Seger knew that Rugad was no longer in Sebastian's body.

Her heart was pounding and her fingers were shaking. They didn't have a lot of time. The moment Rugad discovered what they were doing, he would try to stop it. Somehow. Some way.

She hoped Coulter was having good luck.

She glanced at the table across the room. She had brought some clay from the Isle and stone, in hopes of success. In her left hand, she held a stoppered glass jar, lined with blood she had taken from the store the Spell Warders kept. With the help of Red Caps, Warders maintained stores of magic supplies, including the blood of enemies, and blood tainted with old magic. She had lined the jar with both, knowing that blood attracted a wayward soul. She hoped it would do the same with a soul's voice. The last time she had taken Rugad's voice, she had done so with his permission. This time, she would have a fight on her hands.

"Hur-ry," Sebastian said. "I . . . do . . . not . . . want . . . him . . . to . . . come . . . back."

Sebastian had confirmed her earlier suspicions. Rugad had opened the Link between Sebastian and Arianna and was traveling back and forth. When Arianna had returned the last time, to tell Luke all she could, Rugad had been in Sebastian.

Soon, Seger knew, Rugad would become skilled enough to run both bodies at the same time. They were lucky that he wasn't ready. If he had had another ten years, there would have been no defeating him.

She turned to Con. "Are you ready?"

He nodded. He clutched the sword so hard, his knuckles were white. His blue eyes were wide and frightened, but he didn't move.

She admired that.

"Hur-ry," Sebastian said again.

Seger nodded. "Remember to move quickly," she said to Con. She didn't want the voice to thread back through the stones.

"I will," he said.

She put her hands on Sebastian's cool skin. Thank the Powers that he was himself at the moment. She believed she would be able to tell if Rugad were inside him. She hoped. She and Coulter only had one chance at this, and if one of them failed, she didn't know what they'd do.

She didn't want to admit to herself that there might not be the possibility of success. The voice might be threaded too deeply within Sebastian's stone, and the construct might have taken complete control of Arianna. If that were the case, both Seger and Coulter would be in trouble.

The entire world would be in trouble.

Rugad would go for the Triangle of Might, and nothing would be the same again.

Con stood, one hand clasping the hilt of his sword.

"Are you ready?" Seger asked Sebastian.

"Yes," he said.

It all rested, ultimately, on Sebastian. He had to keep Rugad out, and he had to shatter at the right time.

"You'll feel a tug," Seger said. "The instant it becomes extreme is the moment you shatter."

"What . . . if . . . Rugad . . . comes?"

She had already thought of this. "Shatter then and destroy your Link to Arianna."

"Des-troy?" He sounded as if she had asked him to cut out his heart.

"Yes," Seger said. "It's critical. He needs to be trapped outside of you and Arianna."

"He . . . will . . . use . . . me," Sebastian said.

Seger shook her head. "If that happens, we won't re-assemble you until we find the construct."

"And . . . if . . . you . . . do . . . not?"

She didn't want to tell him what they would do. They would have to leave him disassembled forever. "I'll leave that up to Arianna and Coulter. They'll be able to handle the magic better than I will."

"I . . . could . . . hold . . . him . . . and . . . shat-ter . . . again."

He could, she knew, if Rugad didn't overtake him completely. But she had seen Rugad now, with a young man's body and a young man's strength, and the naked ambition still shining in his eyes. Sebastian had surprised Rugad years ago and gained advantage. She doubted Sebastian would surprise him again.

"If we reassemble you and he's there, then that's what you must do," Seger said.

Sebastian nodded slowly. Con took a step closer.

"I think you want to stay back," Seger said. "The shards could hurt you."

"I'll be all right," Con said.

She met his gaze. He too cared about Sebastian, just as Arianna did. Amazing that a creature created out of stone could inspire such loyalty. Even she felt it, some-times against her will.

Seger took a deep breath. She put the tips of the fingers on her right hand against Sebastian's naked chest, and wrapped her left hand gently around his throat.

"Here goes," she said.

CHAPTER TWENTY-NINE

*T*HE VOICE WAS as familiar as her own, but Arianna couldn't believe she was hearing it. Rugad was tormenting her, plucking her memories and playing them like strings. He had to be.

She was deep within herself, being held in place by a mental force beyond her capability. It felt—if feelings were the correct way to describe things that happened to a part of her that had no actual body—as if a giant hand were pressing on her, flattening her, keeping her in place. She had changed form countless times, from Fey to water to air, and still the pressure came.

Rugad was holding her back from inside the core of herself, using her own powers to contain her, and she had no idea how to fight him. He anticipated her every move, knew her every thought, and occasionally tortured her by giving her a small success and then quashing it.

An Islander who looks Fey, Rugad said in both Islander and Fey. Arianna felt a jolt of surprise. That described Coulter's vision of himself so perfectly. The first time she had seen him had been inside her own mind, when he had been perfect energy, represented as he imagined himself: a tall blond Islander boy with upswept eyes, high cheekbones, and pointed ears. She remembered thinking she had never seen anyone so handsome.

That thought hadn't changed when she saw what he really looked like: short, blue-eyed, round-faced, and dear. So dear. He had left her after she had become Black Queen, promising to return one day, but he hadn't come back, and she had been too proud to send for him.

Was he really here now?

He had to be. Rugad was still talking, and using a different tone than he had ever used with her. A mocking, challenging tone.

. . . It's pathetic how much you want to be Fey. Is that why you're in love with my great-granddaughter? Or is it because she's the female version of my great-grandson, the one you're Bound to?

My name is Coulter.

He was here. He was. He had come for her.

"Coulter!" she cried, but the hand pressed on her harder, making her words vanish.

She had to reach him somehow. He had to be able to find her. If he found her, together they could defeat Rugad.

"No, you can't."

It felt as if Rugad's voice were a part of her. For a brief moment, she had forgotten that he could hear her thoughts. But he was speaking to her and Coulter at the same time. He had never done anything like that before.

"It takes ninety-two years of living before you can do anything like that," he said, but the thoughts were still bleeding both ways. Rugad was lying. All it took was practice.

And misdirection. She had to get him to think of something else.

"Like your precious Enchanter?"

His words to her overlay the words he was speaking to Coulter.

You have come to save your precious Arianna. But it's too late. I've already built my encampment here.

"But he's not done!" she shouted.

"He can't hear you," Rugad said. "No one can hear you. Your voice is mine now."

Her voice was his. And his hers? His power had to be less if he was dividing it between two places. She concentrated, tried to dislodge him, and felt her physical body shudder.

Rugad cursed her.

I shut the door to the Link, he was saying to Coulter to try and cover the shudder, *and we're both trapped in here.*

She shoved on the hand, shoved with all of her strength. It moved slightly. She shoved again, and it moved some more.

She could hear Coulter speaking to Rugad, but couldn't concentrate on the words. She needed to ooze out, needed to—

And then she realized what she had been doing wrong. If Rugad could divide himself, she could too. He had been lying about the time it took to learn these things. Lying.

The hand slammed her harder and she separated into two pieces. The hand moved through her, and she was on either side of it. She decided to put most of herself into the silent part of her, and to use the other part to distract Rugad.

"Coulter!" the smaller part of her shouted. "Coulter! I'm here."

The hand caught that part of her, pushed it so hard she thought she was going to get squashed. She divided the silent part of her into two pieces and sent one toward the voices.

Where's Arianna? Coulter asked. She could sense him. Part of him was close to her, and it wasn't the part that was speaking. Had he separated as well? She couldn't see him and she didn't want to risk shouting for him.

"Hiding from me will do you no good," Rugad said to her. "You have nowhere to go."

He couldn't find her, and with other parts of her floating about and thinking as well, he wouldn't know where to look. She still felt the hand on the smallest part of herself and she made that part scream. It became one long, drawn-out, loud scream that hurt her own ears—all six of them.

Did you think I'd harm her? Rugad was saying to Coulter.

You can't harm her, Coulter said. *If you did, she'd die and then you'd have no body.*

Ah, Coulter. That was wrong. Rugad could kill her, and would as soon as he figured out how to resurrect his own Vision.

The sense of Coulter was even closer. She didn't know how to measure distance in here, but it seemed as if he were around a corner, a corner she couldn't see.

Her third self edged closer to the conversation. She saw the physical manifestation of Rugad standing with his feet apart, military style. Coulter—the one she had first seen, the Islander Fey, but so much older and sadder—was floating, his feet hovering just above the surface of her mind.

You couldn't. Coulter sounded panicked. What had Rugad said? She hadn't been paying attention. *You'd do that blood thing.*

Rugad laughed. *Black Blood against Black Blood? It only refers to physical blood. It's very literal. And you've even seen how the blood creates itself.*

Her second self was hurrying toward that corner, following the sense of Coulter. Her third self was gasping for nonexistent air. You can scream forever, she reminded herself. Scream. The hand was crushing her, destroying her, but she wouldn't allow herself to get pulled into that third self. Not when she was so close. Not when Rugad didn't know where parts of her were. He was too distracted.

Coulter had provided her the first opportunity she had had since the headaches began. She had to make the most of this.

"Will you stop screaming?" Rugad's voice, the one he was using with her, was coming from far away. How far had she come from her third self?

Instead of answering him, she screamed louder. There were no limits to the volume she could use on her voice, not here. She could deafen them all.

Even though Coulter didn't seem to be hearing her.

You forget, Rugad was saying to Coulter. *I am not an invader like you.*

Arianna had almost reached that corner. The sense she had of Coulter was so strong she wanted to cry out. But she kept this part of herself silent.

I own her.

Then she saw Coulter, a ghost of him, like an outline against the blackness of her mind. She had to touch him, so that she didn't speak to him but so that he felt her.

Her second self saw Rugad stop speaking and look suddenly angry. Then he vanished. Coulter didn't seem to notice.

She reached for Coulter's ghost self, her fingers nearly touching him, when he too vanished. And then Coulter's larger self, the one that had been talking to Rugad, disappeared as well.

The corridor she was in, blocked on all sides by Rugad's walls, felt empty. The space where Rugad and Coulter were speaking felt empty as well.

All she could feel was that hand crushing her third self. And then that disappeared.

What was happening?

She coalesced into one self, felt in the remains of her mind, and saw them fighting at her Link doors. Coulter broke free, and locked his door. The door to Sebastian, the one Rugad had opened without her permission, was shut and locked.

She floated toward them, silently. They appeared to be talking. She separated a tiny part of herself and left it where the hand had been so that Rugad would look there first, he would find her, as he expected. She made that part lie down and feign defeat.

You have no Vision here, Coulter was saying. *That magic belongs to Arianna, and you have no body of your own. You can't appropriate her Sight.*

So he did understand at least parts of this. She made herself ghostlike, even more invisible than Coulter's ghost self had been. Then she snuck behind Rugad, containing herself like a person trying not to breathe. She hoped that if he sensed her, he would think that the normal consequence of being inside her mind.

I don't have to appropriate her Sight. Rugad was concentrating on Coulter. Coulter had done something that hurt Rugad. Rugad had spread himself too thin, and he had made a mistake. *She shares it with me. She shares everything with me. Are you jealous of that, Islander?*

She had finally reached Coulter. She had to get his attention without drawing Rugad. What would Rugad do if he were in her position?

The boldest possible thing.

She made that little part of herself feign waking up, moaning as if in great pain, and then she sat up. She would walk toward them, and that would distract Rugad.

It already had. He cocked his head slightly. She had no more time for thinking.

She meshed her imaginary body with Coulter's. He jolted, startled, and a bit frightened. She could feel him now, as if he were part of her. *Shh,* she thought. *Hold on to me, no matter what happens.*

She felt more love than she had ever felt in her life. It wrapped itself around her, clung to her, made her part of Coulter. *I have you,* he thought. *What about Rugad?*

I can distract him. She made her other part start to run toward them. A part of Rugad reached out and built a wall in front of her. But she could go through walls if she concentrated, and she did. He apparently didn't want to use the strength to fight her.

Part of him was watching Coulter as if waiting for a response. Coulter didn't remember what Rugad had last said to him. She sent the memory, the bit about jealousy.

"I'm not jealous of you," Coulter said to Rugad, while asking Arianna, *Where does the construct live?*

In my core.

Show me.

She did. She showed him the center of herself and how to get there through the labyrinth that Rugad had established in her mind.

"Of course you're not jealous," Rugad said. "You haven't seen her in so long, you have no idea what she's become. She's more like me than you could ever imagine."

"You lie," Arianna said through Coulter's mouth, using his voice. *Sorry,* she sent. He was smiling inside.

I was going to say the same thing.

Rugad frowned. Had he heard her? She couldn't tell. She had to act now. She sent her other part through the wall Rugad had built. He whirled as if feeling the violation, and then he vanished.

We only have a moment, Coulter thought.

Not even that. Arianna called the other part back to her, and as she did, felt a whoosh of power. Rugad's giant hand had nearly crushed her again.

Coulter started to separate from her.

Stop, she thought.

No, he said. *We do this my way.*

He sent a picture to her of what he wanted to do. Before she could protest, he separated from her, unlocked his Link door, opened it, and shoved her through it, closing the door behind him. She was standing in the Link, in the tunnel of light between their two bodies. She was no longer inside herself.

She thought of pounding on the door, but it would do no good. She stood in the tunnel of light that was the Link between them. It was still healthy and strong despite the years, despite everything.

He wanted her to wait there while he fought Rugad. Coulter was going to the place Rugad had infiltrated, the place Rugad had conquered, and he was going to pull Rugad out. Coulter was going to tie him up, using Enchanter's tricks, and then Coulter would open the Link door again. Arianna would return to her own body, and Coulter would leave, pulling Rugad out with him.

It was risky. It was so very risky. If Coulter lost, he died, and Arianna would never be able to return to her own body. There was also a chance that Rugad would find her here, drag her back inside, and imprison her again.

But she felt stronger than she had in days. She had help, good help. Coulter's help. And with it, she would return to herself.

But this was the hardest part. This was the part where all she could do was wait.

Chapter Thirty

EGER CLOSED HER eyes. The fingertips on her right hand brushed Sebastian's hard chest. His neck was cool beneath her left hand. It felt odd to hold a neck and not feel the heart beat, the blood pulsing through the veins.

Sebastian was completely still. He didn't even breathe just to be polite, like he usually did. He was as motionless as she had instructed him to be.

The voice was threaded through each part of his stone. The blackness looked thicker than it had before, as if it had gained more space, as if there were more to it than a simple voice.

She used her right fingernail to pry some of the blackness loose. She expected Rugad to speak, or the blackness to do something, but nothing happened. She was able to pry a bit of the blackness loose as if it were a thread coming out of an old sweater.

With her index finger and thumb, she pulled on that strand of blackness. The last time she had done this, the blackness had pulled back. This time, it didn't. This time it stretched, as if it were made of clay. By pulling it, she realized, she was making it stronger.

"Con," she said without opening her eyes, "put the jar next to me."

"Open?" he asked.

"Yes, but have the stopper ready."

It meant he had to set down the sword, she knew, but that was an acceptable risk. She heard his clothing rustle as he moved, heard the pop of the stopper as it pulled out of the jar, and then felt his warmth beside her.

"Ready," he said.

The blackness had not moved. It didn't feel alive like it had last time. Last time, she had gotten the sense of a hidden intelligence. Rugad must have been monitoring it from Arianna. With luck, he was so preoccupied with Coulter, he wasn't paying attention to Sebastian.

Seger's heart pounded. There wasn't much time.

She twisted the blackness around her finger, then let go of Sebastian's neck. With her other hand, she pinched off that bit of blackness.

"Move the jar beneath my right hand," she said. If she opened her eyes, she would lose the healing vision and have to start over. She didn't want to do that.

She felt the lip of the glass against her skin. She stuck her finger inside the glass and pushed the blackness off.

"Cover it," she said. "When I hold my hand like that again, we repeat until Sebastian shatters."

She twisted more blackness, pinched it, and dumped it in the jar. She did this for what seemed like forever. The blackness threading through him was growing thinner. Rugad had used some of Arianna's Shifting ability to modify this voice. Normally, Seger should have been able to tug it free, but he had given it some sort of elasticity, something that made it even more difficult to remove.

He had anticipated her.

She worked harder, using some of her weaker Domestic abilities to work the thread. Instead of wrapping it around a finger, she wrapped it around her entire hand.

The work was exacting, tiring, and she could feel sweat pouring off her forehead.

Finally the blackness started to pull through Sebastian like real thread.

"Hurts," he whispered. That surprised her. Nothing was supposed to physically hurt him.

"Remember what I said." Seger couldn't say more than that, in case Rugad had joined them.

The blackness kept pulling, actually cutting through Sebastian's stone skin. Even if he didn't shatter, the thread would cut him in half.

Around Sebastian's stone, Seger saw light. Con inhaled sharply. Apparently the light was visible on the real physical level as well as the healing level.

It was a golden light, very strong, very pure, and very powerful. It seeped through the cracks in Sebastian's skin, covered the blackness like water pouring over sand, and illuminated the air around it.

Seger had to concentrate to hold on to the blackness. She stuck both hands in it, wrapping it around her fingers, and clenching her fists. The golden light was growing, making the darkness harder and the stone brittle. The blackness seemed slipperier than it had before, but she clung to it with all of her strength.

The light expanded all the cracks in Sebastian's skin. Seger squinched up her eyes, forgetting, for a moment, that she had them closed. With her healing vision alone, the light was almost too powerful. It felt as if it would blind her.

Then, suddenly, Sebastian exploded. Shards of stone flew everywhere. She had to use all of her strength to remain standing. The stone pelted her, cutting into her skin. Her face felt as if it were shredded. But she kept her eyes closed and her hands clenched.

Beside her, Con made a small sound. Bits of stone hit the floor like hail. A wind enveloped them, and then disappeared.

And the light was gone too.

But Seger remained standing. Blood was warm against her skin, and she was covered with pinprick pains. But she still held the blackness. It formed a man's shape made out of thread. Not Sebastian's shape, but Rugad's when he was younger, lanky, and tall.

"The jar," she said, her mouth not working quite right. "I need the jar, Con."

She felt it bump against her elbow.

"Sorry," he said. He sounded shaky too.

"Hurry!"

She heard a small clang, had a horrible moment when she thought the jar had broken, and then Con said, "All right."

Carefully, she moved her hands over the jar, hoping that the blackness, the threadman, would be lured by the blood around the lid, not the blood oozing out of her cuts. For a moment, the blackness seemed to hesitate. Then she heard a cry in Fey, a man's cry of protest—

Nooooooo

—as the threadman swirled into a large black mass, and then was sucked into the jar.

She kept her eyes closed. There was no blackness on her hands. She opened them to make sure, but no residue remained, not on her skin, not in the air.

"Cover it," she said, and heard the stopper pop into place.

"Done," Con said. "Now do we help Sebastian?"

"Not yet."

She still had her eyes closed. She crouched, felt for a stone shard, and found one. She held it up. There was no blackness threading through it, or the next shard she touched or the next.

They had succeeded.

She sat down and opened her eyes. She was covered in bits of stone and blood. She looked at Con. Blood ran down his face like tears. His clothing was ripped and there was a long laceration on his right arm. But he held the jar that, to her normal sight, looked empty.

Seger held out her hand. He gave her the jar. She set it on the nightstand, and then brushed herself off. "Remove any shards from yourself that you find," she said. She would have to treat both of them later, to clean out the magic residue. But right now, she was worried about Sebastian.

She picked the clay off her table and set it on the ground in the middle of most of the shards. There were bits of cloth all over the floor as well from the wrap Sebastian had insisted on wearing. Con was gingerly brushing at himself. With his left hand, he removed a sliver the size of a knife from his laceration. They piled the shards around the clay, and then she looked at him.

"What's the clay for?" Con asked.

"In case we've lost some of him," Seger said. And to replace parts he had already lost in previous shatterings. Her mouth was dry. What she hadn't told either of them was that, sometimes, Golems couldn't be reassembled. Too many shatterings, not enough strength, not enough original stone. Anything could cause the destruction. And if Rugad had bled off some of Sebastian's strength, Sebastian might not be able to come back.

"Are we ready now?" Con asked. He had a large cut at the base of his lower lip. It made him speak cautiously.

She glanced at the jar, then scanned the room. Except for the stone shards that had fallen everywhere—the floor, the bed, the tables—it looked the same as it had before. The air tingled slightly, hinting at another presence, but the presence felt friendly. That would be Sebastian. She couldn't sense Rugad anywhere. She hadn't sensed him inside Sebastian either.

"I guess we are," she said.

Con nodded once, then picked up the sword. "Better move," he said to her.

She backed away, careful not to stand on any small bits of stone.

He placed the sword on top of the main stone pile. The room spun and the air was sucked away. Seger slid backward and slammed against the bed. Con flew in the opposite direction and hit the wall. Thunder boomed once, twice, and a third time.

Then the air came back.

Seger glanced at the jar first. It remained closed and unbroken. She took a deep breath.

Sebastian was sitting on top of the sword, the blade against his heels. He was nude. Her repair magic had worked. All the cracks in his skin were gone. He looked younger and, if it weren't for the grayness of his skin, exactly like Gift.

Slowly he touched his throat. "It . . . is . . . gone."

Seger let out a sigh of relief.

"Praise God," Con said.

"You . . . are . . . hurt," Sebastian said, looking from one to the other of them.

"It's nothing I can't fix," Seger said. She got up, feeling aches in muscles she didn't even know she had. Some of the blood had dried already, and it pulled against her skin.

She picked up the jar.

"What are you going to do with that?" Con asked.

"Take it back to the Domicile and destroy it."

"Now?" Con asked.

Seger nodded.

"Shouldn't we see how Coulter is doing?"

Seger held the jar tightly. "Not until this is completely gone. Then, when no physical part of Rugad remains, perhaps it will be easier for Coulter to destroy the construct."

"But . . . Ari," Sebastian said.

"The best thing we can do for her is take care of ourselves." Seger stood and extended a hand to Sebastian. He took it, and she pulled him to his feet. The extra clay had made him more supple as well. Not much—he still moved like Sebastian—but enough that he would notice the difference.

"You . . . fixed . . . me," he said and smiled.

She smiled back. "It seemed the least I could do."

CHAPTER THIRTY-ONE

*C*OULTER FLEW THROUGH Arianna's mind, following the map she had given him. Touching her, knowing
that she was alive and safe, had given him a strange
joy and a willingness to do whatever he could to save
them both.

He had no idea where the core of her really was, only
where her map led him. The maze of walls erected by Rugad confounded Coulter's sense of direction, which
might have been skewed anyway, given the nature of this
place. All he knew was he had to find Arianna's center,
and when he did, he would pull the construct from it, bit
by bit.

He felt Rugad behind him, flying as well, moving as
fast as Coulter, trying to keep up with him. But Coulter
went faster, imagining himself always ahead of Rugad,
knowing that would make it so.

Finally, Coulter reached the part of Arianna's mind
that was uniquely her. It was a comfortable room with
soft walls and golden light. Everything she loved was
there—portraits of her father and Sebastian and Gift, and

beside the warm bed, a portrait of Coulter. He stopped, stared at it. It was a portrait of him as he looked now.

There were other fragments here, a robin's feather, a cat sleeping in a chair, bits and pieces of things he didn't have time to look at. The sense of her was strong, so strong that he wondered how the construct was in here at all, until he remembered Seger's story.

Arianna had picked up an infant and carried it here, thinking it was Sebastian. Coulter couldn't look for a building or a fake man. He had to look for a child.

Then Rugad flew into the room and tackled Coulter. Rugad's physical strength was great, and it knocked Coulter against the far wall, sending some old and dusty portraits crashing to the floor.

Coulter had had enough. They had been playing at this as if they were in the real world, not some imaginary place. And if they were in the real world, a teenage boy probably would have more strength than Coulter. But Coulter would be smarter.

He imagined himself throwing Rugad off and, to his surprise, it worked. Rugad flew backward and bounced on the bed. Coulter created a wall of fire between them, one that destroyed nothing, but which would burn Rugad if Rugad touched it.

That would keep Rugad busy for a while. Coulter was tapping into his own magic, and Rugad had no tools with which to fight that.

Coulter scanned the half of the room he was in. What would people do with a child in this place? They would create a crib, care for the child, and watch it grow.

It would outgrow the crib and, as it grew, need a place of its own.

Almost as if he'd had the thought, a door appeared. Rugad screamed and pushed at the fire, trying to come through, and screamed again.

Coulter ignored him. Soon Rugad would figure out how to defeat that wall of fire and follow him, but by then, maybe, Coulter would have found the construct.

He opened the door and saw a plain room with stark

decor. The austere feeling reminded him of the military garrison he'd grown up in, a magic-made place called Shadowlands designed by Rugad's son. There was a bed that was little more than a cot, chairs beside it, and bare walls.

Or at least, they seemed bare until he approached them. Then he noted the weapons on them: arrows, swords, knives—all of them decorative, all of them clearly made by different cultures. He felt a chill, wondering if they were trophies of the places that Rugad had conquered.

Even though the room was empty, it did not feel empty. It felt as if Coulter had walked into Rugad's brain, not Arianna's. And then he shivered, realizing what danger he was in. The image outside was not Rugad. The construct lived here, grew up here, existed here.

And Coulter had to remove it.

Coulter put his hands on the walls. They had been built by Arianna for the infant she had brought here, but they no longer felt like hers. Running through them was a hum of someone else, majestic and powerful.

Coulter had found the construct.

At that moment the door banged open and Rugad's image staggered in. His clothing was still smoking and a section of his hair was on fire.

"You're good," he said, speaking Fey.

Coulter turned his back on him. The image couldn't hurt him. Not in here.

"You play on primitive fears. I can do the same."

Coulter blocked his mind to that voice. He searched for the hum with his fingers. It skittered away from him.

Suddenly, the room vibrated and he heard a faint *Nooooo!* cried in Fey. A man's voice. Then he felt echoes of pain. Not real pain, but the pain of separation.

Seger. She had succeeded.

Everything in the room froze except Coulter. He reached through the walls, touched the hum, and wrapped it in light. Then he pulled it free.

What he got was a squirming man—fully grown, and much older than the image—but visible only because he was wrapped in light. Coulter slung the man—the construct—over his shoulder.

Rugad's image shouted at him, but the words faded to nothing as the vibration from outside continued.

Then Coulter stepped through the door, and into Arianna's room. There was no vibration here, no feeling of separation. Only a lingering sense of her as if she had walked through the room and just a trace of her perfume remained.

Seger had given him a chance. Coulter meant to take advantage of it.

He flew through the maze as he had done before, hands wrapped around the writhing construct. With great effort, the construct stuck out an arm, letting fingers trail across the maze.

The wiggles grew more powerful, until Coulter was having trouble holding the construct. Coulter increased the light, did an Imprisonment spell that would have worked in the physical world, and made himself go even faster. He would have appeared near the Link doors, but he was afraid of getting lost, even now. He didn't know exactly where they were located from this maze, only that there was one path to getting there.

Too late, he realized that Rugad was regaining strength by touching the maze. Coulter grabbed for Rugad's hand, but he couldn't reach it. So Coulter concentrated on holding Rugad and flying.

Finally, they tumbled out of the maze. The construct fell out of Coulter's grasp and before he could pick it up, Rugad broke through some of the bonds of light. Coulter repaired them, then grabbed his own door and opened it.

As he did, Rugad seized him. Coulter struggled, but Rugad moved too fast. Rugad gripped the bonds of light, the bonds Coulter had made, and used them like rope to wrap Coulter.

"You're an amateur, boy," Rugad said, shoving Coulter toward the Link. "You'll never be able to win against me."

Chapter Thirty-two

*T*HE DOOR OPENED and Arianna stepped back. Blinding light the same color gold as the Link poured in, and behind it, she could hear Rugad's voice, but not his words. She pressed herself against the walls of the Link, staying out of sight as Coulter had warned her to do.

Then Coulter fell out, wrapped in light. The light trussed him, binding his hands, his feet, his entire body. He cursed, then shook the light off. The bonds dissolved. He stood, and went back through the door, closing it behind him.

She clasped her hands together, hearing pounding and cursing on the other side of that door. Voices raised and lowered, someone cried out in pain. Then the door opened again, and this time, it was Rugad who hovered there, ropes made of light hanging from his wrists. He was facing backward, and did not see her. He used the edges of the door to brace himself, and to launch himself inside.

The door closed again. Arianna paced. She wasn't used to this. Coulter was fighting her battle. She should be helping, but she had promised him she wouldn't.

She threaded her fingers together, heard the yelping and thudding on the other side. Why, when they could do anything they imagined, did they imagine a simple fight? If she were to go in, she would imagine something greater.

As if that had worked. Everything she had imagined after she discovered Rugad had failed.

The door opened, and this time, both men fell into the Link. Rugad had his hands around Coulter's neck. Coulter erupted into flame, and Arianna jumped back as if she could get burned. But Rugad continued to hold on, his fingers squeezing tighter and tighter.

She recognized this. She had felt it. If she could just grab Rugad and pull him off, then Coulter would have a chance.

But she would give him a better chance if she cut off the source of Rugad's power. She had to risk it.

She had to run for the door, even though Rugad didn't know she was here, even though he would see her.

Coulter turned into water, and Rugad lost his hold for a moment. Then Rugad became glass and started to contain the water.

Soon Coulter would run out of tricks. Rugad seemed to be keeping pace with everything he did.

Arianna leaped past them and sprinted for the door. Rugad lifted his head out of the glass and then became Fey again. Coulter turned into himself as well.

"No, Ari!" he yelled in Islander. "Not yet!"

But she couldn't turn back now. She Shifted, became a robin, and flew through the door. She reached for its knob and realized she couldn't do that with wings.

As she Shifted back, she remembered that she could have done anything she wanted. This rigid thinking had trapped her once before.

She reached for the knob as Rugad threw his weight against the door. Coulter grabbed him, and Rugad shook him off. Rugad seemed twice as strong as Coulter, even stronger than Arianna had thought he was.

Rugad became water himself and slipped inside.

Arianna couldn't close the door now; she'd trap herself with him.

Coulter reached for her. She took his hand, and he pulled her into the Link as Rugad slammed the door closed.

"No," Arianna said. "No. He can't be in there alone. He can't. I'll die."

"No, you won't," Coulter said. "He needs your body. You'll be fine as long as the body's fine."

She grabbed the knob and tugged. The door was locked. "He can't shut me out of there. That's my own body."

"He has shut you out, Ari. At least now he won't kill you."

She turned. "But I have nowhere to go. Don't you understand, Coulter? He's me now."

Coulter stared at her for a moment. "Yes," he said finally. "To the world, he's you. But he didn't take complete control, and now he's going to rule without Vision. I think even Rugad will have trouble with that."

"It doesn't matter." She slipped down the side of the Link, leaning on the wall as if it were her only support. "He'll never let me back in."

"That's right," Coulter said. "He'll never let you. But you didn't let him in either. There are other ways, Ari."

She raised her gaze to his. "But I have nowhere to go. I don't exist, Coulter."

"You exist." He held out his hand to her. She took it and let him help her up. He put his arm around her and pulled her close. There was comfort in his touch. "You can stay with me. Or we can get Seger to build you a Golem."

Like Sebastian. Only hers wouldn't be able to Shift or to even move well. She, who had always been so quick and athletic.

But here, she would have no control at all.

She turned and tried the door one final time. It still did not open.

"Do you have ways of testing whether or not he's locked it?"

"If he hadn't locked it," Coulter said, "you'd be able to open it."

Rugad was solidifying his hold on her body now. She knew it as if she were still there. He had her completely, all except the part of her that really counted. He had her body, but not her soul.

She moved away from the door. She hadn't been able to hear more than muffled yelling from the Link, but she didn't want Rugad to hear any more.

She took a deep breath. She didn't like any of her choices. But she had to make the right one, for herself, and for her people.

Arianna was shaking. She wanted to turn and fight, but there was no fighting this. Not here. To try would only make things worse. She knew that much. She had to outthink him somehow.

Or destroy herself.

Would that be Blood against Blood?

Coulter took her hand and led her away from the door. He seemed to be having the same thought, or maybe their thoughts were already leaking. When he reached the door into his own body, he pushed her through.

Coulter's mind was warm and disciplined, filled with dark places and places of light. She felt at home here, even though she had never been here before, and yet it was so very different from her own mind.

His brain had small walled-off areas, and Link doors that were still open. There were memories tossed in a corner as if they were left there after the last time they were used. She touched one. It was of a red and gold sunrise behind the Cliffs of Blood.

He shut the door to the Link between himself and her.

"Now's the time to decide, Ari, what we do with this part of you."

He meant that she had to choose where her soul would reside while Rugad had her body. She couldn't live in the Link between two bodies forever. And now she was in Coulter's mind. She had to find a place to survive, until she got her own place back.

She kept her hand in his. "If Seger makes me a Golem, Rugad will know where I am. If I'm with you, I can go other places, do other things, and he'll never know."

"That's right," Coulter said.

"And if I'm in you, he can't kill me."

"He won't even try," Coulter said. "Not anymore. He's going to need Vision, and I don't think a construct has any. I think he was going to try to take yours somehow, and now that you're here, he can't touch you."

She sat down just inside the door. The idea of living inside someone else's mind frightened her. But this was Coulter. She cared for him. This couldn't be worse than having someone like Rugad inside her mind, sharing it against her will, trying to take it over.

Arianna bent her head. The best thing would be for this nightmare to end, for Rugad to leave, and for her to get her body back. But that wasn't going to happen without work.

She sighed. "I'll stay here."

Coulter studied her for a moment. He was planning something, but she couldn't tell what it was. "Are you sure about this decision?" he asked. "Because I need to know now."

"Why now?" Arianna asked.

"Because if you stay with me, I can prevent Rugad from ever touching you—this part of you—again."

She thought for a moment. Coulter loved her. He would protect her until she figured out a better plan. And she would find one.

She had to. She couldn't live like this.

"Yes," she said. "I'll stay."

He smiled. "Good," he said. Then he opened the door, and leaned out. His right hand became scissors. As she watched, he reached down and severed their Link.

It felt as if he had broken something inside her. The pain was swift and intense. It was all she could do not to double over. The Link itself floated in the air for a moment, then it fell against the door that Rugad had just closed—her door—empty and lifeless.

Coulter closed his door, his hand no longer scissors. He put his arm around her.

"What did you do?" she asked.

"We can't have our bodies Linked. He could use that. Now he can't."

She turned her face toward his. "But we—"

"Right now, we don't need the Link. We're together here. We'll be fine."

But she had the awful feeling that they wouldn't be fine, that he had done something irreparable, something even worse than what Rugad had done.

"Coulter—" she started, but he put a finger on her lips, then bent over and kissed her. It was a warm kiss, a good kiss, a kiss like nothing she could experience with her physical self.

Then he eased back. "We'll be fine," he said again.

She hoped, for both their sakes, that he was right.

CHAPTER THIRTY-THREE

*C*OULTER WANTED TO stay with Arianna and comfort her, but he had to move out of his own mind, become one with his body again, and he had to do it quickly. He could feel the time passing, the moments disappearing, and his advantage leaving.

He had to come back to himself before Rugad gained complete control of Arianna's body.

"Make yourself at home," he said to her. "Create a place of your own. I have to—"

"I know," she said. Apparently his thoughts were leaking to her. He smiled and reconnected with his body.

His neck was cramped, his back ached, and Arianna's birthmark no longer throbbed beneath his thumbs. He opened his eyes. Xet'n was staring at him.

"Get out of here," Coulter whispered.

"But there's no—"

"I know," Coulter said. "I failed. Now get."

He didn't want to use Xet'n's name in case Rugad could hear. The eyes on Arianna's body were closed and she looked no different. But it wasn't her any longer. He could sense that somehow. Something in the set of the face, the line of the shoulders, made it clear that Arianna wasn't there any more.

Xet'n picked up his lamp and snuck out of the room. Coulter sat up. He had been in that position a long time. His body was cramped.

He got up, heard his knees crack, and opened the window, creating what he hoped would be a diversion. Then he let himself out of the bedroom.

Luke was still standing by the door of the suite. "How'd it—?"

"No good," Coulter said and ran past him. Coulter wasn't worried about Luke. Luke could take care of himself. There was no way that Rugad would know that Luke had been involved.

But Rugad would know about Seger, and Sebastian.

Sebastian?

The thought seemed to come from inside him, but it had a different feel to it, not a thought of his at all. Arianna, then.

He'll be all right, Coulter thought. It only took him a moment to get to Sebastian's suite. He entered. Both rooms were empty. There were holes in the blanket on the bed, and blood drippings all over the floor. Several shoes had left prints.

I thought you said he'd be all right!

Coulter wasn't going to answer her. Her panic was feeding his. Seger had said they would return to the Domicile if they were successful. He would look there, and then he would worry.

He left the suite at full run, and headed down the steps. Luke was behind him.

"Tell me what happened," Luke said.

"Nothing," Coulter said. "It didn't work, and now he knows I'm here. I've got to leave. Can you get my driver?"

"Driver?" Luke asked.

"I have a carriage and an Islander named Dash got me here. Can you find him?"

"Yes."

They had reached the bottom of the stairs. Luke put a hand on Coulter's shoulder, stopping him.

"I've got to hurry," Coulter said.

"I know," Luke said. "Look, I'm sorry about what I said. About failing."

Bitterness twisted Coulter's stomach. He didn't want Arianna to hear this. "Looks like you were right."

"No," Luke said. "It takes courage to try."

Coulter didn't want to hear it. "Was Seger successful?"

Luke nodded. "They're in the Domicile."

Coulter could feel Arianna's relief layering his own. "I need my driver and carriage as fast as you can get them."

"Consider it done," Luke said. "They'll be waiting for you the moment you get out of the Domicile."

Coulter nodded, and ran down the hall. He thought he had forgotten the way, and then he realized that it was Arianna who was guiding him, Arianna who was showing him the shortest routes. She was pushing him harder than he would push himself.

He burst through a side door, ran across a part of the courtyard littered with dogs eating kitchen scraps, and then up the stairs in the Domicile.

A Domestic was holding newly spun yarn, its magic spilling like water around her hand.

"Where's Seger?"

The Domestic pointed down a long hallway. Coulter ran its length, excusing himself every time he nearly bumped into someone. There were Domestics everywhere, carrying medical supplies and clothing and food. He finally realized they were going where he was.

A door was open at the end of the hall. Inside, Con sat on a bed, his face tilted upward, his eyes closed. A Healer was bent over him, removing tiny bits of stone from his severely cut face. Seger was on the next bed, lying on her back while another Healer worked on her chest and arms.

Sebastian stood at the window. He turned when he saw Coulter, and Coulter gasped.

"Gift?" he asked.

"No," Sebastian said.

His cracks, Arianna said. *They're gone.*

"What happened to you?" Coulter asked.

"Se-ger . . . fixed . . . me."

There was a noxious odor in the room. Coulter turned toward it, saw a melting jar in the fireplace, and several magical screens in place before it, so that nothing leaked out.

"We destroyed the voice," Seger said, "and we are getting rid of the container. It should be gone soon."

"We don't have soon," Coulter said. "I didn't get Rugad out of her. We have to go and we have to go now."

You're not telling them about me, Arianna said.

Not yet, Coulter said. *There are too many ears here.*

"If we could finish the treatments," Seger started, "then—"

"No," Coulter said. "If he finds you, he'll know what happened. He'll kill you, Seger. And you, Sebastian. You've defeated him twice before, not to mention this time. He'll destroy you, like you've destroyed that voice."

"And you," Seger said.

Coulter shook his head. "He'll probably torture me for a while, so that he can keep Arianna in line."

It was true enough as far as it went. He wasn't going to say any more about that.

"Come on!" he said.

"What about me?" Con asked.

"He doesn't know about you," Coulter said. "It's your choice."

"He may know," Seger said. "It depends on how powerful that voice was."

Con stood and picked up his sword. His eyes were sad. "Where are we going?" he asked.

"Out of here." Coulter wasn't going to give the other Domestics any more information. They served the Black Throne and would answer to the person they thought to be its Queen.

Seger stood as well. Con put an arm around Sebastian and hurried him forward.

It took longer than Coulter wanted to get the group out of the Domicile and to the stables. The carriage waited with fresh horses. Dash sat in front, reins in hand.

He peered over his shoulder at them. "This thing wasn't built for an army," he said to Coulter.

"Well," Coulter said, "it'll have to do."

Con was helping Sebastian into the carriage. His weight tilted it slightly. Seger got in, and then Con.

"Get up front to help balance this thing," Dash said. Coulter climbed beside Dash. The driver's bench was barely big enough for both of them.

"I hope these horses are quick," Coulter said.

"They'd be quicker if we dump one passenger."

He wants to get rid of Sebastian, Arianna said.

He won't, Coulter thought, and then said aloud: "Just drive."

Dash clucked at the horses and they started across the courtyard. Coulter glanced behind him. So far, no sign of Rugad. That was good. It meant he didn't yet have as much control as he needed, and perhaps the loss of the voice had hurt him as well.

As they passed through the gates, Dash asked, "Where are we going?"

To the only place they could get any strength, Coulter thought. The only place with power enough and magic enough to fight Rugad.

Coulter said, "We're going home."

THE BLACK QUEEN

[Two Weeks Later]

CHAPTER THIRTY-FOUR

*B*RIDGE STOOD IN the small room off the audience chamber, his hands clasped behind his back. Lyndred sat in an overstuffed chair. No fire burned in the fireplace— it was a warm spring day, and even warmer in the palace— but the window was open, revealing a charming garden whose early flowers were just beginning to bloom.

A man could get used to this place. It had a simple charm that seemed to have been bred out of most parts of Galinas.

Bridge paced from the window to the door. He and Lyndred had been here for much of the afternoon. Somehow he hadn't expected rudeness from his niece. He had heard that she was warm and courteous, but so far he had seen none of it. She had even put him off when he got here yesterday, telling him he needed to request a formal audience.

He had requested the audience, although Lyndred said he shouldn't. Lyndred believed he should have charged into the Queen's room, demanding time. But Bridge knew his place. He also suspected that his niece was making certain he remembered it.

He wasn't sure what he had expected—royal treatment, perhaps? A friendly welcome? An embrace? Instead, she was proving herself every bit as difficult as her predecessor. It didn't matter that Bridge had made a long journey to get here, nor that he had whipped his crew to near exhaustion to make it. All that mattered was her schedule, and the time she had to see people she hadn't planned on.

It was not a good way to begin the relationship.

Lyndred sighed behind him, then slumped in the chair and closed her eyes. She had been quiet for the last two weeks, ever since Bridge had sent Ace to find Gift. The closer that the ships got to Blue Isle, the tenser Lyndred had become. When their Navigators and Nyeian experts negotiated the Stone Guardians, the dangerous rocks that protected Blue Isle's natural harbor, Lyndred hadn't even watched. She had stayed below decks and refused to see anyone.

Bridge was worried she wasn't going to come with him to this audience. But she had. They had walked across the city of Jahn together—the distance from the harbor to the palace wasn't that far—and it gave them a chance to see the city close-up. It wasn't what Bridge had expected. He had thought it would be something like Nye, all frill and business, only he had expected the frill to be weird religious trappings.

He saw no religious trappings at all. The buildings were simple structures covered with bright paint, and signs that notified someone if there was a business. The road was full of Fey and Islanders, and a handful of young people who looked like they could be a combination of both. There were no signs of war, no remnants of the violence that must have held Blue Isle in thrall over a decade before—at least none he could recognize. Of course, he didn't know how this city had looked before the Fey arrived, so he had nothing to compare it to.

Behind him, a door opened. Bridge turned. Lyndred

sat up and opened her eyes, then stood as a woman walked into the room.

The woman was in her early thirties. She had a regal face. There was some softness to the cheeks, and her skin was a light brown instead of the dark brown that most Fey had. But it was her eyes that were startling: a vivid blue against the dark skin. The color made them seem colder than any eyes Bridge had ever seen before, like chips of blue ice. There was no fire in them at all.

The birthmark proved her to be Arianna, Black Queen of the Fey.

"So," she said in haughty, unaccented Fey. "Bridge arrives at last."

There was a certain familiarity to her tone, a way of speaking that reminded him of his grandfather Rugad. As she watched him formulate his response, her blue eyes glinted with amusement.

What had his daughter said about her Vision of Arianna? *The Black Queen has a very cruel face.* It was accurate, more accurate than Bridge wanted to acknowledge.

Bridge tilted his head. He had to look up at her slightly. How powerful was this woman? "I thought perhaps you'd welcome us to Blue Isle."

"Welcome you?" she asked. "The man my greatgrandfather rejected for the Black Throne?"

Bridge's mouth was dry. How had he made such a miscalculation? He had thought this woman would need his help, that she would be more Islander than Fey, that she probably had no idea how to run the Empire, which was why she was changing everything. But he was wrong. She was pure Fey and as blunt as Rugad, maybe more so.

Lyndred was watching with a keen interest. It was for her, not for him, that Bridge decided to fight back.

"Perhaps I have wasted too much time on Nye," Bridge said. "I expected courtesy when I arrived here."

"We only extend courtesy to those who deserve it. What's your business here?"

"Apparently I have none," Bridge said. He didn't wait

to be excused. Instead he pushed past his niece and headed for the door. Lyndred followed him.

"And who's this?"

Bridge turned, hand on the doorknob. Arianna had a hand on Lyndred's arm. They were of a height, and they looked amazingly alike, except that Lyndred's face was narrower, her skin darker, and her black eyes were filled with life.

"My daughter." Bridge turned the knob. "Lyndred. Come on."

"Lyndred." Arianna hadn't let go of her arm. "You were an infant when Rugad left Nye."

Lyndred's eyes narrowed. "So?"

Bridge took his hand off the doorknob. He hadn't expected this.

"And you hadn't come into your magic yet." Arianna took Lyndred's face and inspected it. "You look like Jewel."

It was strange to hear her refer to her mother that way. And she seemed to sense it, because she added, "There's a portrait of her upstairs that could be you."

That was it. Arianna favored her mother, and Lyndred had the same look. They could have been sisters.

"What kind of magic did you end up with?"

Lyndred yanked her face out of Arianna's grasp. "I'm a Visionary," she said. "And from what I've seen around here, I'm a better one than you."

Bridge sucked in his breath. His impulsive daughter also acted like Jewel sometimes. Speak first and think later.

A slight color touched Arianna's cheeks, but to Bridge's surprise, she smiled. "Do you think so?" she asked in that haughty voice. "Maybe we should compare Visions."

Lyndred raised her chin, apparently unaware she had been baited. "I Saw you long before I came here. And you're surprised by me."

"Perhaps you're not important to my life," Arianna said. "Or to the Empire."

Bridge let out the breath he was holding and almost— almost—argued with her. But after this, he wanted nothing from her. He had wasted a month of his life traveling here, and for what? A few insults, an embarrassing meeting with a woman too proud to know she needed him?

"Come on, Lyndred," he said again.

Lyndred shot an angry glance at Arianna, then started to follow her father.

Arianna watched them both, the amusement Bridge saw earlier still glinting in her eyes. "You came here for something. Did you need my help in some way? Do you want another small assignment? Are you tired of Nye?"

"I don't need you. And what I came here for no longer matters." But because he was angry, he added, "I will give you one piece of advice, completely for free. The next time you send a Gull Rider on an important mission to Vion, send an experienced one."

Those cold blue eyes grew even colder. "I sent no Gull Rider to Vion."

"She said you did." Lyndred spoke with obvious relish. "She said you were sending for Gift."

The blue eyes were terrifyingly cold now. Bridge had seen that look before. He had learned how to watch for it in his grandfather's eyes, and how to get out of the way when Rugad was that angry.

"Is that why you came here?" Arianna asked. "To put in your bid as the Black Ruler should I die?"

"No," Bridge said. "We were already halfway between Nye and Blue Isle when the Gull Rider crashed on our ship. She never would have made it across the sea if it weren't for us."

"I did not send her," Arianna said. "I would have sent someone competent." She folded her hands together. "So someone sent for Gift. Someone has been worried." Her smile was small. "I know how to take care of this."

"Good," Bridge said. "Then at least we served some purpose here. I hope you don't mind that we stay and explore the Isle. My crew is tired, and I really don't want to tell them to turn around and go back."

"That was always your problem," Arianna said as if she knew. "You never wanted to confront the hard issues."

Bridge stared at her. That had always been his problem. He had too much compassion for a Black Ruler. But he had no idea how she had known that.

She clasped her hands behind her back. "You've come this far. I suppose I should be hospitable and give you rooms in the palace. Bring your things here. Keep your ships in Jahn harbor. We may have use for them."

Lyndred looked at Bridge in confusion. Bridge didn't move. He had a feeling that moments earlier, Arianna had been ready to send him away, to never see him again. But something changed that. The mention of Gift? Or was it something about Lyndred?

"Thank you for your offer," Bridge said. "We would love to stay here."

Lyndred's eyes widened, and then she shook her head slightly. But Bridge wanted to stay. Something was unusual here, just as he had suspected. He wanted to find out what it was. He added, just so that Arianna knew he was aware of her change in attitude, "We're grateful for your courtesy to unexpected visitors."

Arianna laughed. "I don't believe in courtesy," she said. "I believe in expediency. It's obvious you have information that might be useful to me. And it's been a long time since I've seen family. Too long."

She was looking at Lyndred, her expression speculative. Bridge wasn't sure he liked it. Maybe Lyndred had been right. Maybe coming to Blue Isle had been a mistake.

He just wished he had enough Vision to know.

CHAPTER THIRTY-FIVE

*C*OULTER STOOD AT the edge of the magic yard, watching Matt work on his fire spells. In the two weeks since he'd taken up permanent residence at the school, Matt's fire spells had grown in complexity. He could now create a fireball and change it into something else without calling it back to his hand. This afternoon, he was creating fireballs that did not consume anything in the physical world. He was rolling them across the dirt to test this, and if they left a burnt trail, he knew he was doing something wrong.

So far, he had only gotten about fifty percent of the fireballs right.

The boy had incredible talent, more than Coulter remembered having at that age. The only difference between them was that Coulter had spent his first five years among the Fey, and he had known through observation that there were no limits to a good Enchanter's magic.

Matt had spent most of his life in a family that had taught him to deny what he was. Some magics still scared him. Coulter worried that they always would.

Matt had a lot to overcome. He wasn't talking about the death of his father, although Coulter had asked him for details. Matt had told him what he knew, and Coulter explained the Mysteries, Jewel, and the long fights she had had with Matt's father. And then Coulter had calmly told Matt that his father had been right; once inside the Roca's Cave, Jewel would not let him out alive.

Matt had taken the news calmly, just like he took everything else. And that calm was the most dangerous thing about him. He should have been angry or unable to stop the tears. Coulter felt that way even more when he realized that Matt had cut himself off from his family, and wouldn't speak of them. The boy had lost everything, and pretended as if nothing happened.

Over the next few weeks, in addition to all the preparations Coulter had to make, he had to take care of Matt. The last thing he wanted was for Matt to become as twisted and dangerous as his father had been.

Matt looked up from his work, saw Coulter, and waved. Coulter waved back. Then Matt absorbed the fireball into his hands, brushed them together, and held them out to show Coulter that the ball was gone. Coulter nodded.

Matt walked up to his side. The boy seemed to have grown just in the time Coulter was away. "Seger's been looking for you," Matt said.

Coulter suppressed a grimace. The work he had been doing with Seger had been tricky and tiring. He wished he had time to rest.

So take some, Arianna said.

He started. He had thought she was in the small house she had made for herself inside his brain.

I'm doing this for you, he thought back to her.

No you aren't, she said. *You're tired of having company in your head.*

There was more truth to that than Coulter wanted to admit.

"You all right?" Matt asked.

Coulter then realized he hadn't responded. He had

been doing that a lot lately, ever since Arianna had joined him. No one except Seger, Sebastian, and Con knew that she was a part of him. He thought it better that way.

"I'm fine," he said. He put his arm around Matt. Coulter had been making such gestures since he'd come back. He didn't know if it was Arianna's influence or his worry about Matt that was making him do so.

"You done with your practice today?"

"I have to do water drills, and then I'll be done," Matt said.

"Well, then," Coulter said, squeezing Matt's shoulder and then releasing him. "Go to it."

Matt nodded and ran back to the yard. There was a section of dirt that flowed downhill that was especially useful for water spells.

I worry about him, Arianna said. *He's so lonely.*

Coulter didn't answer her. She already knew how Coulter felt about this. She knew everything about him and, strangely, that wasn't what he minded about sharing his brain with her. Sometimes he just wanted to have a thought all to himself. His love for her hadn't changed. If anything, it had grown. He was just realizing how important privacy was.

He walked to a side door and let himself into the workshop he had set aside for Seger. She looked up from the table covered with unformed clay. Sebastian sat by the door like a guard, his handsome face immobile.

"We're ready to try again," Seger said. "Sebastian thinks you need to be here."

They were trying to make a Golem, something that hadn't been done in centuries. Usually Golems formed from changelings, but they didn't have time to grow a body for Arianna. They had to create one. Seger's magic could do some of it and Coulter's the rest, but the first two that they tried, using, as Seger said, spells so old they creaked, had shattered when Arianna tried to enter them.

"Of course I need to be here," Coulter said. "I'm helping make this thing."

"No." Sebastian turned toward Coulter. His gray

eyes sparkled in the dimly lit room. "Se-ger . . . asked . . .
what . . . kept . . . me . . . a-live. I . . . have . . . thought . . .
on . . . it . . . and . . . this . . . is . . . the . . . an-swer."

Coulter waited. Sebastian's slow speech patterns always drove him crazy. If he ever got time, he would try a
spell of his own to repair that.

"I . . . was . . . created . . . through . . . Gift's . . . Link . . .
to . . . me . . . and . . . his . . . fam-i-ly. I . . . con-tin-ue . . . to
. . . ex-ist . . . be-cause . . . of . . . those . . . Links . . . and . . .
love."

"Love?" Coulter asked.

Seger nodded. "People have cared for him enough
that whenever he shatters, he wants to return. He loves
them enough to know that they will be hurt without him,
and does not want to do that. This body we're creating
has no love, and no one to love it. I was wondering if you
could create a Link to it before we finished it, and then
we could try to love it for what it is."

No! Arianna sounded frantic. *No! I have a better idea.*

What is it? Coulter asked.

Let me be part of the Golem as you create it.

No, Coulter thought. *It would be too dangerous.*

*I am used to different bodies from my Shifting. I
would be all right. You know that.*

"What?" Seger asked.

Coulter explained Arianna's idea.

Seger nodded. "It might work, but I have no idea how
to go about it."

I do! Arianna snapped. She was impatient. Her mood
rocketed through Coulter, making him queasy. *We use
my Vision. I still have that. It's with Vision that constructs are created, and through Vision that a person can
travel across the Links. You don't need to Link to that
body, Coulter. I do. When the body is ready, touch it, and
I'll create a bond between you and me and it that will
give it the vibrancy it needs.*

It made sense. It made complete sense. Coulter explained her idea to the others.

"Yes," Sebastian said. "That . . . is . . . what . . . I . . .

i-ma-gined . . . I . . . just . . . did . . . not . . . have . . . a . . . way . . . to . . . cor-rect-ly . . . des-cribe . . . the . . . ma-gic."

"This will take some work," Coulter said. "First we have to finish the Golem, and then we'll have to make sure it's perfect. We'll need your help with that, Sebastian. Then Ari will make her attempt. If this doesn't work, we'll keep trying until we get it."

He figured Arianna could live in both places, the room she had created in his mind and in the Golem's body. That way, if Rugad ever caught up with them—and he would—he wouldn't know where she was.

Rugad had been on Coulter's mind ever since they left Jahn. They had to get the construct out of Arianna's body while leaving the body unharmed. Once Coulter had had a fleeting thought that perhaps it would be easier to destroy her body and let her live in a Golem's body, and Arianna had been so angry that his entire being felt like it was being shredded from the inside. He had never made that suggestion again, and tried not to think about it even though they both knew it was an option.

Coulter had sent Con to the Place of Power to study the artifacts in it. With his knowledge of Rocaanism and its own twisted magic, Con might find a way to dislodge Rugad using a Place of Power itself.

Coulter had also put a large contingent of guards—all Islanders—on the Place of Power. He wanted to put some in the Vault as well, but for that he would need Matt's help, and Matt wasn't ready. But Coulter figured he had time. He doubted Rugad would come here—the place where his physical body had died fifteen years ago. Coulter knew that Rugad was strong, but he doubted any man was that strong, strong enough to face this kind of power for a second time.

If he did, then Coulter would take Arianna and the students and barricade them in the Place of Power. He and Arianna had lived that way once before. They could do it again.

The fact that he had her, that Arianna herself was safe, relieved him more than he cared to say. It also gave him hope. As long as she had been under Rugad's thrall, she might have changed into something unrecognizable. Here, with Coulter, she remained herself—and she had the one thing that Rugad needed, the one thing he couldn't rule without. She had Vision.

"Well," Seger said, watching him, obviously knowing that he had been having dialogues within himself too much lately. "Should we get started on this?"

Yes! Arianna said.

"Yes," Coulter echoed.

Seger smiled. "This time," she said, "we have the right combination. This time, our plans will work."

Coulter hoped she was right. Not just about the new Golem. But about all of their plans.

She doesn't have Vision, Arianna warned.

But you do, Coulter thought. *Will we be all right?*

He felt a warmth that came from her. *I still See a future for all of us,* she said. *I think that's a good sign.*

I think that's a great sign, he thought. And then he went deep inside himself, just so that he could hug her.

She looked startled. *What was that for?*

The future, he said, *and the fact that you have just given me hope.*

CHAPTER THIRTY-SIX

*G*IFT SAT IN the wide chair in the center of the barge, a cool drink that tasted faintly of lemons in one hand. He tapped on the chair's arm with the other. Skya gave him an annoyed look from the chair beside him. She had been annoyed at him ever since they got on this ship. Which was fine with him, since he had been annoyed with her.

Xihu wisely stayed away from both of them.

After eleven long and strange days, Skya had brought them to Btsan, at the southernmost tip of Pitka. She wouldn't let them leave her side, and took them directly to the harbor. That had been strange enough. There, people wore nothing more than pants, both the men and the women, and their torsos were covered with nothing more than jewelry. The smell of fish was so strong that Gift wanted to gag.

It hadn't taken her long, using his name, to commandeer a boat. But when Gift saw it, he hadn't wanted to set foot on it. That had been their first fight.

The ship wasn't really a ship at all, not by Nyeian

terms. It was as long as a Nyeian ship, but sat differently in the water, and it didn't have a sail. Instead, a hundred men sat on benches on the lower levels, handling oars in unison, following commands barked in rapid Pitakan. When Gift asked what kind of man would willingly do that job, Skya had looked away. So it was up to Xihu to find out.

The men were indentured servants, only one step up from slaves. They were contracted to the shipping companies, and worked off that contract in years, not in money. Gift refused to sail on the ship and Skya laughed.

"Then how do you plan to sail out of Btsan?" she asked.

"If you had told me this was how business was conducted here, I would have insisted that we go by land," Gift said.

"And lose all that precious time?" She put her hands on her hips. "If we go by land now, we will add several weeks to our trip. We've gone a long way out of our way to do that route."

He knew she was right, and eventually, he gave in. But he hated this, and he knew when he returned to Blue Isle, he would ask Arianna to put an end to this loathsome Pitakan custom the Fey had seen no need to change.

As they had sailed, he had learned that only half the men rowed while the other half rested. Because of him, the ship's owner had put on twice as many oarsmen as usual. They promised to get him to Tashco in record time.

It seemed that they would. The water was relatively calm here—they were going along protected channels just off the main part of the sea—and the weather was surprisingly warm. No one on the ship would let Gift do anything except sit—he was royalty, after all—and if he tried to get something for himself, someone blushed and fetched it instead.

So he had spent the last two days studying Skya's strange map, which she had picked up for them along the way. It was a beautiful bit of work that showed the Fey Empire from Blue Isle to the farthest corners of Vion. There were notations in a language he couldn't read, and a small symbol in the upper right-hand corner that, when he first saw it, made him shiver.

The symbol had a single heart resting on top of a single sword, with a crown floating above them both. He wished he knew what the symbol meant, but when he asked Skya, she had shrugged.

"I told you what I know of the Dorovich," she said, "and now I've given you my map. You have all my secrets."

Gift doubted that. He doubted he knew enough about her at all. As irritated as he was at her, she had proven herself very competent these last few weeks. Competent, elusive, and increasingly beautiful. He and Xihu would never have made it this far without her.

He looked out to sea. The water was a soft blue, almost flat, and the only sound around him was the splash of fifty oars hitting the surface in unison.

At moments like this, he knew he would make it home safely. He knew that whatever had gone wrong there—and something had, he could feel it—he would be able to put it right.

He took a drink from the glass in his hand. The lemony taste quenched his thirst even as it made him wince. It was like he imagined his homecoming, both bitter and sweet.

He no longer regretted his years in Protectors Village. Even though he hadn't been able to become a Shaman, he had learned patience there. Patience and a certain trust in the fact that things would go the way that they must. He had also gained a confidence he had never had.

I'm coming, Arianna, he thought, and wished they hadn't closed their Links, so that he could let her know he was on his way. *I'll be there as fast as I can.*

Maybe by then, she wouldn't need him. Maybe by then, everything would be all right.

But he had a hunch he was the missing piece to a puzzle even he didn't understand. He just knew that whatever waited for him on Blue Isle, he was strong enough to face it. And he knew that whatever happened, the path he was on was the best one—for everyone involved.

DON'T MISS THE NEXT RIVETING BOOK IN THE BLACK THRONE SERIES:

The Black King

by Kristine Kathryn Rusch

With Ariana now banished from her body, Rugad rules the Fey Empire. And Rugad is not the pacifist his great-granddaughter was. He wants conquest and power. He wants Leut so he can someday locate and control the Triangle of Might. And he will stop at nothing to achieve his goals—even if it means destroying Arianna's essence completely.

And yet . . . Is the destruction of a soul the same as the destruction of a person? If he moves against Arianna, will he be invoking that ancient curse of Black Blood against Black Blood which could annihilate the world in its fury? He badly needs a ruling from one of the Shaman, but will they be inclined to listen to a Queen who once ignored them? And how can he phrase that question without revealing the truth of his new existence? Especially since the Shaman have their own plans for Leut and the Triangle which do not involve the Black Family.

Worse, into this growing chaos comes Gift: a Shaman in training who abandoned his dream of peace in order to come to his beleaguered sister's aid. And little does he realize that he will be confronting not his sister, but Rugad. Thus the stage is set for the dire warnings of the all the Visionaries. Blood against Blood has never been more possible, and the fate of a world hangs in balance because of one family's impossible struggle. . . .

Coming in Summer 2000

ABOUT THE AUTHOR

KRISTINE KATHRYN RUSCH is an award-winning fiction writer. Her most recent sf novel for Bantam Books, *Alien Influences*, was a finalist for the prestigious Arthur C. Clarke Award. She has published five other novels about the Fey, as well as twenty nonrelated novels. Her novel *Star Wars: The New Rebellion* and several of her Star Trek novels have made the *USA Today* bestseller list. Her short fiction has been nominated for the Nebula, Hugo, World Fantasy, and Stoker awards, and recently won *Ellery Queen's Mystery Magazine*'s Readers Choice Award. Her novella *The Gallery of His Dreams* won the *Locus* Award for best short fiction. Her body of fiction work won her the John W. Campbell Award, given in 1991 in Europe. *The Fey: Sacrifice* was chosen by *Science Fiction Chronicle* as one of the Best Fantasy Novels of 1995.

Until 1997, she edited the *Magazine of Fantasy and Science Fiction*, a prestigious fiction magazine founded in 1949. In 1994, she won the Huge award for her editing work. She started Pulphouse Publishing with her husband, Dean Wesley Smith, and they won a World Fantasy Award for their work on that press. Rusch and Smith edited *The SWFA Handbook: A Professional Writers Guide to Writing Professionally,* which won the *Locus* Award for Best Non-Fiction. They have also written several novels under the pen name Sandy Schofield.

Her next book for Bantam is the second book in The Black Throne Series: *The Black King*.

Enter the thrilling world of

⊷ THE FEY ⊷

by Kristine Kathryn Rusch

*A rich tapestry of enchantment and betrayal
from one of our most exciting new
fantasy talents*

THE SACRIFICE
___56894-9 $6.50/$8.99 Canada

THE CHANGELING
___56895-7 $5.99/$7.99

THE RIVAL
___56896-5 $6.50/$8.99

THE RESISTANCE
___57713-1 $6.50/$8.99

THE VICTORY
___57714-x $6.50/$8.99

Ask for these books at your local bookstore or use this page to order.

Please send me the books I have checked above. I am enclosing $____ (add $2.50 to
cover postage and handling). Send check or money order, no cash or C.O.D.'s, please.

Name _____

Address _____

City/State/Zip _____

Send order to: Bantam Books, Dept. SF 47, 2451 S. Wolf Rd., Des Plaines, IL 60018
Allow four to six weeks for delivery.
Prices and availability subject to change without notice.   SF 47 11/98